I0830787

Gulchekhra-Begim Makhmudova

FLASK OF THE CRYSTAL HOOKAH – III

THE MYSTERY OF THE KOH-I-NOOR DIAMOND

London 2025

Published by Hertfordshire Press Ltd © 2025
e-mail: publisher@hertfordshirepress.com
www.hertfordshirepress.com

FLASK OF CRYSTAL HOOKAH-III
or THE MYSTERY OF THE KOH-I-NOOR DIAMOND

by Gulchekhra–Begim Makhmudova ©

English

Translated by Yelden Sarybay
Edited by Timur Akhmedjanov
Design by Alexandra Rey

---

*British Library Catalogue in Publication Data
A catalogue record for this book is available from the British Library
Library of Congress in Publication Data
A catalogue record for this book has been requested*

ISBN: 978-1-913356-94-1

*Dedicated to my parents – Matluba and SaidJalol
who have taught us – their children, grandchildrens
and great-grandchildrens in their lifetime
to show Love and Kindness…*

"Flask of the Crystal Hookah III: The Mystery of the Koh-i-Noor Diamond" is an adventure-detective drama that explores the destinies of women in both modern Uzbekistan and the ancient world of the Saka-Massagetae tribes, once led by Queen Tomyris — the first regal Amazon and ancient guardian of the legendary Koh-i-Noor Diamond. Myth and history intertwine with the present-day adventures of the descendants of the great forefathers of the Uzbek land…

The novel is intended for a wide audience.

It is always a source of pride and joy to witness, year after year, the growing interest in the most remarkable chapters of Central Asian and Uzbek history—alongside a deepening appreciation for how our cultural heritage has shaped global progress and marked pivotal milestones in the development of human civilization.

The outstanding figures of our region—from the first Amazon warriors of the ancient Massagetae to the rulers and heroes of the Greco-Bactrian and Kushan kingdoms, and later, the luminaries of Maverranahr (Transoxiana)—all paved the way for the conquests of half the known world by the great commander Amir Timur and for the remarkable scientific achievements of his descendants.

These include Mirzo Ulugbek, with his creation of the world's first astronomical map, the Gurgan Zij; the groundbreaking work of Ibn Sina and Al-Biruni; the profound philosophy of the first Sufi of the Naqshbandi order; and a continuous stream of discoveries of universal significance. The Uzbek land has birthed so many brilliant minds that listing them all would be nearly impossible. Truly, ours is a Sacred Oasis.

The earliest mentions of treasures such as the Koh-i-Noor Diamond (from the Persian, meaning "Mountain of Light") date back to the time of Queen Tomyris in the 6th century BCE — ruler of the Saka-Massagetae, a tribe that once inhabited much of present-day Uzbekistan.

This 105-carat diamond has travelled through the centuries, bearing witness to countless adventures. From adorning the turban of the Indian Sultan Alauddin, it passed into the hands of the great

Emir Amir Timur and his descendants in India, and ultimately made its way to the treasury of Great Britain, where it continues to sparkle in the crown of Queen Elizabeth II.

The book, Flask of the Crystal Hookah III: The Mystery of the Koh-i-Noor Diamond, offers one version of the diamond's origin and chronicles its extraordinary journey — along with the story of its ancient guardian, Queen Tomyris. She was the first regal Amazon: a fearless warrior with the tender, romantic spirit of a true Woman.

Historical events in the novel are interwoven with modern narratives, bringing the ancient past of our region to life and allowing it to resonate with the present day. As though history itself were awakening — reborn in today's world.

Gulchekhra-Begim Makhmudova

Tashkent, Spring 2012

A witness to great history—born at the close of the nineteenth century, having weathered the turbulence of the entire twentieth, and now peacefully contemplating the dawn of the twenty-first— the noble and statuesque Feruz-begim felt the time drawing near. Soon, she would slip into eternity, leaving behind this beautiful yet transient world…

In the grandest room of her home, Feruz-begim's entire family had gathered. Her great-granddaughter Sitora and her husband Said—who lived with her—were joined by visitors: Sitora's mother, and her cherished daughter Shahlo (already in her sixties) with her husband Kadir; their granddaughter Malika, with her husband Bahadir and their adopted daughter Samira (taken in after the early passing of Bahadir's sister, Rano); as well as Bahadir's brother Amin, his wife Dilshoda, and the parents of both brothers—Abdulla and Mukhabbat Fattakhov.

The mistress of the house reclined on the luxurious kurpacha blankets near her beloved crystal hookah, its bowl fragrant with aromatic herbs from the banks of the Amu Darya and the mountains of Chimgan. Slowly, she cast a wise and meaningful glance over those gathered before her.

Her family never tired of admiring her. Even at more than a hundred years old, the venerable woman—though physically frail—retained a sharp mind and an impeccable memory.

No one knew—and Feruz-begim was in no hurry to reveal the secrets she kept—whom she was awaiting… but it was clear she was waiting for someone important.

Who was he—or she? Everyone watched her with anticipation and curiosity.

Then, through the delicate haze of the hookah's smoke, she began to chant softly, reciting the verses of her beloved Omar Khayyam:

Do no harm, for it will return to you.
Don't spit into the well, for you will drink its water.
Don't insult one of lower rank—
What if you ever need to ask their favor?
Don't betray your friends—you cannot replace them.
And don't lose those you love—they cannot be recovered.
Don't lie to yourself—you'll learn the truth in time.
For in that lie, you betray your very self…!

There was a palpable sense that Feruz-begim's soul was steeped in a lyrical and philosophical anticipation—something mysterious, something beyond the ordinary family gathering.

He who has been beaten by life achieves even more.
He who has tasted salt, cherishes the sweetness of honey.
He who has shed tears, laughs all the more heartily.
He who has died, understands what it means to truly live.

As her humming continued, suddenly, the sound of footsteps—firm, yet unhurried—echoed through the hall as the doors slowly opened…

1

Tashkent, 2012

"How come you're glowing like a cut diamond?" asked Dilshoda, the wife of businessman Amin Fattakhov. "Has something good happened?"

"Yes!" Amin replied, nodding exuberantly. "Can you imagine? I recently discovered that there are other direct descendants of the Great Mughals living in our country! And among them is an incredible woman—our distant relative. Her name is Tamilla Mahkamova. She's the head of the International Foundation for Gifted Youth and a United Nations Goodwill Ambassador. We met at an event and were both thrilled to learn about our kinship. She's truly fascinating—I've spoken with her a couple of times, once in person and once on the phone."

"A UN Goodwill Ambassador? She must live abroad, doesn't she?"

"No, why would she? Tamilla Sardorovna is a local. She called me two days ago and said she wanted to share something important about our common ancestor, Shah Jahan. She was recently in India and uncovered new historical information! And you know how much that kind of thing interests me. So, dear, we've arranged to meet this evening at a restaurant she recommended. If you'd like, we can go together."

"I trust you completely, my dear husband, I think I'll come along—mainly because I'm very curious to speak with someone like her!"

"Exactly—there's nothing to worry about. First of all, she's old enough to be my mother. And secondly, you know I love you!… But it's odd—she still hasn't called."

"Maybe this Tamilla isn't very reliable?"

"Oh, not at all! That would be completely out of character for her. She's such a positive, honorable woman. I wonder if something's happened. Well, let's wait patiently—it would be awkward to pester someone like that."

***

Tamilla had tried calling both the mobile and work phones of her husband, Rashid. He hadn't answered for over three hours, and that deeply troubled her. In more than thirty years of life together, this had never happened. Of course, she considered the possibility that his phone battery had simply died. But then again, Rashid was a meticulous, extraordinarily organized man who always kept everything in perfect order.

No—something was clearly wrong.

Suddenly, an unknown number flashed on her screen.

"Hello, is this Mrs. Mahkamova?" a stranger asked. Tamilla sensed a trace of mockery in his tone. "Listen to me carefully and don't interrupt. Your husband, Rashid, is with us. You will come for him immediately—I'll send you the address of the holding cell in a moment. Bring us all the diamonds you have. And most importantly—the Koh-i-Noor Diamond."

"What?! A diamond? But it's—" Tamilla began to protest, stunned by the bizarre demand. But the man didn't let her finish.

"Hurry up, ma'am!" he snapped, almost taunting. "And if you go to the police or the prosecutor's office, you will never see your

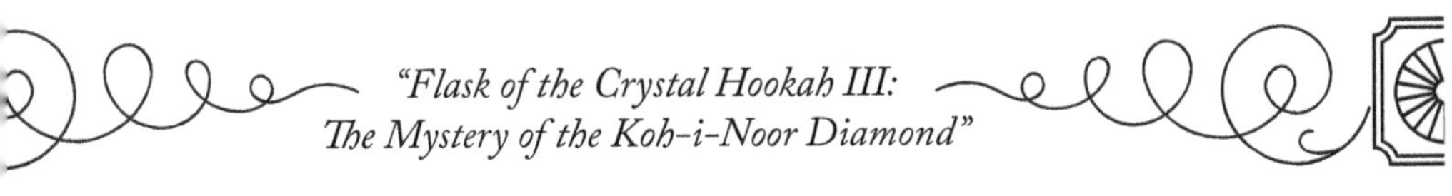

husband alive again!"

He hung up abruptly, about a minute later, a text message appeared on her phone…

* * *

Having retrieved all her precious jewels from the bank's safety deposit box, Tamilla tried to compose her thoughts in the car. First and foremost, she decided, she needed to call her daughter—after all, the girl would surely be worried.

"Saltanat, my dear, I just got a call from someone—well, from a man—who said he might be able to help find your father!"

"What kind of person? Where can he be found?" Saltanat asked nervously. "And where *is* Papa, anyway?"

"Well, I… haven't figured everything out yet. I'm on my way to a meeting right now. Don't worry about anything, alright? And always remember—your parents love you very much! You're our dearest girl!"

"Mom, I'm already grown—I even have children of my own. Why all the sweet talk all of a sudden?" she asked, slightly confused. "The most important thing is to find Dad!"

"Yes, yes, of course—you're right. That's what matters most. Don't call me for the next two hours, okay? I'll try to reach out to you myself. And if…" she hesitated for a few seconds, "if for some reason you can't get through to me, then call the police. But not now. Do you understand?"

"That's strange. Why wait? We should call the police right away…"

"No! Absolutely not—I forbid it."

"Alright then… I'll do as you say."

"Good girl. That's all for now, my dear—I'm sending you a kiss. Take care of the children!"

***

Something must be done! Tamilla thought, panic rising in her chest. Dozens of ideas for how to rescue her husband whirled through her mind like a storm. *Of course, I'm a strong and brave woman—but I'm no secret agent, no military general! I can't face armed bandits on my own… Could Rashid be suffering right now because of me? Locked in some foul dungeon, bound and helpless? Is it because I happened to come into possession of these cursed jewels?… Wait— how did they even find out about them? I certainly wasn't flaunting anything… Oh—of course! The queen and I were shown on television when I wore that headpiece… But still, why assume… Could Rashid's enemies have played a part in this?*

In any case, I can't do this alone. But who can I turn to, if going to the police isn't an option?

Wait—yes! There's only one man who might be able to help…

Without hesitation, she dialled a number saved to her speed dial.

"Hello, Konstantin Ivanovich? Good evening. Well—actually, it's not a good one. May I get straight to the point?"

"Of course, dear Tamilla. Speak freely—say whatever you need to. You know I'll do everything in my power to help. I'm listening. What's happened?"

"I'm in serious trouble. My husband has been kidnapped! I believe it's the work of some criminal gang…"

"Your husband?" Konstantin repeated, clearly startled. "But what could they possibly want from such a modest, good-natured man?"

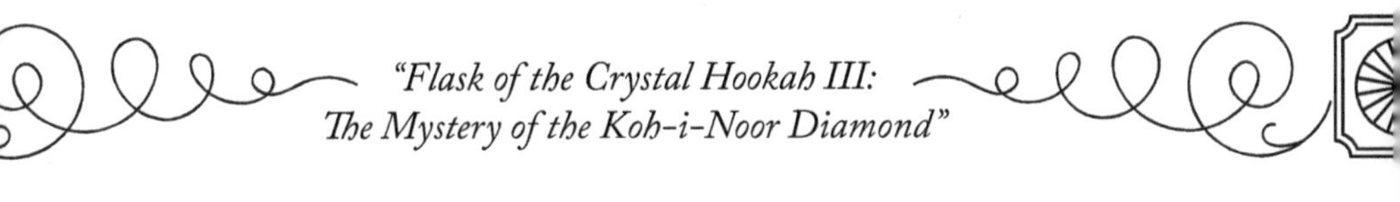

"They said… they said they might *kill* him!"

"But why? What do they want? Do you know who they are?"

"No, of course not. They never identified themselves. They're demanding… they want *everything*… all of my jewels!"

"Forgive the bluntness, Tamilla," Konstantin said delicately, "but—do you have many?"

Tamilla could hear the tension creeping into his voice. Konstantin Romanov, their longtime Russian friend, was clearly growing anxious on her behalf. She was deeply moved by his genuine concern—for Rashid, and for her. After all, she knew from experience: true compassion for another's fate is a rare thing in this world.

"Not really, not very many. But I'll be honest, since I trust you: among my jewels, there are a couple… very, *very* expensive ones with rare diamonds. And somehow the criminals found out exactly which ones. Although they made a mistake in—"

She couldn't finish her sentence, as a sudden burst of noise crackled over the line.

"I'm on… my way to… you now…" Konstantin said, his voice barely audible over the rising static. "Don't worry, Tamilla—I'll help you. But I must warn you right away that, for the sake of your husband's life… you might have to give these bastards all your jewels! And I—"

"Yes, yes, of course," Tamilla agreed without a trace of hesitation or doubt. "For Rashid, I won't spare anything. But please—I beg you—come as soon as possible!"

She then dictated the address provided by the kidnappers.

"What? I'm sor—what did you say…" His words faded, swallowed by even louder static. Short beeps followed, and the call disconnected.

Once again, she was unable to reach him.

What kind of day is this?! Tamilla thought in despair. *I need to pull myself together… Alright, let's hope he caught the address—and that he'll rush to help us. Maybe not alone, but with a group of strong men! After all, this is the 'all-powerful' Konstantin Ivanovich. He has such vast connections and resources! No wonder he sends so many young people abroad to study and work… God willing, he'll sort everything out!*

2

Moscow, the Same Year

Businessman and philanthropist Alexei Vadimovich Irmanov called his young assistant, Nastya—the daughter of his wife, Aleksandra Veniaminovna—into his office.

"Nastya, could you call Rashid Kudratovich from the city line once again? He still isn't answering my calls."

"He isn't picking up, Alexei Vadimovich," Nastya said, shaking her head. At home, at Alexei's request, she sometimes addressed him as *Papa* (though still using the formal *you*), but at work, she always used his first name and patronymic.

"I keep dialling him—but it's all in vain. He just won't answer."

"What on earth is going on?" Alexei exploded, his nerves clearly frayed. "In just a few days, the Young Performers Festival begins. How can someone take the funds entrusted to them for organizing the event—and then vanish with them?" He fumed. "And he's an old friend, someone I've trusted like a brother for years!"

"But maybe it wasn't him who took them?" suggested Nastya. "That just doesn't sound like Rashid Batyrov at all…"

"Well, you're a know-it-all," Irmanov grumbled. "Who else could it be? I transferred the money directly into his bank account! Or… perhaps you mixed something up with the transfer? Could the funds have… accidentally… ended up with someone else?"

"No!!" the girl exclaimed, her voice trembling with agitation.

"Why are you shouting like that, Nastena? Alright, you said 'no.' I hope so… Have you called your mother?"

"Yes, she's fine. She's already prepared dinner and is waiting for you… both of us."

"What dinner? I haven't got time for that now! Millions have just disappeared! Of course, I'm by no means a poor man…" Alexei snapped.

"Well, everyone thinks you're an oligarch…" Nastya began.

"Oh, come off it—drop those trendy labels! That's not the point. Maybe not everyone understands this: if I frittered away my money left and right—whether big or small—I never would've reached the position I'm in today! Besides, I have competitors, even outright enemies. Give some people the slightest reason, and they'd smear my name with a load of sh—sorry, never mind. Now, Nastya, get through to Rashid!"

* * *

Tashkent, the Same Year

Rashid Kudratovich was a respectable man with a solid presence, who had served for many years as the head of the Department of International Cooperation on Youth Affairs at the Ministry of Culture. Having lost his parents long ago, he had achieved everything in life through his own intellect and hard work. And when he married Tamilla, it was his wife who always helped him maintain his image.

But now, bound hand and foot by a gang of psychos and dragged into some old, foul-smelling basement, he was scarcely recognizable. His jacket was gone, his shirt torn to shreds, and blood streamed down his grimy face. The bastards had beaten him several times. Had he faced any one of them alone, he could have easily overpowered the foe—but there were several of them, some armed with clubs and one brandishing a knife.

"I'm sick and tired of you, old man!" one of them spat out irritably, pretending to be the boss. "I've asked you for the umpteenth time: where's your wife's bling?"

"They're diamonds, Bahrom," the second gangster replied calmly.

"What difference does it make!" Bahrom snapped, his tone still edged with anger. "This stubborn old coot is driving me crazy. A serious, grey-haired man like him—and he won't tell us the truth!"

"I already told you: the diamonds are in my office safe," Rashid Batyrov managed to say between laboured breaths.

"You know, you bastard, Nikolai already went to your workplace and checked everything. There isn't a trace of any ice there!! I mean, no diamonds. Don't take us for fools!"

In truth, Rashid had no idea exactly where his wife stored her precious jewels. He loved and respected Tamilla so deeply—and valued her personal freedom so highly—that he deliberately steered clear of meddling in her private affairs, especially when it came to her belongings. If she asked him to buy something, he would always do so. He even took every opportunity to spoil her with expensive and delightful souvenirs—either brought back from business trips or purchased especially for her in Tashkent.

As a true gentleman, he considered it improper and unchivalrous to intrude upon his wife's personal "possessions," and so he never did. And now, in front of these thugs, Rashid was doing everything in his power to protect Tamilla from further harm.

If need be, I'm ready to die—just as long as my family remains unharmed, he thought.

"Enough of your drivel, old man!" Bahrom snarled. "I'm tired of waiting. I summoned your wife—and she's already barrelling over here at full speed to rescue her husband!"

Rashid hadn't known any of this. He was dumbfounded.

"No!!" he shouted. "I'll tell you everything and give you everything I have. But leave my wife alone—don't you *dare* lay a hand on her!"

"Don't boss me around, old man. And it's too late for that now. It'll be easier for you two to think it through *together* and give me not some made-up answers, but the *real* ones I expect! Now—remember—where did you hide the bli… diamonds? And as for your dear wife, our bo—erm, I mean, *I* have another interesting idea. But that's no longer any of your concern."

***

The robbers immediately searched Tamilla as soon as she arrived. They snatched her purse and removed all the jewellery she was wearing at the time.

"But that's just trifles. Where's the rest?!" Bahrom demanded irritably. "Tie her up!"

They hadn't seen her driver since she had let him go earlier, and she told them she'd arrived by taxi.

Tamilla, bound back-to-back with Rashid, held herself with steadfast courage. She was both worried and surprised that their friend Romanov hadn't shown up yet.

Perhaps he'll be here soon to help us! she thought hopefully.

"You sure have a beautiful wife, old man—though she's no longer a girl!" one of the bandits sneered boldly. "Bahrom, how about we take her into our harem for a while? Borrow her from that old man for a bit? He's hardly capable of pleasing this lovely lady on his own anyway!"

Tamilla bristled at the fact that these scoundrels still referred to her not-yet-old husband as "old man." As for their insolent banter, she trusted that her husband would never let anyone harm her—that he would protect her. As long as he was by her side, her honour would remain untarnished.

"My love, you shouldn't have come here," Rashid whispered in her ear. "I would've handled this alone…"

"No, I couldn't leave you in trouble all by yourself!" his devoted companion replied. "And you know I never could…"

"Thank you. But now it's even harder for me—I'm afraid for you…"

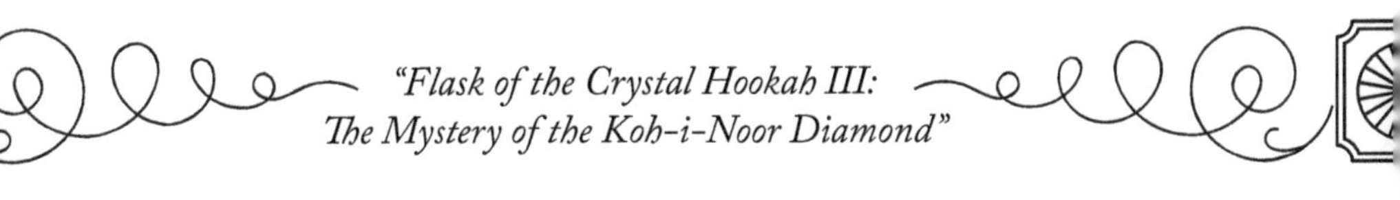

"Oh, oh, would you look at those doves!" Bahrom jeered mockingly. "Just like something out of a movie! Hey, you—what's your name? Tamilla, isn't it? Where's the Koh-i-Noor diamond?"

"I don't have it. I never did."

"What nonsense are you spouting? How can it be that you never had it? And what about that photograph with the English queen? I saw it myself. And an expert confirmed it wasn't Photoshop or any montage."

"Yes, I saw that precious stone in the crown and even wore Her Majesty's crown on my head—the queen herself gave me that opportunity. We even took a selfie together. But that's all there is to it! The Koh-i-Noor remains in London, at Buckingham Palace."

"But we have other, verified information!" Bahrom fumed. "Reliable sources have told us that the diamond cleared customs and was brought into Uzbekistan! In any case, here's how it's going to be: you two sit here and think! We're off to take a break, and tomorrow morning we'll come back. And then—you won't be able to wriggle your way out at all! Dima, you're to guard them."

* * *

"I'm most worried about your life, my love," Rashid murmured quietly to his wife, careful not to wake Dmitry, their guard. "I also want to come out of here alive—the Youth Festival is right around the corner! You know, I bear enormous responsibility, and I can't afford to let so many people down..."

"I understand you. And I worry most about our daughter and grandchildren—how will they manage without us?" Tamilla sighed.

"Please, don't say 'without us'! I believe everything will be all right. These people wouldn't dare kill us. These aren't the savage ancient times or the wild '90s."

"I'm not sure these… criminals think as you do. Understand, I'm not at all afraid for myself. Every person's life is in the hands of the Almighty—what is meant to be will be. And if it's destined that we survive, then we will. Also, I'm worried about the kids…"

"The kids? You mean the young men and women that Konstantin Ivanovich and I sent abroad for internships—and some even for studies? The thing is, I haven't been able to reach some of them for three days now, and honestly, it really worries me."

"And what does Romanov have to say?"

"He assures me that young people often forget their phones somewhere or just don't hear them ring when they're in a noisy group."

"See? And when they eventually pick up their phones, they usually call right back. Isn't that so?"

"Actually, not in this case. The kids can't really afford to call me back from Europe. Although you're right on one point—they could have sent a quick SMS…"

"But none of them have…" Rashid concluded thoughtfully. "That's not very good. But don't worry. Surely there's a reasonable explanation for this! Now, Tamilla, tell me—what's the story with the Koh-i-Noor diamond? You've never mentioned it to me before. Why did British Queen Elizabeth herself place her crown on your head? And why have these bandits suddenly decided that you have a direct connection to the diamond?"

"Actually, it's a long story, Rashid."

"We're in no hurry—we have the whole night ahead of us. I need to know every detail so that I can figure out how we're going to get out of this alive."

"Part of the story is connected with my father, Sardor Shahmuradovich Mahkamov, and some people he knew in his youth. And partly... you know that on my father's side, I'm a descendant of the Great Mughals—the great Babur, Shah Jahan, and Arjumand-Begim..."

"Yes, I remember, my princess..."

"And on my mother's side, our lineage begins with the legendary, yet very real, queen of the Saka steppes—Tomyris. It was in her honour that I was named Tamilla..."

"Wait, my wife! I've read a bit about her. It seems she was a valiant, courageous woman who saved the entire Saka people from the treacherous conqueror—King Cyrus?"

"That's right. In fact, the people known as the 'Saka'—or more precisely, the largest branch of them, the Massagetae—are the ancient ancestors of all Uzbeks. Tomyris lived in the sixth century BCE. She became a great queen and the first Amazon...!"

3

The 6th Century BCE—an era of ancient civilization. In India, the scholar Panini creates the oldest surviving writing system—a Sanskrit grammar. Meanwhile, Buddha Shakyamuni and Mahavira become the founders of Buddhism and Jainism. In the Near East, the Chaldean, or Neo-Babylonian, Empire dominates, having successfully revolted against Assyria at the end of the previous century. The Kingdom of Judah comes to an end when the Babylonian army of Nebuchadnezzar II captures Jerusalem, and the bulk of the

population is forcibly resettled in other lands—ushering in the era of the Babylonian Exile of the ancient Jews. In Iron Age Europe, the expansion of the Celts continues. In the Mediterranean, ancient Greek philosophy begins to take root. In China, the Spring and Autumn Period begins. In East Asia, the Chunqiu period commences. Chinese philosophy assumes an orthodox character—with Confucianism, Legalism, and Mohism flourishing—while Laozi founds Taoism. At the same time, a powerful Persian Empire arises… Nations and states are ruled by authoritative, strong, and independent kings—such as Astyages, Kavad, and Spargapis…

Sakastan, 6th Century BCE

King Spargapis of the Massagetae—the scourge of many chieftains and warriors, descendant of the Ishguz tribal leader Ispakaya and son of King Madyes—lay in his tent, which was hardly distinguishable from the tents of simple nomads. At that moment, he was visited by a most unusual dream.

In the dream, he held his gigantic sword in his hands, its hilt adorned with precious gems, and battled disobedient enemy tribes. Suddenly, it seemed to him that he merged completely with the sword—and then… he himself became the sword! He used his very being to crush and annihilate the foes attacking his people. But the sword-Spargapis began to weaken, as enemies continued their assault on both him and his lands. He seemed to melt away, to dwindle, transforming into vapor and gradually disappearing. The heart of the nomadic king trembled. A man who had never known fear was now gripped by it.

Then, suddenly… something astonishing occurred. From deep within him, from some inner essence or soul, an iron bird burst forth. It touched the blade and hilt of the Spargapis sword, and in an instant… the sword, too, became entirely iron—strong, powerful, indestructible. In his dream, Spargapis felt deep within that his lands were henceforth protected, that they would be safe from now on, and—miraculously—his long-held dream was coming true! Henceforth, all the Saka would be united as one.

All of this was strange and, for now, far from reality…

"What could it possibly mean?" the astonished king of the Massagetae wondered upon awakening.

* * *

Southwest Asia, the Same Century

The first rays of the early summer sun danced restlessly on the velvet pillow—edged with thick golden trim—that adorned the luxurious bed in the finest chambers of the palace. King Astyages of Media, dazzled by those thin, intermittent, yet rather insistent beams, immediately awoke and sprang to his feet as if scalded.

The sunlight did nothing to dispel the dreadful darkness of the night from the ruler's soul.

"Harpagus!!" the king cried out in anguish.

Instead of the military commander—who, at such an hour, was still peacefully dozing in his warm bed—the king's personal servant burst into his chambers. Sleepy and somewhat clumsy at this early hour, the servant, as was proper, merely bowed low before his master without uttering a word; a slave was never permitted to speak first to a king.

"Omar, where is Harpagus?" Astyages asked irritably.

"Forgive me, my lord, but your general has not yet left his quarters—he is apparently still resting, it is early… Shall I order him to come?" replied Omar.

"What, you fool, are you asking? If I am searching for him, of course he must be summoned!

And immediately! Now, run along! And invite the priests—the ones who serve at the palace."

"I shall obey, my lord," the servant replied obediently, softly yet clearly.

Omar was a clever young man and immediately suspected that something unusual had happened during the king's sleep—most likely, an unpleasant dream had troubled him. Yet, questioning the ruler of a great empire was not within his rights. All that remained was to wait for news from General Harpagus and the priests. Even if, during their conversation, the king were to dismiss his loyal Omar at the door, it wouldn't matter—after all, one could always eavesdrop quietly. Wouldn't be the first time…

There was only one thing that troubled the servant: he had noticed that the already surly King Astyages now seemed even more furious, enraged, and distraught.

After the men summoned by Omar entered the king's quarters—and for some reason the attendant servant was not called in but ordered to wait outside—his inner battle between fear for his own life and overwhelming curiosity was eventually won over by the latter. Trembling with apprehension at the thought of being noticed (Omar knew that Astyages might even execute him for such an act!), he crept up to the door leading to the king's chambers,

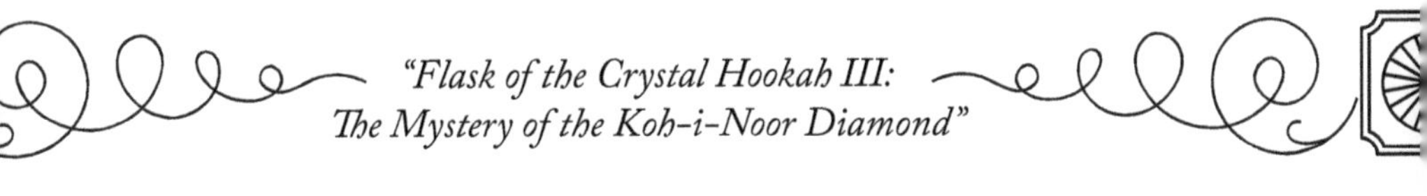

carefully and stealthily cracked it open, and pressed his ear against the cedar doorframe.

"Wizards, tell me," the king impatiently demanded, "what is written in the Gathas about ill dreams? Can you interpret them? I command you!"

The priests—Zartosht, Faridun, and Ardashir—exchanged silent, astonished glances, unsure how to respond to the unlearned Astyages. It was common knowledge throughout Media that, among the Zoroastrians, the word "sleep" meant nothing more than a deep, dreamless relaxation—a state of shut-down consciousness. Nevertheless, improvising an interpretation of a dream on the fly was well within the customary practices of the priests. Ardashir, the boldest and most resourceful of the three magi, ventured:

"Do not be angry, most esteemed ruler. Would it not please you to reveal to us exactly what you dreamed? Then we shall surely find its meaning."

Astyages furrowed his brow. He had expected that, in time, the elders might know the content of his dream… But realizing that it was surely beyond their power, he sighed sorrowfully and said:

"I stood beside my daughter Mandane and saw a grapevine beginning to sprout from her belly… Suddenly, the vine reached out directly toward me—and began to entwine me completely, from head to toe. I felt clearly how that vine was choking and stinging me, like a venomous snake. At one point, it even seemed to me that in just a minute, death would overtake me… But I do not wish to die!! I am a great ruler—and I must live forever!"

"Undoubtedly, my lord," all four visitors bowed in subservience. "You will never die, and without doubt, you shall rule Media for all eternity!"

"Yet the territory of Media might be seized by the Persians," Faridun interjected for some reason. "Perhaps your daughter will bear a boy who will conquer Media, and then all of Asia…"

This was nothing more than a fanciful, careless flight of a priest's imagination—a reckless game of fancy. And who could have imagined that it would incite such a storm of indignation in Astyages's heart! Had he possessed the authority, he would have ordered this insolent priest's head to be severed without delay!

"No, no-o-o-o!! I will not allow it!! This shall never happen!!" roared the king. "Be off from here, you incompetent fortune-tellers! And do not dare show yourselves before me again in the near future!"

The priests, abashed by what had transpired, bowed low to the king and departed. In all the land, there was not a soul who could humiliate them as thoroughly as King Astyages. Yet, being fed from the king's own hands and by his gracious favour, they dared not complain.

Only when Harpagus was about to follow the priests out of the royal chambers did Astyages abruptly halt him with a sharp gesture and sternly added:

"And you, military commander, have not been dismissed or permitted to leave yet. Come here and sit down at my feet."

Harpagus obeyed without question.

From a single glance, the king discerned that the aging warrior was somewhat perplexed: why was Astyages so agitated? After all, it was well known that the daughter of the ruler, Mandane, was not pregnant and had no children at the moment—let alone any sons…

Already sullen, the king's countenance darkened further, and he declared:

"Mandane once allowed her husband, that wretch from Persia, Atradat—now known as Cambyses, prince of Persia—to enter the bed of their maid, Artosta. And that Artosta… well, she is already with child; she is about to bear a son for Mandane!"

Even the experienced Harpagus was taken aback by such news. On one hand, he should have congratulated the king—for it would be the first time in his life that he was about to become a grandfather. On the other hand, it was perfectly clear that after that strange dream, Astyages trembled like thunder at the thought of this as-yet-unborn infant—this Persian spawn!

"My lord," Harpagus finally managed to say, "but by the laws of Media, a Persian can never become the king of Media! So there is nothing for you to worry about!"

"You think so?… Well said. Yet how can one not be troubled by such dreadful dreams?"

"Oh, my king, I beg you, pay them no heed. For it is well known that in Media, what is truly valued is only your judgment and your decisions. Moreover, your faithful servant Harpagus will do everything for his master—for the preservation of your throne and your safety. I pray you, do not trouble yourse—"

"Then, as soon as Cambyses and Mandane bear a son, you are to go immediately to Pasargadae and carry out a secret task of mine…"

"I shall obey, my lord," Harpagus bowed obsequiously before the king had even finished his thought. "Everything you command, everything you desi—"

"Then go—and at once, kill that infant!!"

Harpagus was a warrior, not a murderer, and deep in his soul, he winced: this bloodsucker had already been responsible for the deaths of thousands of grown men, and now he was setting his sights on infants—even unborn ones! What a monster! He would spare not even his own grandchild…

Yet the wise military commander, in the presence of the king, revealed nothing of the inner

turmoil the order had caused him. As he listened to the command, he remained so composed, so calm, and so obedient that King Astyages never entertained the notion that Harpagus might disobey him.

* * *

Sakastan, the Same Century

Kavad, king of the mighty Saka tribe of Tigraxauda—neighbours of the Massagetae—summoned his brother Sakesfar into his chambers.

In the recent battle I aided you, my brother Kavad, thought Sakesfar. *Surely you wish to repay me—either by giving me something valuable or by promoting me. It's high time you made me your Chief Advisor instead of merely the commander of your forces! And to be perfectly frank, your throne should have been mine all along! If only, in our childhood, when you were terribly ill, you had perished…Oh, how foolish I was then, caring for you, tending to you as best I could. After all, you are my own dear, younger brother! I loved you, Kavad… But you grew up—and suddenly so did my detachment towards you. How unfortunate that in our tribe the law decrees that the youngest son inherits the throne. Otherwise, it would have been me—not you—who would be king! All right, let's see what you have to offer me…*

"Leave, Sakesfar!"

Kavad, from the very threshold, angrily addressed his elder brother.

Sakesfar was taken aback—his legs beginning to tremble from the shock of such a reception.

"What?! What are you saying, O king?! You were the one who summoned me, brother…" he protested.

"After all your surprises, I am no longer your brother! Take your wife and your newborn offspring—and scram from this land! The Haomovarga will take you in," Kavad thundered.

"By the gods—then explain to me what has happened!" Sakesfar demanded.

"And he still asks!" roared Kavad. "Who in their right mind would name their newborn son 'Skun'—meaning 'leader,' 'chief,' 'first'? Huh? I'm no fool; I understand exactly what you meant!

That name is a clear hint at your intention, brother, to lay claim to the throne of the Saka-Tigraxauda—that is, my throne! Here, 'first' and 'chief' refer only to me, got it? Now beat it!"

"Well then, dear relative… May you be… You are dooming me and my family to persecution and wandering. May the gods judge us! And I, too, wish upon you no less misfortune. Someday, mark my words, you too will be condemned to suffering! Know that the time will come when my son Skun shall, in truth, rightfully ascend the Saka-Tigraxauda throne—"

"Out! Get out!" Kavad, now completely incensed, cut him off.

Without so much as a bow, and equally full of anger, Sakesfar swiftly departed from the king's tent.

"No—after me, it will be my son who becomes king of the Saka-Tigraxauda!" Kavad shouted after his banished brother. "My wife is already with child; very soon, my Rustam will be born…"

4

"Father, you are the chieftain of the mighty Abii! There are so many invincible warriors in our tribe willing to perform heroic deeds and even die for you—and you… what, are you afraid of Spargapis?" puzzled the beautiful Zaryana, as she sat beside the fire on a bull's hide in the tent.

"Stop it. I fear no one. But I absolutely detest that little king!" replied the grey-haired Tursun to his daughter, spitting out his disdain and tossing more sticks into the fire.

"I don't like it when you talk about someone like that," Zaryana sighed. "But I know you are a good man. That must mean there's a reason to hate him so much…"

"Yes, there is. Spargapis cunningly confounds our simple steppe folk with his unexpected and seemingly 'harmless' maneuvers—intricate schemes that few understand! Many think he acts foolishly, even naively. But I am clear-sighted enough to know that his moves carry a profound meaning: a struggle for power, spiced with his exceptional will to win and absolute confidence in it!"

"Yet Spargapis has long since inherited the kingship…"

"That's true, daughter, it is so. But he fully realizes that not everyone recognizes his authority—only the chieftains of the weaker tribes do. He sees that among the Alans, the Tocharians, and us Abii, he is still not feared, and that many in the steppe are eager to wrest that coveted throne from him… Only by subjugating these tribes and forcing them to bow to his rule could he become the true master of all nomads! And so he fights with all his might,

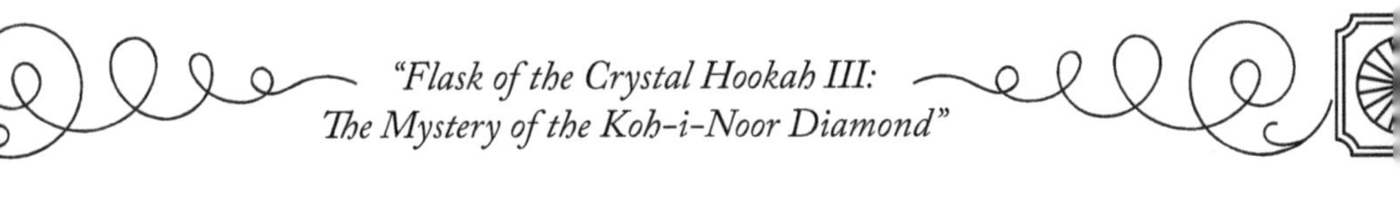

constantly trying to prove himself as the 'master of the house!'"

"I'm not a man, and I don't know everything about the struggles of the Massagetaen tribes. But I'm sure, Father, that it isn't only Spargapis—every chieftain in our tribes dreams of becoming the king of all the Sakas—or at least of the Massagetae. Isn't that so? Then why single out Spargapis for blame?"

"You're right in some measure, my dear. But that sly fox exploits this better than anyone else, cunningly pitting us all against one another, driving everyone headlong into a battle for the coveted title of king! And in truth, he has no intention of surrendering that position to anyone. This man grows ever stronger and increasingly dangerous for the tribes. We nomads were convinced that, as king of the Massagetae, Spargapis would conscientiously extinguish the flames of internecine strife within his hereditary lands. Instead, contrary to our expectations, he acts in the opposite manner. This 'master of the steppe' devises every possible—and even impossible—scheme to further stoke the fires of discord between the tribes and their chieftains. He incites one leader against another, leaving us weakened and forcing us to turn to him for help, yet never fully satisfying the demands of either side; all the while, he slyly sows enmity and discontent, fracturing his still-independent subjects."

"Such a cunning and dangerous strategist?"

Zaryana grasped his meaning.

"Indeed—the most cunning and dangerous of all! Nowadays in the steppe, no one really knows who is allied with whom and who stands against whom. What's more, every chieftain on opposing sides is convinced that Spargapis is on his side, and without once dispelling that notion, the king of the Massagetae leaves us in that delusion. In truth, he stands entirely for only one person—himself!"

"Why does that trouble you so much, Father?"

"Because, in doing so, he deceives, robs, and leaves all the Sakas in ruin! There is no more unreliable and treacherous ally in our steppe than Spargapis. He pits one chieftain against another, crushing his foes without a trace of mercy, sparing no one. And when the defeated, enraged enemy sinks into utter despair, filled with hatred for Spargapis, it is then that he himself approaches. As if not noticing the fury in the eyes of the beaten leader, he greets him and his kin cheerfully, then casually slips into the honored position—shamelessly exploiting the unassailable laws of hospitality among the nomads!"

After mentioning hospitality, Tursun felt a slight hunger. But he had no wife—she had long since passed away—and he didn't wish to burden his daughter with cooking late in the evening. Moreover, Zaryana had already prepared a meagre dinner earlier, which had now been entirely eaten. His compassionate regard for neighbouring tribes prevented Tursun from launching new raiding expeditions or seizing provisions from other nomads; thus, even he—the chieftain of his tribe, like all the Abii—occasionally experienced hunger and need.

Fortunately, he had a wise and sensitive daughter. Catching her father's glance, Zaryana immediately rose, walked over to the part of the tent that resembled an ancient kitchen, retrieved a piece of bread and a small jug of sweet haoma from her supplies, warmed the drink slightly over the fire, and served it to her father. Though he was grateful, out of masculine pride he said nothing.

Zaryana herself neither ate the bread nor drank the haoma; instead, she sipped a little cool water from a vat, wiped her lips, and returned to her former spot.

"It turns out that things in the Saka steppe are not so simple..." the girl mused thoughtfully, her concern unmistakable—not for herself, but for her father and for her kinsmen and fellow tribespeople. "I've heard that a serious war has broken out between the Alans and the Tocharians. The entire steppe now knows that, in terms of bloodshed and cruelty, it surpasses all the previous internecine conflicts of the Massagetae! Tell me, is it true that in this war, one way or another, all our tribes have been drawn in?"

Tursun fell into a gloomy silence and averted his gaze from his daughter. It was hard for him to think about all this too, for he was deeply troubled about the fate of his tribe.

"I'm frightened, Father. I have such ominous premonitions…"

"It is the power-hungry Bikbulat and Zakir who have clashed; each of them wants to sit on the throne and refuses to submit to another king… As for me, perhaps I am devoid of such arrogant ambitions. But do you see what is being wrought because of Spargapis?! And you defended him… That treacherous fiend must know well that I am at odds with the chieftain of the Tocharians, Zakir, and that, sooner or later, I might come to the aid of the chieftain of the Alans, Bikbulat. Therefore, I know that we Abii are thwarting Spargapis. But I swear by my grey beard—we will never surrender to him! Together with other tribes, we are a formidable force. I will join my army with Bikbulat's and march against Zakir's warriors—and then we shall see what that 'king' does…"

"Please, be careful! Mother is gone, and my brother is dead—you are all I have left. I beg you, take care of yourself!"

"I promise, daughter—for your sake and for the memory of those we both hold dear…"

***

"Who is that stranger who just galloped away?" asked Yatim, one of Bikbulat's sons, turning to his father. "He looks like a messenger! And judging by his clothing, could he be from the Abii?"

"That's right, son," nodded the Alan chieftain. "It is the noble Tursun who has sent his messenger to inform us that he, the chieftain of the Abii, is coming to visit us for some important discussion."

"I have a feeling I know what about. I hope he intends to unite our two tribes in the fight against those detested Tocharians?"

"How I wish it were so. We alone can scarcely cope with Zakir's vast army. Moreover, that fierce warrior Sarmak of theirs is no joke. Even my brave riders—all of them tremble at the sight of that shaggy monstrosity, who looks like a bear! And we must, by any means, defeat the Tocharians… You know how it is in the steppe these days—either they get us, or we get them. There is no other outcome."

"But surely the chieftain of the Abii also has designs on the kingship? Won't he usurp you?"

"Who? Tursun?! No, no—he isn't like that; he does not covet the throne. Ever since his wife died, all he has cared about is the happiness of his only and beloved daughter, the beautiful Zaryana. He wishes to unite our armies for one purpose only—to survive, to stand firm in this bloody struggle. And that is understandable. Perhaps he even wants to punish Spargapis for his arrogance. In any case, we will certainly help Tursun!"

"Will you order everyone to prepare properly for the Abii chieftain's visit?"

"You're a smart and capable lad, Yatim—I understand you perfectly. Yes, certainly: order it, in my name, to your younger brothers and all our servants. Prepare the most exquisite feast and the finest gifts for Tursun. Tomorrow he will visit our camp."

"Don't worry, Father; everything will be done in the best possible manner," replied Yatim obediently, bowing to Bikbulat as he quietly departed.

* * *

That very same day, late in the evening, a loud clatter of hooves was heard in the camp of the mighty Alans.

"Who are these riders?" Bikbulat asked discontentedly.

Having recently confirmed that everything was ready for a proper reception of the honoured and dear guest, he had been just about to go to sleep when he was interrupted.

"Chief, envoys from the king are requesting an audience!" burst in the chieftain's armoured attendant, trembling all over with fright. "They say the matter is urgent."

"Why are you so scared, huh?" the chieftain exclaimed in surprise. "You fool! My warriors are all around! How many uninvited guests are there?"

"Only three," the servant answered, still trembling. "But they... they look exceedingly fierce."

Bikbulat smirked.

"'Exceedingly fierce'?!" he mocked the young man. "Nonsense. And what is it that scared you so? We are a tribe of giants and

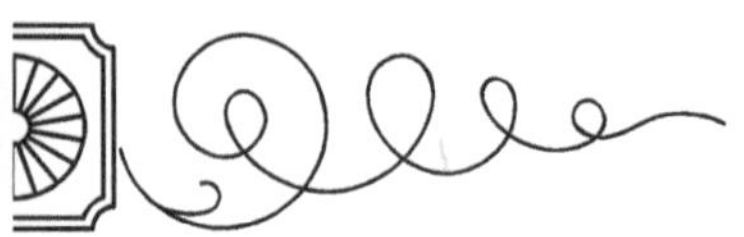

strongmen! Have you forgotten?"

The chieftain dressed and ordered that all the armed guards be summoned, just in case, and then that the equally armed visitors be brought in.

Three envoys of Spargapis entered the tent. Indeed, they looked something fierce! Each had a severed, bloodstained head tied to his belt, emitting a ghastly stench. From the mouths of all the victims, half-cut, bluish tongues dangled. Even the battle-hardened Bikbulat felt a shiver of unease. And what a visit—to come in the dead of night! He understood that they had come with a threat.

Nevertheless, pretending to be respectful and courteous, the guests bowed to their host.

"Why have you come?" Bikbulat asked curtly, without even returning their greeting or offering any preamble. "Does your master require something of me?"

"The noble lord of the Saka steppes, King Spargapis…"

"For now, he is only the king of the Massagetae—and not even of all of them," Bikbulat rudely interrupted.

"The lord of the Saka steppes, King Spargapis," one of the envoys insisted, almost gently repeating, "sends you and the Alans gifts, great chieftain. Please, accept them!"

Bikbulat understood that the word "please" was nothing more than a contrived show of diplomacy and friendliness, leaving no room for refusal or objection. After all, these "envoys of peace and friendship" had bloodstained heads with blue tongues hanging behind them for a reason…

He made a gesture indicating that they could bring in the gifts—he would inspect them. A horrifying thought flashed through his mind: these might also be… parts of dead bodies. He involuntarily shuddered.

Nevertheless, the three stepped out of the tent and, within a few minutes, brought back chests filled to the brim with gold, silver, and very fine, expensive clothing. It was clear that Spargapis needed Bikbulat for something important—and that the king would not accept a refusal. A suspicion arose in the depths of Bikbulat's soul—he wondered what he would be asked to do.

"This is all for you, great chieftain!" declared the second envoy. "Taken from the trophies of the bravest and boldest of warriors— Spargapis himself. There is much wealth here, very much. It is yours!"

Bikbulat tensed, anticipating some sort of "surprise." The envoy continued:

"The king has commanded that I convey his… er… request to you. Do not form an alliance with Tursun, chieftain! He will help you defeat Zakir and the Tocharians himself. Why would you want to make your good and loving friends jealous with this new, unwanted friendship with the chieftain of the Abii? And your best friend from now on is King Spargapis. And if you refuse…"

All three then half-drew their swords from their scabbards, making it clear what would befall him if he did.

"I understand," Bikbulat replied quickly. "But you need not try to scare me! I fear no one, and I am not afraid of death. So pass on my message to the king. I do not like being told what to do or being threatened. I am not one of the weaklings. There are tens of thousands of Alans, and we are truly mighty!"

He glared fiercely at all three. They silently waited for him to finish his speech.

Then, softening his tone somewhat, Bikbulat added:

"But… to be honest, I need that gold and that silver, for lately I have had nothing to feed my warriors and their families… Of course, Tursun was important to me. But if Spargapis will help us defeat the Tocharians without Tursun and the Abii…"

"Well, of course—the king swears by it; he gives his word," nodded the third envoy. "Only you must be patient—for it will take a long time to defeat the Tocharians… By the way, we have not yet had the chance to tell you: Tursun boasted that he can easily defeat you in combat!"

The eyes of the proud and self-loving Bikbulat flared with anger.

"What?! Him?! Defeat me?! He couldn't even defeat his own young daughter, I wager!! If that's the case… Very well. I agree. From now on, Tursun is my enemy, and the Abii shall never be allies of my Alans! Now, begone. I need to rest."

* * *

In Pasargadae, just as Mandane and Cambyses were blessed with a son—a child named Kurush—General Harpagus, by royal decree of the Median sovereign Astyages, ordered his soldiers to seize the newborn at once from his parents and carry him off to Ekbatan. Mandane was furious at her father's monstrous cruelty, yet she could never have imagined that Astyages not only intended to whisk her newborn away from both her and her husband, the Persian prince… but had long resolved to have Kurush put to death!

Meanwhile, Harpagus—ever the ambitious courtier—found that merely holding the post of chief general under Astyages was not enough. He craved more, dreaming of ruling all of Media. However, the clever Harpagus knew that his wealth and influence fell far short of what was needed to seize the Median throne by himself... He never even tried to directly contest Astyages by promoting his own candidacy among the nobles. No, he decided that the path to power must be carved out by other means. But how?

Then, after a conversation with the Median king in which Astyages ordered him to be ready to dispose of the royal infant immediately upon birth, a curious idea began to take root in Harpagus's mind.

What if... oh, yes! The heir to the Persian throne—and by blood also to the Median one—could serve as the perfect pretext for me to seize control of the entire country!

But how could he defy Astyages? Who among the king's subjects would dare ignore such an order? How could anyone possibly refuse to carry out the command to kill the newborn Kurush on the spot?

After much intense thought and calculation, Harpagus devised a daring plan.

His wife, Spaka, owned a modest country cottage inherited from her rural parents. Not long ago, she had been pregnant and lost the child she and Harpagus had conceived—the little one perishing in her womb. Her sorrow was deep.

Returning home, Harpagus explained to her the strange order he had received from Astyages.

"Spaka," he began cautiously, "do you think we could adopt this unfortunate child, Kurush—the very child his own grandfather wants dead?"

"So my friend Mandane has also borne a boy?" Spaka asked, her voice quickening with excitement. "That's wonderful! But where is he now?"

"He's safely hidden away," Harpagus replied. "But we can't keep him there for long; he needs a proper home and family. Besides, Mandane herself did not bear him—her maid, whom she sent for one night as a concubine to her husband, Prince Cambyses, gave birth to him. Still, I promise you, Mandane loves her son as if he were her own; she has long yearned for and awaited his arrival!"

"And how will Mandane manage without him?" asked Spaka, her voice trembling.

"I believe… she will endure—if only we rescue him," Harpagus said solemnly.

Then, with overwhelming grief, Spaka murmured, "My son… my dear little son… Why have you abandoned me? Whom did you forsake? You now lie beneath the earth…"

Her sorrow burst forth in loud, heart-wrenching weeping.

"Please, Spaka, stop!" Harpagus pleaded, striving to break through her despair. "Would you like to have the king's grandson as your own? Kurush will be yours instead of… I mean ours—I mean, we shall become his parents!"

Slowly, the meaning of her husband's words sank in.

"But there is one condition," Harpagus continued when he noticed that his wife was listening attentively and her tears had subsided. "As soon as I bring the infant home, a carriage will be waiting. You must take the boy and go to your parents' cottage—far from the prying eyes of bloodthirsty Astyages! I will visit you often… What do you say, Spaka? Do you agree?"

"Are you abandoning me? Do you have another woman?" she demanded, agitated.

"No, no—come now, think clearly! I just… I only fear for the life of this royal… this little child—Kurush. For his safety, I propose that we immediately refer to him not by his Persian name 'Kurush,' but by the Greek 'Cyrus.' What do you say?"

"You're giving me a son? My dear husband! Have you ensured that your Spaka will not be deprived of the great joy that every woman treasures? I shall be a mother again, won't I?"

"Of course! Praise the gods—you finally understand. Fear nothing; I will protect both of you. The carriage will be stocked with all the necessary provisions and clothing for the near future, and later I shall bring even more."

"Know that your son and I will always wait for you," she whispered through her tears.

"Everything will be fine, Spaka. Do not worry. I have no doubt that we will raise Cyrus to be a strong, brave, and illustrious man—a man who will obey his new father, Harpagus, in all things… And mark my words, someday… yes, someday the throne of his grandfather Astyages will be his! As sure as my name is Harpagus…"

* * *

Tursun, accompanied only by his closest companions, was riding toward the camp of the Alan chieftain. Since he was journeying to see a friend, he had not brought a large force—just a small band of his most trusted warriors.

"I don't understand a thing," grumbled the chieftain of the Abii as they reached the main tent. "My messenger told Bikbulat I'd arrive today. So why is no one coming to meet us?… This is odd."

"Have you noticed, chief, how coldly Bikbulat's guard is staring at us?" one of his men observed.

"I have, Sharif. But what does it mean? Are we not welcome among the Alans? Surely the Tocharians would welcome the assistance of the Abii in their struggle…"

They dismounted, and Tursun's surprise grew when a servant-guard at Bikbulat's tent neither bowed nor offered any greeting. Tursun acted as if he had not noticed the insolent slight and did not take offense.

"Tell your master that Chieftain Tursun has arrived!" he addressed the guard.

The guard merely shot him an indifferent glance.

"I've been ordered not to admit you—the master is resting," he replied flatly.

"What?! How dare you, dog! Don't you know who stands before you?!"

Just as Tursun uttered these words, one of his warriors suddenly drove an acinaces into the servant's belly.

"What did you do? Why?!" Tursun roared. "Now you've set us on the path to slaughter! We are guests here—this was entirely unnecessary! I never gave you permission."

"Forgive me, chieftain—I lost my temper," the warrior muttered, lowering his head in remorse. "How could he speak to you, great chieftain of the Abii?"

"Well, it appears that nobody regards me as great around here," Tursun smiled regretfully.

Within moments, all the men filed into Bikbulat's tent, where the Alan chieftain reclined on soft, warm tiger skins. No sooner had the Abii stepped inside than a throng of Bikbulat's warriors surged in.

"How dare you, Tursun, enter here without an invitation?" snapped the chief Alan haughtily, barely glancing in his direction.

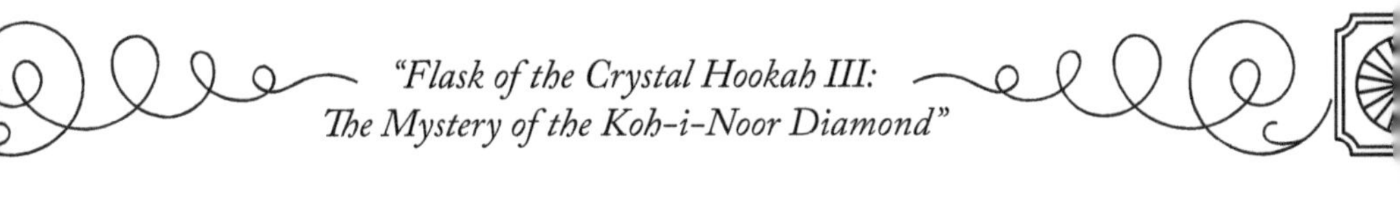

"Didn't my servant tell you that…"

"Your servant is dead," Tursun interjected. "He chose not to announce our arrival—and besides, he was most insolent to me, so my warrior…"

"What?! Is that so? Who gave you the right?" roared Bikbulat. "Alans, seize them all—quickly!"

"Hold on, Bikbulat, don't be foolish," Tursun pleaded. "We are your guests. That's not how things are done on the steppe. Just yesterday, you gave my messenger your consent for our brotherly meeting. And what kind of brother are you now? Is that truly how one greets a brother? Is that the custom among the Sakas? Huh?"

"Who are you, and who am I, do you know? I am richer than you, and King Spargapis himself is my friend!" spat Bikbulat.

"Ah, so that explains the sour mood and biting chill…Spargapis! That wily jackal has meddled in our affairs. He has meddled and spoiled everything! He schemes to turn all the Massagetae against one another. Don't you see, Bikbulat? He's manipulating you to suit his own ends, weaving his intrigues. Mark my words—if you let him, his web will tighten like a noose around your slender neck! And when you call for help, I won't come!"

"Get out of here, you weakling and loser! Let them go—let them ride away. We shall kill them… later," Bikbulat sneered. "Tursun, you're far weaker than I am; you're hardly worth my concern. Because of you, I now have the nuisance of finding a new servant. So ride back to your lands quickly—run, before my warriors slit your throats along with those of your companions, and turn you into stew for their horses!"

Tursun's brow furrowed as anger boiled within him, barely contained.

"Enough! As you say, chieftain of the Alans, your tribe may be strong—but you lack the agility and cunning we possess in battle. The Abii would have been a valuable asset to you. But now… Yet let me offer you some friendly advice: you are wrong to listen to Spargapis. He will deceive you, and you'll end up moaning and whining… That is surely defeat. Is it worth it?"

Bikbulat and his warriors erupted into hearty, resounding laughter, jeering at the Abii as if they were nothing more than a joke.

"As you wish…" the Abii chieftain repeated wearily. "Very well, we are leaving."

And so Tursun and his companions rode away, still reeling from such an unwelcoming reception. *What an arrogant fool!* Tursun mused silently, feeling a tinge of pity for Bikbulat.

***

The food situation in the Abii camp was indeed getting worse. As a cold autumn set in, the seasoned hunters of the tribe noticed that flocks of birds were flying overhead more frequently—it would have been unwise not to take advantage of the opportunity. So Tursun gathered his archers and set out on a hunt. He posted guards throughout the camp and along the borders of his territory to protect his nomadic lands from the fires of internal strife, and then he himself rode off into the wild.

No sooner had the riders covered the first few miles and entered the forest than one of the men spotted several injured foxes lying in their path. It was clear that someone had shot them not long ago, only to be startled and flee—an all-too-common occurrence on the steppe. This, the men reasoned, meant there must be a sizable fox den nearby. They paused briefly, collected the foxes, quickly skinned them, and salted the meat. They roasted a portion over the fire and ate it immediately—the fox meat was surprisingly delicious—while the rest they left to air-dry. Afterwards, they concealed the pelts in the hollow of a large, ancient tree and, taking the nearly prepared meat with them, resumed their hunt.

"Strange," remarked an old hunter, "why had I never noticed foxes here before? Perhaps they've only recently come to our lands? Nature works in mysterious ways. Still, it's astonishing…"

The Abii rangers pressed on, aiming at the flocks that soared high overhead—so high, in fact, that even the most skilful archers had little luck with their feathered quarry. Yet Tursun's mind was troubled by a single thought: back in the main tent, though well-guarded, remained his one and only beloved daughter…

Then, as suddenly as a whirlwind, King Spargapis himself burst into Tursun's camp.

With his band of ruthless cutthroats, he rampaged through the camp, recruiting any of the Abii willing to defect and betray Tursun—and slaughtering those who refused to turn traitor against their tribe and chieftain.

At last, the merciless king of the Massagetae reached Tursun's tent, where Zaryana sat, frozen with fear at the sound and fury of the rampage outside.

Without any warning or invitation, Spargapis, flanked by a couple of his trusted bandits, stormed into the main tent, swiftly dispatching the two guards standing near her. But the moment his eyes fell upon Zaryana, the king halted, utterly astonished… Never before had he seen such beauty in the entire steppe!

"Gather yourself—you will come with me!" he commanded the Abii chieftain's daughter. "And how did Tursun manage to keep such a precious treasure hidden from my gaze for so long?! From now on, you are mine!"

"No!" Zaryana replied firmly, having so far offered no courtesy to the uninvited, imposing guest.

Advancing on her like a wild predator, Spargapis was about to pounce on the object of his sudden, all-consuming desire when Zaryana instantly drew her sharp akinak and boldly pressed its blade against his throat.

"Oh, my—you're scorching hot, like fire!" he marvelled. "I respect that! Very well, I won't harm you without your consent. But tell me, my dear, do you know who stands before you?"

"I do," Tursun's daughter retorted boldly. "A robber, a murderer, a treacherous schemer—and a scoundrel."

"Now, now—ease up!" he said gravely. "Do not enrage me, girl, or you'll regret it. And I don't care that you are so shapely; I will annihilate you. I am the ruler of the Massagetae!"

"Forgive me, King Spargapis," Zaryana said more softly. To her own surprise, the brave and proud face of this uninvited intruder—a brute who had wrought havoc in her native camp—began to stir in her feelings she could hardly explain, filling her with a strange fascination and enchantment. It was as if she were inexplicably drawn to him. "Give me some time to think… I cannot betray my father and my tribe, can you not see?"

"Decide today, right now. You misunderstand—in fact, the fate of your tribe depends entirely on your decision. If you do not agree, I give you my word that I will turn your entire clan to ashes and ruin your father! Incidentally, I ensured he was distracted with hunting at this very moment by slipping him a few complimentary trophies… If you agree to come with me and become my wife, I promise to spare everyone you hold dear. I have been searching for someone like you my whole life. I like you—very much. I always give orders, but for you, I ask. Come, let's go…"

Zaryana hesitated, and then… resolved to leave the camp with Spargapis.

Someday my father will understand… and, I hope, forgive me, she thought.

Later, after Spargapis and Zaryana began living together, sharing a bed with his wife, the king said to her:

"My beloved, I want you to bear me a son—a warrior, my heir! Will you do it?"

"But what if it's a daughter?" Zaryana asked playfully, tenderly stroking his cheek.

He abruptly pulled her hand away and said in a stern tone:

"No—a daughter will do no good. Women are not people; they are worthless, having no rights or authority." After a brief pause, he added, "Of course, I am not referring to you. You, on the other hand, have the luxurious privilege of pleasing me, the ruler of the Massagetae!"

And with that, Spargapis laughed heartily.

5

Tashkent, 1958

Babur Yadgarovich Yusupov had recently launched his own business, and his family was prospering. Then tragedy struck—his wife, Mahsuda, passed away—and as his daughter Maryam blossomed into a lovely young woman, the time had come for her to begin her own life.

"Daughter, I cannot allow you to date a criminal!" Babur declared one day. "I've done my research on him—he served time for shoplifting and has only just been released from prison! You are a kind and intelligent girl, and a man like that is utterly unsuitable for you…"

"Wait, Father," Maryam countered, "don't you remember that many people have suffered the same fate—punished unjustly? Many have been locked up while completely innocent. Sardor Mahkamov loves me, I know it. And I couldn't find a better husband!"

"Daughter, listen to me, you can't trust everyone who's been behind bars. Not all of them are honourable or reliable; many will deceive you cruelly and leave you with nothing!" Babur worried about the young Maryam. "Don't tie your destiny to a dangerous man!"

"I understand, Papa, I really do," Maryam said soothingly. "I know that not everyone who leaves prison is a good person. But Sardor isn't like that. He's neither dangerous nor untrustworthy—he's kind and decent. Besides, he got caught when he was just a

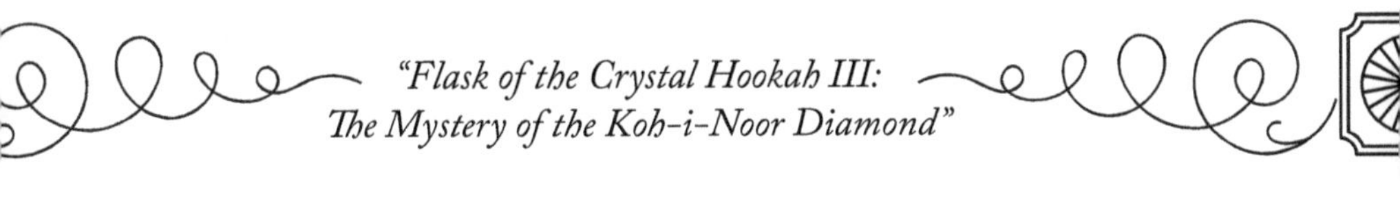

boy—a starving orphan who stole a loaf of bread… merely a victim of deceit by bad people. And if it means anything to you… the moment he was released, he went straight to work at our factory! In just a couple of months, he even rose to become the senior assistant to the workshop foreman! He's hardworking, and the other workers speak highly of him. Not to mention, he promised me that he would make me a real queen—that with him I'd never want for anything! He's a good guy, honestly! In fact, just yesterday… he proposed to me. I told him I'd think it over…"

After some time, Babur Yusupov decided that before the wedding, he must meet the young man and have a word with him.

"Don't think for a moment, Sardor, that I will ever allow you to hurt my daughter!" Maryam's usually affable father addressed Mahkamov with a stern expression. "I've checked you out: you've become the head of a workshop, which, being hardworking, is commendable—but I'm no fool, and I wasn't born yesterday. I'm not as naïve as my daughter. Such rapid career advancement seems slightly suspicious, to say the least. You clearly are a shrewd hustler and organizer… In short, I see in you a dominant, enterprising nature. I don't understand why someone as delicate as my Maryam should be your choice. And if you ever treat her like a mere servant, or heaven forbid if you ever lay a hand on her, I will crush you like a worm and wipe you out—mark my words! I would not only forbid her from marrying you, but I'd forbid her from even setting eyes on you. Still, in our family we have always respected women, valued their freedom, and honoured their choices. But remember—I will be watching you closely, and if you ever wrong Maryam or our entire family, I will punish you with the utmost rigor. Don't worry, I have the strength for it. Do you understand?"

"I understand, Babur Yadgarovich." Sardor offered a modest smile. "And let me add this: I anticipated your concerns, and I'd be surprised if someone like you would simply hand over your beloved daughter without hesitation. Life has already beaten me down enough, and I must confess—I'm no perfect gentleman; I have a rough, complicated character. Yet in all my thirty years, I have never loved anyone as deeply, as wholeheartedly, as I love Maryam. I am convinced that she is entirely my person, my true soulmate. I don't know if you've ever experienced that feeling—when just the presence of another person lifts you up, fills you with a desire to live! We're happy together; we can talk for hours on end. Thanks to her, I've learned more, become more capable, earned more, grown, and striven for success… solely because of her! She is my beautiful diamond—there is nothing, and no one, more precious in the world, and there never will be."

Babur Yusupov was pleased by Sardor's answer, and besides, it wasn't in his nature to refuse an orphan. So the father gave his wholehearted blessing to the union. Before long, they celebrated a modest yet beautiful wedding, and the joy in the eyes of the young couple made it clear to everyone that their new family was founded on genuine love.

***

Tashkent, 1959

Sardor Shakhmuradovich Mahkamov never imagined that he would be so overjoyed by the birth of a daughter! Like any Eastern man, he had longed for a son, an heir. But the moment he saw his

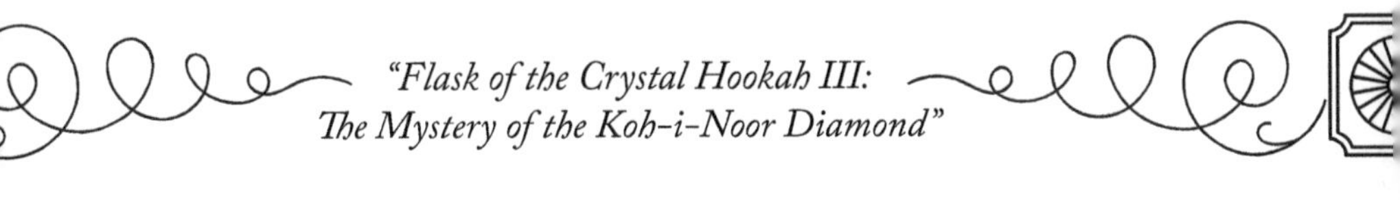

four-kilogram "little one," Tamilla, and cradled her in his arms, he melted with tenderness and bliss.

"Oh, thank you, my dear wife!" he beamed, expressing his gratitude to his beloved Maryam for the precious child.

"Not just a girl—a heroine!" the nurses exclaimed cheerfully in the maternity ward, marvelling at the impressive size and weight of the Mahkamov daughter.

* * *

Moscow, 1963

Colonel Oleg Shamilievich Midiyatdinov of the Soviet Ministry of Internal Affairs was adamantly opposed to the marriage of his younger sister, Marina, to high school geography teacher Denis Persiyev.

And deciding whether to approve this union was, in Oleg Shamilievich's eyes, entirely his business! With both of their parents long gone, Oleg had assumed the roles of both father and mother not only for his full sister Marina but also for their even younger, non-biologically related sister Farida. Of course, Marina's chosen suitor—Denis, affectionately called Dena—was a pleasant, well-mannered young man, and on a personal level, Oleg had no quarrel with him. However, the practical-minded Oleg had grander plans: he intended to secure a far more profitable match for his sister— marrying her off either to the son of an honest, prosperous Soviet magnate with a solid savings account or to the up-and-coming heir of a well-connected official.

Marina, however, had always been a free-spirited, romantic soul, and she had long grown tired of her strict, domineering brother. So even under the threat of domestic retribution, she did things her own way—she simply married Denis! And he, hopelessly in love with this charming girl, promised her "mountains of gold," just as most young men do.

"Marinachka, don't worry—everything will be just fine for us!" he assured her.

And so, with fits and starts, the wedding took place. Oleg didn't attend the ceremony, but he did send a monetary gift to the bride and a modest little "Zaporozhets" to the groom. Denis was over the moon, and Marina mused to herself, *Well, at least my brother is doing something useful.*

However, about three months later, when Oleg visited and saw Marina sporting a noticeable baby bump, he exploded with rage. At that very moment, Denis was still at work.

"Marina, have you lost your mind?!" the colonel roared at his sister. "Why didn't you get an abortion? I'll kill that Denis! You're not supposed to be pregnant—your heart is weak!"

And he was right. There had indeed been a serious risk—Marina's doctors had warned her that it would be better not to give birth. But Marina had longed for a child; she had been dreaming of this son. She was sure it would be a boy who would be just like Denis in every way. She adored her husband and yearned to bear him a son who would be his spitting image.

The force of her brother's outburst left Marina feeling terribly unwell, and Oleg promptly called for an ambulance.

Marina was rushed to the hospital. Miraculously, both she and the child in her womb were saved, yet the doctors warned the entire family once again: given her heart condition, her situation was precarious, and ideally, she should be examined by one of the luminaries of Soviet cardiology—say, Professor Lazar Israelovich Fogelson, head of the therapeutic department at the clinic of the Central Scientific Research Institute for the Evaluation of Labor Capacity and the Organization of Work for the Disabled, TSIETIN, for short. But Denis had already learned that securing an appointment with Professor Fogelson was nearly impossible. The waiting list for the renowned doctor was so enormous that his schedule was booked solid for years into the future. But Marina's heart simply couldn't wait that long.

Later that day, after bringing his sister back home, Oleg said, "Marina, listen—let's talk calmly." In the kitchen, Kostya was quietly making tea at Oleg's request, not daring to interrupt the conversation. "Just don't interrupt me or even think about getting upset. Here's what I wanted…you know I'm over forty and, because of an illness in my childhood, I can't have children. That's just the way it is; you're lucky that fate spared you that misfortune. But…I promise to help you! I'll work something out with that brilliant Professor Fogelson so that he can examine you—and even treat you. But there's one condition… Marina, you must promise me, once you give birth to a son, you must hand him over to me to raise."

Marina was stunned. Not only was Oleg speaking in his usual imperious tone—a tone she had grown accustomed to—but what he was now proposing was utterly outrageous! She had always suspected that her brother was a bit "not all there," but never to this extreme.

"Forgive me, Oleg—but are you out of your mind? No! Never, ever!" she protested. "I'd rather…"

"What, rather?!" Oleg snapped. "You'd rather die, wouldn't

you? You know your condition is terrible—you know it yourself! But if you die, you'll never see your child. Now listen: once you recover, I'll give you another two years to nurse him and gradually wean him from you. And after that, you can visit us and see him whenever you like, no problem. But under no circumstances are you to tell him that you are his mother. Deal? And during that time, once you're well again, you and Denis can have a whole bunch more children! That way, you won't really need this firstborn… and I'll have my own son, whom I can raise exactly as I see fit! Come on, just agree."

I can only imagine how you'll raise him, Marina thought in horror. But she dared not defy her formidable brother—he wouldn't tolerate any dissent, and she was terrified of him. "Alright," she finally whispered, "I'll give birth and nurse him—and then we'll see… Maybe I can even run away somewhere with my husband and our son, far away from this monstrous brother of mine."

"Have you suddenly become very rich?" she managed to ask.

"Not yet… but very soon, don't doubt it! I always get what I want."

6

The Kyzylkum Desert, Bukhara Region, near the city of Gazli, 1965

Classified, Top-Secret Facility No. 57

Chief accountant Natalia Dmitrievna Sokolova burst out of the director's office as if scalded, nearly dropping her folders in her haste.

"Liza!" she cried, fixing her glare on the very young secretary, who was calmly filing her long, painted nails at her desk. "Why didn't you… tell me anything? Why on earth did you call me to his office? Is this some sort of sick joke?"

"What happened?" Liza asked, reluctantly tearing herself away from her nail file. "Why are you yelling like someone's died?"

"Yes!" Natalia shrieked, her voice trembling with hysteria. "Exactly—he's dead! He's not breathing at all!"

"Who?" the sleep-deprived secretary managed to ask. "Who isn't breathing?"

"Our director, Davron Ulugbekovich!" Natalia gasped, her eyes wide as she struggled to breath. "You told me he was calling me— that he was waiting! But now… his head is thrown back… and he doesn't seem to be sleeping! I'm not even making this up—go in and see for yourself!"

"I'm scared," the secretary admitted. "May I call one of our men?"

"Call whoever you want!" Natalia snapped, waving her hand furiously. "Just leave me out of it—don't touch me. And let no one later say that I drove him into a heart attack! We didn't even exchange a single word today."

With that, Natalia hurried out of the reception area.

"Who's accusing you?" Liza called after her while simultaneously dialling the number of the chief process engineer, Burilkov. "Hello! Mikhail Anatolyevich? This is Liza—the boss's secretary. Please come here immediately! What? Oh... no, it's not the director calling—well, not exactly him... I mean... Anyway, come as soon as you can and you'll see for yourself! And bring along one of the men, will you? Don't ask me who—it doesn't matter. Yes, just come."

About five minutes later, while Burilkov and two of his colleagues were making their way from the workshops (which had been inspected earlier that morning) to the director's office, they gathered outside the door.

"So, what was he calling for?" the chief engineer asked, still not fully grasping the situation and hesitating even to crack open the director's door. "Was it something important?"

"More important than anything!" Liza replied grimly. "Just a moment ago, Natalia Dmitrievna practically shot out of there like a bullet," she said, gesturing toward the office. "She insists that our Davron Ulugbekovich is dead. But how can that be? I don't understand! I saw him myself an hour ago when he entered his office. Although..."

"Although, what?" the somewhat brusque engineer asked impatiently.

"He was all red and breathing heavily," Liza explained.

Without another word, Burilkov yanked open the door and stormed into the director's office, his subordinates trailing behind him. There, they found that the plant director, Davron Ulugbekovich Abduhalikov, was indeed dead.

The doctors called by the ambulance later announced that the preliminary cause of death was a cerebral haemorrhage.

The entire workforce was in shock. How could this be? Why so suddenly? And who would now replace the director of this top-secret facility—who was to take over his post?

***

Tashkent, still 1965

Vadim Borisovich Irmanov, the head of the State Depository for Precious Metals of the Uzbek Soviet Republic, received a telegram containing a message that was cryptic yet perfectly clear to him: "The old man has necrosis. The little stars have lit up. The pipe may go out. One spoon of tobacco is missing."

These were bad news—very bad news.

Immediately, Irmanov recalled by analogy the famous phrase from the radiogram sent by the Soviet geologists Khabardin, Yelagino, and Avdeenko from the town of Mirny: "They lit the pipe of peace; the tobacco is excellent..." And now, under Irmanov's wing, things were clearly not as good as they had been in 1955 in Mirny... Oh no, not that!

The words "The old man has necrosis" meant, in his mind, that the director of the diamond factory was no longer alive. *But why did he suddenly die?* Vadim Borisovich thought. "The little stars have lit up" meant that the police were all over the factory—and that the higher-ups were clearly keeping the matter under control.

"The pipe may go out" implied that unless measures were taken, shipments of Yakut diamonds to Gazli might be interrupted, since they were being handled through the deceased director. And "One spoon of tobacco is missing" was downright dismal: a portion of diamonds—more precisely, about a handful worth several tens of thousands of American dollars—had been stolen. Moreover, these were uncut diamonds, for if they were processed, the sender of the telegram would have called them "roses." *I wonder what the investigation has managed to uncover...*

While the head of the Depository was intently mulling over these strange, abruptly unfolding events, there was a knock at his door.

Not very timely, Irmanov thought, but out of habit, he called out:

"Yes, come in!"

"Well, hello, my dear Vadik!" A greyish, scrawny, and slightly stooped man entered the office, his tone laced with irony.

His gaze toward the seated Irmanov was feigned as benevolent, yet Vadim immediately noticed a masked unfriendliness behind it.

The republic's Depository was a division of the State Institution for the Formation of the State Fund of Precious Metals and Gemstones of the entire Soviet Union, responsible for the storage, distribution, and use of precious metals and stones under the Ministry of Finance.

Vadim Borisovich had been appointed head of this division— that is, the republican Depository. This meant he controlled the operations of all the republic's enterprises specializing in the extraction and processing of gold, platinum, diamonds, and other precious stones.

"What brings you here, Stanislav Zakharovich?" Without replying to the greeting, Vadim Borisovich asked tensely.

"Why so formal?" The guest shook his head reproachfully. "We're old friends, aren't we? Or, sitting in that high-backed chair, have you forgotten already?!"

His tone laced with an undertone of threat.

Stanislav Levidovsky, without any ceremony, strode over to the chair nearest to Vadim and, without even asking permission, plopped down into it.

"Tell me, Vadik, why is life so unfair?" Stanislav continued in the same impudent tone. "Some people seem to get everything, while others get nothing! For some, it's a luxurious big house, a car, and a cushy post as a high-ranking official in the Ministry of Finance! And his course mate—his close friend, practically a relative—gets nothing at all! It's just infuriating."

"Stasik, you know that I inherited the house and the car from my late father," began Vadim in a conciliatory tone. "And he got them from distant ancestors…"

"I know, I know. I've heard that your lineage goes back to some wealthy kings—what were they called? Something like Kavad, Rustam, and the others. And since your grandfather and father married Russians, you ended up with a Russian name, even though you're essentially Uzbek."

Clearly, the wealth of those Saka kings was immense if it has reached you! Do you even believe that fairy tale yourself?!" Stasik burst out laughing. "Well, what can I say—the position of head of the State Depository suits you!" he continued, adding, "And by the way, you and I graduated together from the Faculty of Geology at the university and did our internship side by side! Yet somehow you ended up with such a cushy post, while I'm still stuck working

as a senior lab assistant at the research institute. And it's all because I have neither connections nor money—and I couldn't secure a better position for myself."

"Listen, Stas!" Vadim Borisovich could no longer hold back. "It's not about my roots or connections but that I'm used to working hard and taking my job very seriously! We're not playing around here. Besides, when it comes to anything dealing with jewels, you know honesty is valued! We live in a socialist country—we're building a comm—"

"Enough already! Quit the demagoguery! I don't believe in any such honesty. Got it? I bet you pocketed a couple of golden nuggets and a handful of diamonds long ago, haven't you? What, haven't you? Surely you took advantage of your high position? And if you didn't, then you're a fool! And what if I report your vast garden, from which you harvest a ton of produce every year?! Vegetables and fruits—all that counts as 'unearned income.' They won't just kick you out of your post—they might even lock you up!"

"What do you want from me?" Irmanov asked gloomily. "Everything I do is by the book—I have documents for everything."

"Documents! You've surrounded your life with luxury and comfort, and you've secured yourself by being buried under mountains of paperwork, haven't you? Clever—I can't really say anything against that! But that's not enough—you even installed your spineless son as the director of that diamond plant near Gazli, to replace the one that suddenly died. What kind of nonsense is that? Nepotism in your career! Outrageous!"

"How do you know about the director?…" Vadim Borisovich asked, genuinely surprised. "That is completely classified information."

"It doesn't matter—I have my own channels. I'm not some

street rat, and don't forget, I'm a geologist too. If you don't want any trouble, my dear friend Vadik, then appoint me to that position!"

For a long moment, Irmanov looked at Levidovsky very seriously—almost sullenly—and then he couldn't help but burst into a rolling, Homeric laugh.

"You?! You'd have cleaned out everything there in less than a month!" Vadim observed between bouts of laughter, wiping tears from his eyes. "And you'd vanish somewhere, so that no one could ever find you!"

"As it happens, I know geology no worse than you—or your son!" Stanislav snapped back indignantly. "And I wouldn't ste… take someone else's property. I mean, state property."

"Then why do you want the position?"

"Can't you see? It's prestigious. Just listen to how it sounds: 'Stanislav Zakharovich Levidovsky—director of the plant!' Isn't that beautiful? Huh? Why are you quiet? Will you appoint me?"

"No, Stasik, I'm sorry. I must ask you to leave—I have too many things to attend to. I can't entrust you even with the laboratory: give you some quartz samples and you'd swipe them too. So don't even ask about the plant! No, no. I'll help you out with money if you need it. But the director of the plant will be Alexei."

"Then make me your deputy in this administration—in the State Depository of Uzbekistan! Or at least the head of a department… or the deputy director at that plant…"

"No, Stasik, that isn't up to me. Moscow makes the appointments. I coordinated Alexei's candidacy with the Main Administration of the country, and they approved it—since my son, though young, has a good education, extensive knowledge, and the best credentials! Besides, he graduated from the Mining Institute in Yakutsk and is an excellent diamond specialist. The higher-ups trust both of us,

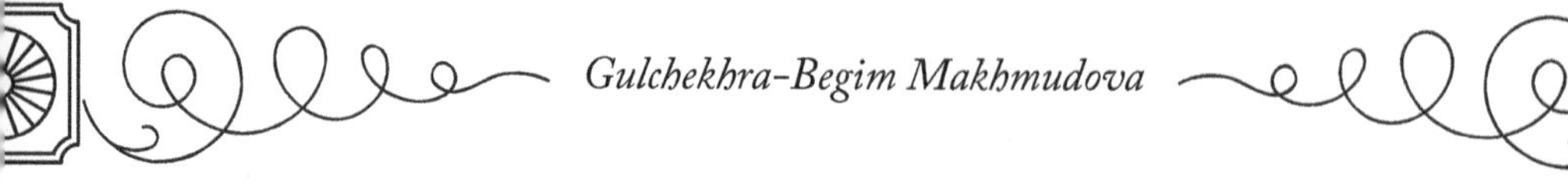

but you—sorry, no one even knows you."

"Yeah, yeah, high and mighty!" Levidovsky grumbled enviously.

"And as for you…" Irmanov continued in an admonishing tone, "if we're being honest—remember how, back in university, you set up our poor professor with the dean, got him punished, and deprived him of a whole month's salary because of you?… You utterly lack moral principles, Stanislav Zakharovich. As such, people like you simply cannot be entrusted with the nation's wealth! Forgive me once more. And farewell."

"So you won't help? I'm asking you one last time!" Levidovsky squinted.

"No, I just can't. I'd be happy to, but it's beyond my power."

"You'll regret this, Vadik!" Stanislav hissed threateningly.

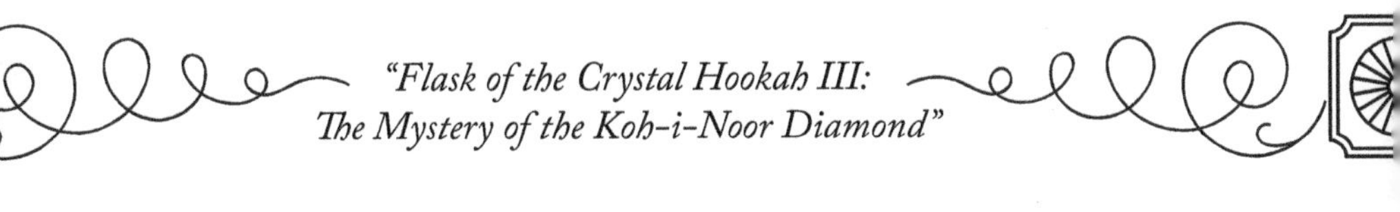

7

Sakastan, 6th Century BCE

The Tocharian chieftain Zakir was in a rage. He had received word that King Spargapis had sent envoys to Bikbulat and the Alans and had even, allegedly, met personally with the Alan leader on their own territory. Scouts had reported that Bikbulat's tribe—long accustomed to a meagre existence and planning an expedition to some southern lands—had suddenly stopped preparing for the campaign. In the Alan camp, however, there was now plenty of well-fattened livestock and an abundance of provisions.

So, it appears that Spargapis has indeed allied himself with Bikbulat and won him over, Zakir thought. *I can understand why Spargapis needs Bikbulat. Every Saka knows that this Alan despises his king and has always dreamed of taking his place—just as I have. But the main point is: why would the king need Bikbulat?... Ah! It all makes sense now! Spargapis plans to use the Alans to wipe out the other tribes and clear a path for himself so that no one can stand in his way as he rules the steppe endlessly. But he'll regret it—he has no idea whom he's messing with. My Tocharians are strong and brave. We'll destroy both Bikbulat and Spargapis!*

Zakir then gathered the elders of his tribe and asked what they should do. How should they punish Spargapis—and, in doing so, Bikbulat as well? Should they attack immediately? Do they have enough strength now? Or should they wait until spring to strike?

"We Tocharians are the strongest when it comes to warfare," replied Aidar, his second-in-command and trusted battle companion. "We can attack right away!"

"Very well, Aidar, I hear you," said Zakir. "But what will my other glorious warriors say? If we fight now, it may not be just another skirmish—it could be our last, for Spargapis is willing to die to wrest his throne from his rivals, the most dangerous of whom is me."

The warriors fell silent in thought. Among the Saka, there had never been cowards, yet who wishes to die prematurely?

Just then, in the midst of the council, the main tent's flap opened—and in walked Spargapis himself! He was unguarded, wounded, caked in dirt, and ragged, his face emaciated and seemingly utterly defeated.

Aidar immediately drew his sword from its scabbard and shouted, "Watch out, you jackal! I've got you now—you came here to surrender on your own! Now you're a corpse!"

"Water… give me something to drink," moaned the king of the Massagetae. Zakir gave a curt nod to one of his attendants, who brought Spargapis a small bowl of clear spring water. Gulping greedily, the stranger looked at Aidar and weakly asked, "Did you, oh famed warrior, defeat me in combat, or capture me on the battlefield?"

There was no arguing his point. In uttering those words, Spargapis had touched a nerve—noble warriors were not meant to claim victory over an enemy without truly earning it.

Then, almost as an afterthought, Spargapis continued, his voice barely above a whisper yet resonant like the toll of a gong:

"Moreover, Tocharians, today I am your guest! I have come seeking your counsel and assistance."

Zakir didn't immediately register Spargapis's words… Then it dawned on him that not only could he not kill this insolent bandit at that moment, but he was also… compelled to receive him with full honours—for the law of hospitality in the steppe was sacred and unbreakable! It was a trap.

Straining to conceal his true feelings, Zakir, through gritted teeth, said,

"Yes, you are our guest, esteemed Spargapis… Please, make yourself comfortable—take the best seat at the head of the tent and rest after your long journey… Your meal will be served shortly…"

"I humbly thank you, O future king of all the Saka, Zakir," replied Spargapis softly and ingratiatingly.

Zakir shuddered.

No one had ever before called him "future king of all the Saka!" And he least expected to hear that title from his greatest rival and enemy—the detested Spargapis! What was happening?

With a signal to his attendants, Zakir dismissed the council, deciding to speak with Spargapis alone. Still, he posted a reliable guard outside—one could never fully trust that snake. Who knew what was in his mind…

"Tell me, Spargapis, why?… You astonish me. Why do you call me king? Are you not yourself a descendant of the royal Ishguz—Iskapaya and Madyes—and the rightful heir to the Saka throne? Why, then, would you so readily yield your position and such high status to me, merely the leader of one of the Massagetae tribes?… It's all very strange!"

"You don't believe it?" Spargapis panted. "I understand. I'll tell you the truth—a secret that's really quite simple. I'm so tired of fighting for my authority, Zakir—constantly having to prove myself! Time marches on, and despite all my efforts, I still haven't managed to rule the steppe all the way to the banks of the Iaksart and the Oxus. Clearly, my strength isn't sufficient… And then there's Bikbulat—whom I hoped to treat as a friend, to whom I extended honour and generous aid—only to be betrayed, attacked treacherously, wounded, and nearly killed… See how I've been maimed by his warriors? I barely escaped. My entire force has been scattered… Will you allow me another sip of water?"

"Of course, illustrious Spargapis! Drink as much as you like."

"Poor, poor me…" After taking another long drink, the guest continued, "Everyone knows that I have no camp of my own, no refuge… And so, you, great King of the Saka, Zakir, I beg for asylum and protection. If you would accept a wretched dog like me, Spargapis, at your feet… if you would avenge me, as a brother, against the treacherous Bikbulat! Then your fame would undoubtedly spread throughout the land, and songs and legends would be sung in your honour! Especially since you alone are invincible among all. And without the help of the Abii—and without my aid—Bikbulat and his giant Alans are as feeble as infants. Alone, however, I cannot overcome him."

"What is it about the Abii that displeased you so, Spargapis, that you set Tursun and Bikbulat against each other? After all, Tursun never laid claim to the throne…"

"He does not love me," Spargapis interjected sharply. "I stole his one and only beloved daughter, Zaryana, and forced her to be my wife. He can never forgive me for that!" After a pause, he cautiously asked, "So, great King Zakir, will you take me—your unfortunate subject, Spargapis—under your protection?"

"Of course…" Zakir replied after a slight hesitation, still not entirely trusting his guest but unable to resist the lure of being called "king" and the prospect of, with Spargapis's help, ascending the

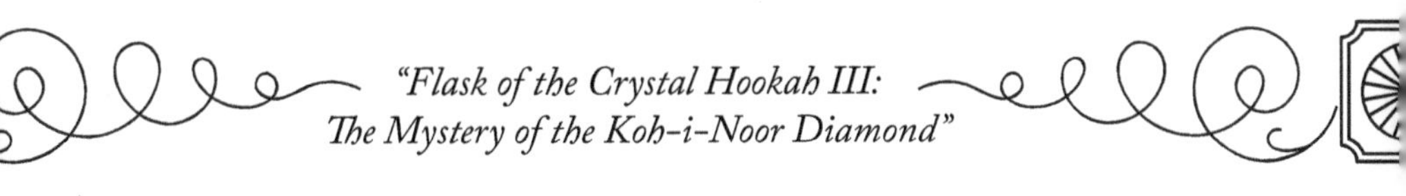

throne in the near future in place of that unfortunate, vanquished barbarian. "Live here, my friend, as long as you wish—even forever! And… if you like, serve as my right-hand man."

It seemed Spargapis had been waiting for this very offer, for he immediately replied with enthusiasm:

"Oh yes, it is a great honour for me! You are so magnanimous, King of the Saka, Zakir!"

"All right, that's enough. After all, no one has officially crowned me king yet—there's been no council…"

"There will be a council. My word is as binding as ever. Since I have declared that you shall be king, so it shall be," Spargapis declared firmly. "Now, what do you say? Will you march to war against those vile, treacherous Alans? And by the way, I almost forgot—I've heard that Bikbulat himself says you, Zakir, aren't even worth his pinkie finger! That he will, at any moment, defeat you and ascend to the Massagetae throne…"

"What?!" Zakir cried, deeply agitated. "He will defeat me?! Never! No man has ever been born who could overcome the brave and valiant Tocharians! I swear, I'll begin preparing my warriors today! In three days, we march against the Alans. I will not be overthrown, not while I am the 'King of the Saka'…"

"Yes, yes, King Zakir, everything is as it should be…" Spargapis murmured, smiling wryly.

* * *

Tigraxauda's King Kavad was a large, tall, and mighty man. He had chosen a wife who was his equal—a lady from a rich, noble family, almost like a princess. She wasn't especially beautiful, but she was tall, statuesque, and strong. Yet just as Aygul became pregnant by Kavad, misfortune struck: after buying some attractive trinkets from passing traders, she inadvertently contracted a dangerous foreign disease—and fell gravely ill. The poor woman barely managed to carry her pregnancy to term, and when she gave birth to a very large boy (her labour being all the more difficult because of his size), she told her husband that she agreed he should name their son Rustam, just as he wished.

Kavad agreed. However, he never expected that his wife would die so quickly—barely recovering after childbirth, she passed away.

The only solace in the king's grief was the beautiful child—a sturdy, rosy-cheeked little fellow with chubby arms and legs.

"This child will grow up to be a true hero—a mighty warrior of Tigraxauda," the king thought. "But I can't remain a widower. I must find a replacement for Aygul soon—I'll have to remarry…"

Kavad's second wife was Balkyz, whom he married not out of love but in exchange for a very large bride price from her family. Balkyz was a frail woman who long failed to bear him any children. She did not love Rustam, resentful of the affection her husband showed the boy.

Yet Rustam, Kavad's son, grew quickly and indeed stood out from all the other Saka children with an intellect, kindness, and strength far beyond what one would expect from someone his age.

"What will become of this splendid boy? Surely he'll be our next king, following in his father's footsteps!" all of Tigraxauda dreamed.

***

The Ruler of Mighty Media, Astyages, was calm and self-assured. He had little reason for worry—after all, his military commander was the loyal and invincible Harpagus, and no one had dared challenge the throne. Despite all the prophecies and omens, even the slain infant grandson was no longer a threat.

"What news? What is happening in the world and in our land?" the king asked one of his advisors, a man named Dinar.

"Nothing remarkable, Your Majesty," replied the official with a bow. "Except that in far-off Hindustan, Prince Siddhartha Gautama Shakyamuni has declared himself 'enlightened'—or, in his own tongue, the Buddha. Now he preaches about some 'four noble truths'…"

"Bah, that matters little," the Media king remarked. "We have our own gods and our own truths! We believe in Ahura Mazda—may he bestow his mercy upon us and help us with our great state affairs!"

Having spoken of matters of state, Astyages suddenly remembered that he hadn't executed or punished anyone in days—and boredom was making his hands itch. He needed a scapegoat, and quickly!

"Servants, bring me that merchant to whom I once owed money—and failed to pay—and who dared remind me of it yesterday! Execute my order immediately!"

The poor wretch was soon found and brought before the king's stern gaze.

"How dare you, you filthy, insolent slave, tell me—me, the great king of Media and Persia—that I have 'forgotten' something, that I

owe you? King Astyages can never have debts! It is you, all of you subjects, who owe him! Do you understand?"

"Oh yes, Your Majesty, please forgive me," the merchant stammered, trembling with fear. "But you pardoned and forgave me last time…"

"Are you arguing with me again? You dare contradict me? Yes, I pardoned you yesterday because I was in a sombre mood, lost in thoughts about the fleeting nature of life. But today I am in high spirits—I want to relax and have some fun… Servants, heed my command: cut off his tongue so that he can never make demands again! And sever both his hands so that he has nothing with which to take what rightfully belongs to me! Everything in this land is mine—and no one else's!"

King Astyages burst into a raucous, sinister laugh as the doomed merchant was led away like cattle to the slaughter—a pitiful soul who had unwittingly fallen into the clutches of a monstrous, crowned, and titled beast with a deceivingly human guise.

"Someday, I shall rule the entire world," Astyages mused dreamily to Dinar. He had begun to feel bored once more. "Having control over just two countries isn't enough—I want to be like Ahura Mazda…"

"To achieve that, great king, you will need… a stone from Hindustan!"

"Again you speak of that country! Why are you so fixated on it?… And what stone are you talking about?"

"I've heard of a precious gem called a 'diamond'—a stone enormous in size, stunningly beautiful, and radiant as the sun. It's said to be worth more than gold or any other jewel! The only problem is, as I've been told, obtaining it is utterly impossible."

"Impossible? Is anything impossible if I, Astyages, so desire it?"

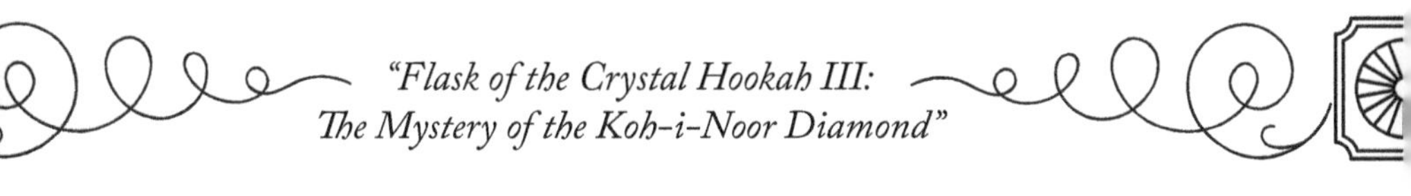

"Oh, Your Majesty, of course not! But the trouble is that this marvellous diamond is owned by... a little Indian boy from a humble background. No one knows exactly where he comes from. He appears unexpectedly—wherever and whenever he pleases..."

"Listen to my command, Dinar: find me this boy, wherever he may be! Promise him all the treasures of Media. Sweet-talk him, deceive him—tell him he will receive anything he wishes. Just ensure that the boy agrees to come to my palace so that I may see him! Then we shall take that stone from him by force and cast him out to the four corners of the earth, or I am not Astyages. If this diamond is as precious as you say it is, then I can possess it! And remember: this matter must remain secret; let no one hear of our conversation. Understood?"

"Understood, my lord. Everything will be done exactly as you command, O king!"

* * *

In the war with the Tocharians, Bikbulat suffered heavy losses. But Zakir, the chieftain of the Tocharians, lost even more. Many of his best warriors fell on the battlefield. And most importantly—in one of the battles with the Alans, his close friend, the valiant hero Sarmak, perished—a man many regarded as a wild bear, a monster, though Zakir had known him since childhood and cherished him.

The chieftain of the Tocharians had never expected such an outcome. He was overcome with grief and raged against Spargapis for having pushed him into this war.

However, Spargapis, like a gentle, enchanting cat, consoled him:

"It's all right, Zakir, it's all right—after all, you still have some warriors left… Moreover, as I promised, you will soon be king! I will manage to persuade the General Council."

Meanwhile, the Massagetae did not take kindly to Spargapis's scheme, even though many both disdained and feared him. But was not the cunning steppe fox plotting something dangerous? Why would he so readily be willing to hand over the royal throne to his fierce enemy and rival?…

Yet when Zakir and Spargapis convened the Council—attended by all the chieftains and elders of the Massagetae—Spargapis himself, having asked the people's forgiveness for all his weaknesses, vices, and mistakes, and having convincingly assured them that the years had passed and he was now far too feeble for supreme authority, declared Zakir king.

The people reluctantly agreed, deciding that, if need be, they could at any time overthrow this rootless king—one who was not a descendant of their common ancestor, Ispakaya—and replace him with another.

The chieftain of the Tocharians was astonished. Well, look at that—Spargapis kept his word! Does that mean he is not as wicked as he once seemed? Can he really be trusted? And what is it that malicious tongues are always slandering the good for? For now, Zakir was king of the Massagetae! A little more, and he would become the lord of all the Sakas, as Spargapis had already begun to call him…

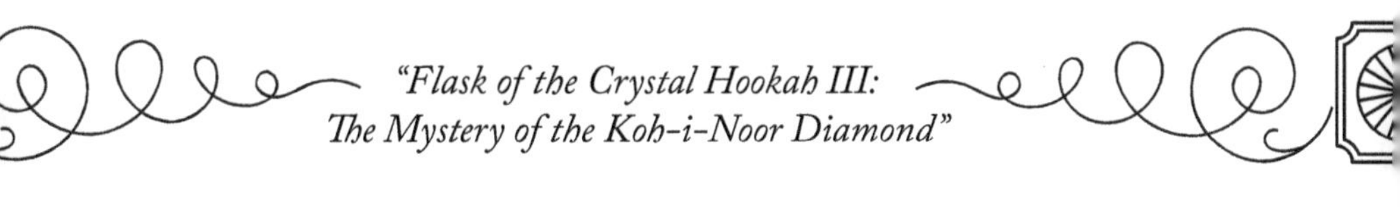

* * *

Spargapis, however, was not as forsaken, poor, and unhappy as he had portrayed himself to Zakir. He had time for both complete freedom and indulgence. Increasingly, he left the encampment of the Tocharians and went wherever he pleased—to his habitual haunts. And often, he would head to the tent of his wife, Zaryana.

Zaryana marveled at herself: she loved this wild reaver with fiery passion. Yet her happiness with him was short-lived, for despite her rare, striking beauty and youth, Spargapis quickly grew cold toward her. She was entirely different from him—pure, luminous, noble, not suited to his nature. The heir to the Saka kings used her solely for his pleasures. And at times, he entertained other women who brought him satisfaction.

But for some reason, only his wife Zaryana became pregnant by that fiend—apparently, it was the will of the heavens that Spargapis, throughout his life, should have only one child...

Months passed, and little changed in their private lives. Finally, the time came for Zaryana to give birth. When word of this reached Spargapis—who was far from his wife—he mounted his fastest horse and galloped to her at the speed of lightning. He desired that child.

Zaryana lay in the tent, with the infant by her side. A midwife busied herself near the young woman, who had lost much blood and strength during childbirth. The midwife was busy wiping both her and the newborn with a clean cloth.

Spargapis entered the tent, smiling broadly and aglow. What a wonder—he was a father!!

"Rejoice, my lord," the midwife blurted out, unable to keep silent in defiance of the law—which mandated that, in the presence of the king, even a former king, all women except his wife must remain mute. "Congratulations—you have a daughter! Look how adorable, such a beauty, and she bears such a striking resemblance to you!"

Slowly, the smile faded from Spargapis's face. He stared intently at Zaryana—and then, suddenly, with fierce anger he roared:

"What?! How can this be?! This is a girl?! Zaryana, what does this mean?! I commanded you to bear me a son! How dare you, you wretch, disobey me?!"

He drew from his garments a thick, tight leather belt adorned with cold copper plates—and began striking the face of his wife, who lay there. The midwife managed to grab the newborn in time and fled from the tent with the baby, shrieking in terror and horror.

At the midwife's cries, the nomads rushed over, but none dared enter the tent of their leader without permission—they were all too afraid of Spargapis.

The hereditary and legitimate king of the Massagetae beat his beautiful wife to death—her strength sapped by childbirth, leaving her unable to resist.

When Zaryana, all bloodied and utterly spent, drew her last breath, Spargapis suddenly came to himself, his consciousness returning. Covered in her blood, he began frantically embracing and kissing the now lifeless Zaryana—the wife he had once loved; the very same woman he had not long ago forcibly abducted from her father, Tursun, the chieftain of the Abii, who had cherished and loved her dearly.

In his despair, Spargapis began searching for the midwife, intending to snatch the infant from her and kill it—he considered the child the main cause of his sorrow, the principal culprit in this

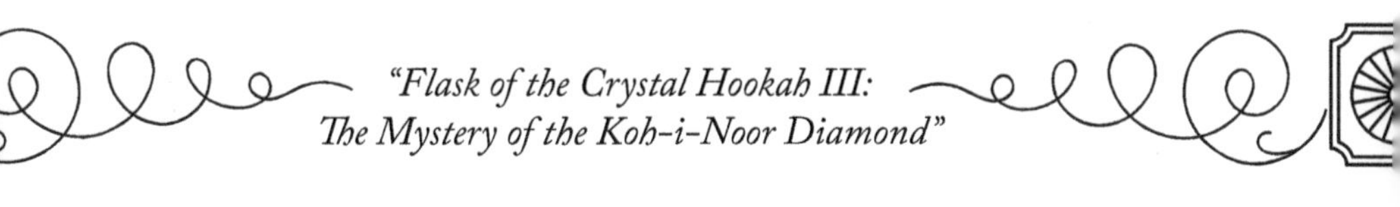

terrible family tragedy. He found her easily; the midwife lived nearby. And as soon as Spargapis entered the humble hut of the old woman—shown to him by the king's attendants out of fear— and raised his hand above the little girl, suddenly, before his eyes appeared… an unfamiliar dark-skinned boy.

The boy looked like an Indian pauper. Yet atop his head, he wore a luxurious turban crafted entirely of pure gold, into which, at its center on the front, was set a huge, exquisitely beautiful, glowing gemstone.

"Stop, King Spargapis!" the boy addressed him. "Do not do this! I am Karna, son of the Sun. In the name of Heaven and the Sun, I command you—do not kill your daughter, spare her life! Name her 'Tomyris,' which means 'Iron Lady.' I see her destiny: she will become the first female warrior, and even the mightiest will count her among equals. She will bring you true paternal happiness and fulfill your long-held dream—to unite all the Massagetae into one tribe. Moreover, she will glorify the Sakas for all time! And when your Tomyris grows up, I alone will reveal to her the secret of my magnificent precious stone…"

And before the astonishing boy Karna vanished, Spargapis— dazzled by the light of the stone—withdrew his hand from his newborn daughter and recoiled, utterly shaken by all he had seen and heard.

8

An old man, dressed in tattered, filthy rags, was making his way across the steppe toward one of the modest Saka villages.

As he approached, a group of boys began spitting at him and throwing small stones, laughing and mocking him because he looked so strange and ridiculous.

Suddenly, an adult man emerged from one of the huts. He grabbed his ten-year-old son by the ear, gave him a good slap, and shouted:

"Never—Vildan, do you hear me?—never even dare to look this respectable man straight in the eyes! And certainly don't slander him, badmouth him, or throw stones at him! Hey, kids, this applies to all of you! If I see or hear that any one of you is insulting the great old man, I'll beat you soundly!! You'll forget your own name…"

"But why, Father?" the boy asked in surprise, his ears still stinging. "After all, he's dumb and so poor! Far poorer than even us… We always laugh at such people, and you've never scolded me for it before! Why isn't it allowed to offend this old man?"

"Son, you don't understand," the man replied. "This is the worthy Tursun, chieftain of the Abii. The poor fellow—having lost his only, dearly beloved daughter Zaryana—has lost his mind… Nothing can console him in his solitary grief. And, in truth, he is wealthy."

"This man is wealthy?!" Vildan gasped even more. "It doesn't seem like it at all…"

"Yes, he is very distinguished and rich; his chests are filled with treasures. When his relatives find him wandering the steppes and villages, they bring him home, wash him, and dress him in sumptuous garments. But they say that at night he discards his clothes again, donning the most miserable, filthy rags, and goes wherever his eyes lead him. For he needs nothing in this world anymore. He is seeking death—like one of the first people on Earth—but he cannot find it…"

"How pitiful the old man is," the boy murmured, deeply moved by the story.

As soon as the old man neared the man's house, the latter bowed low before him.

"Come in, great chieftain! My name is Fuad. My home is your home. My wife has just prepared dinner. Share it with us, your unworthy slaves! It is a great honor for us to receive you."

Tursun said nothing, but almost immediately—far too swiftly for a feeble old man—he entered the house.

He must be terribly hungry, the poor fellow… Fuad thought. It looks like he's wandered for a very long time through the barren, cold steppe… Thankfully, he has arrived in our village.

The old man ate a great deal, greedily and hastily, as if he were in a great hurry to be somewhere.

"I must be off—my daughter Zaryana is waiting for me; I was delayed on the road," he explained, his voice tinged with excitement.

"But your daughter…" began Fuad's not-so-bright wife, Dilara—the keeper of the hearth—who hadn't yet figured out how to speak properly to a distressed, deranged old man.

"Shh!" Fuad hushed her almost imperceptibly, his look conveying that Tursun was in such a state of misery and burden—so overcome that he had lost his mind—that he simply could not face the harsh truth of life… a life without his departed daughter.

"Stay with us for the night," the hospitable Fuad kindly offered.

"Very well," the guest agreed, both gratefully and with a hint of indifference. "But tomorrow I must leave—if I am away too long, my Zaryana will worry! I went out looking for her. She didn't come by your place? Apparently not. So, she must have already gone home!"

Dilara glanced silently at her husband, wondering if it was really worth fussing over a madman. But Fuad was resolute in his decision to accord the guest the highest honors. He ordered Dilara to lay out warm blankets for old Tursun in the best spot of the hut, and she obeyed.

After dinner, everyone retired to rest. Little Vildan tossed and turned for a long time, unable to sleep, his thoughts occupied by the tragic fate of the once mighty and wise man—the chieftain of the Abii.

In the morning, the lady of the house rose early to milk the goat and prepare a heartier breakfast for both the guest and her men. However, Tursun's trail had vanished. No—he had taken nothing that wasn't his; he hadn't even finished his own piece of bread. He had left in the very clothes in which he had come.

"And he didn't even say goodbye!" the woman complained as she roused her husband.

"Don't reproach him, understand? Never!" Fuad snapped. "Not a single harsh word about the old man—no one should ever have to endure such a fate. His whole life has crumbled. He won't even acknowledge his granddaughter, believing that Zaryana perished

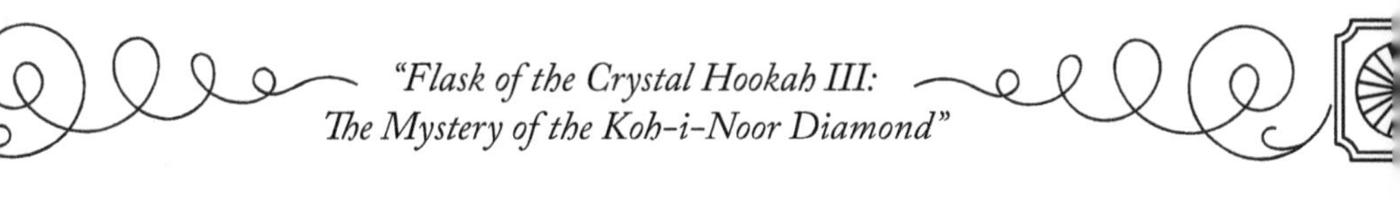

because of her birth. And he despises his son-in-law even more. Rumor has it among the people that Zaryana was done for by Sparga…"

At that, Fuad, interrupting himself, suddenly fell silent in fear. In the steppe, everyone—especially the common folk—revered and feared the mighty father of Tomyris.

* * *

Zakir became the king of all the Massagetae tribes. He received this lofty title as a gift from his "brother" and "closest friend"—Spargapis. The intoxicated Zakir was immensely flattered by it. Meanwhile, the feud between the Tocharians and the Alans continued, especially since Zakir was young and strong. Bikbulat, the chieftain of the Alans, was the most dissatisfied that Zakir had been crowned king. The foremost Alan could not stand Spargapis, but at least he was the hereditary king! And who, by all accounts, was Zakir? What sort of ruler of the Massagetae was he? Thus, Bikbulat made no secret of the fact that he would not submit to that scoundrel for a single moment.

Across the steppe, people marveled at how the former king had voluntarily, without any struggle, yielded his power to another. No sooner had Spargapis proclaimed Zakir king than the tribal chieftains immediately refused to recognize it. No one was willing to obey or submit to the new authority. This infuriated Zakir. He began forcing the chieftains into submission. His punitive campaigns against the villages of the recalcitrant tribes were marked by great cruelty. After these raids, nothing remained but burned huts and heaps of ashes.

The absence of all restraint also corrupted the ranks of the Tocharian warriors—they pillaged, burned, killed, and raped, and some even took the last of what the surviving women had, preying on the misfortunes and losses of others without a thought for anyone. Tasting all the sweetness of power, the outrageously ambitious and arrogant Zakir became utterly unbearable in his dealings with the other Massagetae chieftains, subjecting them to all manner of insults and humiliations. The chieftains started to protest.

Before long, Zakir increasingly disregarded the opinions of his sworn friend Spargapis, acting solely as he saw fit. Yet, out of desperation and despair, the chieftains would sometimes turn to Spargapis with complaints and pleas to shield them from the arbitrary tyranny of their new master. After all, Spargapis had borne the title of king not long ago and was now the chief sardar of the new lord of the steppe.

Spargapis, for his part, knew how to distance himself from Zakir's misdeeds. And when Spargapis publicly interceded on someone's behalf—clearly fawning before Zakir—that young fool, who had unexpectedly come into a vast measure of power, tightened his rein and continued to trample and demolish everything left and right, thereby earning ever-growing hatred from all the tribes.

Zakir, accompanied by his Tocharians, rode far from his native village and camp to wage war against Bikbulat's Alans. Now, after the death of the mighty Tocharian Sarmak, the Alans had grown stronger, and Zakir's retinue had noticeably thinned. Zakir was no coward—he was brave and valiant—but his strength and patience were beginning to fail him. Yet the warrior's pride and honor—and now that of a king—would not allow him to capitulate or be the first to end the war. Moreover, Spargapis frequently goaded Zakir, reminding him that Bikbulat most of all desired to snatch the throne from him, and that Bikbulat was his first blood enemy!

One day, in the lull between battles, a messenger arrived at Zakir's tent—a man the new king had never seen before. The messenger told Zakir that the king had simply failed to recognize him—for he was just the grown-up son of one of his kinsmen, Sadyk.

"Tell me, young man, what is your name?" inquired Zakir.

"Nariman, my lord," the messenger replied. "Your mother sent me. She sends you her greetings and…"

For some reason, the messenger suddenly fell silent.

"What is it? Speak quickly, Nariman, do not dawdle!" Zakir bellowed.

"My lord, I fear I have unpleasant and very sorrowful news for you…"

"Well?! What is the matter? Has something happened in my camp? What does my revered Aisha, my mother, say?"

"The chieftain of the Karats, Kuzybek… attacked the camp and… killed your young son!"

"What?!" Zakir roared in horror at the dreadful news. "My son?! Who?! Kuzybek, my neighbor and close friend since childhood?! Has he lost his mind?! But why, for what reason?!"

"I don't know, my lord. It appears the chieftain of the Karats had drunk himself into a stupor and did not know what he was doing… He was not himself, raging wildly."

"What was he doing in my village in my absence?"

"How?" the messenger asked in astonishment. "As usual, he came as your guest. But it seems that one of the Tocharians, one of your kinsmen, insulted the drunken Kuzybek—and he began slashing at everyone within reach! Your boy suddenly dashed out of your tent right at Kuzybek's feet—and Kuzybek struck him with his sword. Most likely, it was an accident."

"Oh, calamity!!" Zakir wailed, filled with despair and horror.

"Yes, very sorrowful," observed Spargapis, who, as usual, was nearby. "But where can you go now, king of the Sakas, Zakir? It is already evening, and the sun will soon set. Let's ride at first light— for you can do nothing to help your son now…"

"But I know exactly whom I shall 'help' now!" Zakir cried, leaping onto his swift, jet-black horse. "Are you with me, Spargapis?"

"Yes, yes, my friend, of course I'm with you! We are brothers, after all. How could I leave you in such dire straits? Wait—but your camp is in the opposite direction!"

"I'm not heading home. You're right, my wise Spargapis; I won't reach my son in time—for according to our customs, he was most likely consigned immediately to the earth. I could not even say goodbye to him, and never will again. Let us ride to the camp of that repulsive monster—Kuzybek! I want to personally hack him to pieces!! Hey, my warriors, who's with me?"

Following Zakir and Spargapis, several hundred armed Tocharians—who never left their weapons behind during wartime, keeping them at their belts even at rest—mounted their horses and galloped toward the Karats.

Kuzybek was not in his camp (understandably, for he might still have been in Zakir's native village or on his way from it), and an enraged, frenzied Zakir, along with his warriors, annihilated every living thing they found in Kuzybek's settlement! Fortunately, many of the villagers had been out in the fields, tending to their harvest. But without a moment's hesitation, Zakir slaughtered… two of Kuzybek's young children. He took parts of their bodies with him, intending to show them to his once-friend, now detested enemy—Kuzybek.

Yet when, the following morning, Zakir, together with his retinue and Spargapis, rode back to his own village, he was greeted with exuberant joy by his entire family. To the astonishment of Zakir and all his attendants, his beloved young son Jamshid was found… alive, whole, and unharmed.

Meanwhile, everyone noticed that a sack was tied to the girth of Zakir's horse. Shortly thereafter, all the Tocharians learned that inside it were the hacked-up bodies of two unfortunate, blameless young children of Kuzybek…

Deeply shaken by all that had transpired, Zakir ordered an immediate search for the deceitful messenger who had, for some reason, besmirched his friend's honor. However, no one had ever heard of any Nariman.

Soon after, an old friend of his father—Sadyk—was brought before Zakir.

"Where is your son Nariman, esteemed Sadyk?" Zakir asked, restraining his anger, for he had always deeply respected the old man.

"Forgive me, my lord, but I do not have such a son!" the old man replied, puzzled. "I have only five sons—you knew that, though you may have forgotten—and among them there is no youth named Nariman with the attributes your warriors described! I do not know who has so tarnished my family's name! And for what reason should this disgrace be upon my gray head?…"

The old man went on lamenting until he was roughly seized by the attendants and sent away.

No matter how Zakir's and Spargapis's warriors fought and searched for that impostor—Nariman (though they now doubted the authenticity of that name)—they found him nowhere. And when the chieftain of the Karats, Kuzybek, sobered up, his grief and anger knew no bounds. He was ready to tear his friend—and now king of the Massagetae, Zakir—to shreds.

"My dear friend, allow me to find this scoundrel, this false messenger Nariman, and take the scalp from him," declared Spargapis, his voice thick with emotion. It was clear that Spargapis was deeply troubled for Zakir by all that had happened.

"Find him, my friend—yes," Zakir agreed. "I trust you like no one else. As I see it, only you have never let me down or deceived me; only you do I believe. And what now will become of me? For Kuzybek desires my soul, my blood!"

"Fear nothing, I will save you," reassured Spargapis. "But perhaps now you must no longer be king; you must go into exile for a time and hide from everyone."

"Yes, yes, you are right, my friend," replied Zakir, his head bowed—the once-mighty warrior now as weak as a small child from his sorrows. "I will leave and hide from everyone…"

And indeed, the news of that merciless, bloody retribution spread in an instant across all of Saka land. The people were outraged, dismayed, and exceedingly angry with their new king.

"Depose Zakir!" many cried aloud for all to hear. "He is unworthy to be our ruler! Restore Spargapis as king!"

Taking in his compassionate friend's words, Zakir himself gathered several dozen of his bravest warriors and his finest horses—and disappeared into regions known to no one except Spargapis, the most loyal and trustworthy in Zakir's eyes. It was to him that Zakir had revealed where he could be found once the storm subsided and all was settled.

The people themselves unanimously proclaimed Spargapis king of the Massagetae.

"Now, listen, people, don't go complaining about me later," Spargapis said quietly, through gritted teeth, as he once again ascended the royal throne. "There are no longer any serious obstacles for me!"

***

Mandane, the natural mother of Cyrus, who had been convinced that her child was dead (her father, Astyages, had even invited Mandane to the funeral in a bid to show extra loyalty—and he himself did not know that they were bestowing great royal honors not upon his true descendant and "heir" Cyrus but upon the deceased son of Spaka and Harpagus!), could never, not for a minute, forget Cyrus. The only person who understood her and, in his own gruff, matter-of-fact way, shared her sorrow was her husband, the Persian prince Atradat, whom King Astyages styled as "Cambyses" in his own tongue.

As for Aryenis—the wife of Astyages and daughter of the Lydian king Alyattes—she was utterly unaware of her royal spouse's treacherous deeds and, just like her daughter Mandane and son-in-law Cambyses, was convinced that Cyrus was dead. However, she was still quite young and in no hurry to become a grandmother and play with grandchildren, firmly believing that her youthful and healthy daughter would later bear as many children as she wished.

Meanwhile, Harpagus's wife, Spaka, nursed Cyrus at her breast and loved him as her own son. She had already consoled herself over the loss of her own infant and recalled him less and less with each passing day. Harpagus, on the other hand, was completely

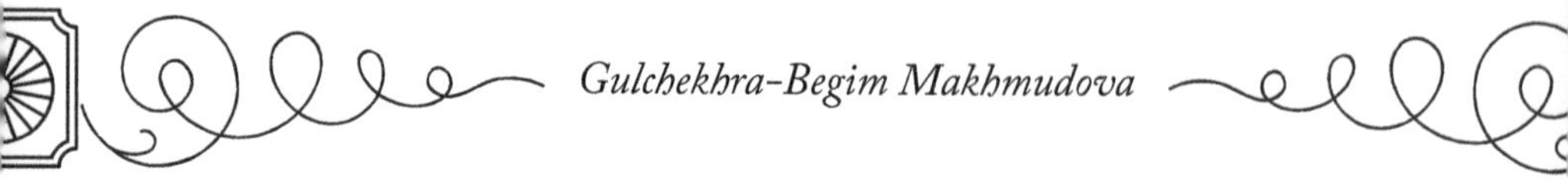

indifferent to children—whether his own or others'. A warrior through and through, he craved great royal power and therefore needed Cyrus as a pupil and protégé who, when grown, would obey him in every respect and "eat out of his hands." Such was the conviction of the Median general. Accordingly, he had already decided that as soon as the boy began to grow, he would personally instruct him in all the intricacies and nuances of military art, as well as the fundamentals of ruling a nation.

"Grow, grow, boy," he would say to Cyrus, occasionally rocking him in the cradle in their secret little house far from the capital of Media, "I will make a great king and army commander out of you—one who will conquer the entire world! Just wait and see, Cyrus, tribes and peoples will long speak of you…"

9

Tashkent, 2012

Saltanat remembered the agreement she'd made with her mother and, instead of dialing the police, after two and a half hours she called her mother. However, for some reason, a man answered the phone.

"Hello! Who is this?!" the daughter of Rashid Batyrov and Tamilla Mahkamova asked anxiously. "I need Tamilla Sardorovna!"

"Hello, Saltanat? Hello. This is Shukhrat, your mother's driver. She just left her mobile with me for a while."

"Ah, Shukhrat, yes—now I recognize you. What do you know about Mom and Dad? Something very bad must have happened to them, right?!"

"Unfortunately, it appears so. You know I'm just an employee, and my duties include following orders without question…"

"Don't beat around the bush, Shukhrat—can you get to the point? Where is Mom?"

"As Tamilla Sardorovna instructed, I took her to a strange, suspicious place. Some people had been calling her, making threats…"

"What kind of people? Who are they?!"

"I'm sorry, I don't know. She told me to leave immediately and said that if she didn't call me in exactly three hours, I should let you know. I was just about to call you—and you beat me to it!"

"What could be happening to them?… Do you know anything else?"

"It seems to me, Saltanat, that both of your parents are in the hands of some gangsters; otherwise, Tamilla Sardorovna would have contacted us long ago! You know how punctual and reliable she is—you can set your watch by her at airports, train stations, even on the metro. She looked alarmed. No, she didn't look frightened—can anything really scare your mom? She's brave! But the situation appears very serious and dangerous…"

"Yes, exactly. So what are we going to do? I'm calling the police!"

"In my opinion, we shouldn't do that yet—it's too dangerous. The bandits might get ahead of the operative team, and then your parents will suffer. They could simply be…"

"Don't continue—I understand! I'm afraid you're right. But still, in this situation, I can't just sit back idly!! Send me the location of the place where you left her, immediately."

"Alright, Saltanat, and here's what I propose: let's wait a little longer—maybe Tamilla Sardorovna will call me or you? And if not, then you can mobilize all your contacts! Again, I say this so that with our decisive actions…"

"Alright, Shukhrat. This is very serious! And we mustn't inadvertently harm my parents. But I'm so scared…"

* * *

Despite the summer heat outside, in the damp basement—where they had been sitting motionless for so long—Tamilla began to feel cold. And that wretched dampness… Soon she started coughing. If only Rashid weren't bound, he surely would have warmed her in his strong embrace. Both of them began to subconsciously feel hunger and thirst, though their desperate situation so consumed their thoughts that they didn't immediately realize that for several hours, neither a single drop of moisture nor even a sip of water had touched their lips.

It had already been about five hours since Tamilla's detention (and she, distraught over her husband, hadn't eaten anything for several hours before), and about seven or eight hours since the bandits had taken Rashid, shoved him into their car, and held a knife to his neck—so that by now, both were unbearably hungry.

Their guard, Dmitry, woke up, got to his feet, and immediately went over to the couple. He checked all the ropes binding Rashid and Tamilla—to see if they had loosened—and wherever he deemed it necessary, he tightened them again.

"Our Bahrom is a wicked moron!" he declared bluntly to both of them. "He wouldn't let them feed you or give you any water! Neither he nor the other guys realize that if you snuff it here, we won't get a damn thing out of you! And the boss will scold us all!"

With that, Dima went off somewhere.

Their boss isn't Bahrom, thought Rashid Kudratovich.

"Apparently he's about to bring us something," Tamilla guessed.

And sure enough: a few minutes later, the guy reappeared beside them, carrying a teapot, a plastic mug, and some kind of bag.

"I'm not going to untie you—so please forgive me! In fact, I wouldn't have kept you here at all, but I'm not the one who makes all the decisions. Please excuse me."

Well, isn't he polite! remarked Rashid Kudratovich. *We might be able to use that later!*

Dmitry poured tea into the mug and offered it first to the woman, then to the man. The warm tea immediately made Tamilla and Rashid feel a little better. Tamilla was surprised that, in such a

damp place, the tea hadn't cooled off much.

Apparently, he transferred it from a thermos into the teapot, she deduced. And since these people brought a thermos here, it means they were prepared for our capture in advance!

"…And Bahrom isn't the one calling the shots here!" continued Dima, "even though he acts like a big shot!"

"And who exactly is your boss?" Rashid Batyrov didn't miss the opportunity to ask.

"I simply can't tell you that," Dmitry replied decisively, waving him off. "Otherwise the boss won't care that I'm his relative and will quickly take my head off! And, excuse me, I still want to live."

After that, he pulled a soft flatbread out of the bag, broke it into pieces, and handed a piece to both Tamilla and Rashid. And since their hands were firmly bound, Dmitry decided to feed them himself. Although most of the food ended up on the floor, the bound captives still managed to eat a little and muster some much-needed strength. They weren't even dreaming of any meat or vegetables.

Finally, their guard sat back down in his chair and promptly fell sound asleep again.

"Rashid!" Tamilla called softly, momentarily pausing her interesting story.

"Yes?" he replied, trying his best to sound cheerful in order to support his wife.

"Can't we take advantage of this guy's sleep and escape?"

"No—we're tied securely to the chairs, and we don't have anything to cut these ropes with! Besides, I don't see anything sharp nearby. Do you?"

"No, truly, nothing of that sort, unfortunately… Listen, husband, I just remembered that I was supposed to call a good person today.

He's a distant relative of mine whom I recently met. His name is Amin Fattakhov, and he, too, is descended from Babur and Shah Jahan. We were supposed to meet this evening and discuss the materials I brought from India. But we couldn't meet—all because of these captors! I'm slightly embarrassed because of this…"

"I think you'll explain everything to him later. And if he really is—as you say—a true aristocrat, a descendant of kings, Timurids, and Baburids, then he will surely understand you and never blame you!"

"Yes, you're right, of course. And I heard that in their house there was a unique item that could help us…"

"What do you mean? What kind of item? Some sort of talisman or amulet?"

"Something like that—but even better! Amin said that the wife of his maternal younger brother had a great-great-grandmother named Feruz-begim. This amazing woman possessed a wondrous, almost magical vessel—the Crystal Hookah. It wards off all misfortunes and calamities! By the way, it's a relic that Feruz herself inherited through generations and centuries from Shah Jahan's wife, Arjumand-begim, and which later passed on to the wife of the Emir of Bukhara. The smoke from the burning, healing, and aromatic herbs in the hookah scatters evil spirits… With its help, all evil vanishes!"

"You're a modern businesswoman, Tamilla Mahkamova—and you believe in this?"

"I wouldn't have believed it if it weren't for the many confirmations. Amin's family—the one I'm talking about—has been through so much, faced such hardships and dangerous adventures! And now they're all well and prospering. This hookah would be a

tremendous help to us right now!"

"Suppose so. Although, to be honest, I'm not inclined to believe in mysticism. But right now, the Crystal Hookah is not with us—as I said—I must try to figure out who is behind these guys! And what it is they really want from us! We can't just sit here forever. Now, tell me the rest of the story."

"Alright, listen… My father, Sardor Shahmuradovich Mahkamov, had a bosom friend—Zakhar Khaev. This Zakhar, from his youth, was accustomed to playing double games and maintaining duplicitous relationships with people. He realized he had every right, deep down, not to love—or even to hate—whomever he wished. Yet outwardly, he never showed it. On the contrary, Zakhar had many friends—even among his enemies or those he simply didn't like. He was ambivalent toward my dad, his factory comrade Sardor Mahkamov. Both of them, almost simultaneously back in 1957, became heads of workshops at a porcelain factory: my father, Sardor, was put in charge of the glass and crystal services workshop, and Zakhar—the sculpture and figurine workshop. And in 1965, my father was highly regarded: he was appointed deputy director of their enterprise."

"Yes, I remember—wasn't he immediately made first deputy, responsible for production?"

"Exactly. The positions of second deputy, in charge of personnel and product sales, and third, responsible for public relations and internal security, had long been filled. Zakhar was annoyed and dismayed that it wasn't he who got so lucky, but Sardor—whose salary also increased significantly. However, when at the beginning of 1967 the position of third deputy became vacant, my dad, Sardor Shahmuradovich, did the following…"

***

Tashkent, 1967

Sardor Shahmuradovich Mahkamov knocked on the office door of the porcelain factory director, Nikitin.

"Who is it? Come in!" shouted the director.

"Semyon Petrovich," Mahkamov began, "I'm here on a matter. I propose that we appoint Zakhar Khaev, the head of the workshop, as your third deputy! He's a competent and reliable employee—someone you can count on. What do you say?"

"Do you really think so?" Nikitin asked thoughtfully. "Well, perhaps…"

Semyon Petrovich weighed everything, confirmed Zakhar's fine organizational skills—and, with Mahkamov's vouching, soon appointed him as his third deputy.

***

Without knocking, like an old friend, Zakhar entered Sardor's office.

"Well, Mahkamov, my friend, give me five! Thank you so much for your help! Of course, in a year or two I would have risen on my own without you. You don't think I'm talentless, do you?"

"What are you saying?!"

"But, to be honest, Sardor, I don't like to wait too long. Shall we celebrate the appointment, brother?"

"Not today, Zakhar, alright? Don't be upset."

"Alright, as you say—I'm not upset. After all, we'll still watch football together and get together with our families on holidays, right?! You know our wives, Maryam and Vika, also love to socialize."

"Of course!" Mahkamov nodded to his friend.

Vika's birthday was approaching, and at the request of his wife, Zakhar had already invited both their relatives and Sardor along with his wife and little daughter to join them a week in advance. Since it was going to be on a Friday evening, with the weekend ahead, the plan was to celebrate especially festively and joyfully.

"You'll come, and we'll get the party started," Zakhar winked at Sardor and gently commanded in a friendly tone, "no objections or refusals will be accepted. When else will you ever get the chance to drink like a man, relax, and unwind? With this job, you never get any rest!"

"Alright, my friend, as you say!" Sardor replied with a good-natured smile of gratitude. "None of my friends cares for me as much as you do. You're the best!"

***

Two days before that celebration, something unexpected happened at the Tashkent porcelain factory. The plant's director was dismissed—officially, it was explained as "failure to meet the annual state production plan on time." In reality, everyone knew this was just a standard phrase, because thanks to the considerable efforts of Sardor Mahkamov and other conscientious workers, the factory was actually doing very well in fulfilling the state quota.

There was something else going on.

Could it be that our Nikitin was stealing, and I never noticed?
Sardor wondered. No, on the other hand, I couldn't have missed that!
Most likely, he was paying someone off from time to time to avoid
inspections. And now, maybe he didn't grease enough palms…

However, he quickly realized that Semyon Petrovich might
have been dismissed because of his advanced age. The higher-ups
could have decided it was time to give younger staff a chance.

The factory workers were told that a party meeting, chaired by
one of the city executive committee leaders, could be expected any
day, at which the name of the new director would be announced.

The third deputy, Zakhar Khaev, was visibly nervous. He kept
running around with folders and documents, trying to organize
something, to negotiate something with someone.

"Listen, Zakhar," Sardor caught him in the corridor, "would
you like me to speak to the bosses? As acting director, I can propose
you for the position."

"I've looked into it: most likely, they're going to appoint
you!" Khaev shook his head, trying to hide his disappointment
and discontent. "What's the point in all this trouble? You really
are the most qualified of us all. You have plenty of experience and
knowledge. Above all, you'll definitely be able to set up production
so well that any plant in the republic would be envious! And me?
Who am I?"

"Don't talk like that. You're a leader too, and a competent
manager. When it comes to discipline in the workplace, there's
no one better than you. Besides, Zakhar, you know perfectly well
that I'm not a careerist, and those endless meetings and briefings
the director has to hold—all that paperwork—isn't for me at all.
I've always been a working man, and I still am, even though I've
climbed the ranks. You go ahead and run the factory, and I'll help

you with production issues as your first deputy."

Zakhar's face lit up with ambition.

"You really would support me?" he asked, smiling happily, as if he had already been appointed. "Are you sure they'll listen to you?"

"Of course!" Sardor said, shaking his friend's hand. "I sure hope so. Unless… they bring in one of their own people from some other plant…"

"Yes, they might do that," Khaev grimaced. "By the way, I hope you haven't forgotten that today is Friday, and we're expecting you and your family to come over?"

"Of course I remember, my friend! We'll give your wife our warm congratulations and finally get to relax! Thanks. Listen, my secretary's calling me. What is it, Anya? They're calling everyone? To the big hall, for a meeting?… Already—today, right now?! But how…"

Sardor hadn't expected this. He knew that important announcements, especially changes in the life of the plant, were usually made on Mondays or Tuesdays, certainly not at the end of the workweek, when everyone just wanted to relax and switch off from work. But the party's decisions were not subject to discussion or appeal. If they said the meeting was today, then so it was.

"Dear comrades, party members, and other workers," began the second secretary of the city executive committee, Dilshod Kasymov, in a solemn tone, "today we have only one matter on the agenda, but it is a very important one: the appointment of a new director of the porcelain factory, to replace… ahem… retired—on well-deserved rest—our production leader, Semyon Petrovich Nikitin."

The audience listened in silence, not knowing how to react. The secretary continued:

"We thanked Semyon Petrovich for his many years of service at this enterprise and wished him good health. Comrade Nikitin was informed of the party's and the republic's—indeed, the entire country's—principal position: a firm course toward younger leadership. As the saying goes, our elders deserve honor, and our youth deserve the path forward. Comrade Nikitin had no objections. I hope you, comrades, will also support our decision. So, who agrees that the factory needs a new, younger, more energetic director? Please raise your hands."

At first, the workers raised their hands slowly and reluctantly, one after another, but in the end, every single person did.

"Who's against?" Comrade Kasymov asked, seemingly only for the record.

Not a single hand was raised.

"Who abstains?"

Again, not one hand.

"So, it's unanimous!" the city committee secretary announced triumphantly. "Now, we'll put to a vote the candidacy of the new plant director, appointed by the First Secretary of the Tashkent city executive committee, our esteemed comrade…" and Kasymov pronounced a last name familiar to many. "The new director of the porcelain factory will be… party member, respected by everyone… Comrade Sardor Shakhmuradovich Mahkamov! Who's in favor? Please raise your hands."

In this case, the reaction was predictable for many of the workers and shop foremen, but unexpected for Sardor Mahkamov himself, for Zakhar Khaev, and even for Dilshod Kasymov. The vast majority raised their hands in favor of Sardor with enthusiasm and joy. He knew his work inside and out and treated people so well that practically everyone at the factory respected and liked him.

It turned out (as Kasymov privately told Mahkamov) that the order appointing him had been signed earlier that morning, and the meeting was just a necessary formality—so to speak, to hear the "voice of the people" and secure the backing of the working masses.

Thus, on the birthday of Viktoria Khaeva, her husband's old friend—Sardor Mahkamov—became the director of the porcelain factory. He truly did not like all the "paper-pushing." But on the other hand, he was glad to get the appointment for a simple reason: he could now really lift the factory up, make production more profitable, and set up shipments to other republics and countries.

"And I'm not going to bribe anyone," Sardor muttered under his breath. "They can forget about that! I'd rather spend the saved money on bonuses for the staff."

* * *

Sardor very much wanted to mark his honourable yet also highly responsible appointment as the new director of the factory in the company of his family—his wife, daughter, and parents. But he suddenly remembered that he had promised Zakhar that they would come over to his place that evening. He just needed to confirm the time once more and talk to Khaev about this sudden turn of events.

However, to Sardor's surprise, Zakhar was nowhere to be found. They searched everywhere, checked all the rooms, but they couldn't locate him. In the meantime, with Kasymov's approval, Sardor immediately got down to urgent current matters and ended up working on them until seven in the evening.

Finally, after wrapping up somewhat and putting off the rest until the following week, Sardor decided to call Zakhar's wife.

"Vika, dear, hello! It's Mahkamov, Sardor. Happy birthday, I wish you all the very best! My family and I are getting ready to come over—"

"Sardor, forgive me, but don't call here anymore. All right? And please don't come over either," Vika answered unexpectedly, her tone sharp and cold.

"Wait… But why? What happened? And by the way, where is Zakhar? We can't find him anywhere! Is he at home?"

"No. He was here, but he left—more accurately, he drove off. He said his life was a failure, that he's a miserable loser, and that he's leaving me and the kids. And it's all because of you, Mahkamov!!"

"What did I do? Listen, it's not my fault that the higher-ups decided I—"

Enraged even further, Viktoria slammed the receiver down.

Well, this is something! Sardor thought in amazement. I always considered them to be close to me. I assumed they'd be happy for me, that Zakhar and I would work together again just like before. But they both got so upset, they didn't even let me explain. So much for friendship…

10

Tashkent – Gazli Outskirts, 1968

"Hello! Hey there, son."

"Hi, Dad. How are you? How's your health?"

Vadim Irmanov didn't pick up any enthusiasm or especially warm feelings in Alexei's tone.

"It's all right. Alexei, my boy, why didn't you come to my wedding with Oksana? Were you really so swamped with work?"

"Yes. I'm sorry. You know I'm not into those kinds of events. But I'd like to congratulate you again," his son replied, still in a measured voice.

"Of course, I understand that you loved your mother..." Vadim Borisovich began to justify his remarriage. "But she's been gone for a long time, and I—"

"Don't dwell on it, Dad. It's fine. It's just—you know that after I organized deliveries of Yakut diamonds to us and covered all the state's losses over that stolen shipment of diamonds that was never recovered..."

"The same ones they apparently killed the previous director, Abdukhalikov, over?"

"Well, yeah! Well, that gave me the opportunity to explore and develop local geological resources. And it turned out that the carbonatites in the Chagatay trachyte-carbonatite complex in the southern Nuratau area... actually contain graphite and diamonds!

Until recently, no one even believed that Uzbekistan might have its own diamond deposits. As you know, I built a mine and an open pit, and they're already up and running. We're going to boost our enterprise, Dad. We may not find a Koh-i-Noor–type diamond, but still…"

"Alyosha, that's a real accomplishment!" rejoiced Vadim Borisovich. "You're doing great; I'm proud of you. This is a sensation! But for now, don't broadcast it to everyone, okay? There are plenty of envious and hostile people around. I don't want the higher-ups to 'freeze' your mine and pit! Tell me how I can help from the center. I'll try to secure funding and involve the right people."

"Maybe you shouldn't, Father. I wouldn't want them accusing you of 'nepotism' or 'corruption'…"

"Nonsense. You're doing important work that benefits the entire republic! And I'm doing my part, too—so our homeland can grow wealthier! By the way, tell me: did the police ever find the thief who stole those Yakut diamonds from your factory two years ago?"

"Yes, I think so, but they couldn't arrest him. If I got the name right, it was someone named Levidovsky…"

"What?!" exclaimed a shocked Vadim Irmanov. "Not Stanislav Zakharovich, by any chance?!"

"Yes, apparently so. You know him?"

"Unfortunately, yes. I'm acquainted with that fellow. But how did he pull it off?"

"I don't know all the details. But they told me that Stanislav Levidovsky went to London with our diamonds and sold them there for almost a billion dollars. So he got incredibly wealthy, opened his own diamond-cutting factory, and started some gemological firms. There's no way to reach him now because he's a British citizen."

"Could he have been the one who killed Abdukhalikov?"

"I'm not entirely sure. Maybe it wasn't Levidovsky himself. Someone helped him."

"I see. That's quite a story you've told. Good luck, son. And call me more often."

"Thanks, Dad. All the best to you, too. I'll let you know if there's any news about the diamonds."

* * *

Moscow, the same year, 1968

"To Colonel of the USSR Ministry of Internal Affairs, Comrade O.Sh. Midiyatdinov.

Dear Oleg Shamilievich, you are being written to by pensioner Yekaterina Bayanova. My 16-year-old daughter, Lyudmila, was arrested—allegedly for dealing drugs. But she's a good girl and has never used drugs! She doesn't even drink alcohol. We're a respectable family. I think my Lyuda just happened to be around some bad kids who planted that filth on her. But the investigator says she's facing real jail time. Please help so that this doesn't go to court and my daughter is released! She's completely innocent!"

...

"Esteemed Comrade Colonel of the Ministry of Internal Affairs, you are being written to by the sister of inmate Pavel Zhidkov. My brother was taken right in broad daylight while walking to the store and detained for 'parasitism' (i.e., being unemployed). Please look into this! Pasha isn't a parasite; he's had cerebral palsy since childhood and can't work normally. But he is a poet, he writes beautiful verses, and he

102

also makes handcrafted items to bring people joy. We were told we should be grateful they haven't added a charge of 'unearned income'—and that's only because they couldn't prove he sells his crafts. But he really never has sold them; he gives them away to children and to people who, like him, suffer from illness—or to those in an even worse situation. My brother is no criminal or parasite; please release him! I beg you, Officer, please help!!"

* * *

Colonel Midiyatdinov had plenty of such letters on his desk—he received them every day. He would glance at some of them now and then, just enough to keep up appearances for his superiors and to avoid giving them anything to nitpick about.

"What am I to all of them, some humanitarian aid department or goodwill mission?!" Oleg Shamilievich muttered under his breath. "They've gotten used to it—always asking for favours! 'Please help,' 'permit me,' 'let them go,' they say… And the main thing is, they all want it for free, for nothing. How does that benefit me personally? Will I get richer from that, make more connections?… Sure, if some relative of the detainee pays well, that's an entirely different story—then I can help, review the case. But otherwise…"

Midiyatdinov summoned the head of one of the Moscow police departments to his office.

"Vladik, why's your crime-solving rate so poor?" Colonel Midiyatdinov demanded sternly of the Major. "How long will you drag out this jewellery store robbery case? You've been interrogating Uvarov, I know. The evidence is pointing at him, plus there are witnesses…"

103

"Oleg Shamilievich, it's not that simple. That man is obviously innocent. There's no solid proof."

"What do you mean 'innocent'? Stop pulling my leg, Vladislav. You're ruining the stats in your district. Hurry up and pin this crime on him—find some evidence… or plant it yourself. It's no big deal! Close the case quickly and send it to court. The year's almost up, and I need high performance numbers! I don't want any unsolved or botched cases. Got it?"

"I got it, Comrade Colonel. But—"

"That's it, off you go, get it done. Don't keep me here. I have no time—I need to get home early today. It's my son's fifth birthday, and guests are coming."

* * *

That same evening, Farida, Marina, her husband Denis, and their two-year-old daughter Sasha arrived at Oleg's place.

"Brother, your table is as lavish as ever!" Farida remarked as she walked in. "And where do you get all this money from? You could share with the family once in a while!"

"You'll manage," Oleg joked good-naturedly. "Come on in; I'm about to serve dinner."

Awaiting them was five-year-old Kirill. The boy still had no idea that Marina was his mother and Denis was his father. Oleg had strictly forbidden them not only to say it out loud but even to think about it.

"Aunt Marina, did you bring me presents?" the boy asked immediately, without any shyness.

"Of course we did, sweetheart! We love you very much and

never come empty-handed. Especially since today is your special day—a little anniversary."

"Did you bring me money, too? My dad Oleg always gives me money, and I'm saving it! I already have a lot. When I grow up, I'm going to buy myself a military airplane."

Kirill revealed his secret to the guests: he showed them a small box filled with real banknotes.

Denis and Marina were perplexed. Why did a five-year-old child need that much money? They wanted to ask Oleg but didn't dare interrupt him. Oleg had invited some young floozy that evening and was devoting almost all his attention and time to her, paying little heed to his relatives' conversation.

"Why do you need an airplane, darling?" Aunt Farida asked Kirill.

"So I can bomb rebellious peoples and countries! I already have a gun…"

"A gun?" Marina said, alarmed. "I hope it's a toy?"

"Yes, with a built-in flash drive. Here it is! Bang-bang!! Uncle Denis, that's it—you're dead. Bang, bang!! Aunt Farida, you're dead, too! Bang, bang, bang!! Aunt Marina, you too…"

"Please, Kirill, sweetie, no! I'd still like to live a little while longer."

Marina understood that the child was just playing—that he was a little boy, and all little boys love "shoot-'em-up" and "war" games, whether with toy guns or on a computer. Yet something about it set her on edge. Long after her son's birthday, she kept thinking about it, and then it hit her: what had really shaken her was Kirill's overly serious tone and the cruel, malicious look he had when talking about killing. She had a sudden feeling that the child was being turned into a terrorist-fighter. And that worried her.

What does my brother plan to make of Kirill?! Marina thought in horror.

* * *

Tashkent, the same year—1968

The director of the Tashkent department store, Babur Yadgarovich Yusupov, fell seriously ill—a kidney stone had moved, causing terrible pain. As a good daughter, Maryam immediately rushed to his side, got him admitted to the hospital, and tried to visit and care for him as often as possible. Babur Yadgarovich underwent surgery, and the dangerous stone was removed.

Yusupov began to recover. Maryam brought him all the necessary medication and delicious food. Sometimes her younger brother and sister took turns helping.

"I can't really have all this, my dear," Babur said with a smile when Maryam arrived again. "I'm not allowed fatty foods, so please don't bring any more roast dishes, all right? If you don't mind, just make some steamed cutlets and chicken broth. The hospital has everything else."

"Of course, Dad; it's no trouble at all, as long as you get well soon!" Maryam Mahkamova replied, worried about him.

"Listen, my dear daughter," Babur Yusupov took off his glasses and looked closely at Maryam. "I want to tell you something important. If I should die…"

"Dad!!" Maryam didn't want to hear such talk. "Please don't! You're all right now."

"Hear me out; don't interrupt, please. You see, lying here, I have plenty of time to think about everything. While I was in intensive care after surgery, my whole life flashed before my eyes like a kaleidoscope. Naturally, I remembered your late mother, Makhsuda, a lot. I miss her so much; it's unbearable! I feel her absence so deeply…"

The older man couldn't hold back his tears. Maryam, too, was close to tears; she had loved her mother as well and often felt she was with her in spirit.

"Maryam, my dear daughter! Tell me honestly—this is important: Does Sardor treat you well? I know these men in leadership positions. They can start bossing everyone around at home like despots. I myself am sometimes like that—your brother and sister get an earful now and then…"

"No, Dad, not at all! My Sardor isn't like that. He really loves me and cares for me."

"Well, thank God. I'm glad to hear it. But I'm still worried about my granddaughter, Tamilla. Don't you think she's a bit too headstrong and independent for a girl?"

"But that's a good thing, Father! She's strong-willed, developing a real backbone…"

"Yes, in a way, but she ought to be interested in more girlish things—dolls, dresses. Instead, whenever she comes to our department store while you're shopping and chatting with the sales clerks, she 'disappears' into the economics section, studying the difference between cost and retail price! And then she organizes paid movie showings in the courtyard, and with the proceeds, she buys new, hard-to-find films… That's hardly kid stuff. Of course, I'm pleased that your child is so bright and beyond her years, but I don't want her missing out on childhood…"

"She's a perfectly normal child, Father," Maryam said with a reassuring smile. "She gets into just the right amount of mischief, and like any young lady, she's learning about the world in her own way… And at my culture centre, when my ensemble performs, she quietly sings along backstage. Sometimes she even gives my performers tips on how they should be singing! She really does have a talent for it—and a powerful voice to match. So please, don't worry—my daughter is doing just fine!"

Maryam smiled warmly, glad that her father, as always, cared so deeply about the whole family.

"So you think there's nothing to worry about?"

"No, absolutely not. It seems to me our Tamilla has good genes. Maybe, like her grandfather and father, she'll become some big boss one day!"

They both laughed heartily. Babur Yadgarovich felt much better, and just a few days later, he was discharged and went home.

* * *

Tashkent, 1972

A voice came through the intercom in the director's office at the Tashkent Porcelain Factory—his secretary, Lida:

"Sardor Shakhmuradovich, there's a whole delegation here to see you. Should I let them in?"

"A delegation? About what?"

"They're factory workers—mostly the department heads. They say it's urgent."

"Well then, send them in."

As the group entered, for a fleeting moment Sardor Mahkamov thought he saw… Zakhar Khaev! That same friend Zakhar who had vanished so long ago… An intensive search had yielded nothing. The police had tried everything but never found him, as if he had vanished into thin air. Sardor rubbed his eyes: no, Khaev wasn't there at all.

"Our dear and much-respected director," began one of Sardor's deputies, Sadreddin Utkurov, "it's now been exactly five years since you started heading our factory—five successful years! Thanks to you, our work here has truly taken off. Everyone gets their wages and bonuses on time…"

"And what's more," interjected another deputy, Ilya Vorobyov, "we all know, Sardor Shakhmuradovich, that under your leadership, the factory has begun producing even higher-quality and more competitive products. The variations of the 'Pahta' and 'Pahta-Gul' patterns, created by our master artisan Rauf Aripdzhanov—whose creativity you supported—have become very popular throughout Uzbekistan and far beyond!"

"By the way, those gorgeous designs now even appear on inexpensive, everyday tableware that the masses can afford," chimed in Karim Abdullaev, one of the workshop heads. "And as we know, we've also come out with wonderful gift bowls made of beautiful 'blue porcelain,' as well as the 'Kuk Atlas' set, which includes a lyagan platter, a teapot, a plate, a qas bowl, piyalas, and many other fine items…"

"In short, we're on an upward trajectory," summed up Utkurov. "We congratulate you on your five-year anniversary! Here is a modest token of our appreciation for you and your family."

They presented their director with one of the most beautiful and expensive sets produced by the Tashkent Porcelain Factory—

the magnificent "Golden Deer" dinner service.

"Thank you, truly, thank you, comrades… my friends!" Sardor said, touched. "I honestly didn't expect this… I'm very grateful! I value every one of you… Ilya, if you don't mind, please stay a moment."

Once again, through Vorobyov, Mahkamov passed on confidential financial assistance to Zakhar Khaev's wife, Viktoria, who had been in dire straits since her husband's disappearance.

Sardor Mahkamov truly managed to get by without paying bribes or "taking care" of anyone in the "upper ranks." He was fortunate that new, honest officials had come into the city executive committee. They had, for the most part, removed the former director, Nikitin, precisely because he had been bribing his superiors and sometimes accepting bribes from subordinates himself, doing nothing to stop the corruption. Now, that was all in the past—Mahkamov was an entirely different type of person.

Sardor understood that his actions were being observed by his beloved daughter, Tamilla—now a teenager—who often came to see him at the factory to spend more time with him. He wanted to be an example in everything, striving to be the best father he could.

Meanwhile, his wife, Maryam, served as the director of the Palace of Culture affiliated with the porcelain factory, organizing concerts by amateur performers drawn from among the factory workers and their children. Their daughter Tamilla increasingly helped her mother with these events. The girl excelled in school and won prizes in numerous competitions in both her native language and English. She also studied music and sang, thoroughly enjoying any chance to perform—be it on amateur stages at the cultural center.

"Just wait and see, Mom," she said one day with confidence, "in a few years, I'll have my own music group!"

"What are you thinking up now?" Maryam asked, amazed by her daughter's creative enthusiasm.

"Yes, yes—my very own ensemble… We'll give concerts all over the world!" the young Tamilla insisted, refusing to abandon her dream by even a single step.

* * *

Moscow, still 1972

"Kirusha," the nanny said kindly and very cautiously—trying not to provoke the older son of Oleg Midiyatdinov, now a middle-school student—"please, after you eat, clear your plate and wash it once in a while, all right? Otherwise, what would your aunts Marina and Farida say if they found out our boy is messy?"

"I don't give a damn what they say!" Kirill shot back rudely, not even considering the nanny's request. "And I'm not 'yours'—I'm my dad's, and this is our place! And I don't give a damn what you say either, Aunt Nadya! Have you forgotten you're just our servant? So you clean up after me!"

"Well, first of all, my dear fellow, I'm not your servant; I'm your nanny and caregiver," responded Nadezhda Pavlovna in a mild but instructional tone, striving to control her emotions so she wouldn't lose this well-paid and prestigious position. "And second, in case you didn't know, serfdom was abolished back in the nineteenth century. You can't talk to adults like that—saying 'I don't give a damn.'"

"I can do anything I want!" the teenager screeched hysterically.

"And still—where'd you pick up such a bad word, Kirill? After all, your aunts have always been kind to you, especially Marina. She loves you so much!"

This time, young Midiyatdinov said nothing at all. He simply gave the nanny a contemptuous, superior look, then walked off to his room and sat down at his computer to play his favorite shooter games.

"Kirill!" Nadezhda called after him. "Your father told me that after school, once you've had lunch, you have to start on your homework right away. He's going to ask about it when he comes home."

"That's none of your business," Colonel Midiyatdinov's kid barked again. "If I want to do my homework, I will; if I don't, I won't. I'll just play. I know what to tell my dad."

He had long since realized that his father would never truly punish him harshly, and that if anyone was going to be scolded for failing to carry out the orders of the head of the family, it would be the nanny herself.

That evening, Oleg Shamilievich came home early from work. On his way in, he noticed a small crowd of people in the entryway of their building—a commotion of sorts.

"What's going on?" he asked his neighbor, Vera Stepanovna.

"As if you don't know!" the woman exclaimed, waving him off.

"What's that tone? No, of course I don't know. What's the matter? Why is there a crowd?"

"It's all because of your son, Oleg!" Vera Stepanovna snapped angrily. "Our neighbor, old Mrs. Inna Alexandrovna Dubonosova, passed away today."

"So? She was an old woman, lived her life. She died—that's that…"

"Listen to yourself! How can you be so indifferent?… Everyone feels sorry, but you don't? And let me tell you, it was your son Kirill who drove her to tears the other day! She was walking past your garden, where branches from your apple tree hang right out into the street. Sometimes apples fall into the shared courtyard. Well, the poor old lady picked up a few that had dropped. She wasn't the only one. But your son, on his way home from school, saw her and berated her so horribly—actually swore at her—that she felt heart pains afterward. She already had a bad heart. And now, look—she's dead. You really should keep a closer eye on your kid, discipline him! He's turning into some kind of monster."

"Get lost, you idiot! None of this is your business, got it?!" Oleg Shamilievich retorted, matching his son's insolence without shame. "He's just a kid—what's there to hold him responsible for? And anyway, nobody should be stealing what's not theirs!"

Then, forgetting the entire exchange, he calmly went upstairs to his apartment.

11

Sakastan, 6th Century BCE

Several years had passed since the death of King Spargapis's wife. All this time, Tomyris had been at her father's side and was now growing up. The terror of the Massagetae had never imagined he could become so attached to a child—especially a female! Yet he had not forgotten that he had once mercilessly punished Zaryana precisely because she had failed to bear him the son he had so desired at the time—an heir, a warrior, a future king…

It was not that Spargapis cursed or blamed himself for what he had done to the woman he had once loved… No—this half-man, half-beast was utterly unacquainted with pangs of conscience. But he did fear that, despite his strictest orders forbidding everyone from telling Tomyris the truth about her mother's departure to another world, someone might crack and let the secret slip. He understood that his daughter might not appreciate such a bitter truth, no matter how much she loved and honored her father.

As for the midwife, Spargapis had secretly killed the poor old woman right after Tomyris was born—taking the infant from her arms by force—so that she would have no chance to say anything unnecessary to his heir.

"Father, tell me: how did my mother leave this world?" Tomyris asked Spargapis one day. "You know, I need her so much…"

"Daughter, why these questions? I realize it's not easy for you without a mother. But don't torment yourself. Am I a bad father? Aren't I enough for you by myself?"

"You're wonderful, and I see that you love me! But if my mother were alive… So, what happened to her? Or is it some terrible secret of yours?"

With that, Tomyris made a mock-stern face, then gave an innocent laugh at her joke.

But her father found the joke unsettling.

"Well… Her name was Zaryana."

"Zaryana…" Tomyris repeated, clearly liking the sound. "How beautiful! And then what?"

"She was a sweet, kind, and brave woman. We loved each other," the King of the Massagetae hesitated, not wanting to speak to his daughter of his affairs with other women or his infidelities, all of which were in the past.

"What happened next?" the king's young daughter insisted stubbornly, refusing to let it go.

"Your mother was expecting a child—you. And… before giving birth, she suddenly fell gravely ill. And after giving me you—my joy—she, alas, passed away…"

"What a sad story… I feel so sorry for my mother," Tomyris murmured, tears appearing in her eyes for the first time in her life.

* * *

Time went on. Whether it was that Spargapis himself was steeped in the spirit of war and fierce battles, or that such a spirit had been strongly passed on by blood, Tomyris also would speak of nothing but battles and victories. In appearance and behavior, she was scarcely different from the boys her age—except that she was stronger, braver, more daring, and more warlike than all of them. Her father taught her to use both the acinaces and a large sword; he was amazed at how quickly the still-young Tomyris was mastering the art of war.

One day, while play-fighting with his daughter (and taking it easy on her for fear of accidentally wounding her), Spargapis remembered his long-ago dream in which an iron bird flew out of his soul. It touched the sword—Spargapis itself—its blade and hilt, and instantly, the sword became iron all over, indestructible.

That bird must be Tomyris! the leader of the Massagetae realized. So she is the one who will protect my people! Excellent… excellent.

* * *

King Spargapis convened a council of the chieftains and elders of all the Massagetae tribes and loudly proclaimed:

"Hear me, Massagetae, and don't dare say you didn't hear this! I, your ruler, have thought long and hard, and here is my decision. I am a descendant of Ispakaya and Madyes, king and rightful heir to the Saka throne! I have no son, and as I see it, I never will—though I hoped to the last that one might be born. But my marvelous daughter, Tomyris, now seven years old, is the equal of our bravest men in talent, courage, strength, and intellect. Therefore, my heir and the Massagetae queen after me shall be—Tomyris!"

In the tent where the council was gathered, a tense silence fell. Yes, everyone knew that Spargapis taught his daughter the tricks of warfare, yet the people still viewed Tomyris as merely a child. Nobody took these royal "games" seriously, assuming that this wild "steppe dog" king was simply playing with his daughter because he knew no other way to occupy her. And now—this! He wants to make Tomyris queen. But she was just a girl!! If enemies attacked—which had always been the Massagetae's lot—how would this pampered maiden defend the people? Would she fight off fierce invaders with her dolls or perhaps with some toy sword, however tiny?

"Great king, that was a good joke!" Suddenly, the elder of the Yati tribe, Nizam, burst out laughing, fearlessly hoping to relieve the tension.

Spargapis, outwardly calm and impassive, slowly approached Nizam. In a flash, he drew his sword from its sheath and, in one lightning move, cut off the joker's head.

A deathly hush settled over the tent.

Seeing such a thing in the steppe was not unusual, but typically it happened on the battlefield, not at a peaceful council. Everyone present froze in fright, stunned. Yet no one screamed—they weren't women.

"Anyone else care to laugh?" Spargapis snarled, baring his teeth.

No one answered. It was plain: in all seriousness, after the death of this beast of a king, his only offspring—his beloved daughter Tomyris—would succeed him. Changing this would be difficult, for he had proclaimed it before the entire council, and she was the direct heir to the throne. The Massagetae had never before bowed to a mere girl. What fate awaited them?…

* * *

Meanwhile, among the Tigraxauda Saka, King Kavad and his second wife, Balkyz, had a son named Zogak. Zogak took after his mother's side: it was evident from the start that, unlike his older brother Rustam, he was no mighty warrior. He was a skinny, frail boy, but his mother loved him dearly. His father, however, seemed not to place much importance on his birth, for he already had a favorite son and heir—Rustam. And though nine-year-old Rustam quickly grew to love his only younger brother, Zogak's mother, Balkyz, continued to detest her husband's firstborn by another woman. She feared that, contrary to Tigraxauda law, the next king after Kavad might accidentally be the father's and the people's great favorite—Rustam. It never even occurred to her that Rustam had no thoughts of ruling. He had dreamt of a splendid and brave young Massagetae girl with luxuriant black braids and eyes as green as the waters of the Oxus. Rustam decided that no matter what, he must meet her! He must spend his life at her side, protecting this beauty from every danger.

From then on, as he grew, Rustam thought of her more and more often. For now, he did not know that the beautiful maiden in his dreams was also of royal blood—or that her name was Tomyris…

* * *

Media, Ecbatana, the same period

Meanwhile, Cyrus also grew up in the family of Harpagus and Spaka. Astyages had nearly forgotten about his grandson. Cyrus spent his days playing with the simplest of children—those who were slaves of the royal household. At times, children from wealthy families or even high-ranking officials would join in their games.

One day, when Cyrus turned ten, during a children's game he was chosen "king," because his strength and agility inspired respect among his peers.

"Now you all must serve and obey me!" the young Cyrus declared with a serious face, not yet realizing that royal blood truly ran in his veins.

"Who do you think you are?!" shouted Fraort, the son of a wealthy Median man who served in Astyages' retinue. "I'm not going to take orders from some commoner!"

Like a real "king," Cyrus punished Fraort on the spot. He found a large whip and ordered that the rebellious troublemaker be flogged. The other boys, as though they were actual "subjects" of a real ruler, willingly carried out Cyrus's command.

When Fraort's father learned of the incident, he complained to Astyages, saying that some "lowborn, worthless" boy was beating the children of the king's courtiers. The nobleman was convinced he was dealing with the son of an ordinary shepherd. He had no idea that Harpagus, the king's own general, was raising the boy in secret, having never revealed to anyone that he had a foster son.

However, even that courtier could not deal with shepherds arbitrarily, for they were considered the king's property. Thus, he brought the matter to the palace. As a result, Cyrus was summoned before Astyages to be punished.

When Astyages laid eyes on the boy, he couldn't figure out who he reminded him of. The king recalled how, years earlier, together with his minister Dinar, he had failed to capture or outwit a boy from India named Karna, who claimed to be the son of the Sun itself! That was long ago… The boy Karna possessed a miraculous gem the likes of which did not exist anywhere else in the world. No matter how much Astyages and his retinue tried to catch him,

Karna somehow got wind of their plans and disappeared—vanished as if into thin air. No one in Media had ever seen him again…

And now there was yet another unknown boy before the King of Media and Persia. People said he was likely the son of a shepherd or some other laborer. Yet his clothing was neither ragged nor beggarly—not lavish, but sturdy, clean, and decent. Clearly, his parents were not poor.

"How dare you beat the son of a noble?" Astyages asked Cyrus sternly, though not viciously. "You are a slave, and you raised your hand against your master?"

"I was chosen king by all the others," Cyrus replied proudly and calmly, "so I was the master, and that boy Fraort was my subject—my slave. How could he have dared disobey me? Tell me, O King—would you not have done the same?"

"I would have had him executed on the spot… Mmm… Yes, but you, you brat, are no king!"

"Once they chose me as king, then a king I was," said Cyrus unflinchingly and with confidence.

Suddenly Astyages, peering more closely at the boy's face, was stunned: this unknown lad was the spitting image of Astyages' own father, Cyaxares!

How can that be?! thought Astyages in alarm. *Could this be Cyrus? But years ago, I ordered that he be put to death! Who dared disobey me?!*

"Summon Harpagus!" Astyages ordered his servant.

Harpagus appeared before the king at once. Cyrus, by the king's command, was taken to another chamber to await His Majesty's decision.

"Harpagus, tell me plainly—is the boy who just stood here in my chambers my grandson Cyrus? Don't you dare lie. Not only do I hear that he calls himself 'king,' but my courtier also said all the children refer to him as 'Cyrus'! What is the meaning of this? Huh? Tell me! What's more, that scoundrel is the very image of my father!!"

When Harpagus saw his foster son in the palace, he gave no sign that he recognized him. Cyrus played along, having been warned by his foster father never, under any circumstances, to reveal their shared secret—not until Harpagus gave him leave. Yet after Astyages' words, Harpagus involuntarily flinched. He was not afraid for himself but dreaded what might happen to his household. Bowing his head humbly, the general spoke:

"Yes… it is he, my lord," Harpagus said, realizing it was now futile to deny it. Too many things pointed to the truth.

"How could you disobey my order and fail to destroy Cyrus?!" the enraged king roared at his commander. "I should have you hanged this instant!"

"Forgive me, I beg you, my lord," Harpagus pleaded, dropping to his knees before the king. Then he quietly added, "But consider: as you recounted, Cyrus has already been 'king' in your lifetime, if only in a children's game. Thus, your dream is fulfilled. Your throne is in no danger from him now! Perhaps… you might simply send your grandson away to Persia?"

Astyages pondered this and also consulted his mages, sorcerers, and astrologers, who agreed with the wise general. Indeed, they all confirmed that the king no longer needed to fear Cyrus. And so, Cyrus's life was spared.

Nor was Harpagus—so essential to the king as a brilliant warrior and general—put to death. Yet Astyages still punished him: he summoned Harpagus' wife—Cyrus's foster mother, the beloved Spaka who had nurtured and raised him with great affection—and

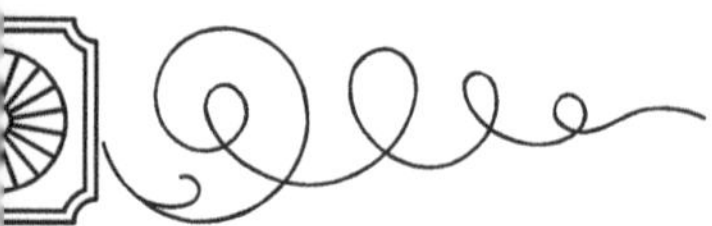

had her executed.

Both Harpagus and Cyrus mourned Spaka deeply. But the king's grandson had little time for grieving; Astyages indeed sent him away to the Achaemenid capital of Pasargadae, to his true parents: his father Cambyses and his mother Mandane.

No matter how hard they tried to be kind and gentle to him—overjoyed that their son was alive and unharmed—Cyrus could not truly love them in return. They remained strangers to him. But he never forgot Harpagus and Spaka…

12

Both Rustam and his younger brother Zogak had grown into mature youths and were now taking part in battles to their full capacity.

…The Saka men—both the Massagetae and the Haomovarga, as well as the Tigraxauda Saka—were at war almost constantly. Warfare filled their entire lives because it brought significant benefits to the tribal leaders. The Saka had grown accustomed to living this way. Prisoners were turned into slaves and used for domestic work. But the Saka did not always win; at times, they themselves were defeated and taken captive by foreigners. For a long time, therefore, the Saka people had been in need of their own heroes—true champions…

In the beginning, Zogak loved and respected his brother. He admired Rustam, was proud of him, and was grateful for the military lessons—after all, it was Rustam who taught Zogak the arts of war. However, after one particular skirmish against the Sarmatians, when the Tigraxauda Saka returned to their camps and settlements, everything changed abruptly.

And then one day…

"Zogak can defeat hundreds, but Rustam defeats thousands!"

That's what men, women, and even children in the Tigraxauda camps began to shout, joyfully echoing the adults. "If not for Rustam, our clan would have met certain death at the hands of the Sarmatians! Rustam is a great hero; Rustam is our defender and savior! Rustam is the future great king of the Tigraxauda!"

Zogak's servant barged into his tent without an invitation.

"Forgive me, my lord!" he said tensely and nervously. "Do you hear what the people are shouting?"

"Yes, I hear it," muttered the younger son of King Kavad in deep displeasure. "They're just a stupid crowd. What they say means nothing! These people are like livestock; they understand nothing! You have to feed them and lead them in whatever direction you choose. But to do that, the one leading them must have power, strength, and all the rights of a king! Soon—when I become king…"

"May the gods be merciful to you, my lord Zogak—you shall be king!" the servant nodded eagerly, truly believing in his heart that this was how it would be.

"…Then I'll show everyone who truly rules this steppe!! I'll let each one of them experience my whip and my sword to the fullest! But right now is not the time. Let them shout and praise that… Rustam. One way or another, I won't let him ascend the throne. The kingdom will be mine!"

***

Tomyris, too, had grown into a strong, agile, and quite attractive young woman. Were it not for her fearsome father, who struck terror into all around him and kept his child from prying eyes, no doubt more than one man would already have tried to gain her favor—or even her maidenhood.

But for her part, Tomyris had not yet developed any real yearning for love, nor did she fully understand what it was… Of course, she lived among people and had already noticed how many women in the camp behaved. She saw that sometimes, without any shame about being seen—like wild lionesses—they would enter the men's sleeping quarters in the tents, sometimes without anyone's permission or invitation, even in front of the men's relatives. At first, the typical reaction of a Massagetae warrior was surprise and anger. But the sight and scent of a woman's body nearby could rarely leave any Massagetae man indifferent. And like male lions, the men would yield to this passionate game, also giving free rein to their natural desires!

Thus, the Saka tribes had many children. Yet most of these children died—either from malnutrition or from the unstable nature of their parents' nomadic life.

The Saka did know many ancient, simple, and reliable methods to prevent untimely conception, and they used those methods as needed. Sometimes, however, the methods failed, and the number of children born remained high—only for many to perish later. The women continued to entice the men, who were in the minority due to constant wars and battles. Whether some of those men and women truly loved their partners, Tomyris could not say.

Tomyris believed with all her heart in one thing: that her mother and father had loved each other deeply, and she—their only daughter—was the fruit of their great affection!

Tomyris noticed that recently her father, Spargapis, King of the Massagetae, had been discussing something in his chambers with the new leader of the Alans—a short, stocky, large-headed man called Haidar, who, to Tomyris's mind, might have been only ten years younger than her aging father. Haidar struck her as an unpleasant character.

One day, by chance, Tomyris overheard part of their conversation and was horrified.

"Mighty king, you know we Alans all hold you in the highest esteem," began Haidar in a sickly-sweet, grating voice, reminiscent of an ungreased cartwheel's squeak. "But forgive me—you are at a venerable age now; your strength is leaving you, while I am still full of vigour and quite wealthy!"

Spargapis smirked at the self-assured boldness of his guest but kept silent, deciding to hear him out.

"So," Haidar went on, "if you would be so kind as to give me your daughter Tomyris in marriage, then I promise you that I and my Alans will guard and protect you for the rest of your days. You shall never want for anything! As for Tomyris—there's no doubt that I am the finest match she could ever hope to find! I'm clever and very well-off. I have the strongest warriors, who can protect her—especially if enemies attack. I'm not like Bikbulat…"

Hearing that name, Tomyris recalled what had happened to the previous Alan leader, Bikbulat, some years back, when she was still just a girl.

Bikbulat had quarrelled seriously with Spargapis—because the king had ruthlessly set him against the Tocharians and their leader, Zakir.

Bikbulat fled to the Sarmatians, taking with him most of his bold warriors. The Sarmatian ruler, Queen Kiana, was a distant relative of Bikbulat, so she could indeed help him in his hour of need.

But near the border of Sarmatian territory, the Alan tribe fell into discord—some of the warriors flatly refused to leave their homeland, their loved ones, and their kin. Bikbulat threatened dire punishment, yet they stood firm in their resolve to stay put, even at the cost of their lives. The defeat and disorderly flight of the tribe's leader from Massagetae lands undermined Bikbulat's authority, as well as the Alans' cohesion and resolve.

Meanwhile, Bikbulat realized that trying to crush the "rebels"—who would surely fight back with desperate strength—would mean incurring heavy losses. And soon enough, Spargapis would catch up with them… But arriving in Sarmatia with only a fraction of his warriors still alive meant coming not as equals, but as fugitives who would provoke pity or condescension! It would mean becoming a humiliated beggar. That was unacceptable. So, hurling curses at the defectors and traitors, Bikbulat crossed the Sarmatian border with the majority of his warriors. Thus, the Alan tribe split into two.

Bikbulat desperately begged Kiana to join him in attacking the war-weary forces of Spargapis. But Queen Kiana refused those pleas, advising her kinsman instead to rest in her camp and recover his strength among her Sarmatians, who were friendly toward the Alans. Kiana understood well that defeating Spargapis was entirely possible, but it would spark a drawn-out war with the Massagetae. That was not in the queen's plans—she had other worries: the Scythians were moving against her. A war on two fronts, fraught with danger, was the last thing she wanted.

Meanwhile, three thousand Alans who had remained behind at the border elected an enterprising man named Haidar as their leader and headed back to meet Spargapis, intending to ask for his mercy. Spargapis welcomed Haidar. He believed Haidar was wholly dependent on him—meaning he would be grateful for the king's aid and remain forever loyal.

When Spargapis, pursuing Bikbulat and his Alans, reached the Sarmatian border, Bikbulat was already gone. There at the border, in battle formation, stood the well-armed Sarmatian cavalry—vastly outnumbering the combined army of Spargapis, Haidar, and the other Massagetae chiefs.

The Massagetae halted. Spargapis and a small retinue of leaders rode straight up to the Sarmatians' commander—Queen Kiana.

"Welcome, welcome, great grey-bearded King Spargapis!" Kiana greeted the Massagetae ruler warmly. "Pray tell, what brings you here to my land? To what do I owe such an honour?"

Spargapis thought he detected a barely perceptible smirk behind her polite, flowery words.

"I express to you my deepest respects, O Queen, though you are younger than I," said Spargapis with a nod, doing his utmost to remain courteous and restrain his impatience. "I have but one request of you, fair Kiana. Surrender the traitor Bikbulat, guilty of crimes and violence against the Massagetae!"

"What's that you say? A traitor?! Crimes, violence?!" the queen exclaimed in surprise. "That doesn't sound like him at all—he hardly fits the profile of an outlaw! But no matter. Let's set that aside. I won't lie to you, grey-bearded Spargapis, though I was tempted. Indeed, Bikbulat is here with me. Yet he is my guest, and you know that anyone who comes under my roof remains under my protection! Let me ask you—have the Massagetae forgotten the teachings of their ancestors and abolished the sacred laws of hospitality in their own land? That would be strange indeed. But we Sarmatians still honour those laws! Or would you rather try to take something from me by force of arms?"

Spargapis and those around him understood that the Sarmatians would not hand over Bikbulat without a fight, and his people were in no state for war, having already spent their strength on internal conflicts and chasing down the Alans. All the Massagetae tribes were weary and exhausted by internal strife; they needed a respite. And the Sarmatians, despite the queen's ironic tone, clearly did not wish to battle the Massagetae either.

"Very well, Queen Kiana. I regret leaving here without even having visited your camp! But I think we shall meet again—and more than once..."

With that veiled threat, the king wheeled his horse and galloped away from Kiana and the Sarmatians. His entourage of Massagetae leaders followed suit...

From that day on, Haidar grew ever more boastful. How could he not? Now he was a close friend of King Spargapis himself—personally pardoned by him! Surely the king trusted him in all things. Haidar told every tribal chief that he was the most important leader among them, since the king singled him out specially.

But I don't trust this new Alan chieftain one bit! Tomyris thought in despair. *He's an unpleasant, slippery, cunning type. And on top of that, he wants to marry me! That old camel—trying to bribe my father with his wealth... No, I'll never allow it! One way or another, I have to stop Father from marrying me off to this vile Haidar! I'm not planning to wed yet—I value my freedom far more! And even if I do get married someday, it definitely won't be to that gobbler! I must come up with something... but what? Yes... This is how I'll do it...*

* * *

King Astyages held a great feast for hundreds of his nobles and, before their very eyes, drank the most precious wine. Having tasted the wine, Astyages ordered golden and silver vessels to be brought forth—items he had once commanded be taken from a temple and brought to his palace, so that he, the king, along with his nobles, his wife, and his concubines, might drink from them.

At the king's command, the golden vessels from the temple were immediately brought in, and both the king and all his courtiers drank from them. They drank wine and praised their gods—those of gold, silver, bronze, iron, wood, and stone.

All of a sudden, at that very moment—facing King Astyages, his wife, and his nobles—a large, disembodied human hand emerged right out of the palace wall. Its long, bloody fingers began to write on the plaster...

When Astyages saw the hand writing, he started, afraid, and his countenance changed. His arms and legs weakened; he began to tremble all over until his knees knocked against each other.

For some reason, he suddenly recalled the countless innocents he had executed and tormented throughout his life, for no reason at all.

In a loud voice, the king shouted to his servants:

"Bring me at once the wise men, the sorcerers, the magi, and the fortune-tellers!"

When all the sorcerers entered the banquet hall, the king addressed them:

"Listen, O Median sages! Whoever reads the words inscribed here in blood by that human—or perhaps divine—hand, and can explain their meaning to me, shall be clothed in the finest garments, shall wear a golden chain about his neck, and shall be second ruler in my kingdom! Well? Why are you all silent? I am waiting."

"It is written in Persian," said the priest Ardashir carefully and uneasily, "and the same three words appear more than once: *mene*, *tekel*, and *peres*."

"What do they mean?" asked the king. "I may be sovereign over Persia as well, but you know I do not speak Farsi all that well. But for some reason, I am very afraid…"

"*Mene* means: 'The Almighty has looked upon your reign and has put an end to it,'" explained the priest Faridun. "*Tekel*—'You have been weighed in the scales and found lacking.' And *peres*—'Your entire kingdom will be divided; one part will go to the Medes, and the other to the Persians.' It would appear that another man shall soon ascend your throne!"

"But who—who is it?!" Astyages rasped in horror and impatience.

The priest Zartosht bowed respectfully:

"You know it yourself, O King. His name is Cyrus—the future great conqueror…"

13

Tashkent, 1972

When Sardor knocked on the door to his apartment, it was almost eleven o'clock at night. He didn't unlock it himself because he knew his wife would still be awake—she would wait for him all night if necessary. And when she was home, the key was always in the lock on the inside.

Maryam opened the door. Usually, she never reproached her husband for staying late at work. But this time, when he started to explain himself, she couldn't hold back.

"Sardor, don't try to fool me or hide anything: I saw you with her today!"

"With whom?" Sardor tried to evade this unpleasant conversation.

"With Vika, Zakhar Khaev's wife!" Maryam exclaimed, almost in tears. "You were driving her around shopping! Do you two have a thing going on? Is that why you've been gone so often lately?"

"Don't make up nonsense, my dear," Sardor said seriously and wearily.

"Forget about me, but at least have some shame in front of our daughter! You're not a child anymore. Aren't you embarrassed?" she continued bitterly. "Go on, wash your hands, and I'll feed you. Or will you say again that you're not hungry? Sure—your lover must be feeding you Russian borscht and pancakes! How could I possibly measure up to her…"

"Stop talking such drivel," Sardor cut in, his irritation rising. After a moment's thought, he realized he was angrier with himself for not having explained everything to his wife from the start. Meanwhile, he washed his hands, went into the kitchen, and asked, "So, what's for dinner? Kabob? I love it! Give me a good helping, please, and sit down to eat with me."

"I don't want to. Tamilla and I already had dinner."

"Is she asleep?"

"Of course. She has to get up early for school."

Sardor ate quickly and nervously, going out of his way to praise the food enthusiastically.

"All right, listen," he finally said, growing more and more tense. "I'll tell you everything—just promise you'll hear me out to the end."

"Fine," Maryam agreed, seeing how tense he was. "I hope it won't kill me."

"This really has nothing to do with you—I haven't been unfaithful, if that's what you're thinking!" Sardor nearly lost his temper at his wife's distrust. "Yes, I've met with Vika… But it has to do with Zakhar! You know his sudden disappearance has been bothering me for a long time. We were friends. And Vika, for that matter, wouldn't speak to me at all for these past five years."

"Well, imagine that! I'm about to burst into tears. So what changed all of a sudden?"

"Please, don't be sarcastic. She was upset with me for a long time—she blamed me for her husband leaving her… You know we secretly sent her a little money because she was struggling, and she hasn't wanted to remarry or start a new life. She must still be waiting for Zakhar and staying faithful to him. A rare quality nowadays!

So, for the five-year anniversary of our factory, I decided—since we have the means—to give her more than usual this time: extra money and supplies so she could get by for a few months without being in need."

In that moment, Maryam thought about how she'd always been a generous person and wouldn't be surprised by someone aiding another. She'd always been supportive of helping others, because she, too, had helped many. Still, she felt angry now.

"My, how kind you are! Taking such care of another man's wife!" she said sardonically. "Vika wouldn't let me look after her, and she used to be my friend. All because of you—understand?"

"I get it," Sardor nodded humbly. Now his own wife was upset with him. Nevertheless, he continued, "But what's strange in all this is that, throughout our years of friendship, Zakhar never once envied me. On the contrary, he was always happy for my successes and supported me."

"Well, that's because, until the day he disappeared, you hadn't been appointed the general director of a big factory," Maryam pointed out.

"Yeah, dear, it sure looks that way. And that's exactly what he told Vika: he supposedly left because, compared to me, he felt like a total failure! He was running around that day with some papers in hand. But… we talked with Vika today…"

"So I was right—this is definitely about her, isn't it, Sardor?"

"I just helped her sort out the household chores that needed a man's hand. Everything had been falling apart; a bunch of things needed fixing, some had to be thrown out, and new ones bought. She realized on her own that it was me secretly providing her groceries all these years. A couple of days ago, she called me at work."

"And you were delighted by the attention from a pretty lady?" Maryam teased.

"First of all, she's not all that pretty anymore—her hard life without a loving husband has taken its toll, you know. Meanwhile, you, my love, are the most beautiful and astonishing woman in the world, because I'm always with you and I love you deeply!" Sardor grinned. "Second, I've long wanted to ask her more about Zakhar—maybe he sent her some message, or maybe she knows something about him. Turns out someone's been sending her money orders! They're small amounts, but they come in regularly, every month…"

"And you think it's Zakhar who's doing it?" Maryam asked, her curiosity piqued.

"Why not? There's no record anywhere of Zakhar Khaev's death—I checked with the Ministry of Internal Affairs. So he must be alive and caring for her as best he can. He has no idea that I—well, that our factory—has been helping her as well. But it seems he's not doing so great himself, or he'd send more. Yes, yes, it has to be him!"

"All right, I see your point. Still, you could have called to say you'd be late—and told me about this 'mission of goodwill.' About how you keep searching for Zakhar."

"It's not surprising. He's not just anyone to me."

"Yes, he was someone to you—and then he vanished. So either it's him or someone else sending her money…"

"I'm telling you, it's him—a hundred percent. There's no one else."

"Let's suppose that's so. Did you find out anything else?"

"Apparently, before leaving, Zakhar gave Vika a photograph, meant for me."

"A photograph? What's on it?"

"Vika says there's nothing special—just an old picture of Zakhar and me together. We probably have loads of those in our album, so I might even have it, too. But the specific one Zakhar asked her to pass to me is missing now. After five years, Vika says she lost track of it. Without seeing that exact photo, I can't figure out why it was so important or why, on the day he left home, he made sure it got to me…"

"I understand, my husband. Still, let it be known—I do trust you, but it's not exactly pleasant for me when you secretly take care of other women!"

"I'm sorry, my love, I'll keep that in mind. It won't happen again!" Sardor promised. He stood up, approached his wife, and, leaning down, held her tightly in his arms and kissed her tenderly.

* * *

Moscow, still 1972

The "Sunflower" orphanage, overseen by the Ministry of Internal Affairs, was allocated ministerial funds—ostensibly for the orphans, but in reality, it mostly benefited the orphanage's director and the caregivers. For Soviet Police Day, the grateful orphanage was holding yet another holiday concert. According to protocol, Colonel Oleg Shamilievich Midiyatdinov was required to attend.

Even the stern orphanage director, Valentina Nikiforovna Pavlova—whom the children secretly called "Baba Yaga," like the old witch from fairy tales—was somewhat afraid of this hard-nosed officer in uniform. Baba Yaga knew that the real help did not come from Midiyatdinov himself but from his subordinates, and that, on the contrary, he had to be "greased," given kickbacks to ensure he wouldn't shut down the orphanage under any pretext. He certainly had enough power and wrath for that!

"Kirill, get ready quickly—you're coming with me to the orphanage today!" Oleg ordered his nine-year-old adopted son early that morning.

"But what about school, Dad?" Kirill asked, more out of formality than concern. In truth, he was already happy about skipping school, confident his father would arrange everything or already had. After all, Colonel Midiyatdinov never asked anyone for anything—he only gave orders and pressured people.

"Don't ask questions, son. Hurry up and eat your breakfast! You need to see and understand how other children live—those who don't have a family. It'll do you good."

Kirill didn't grasp those final words, but he didn't dare ask his father to clarify.

As always, the "Sunflower" orphanage had prepared a few songs performed by the children and, as the "crown jewel" of the program, a children's play: *The Frog Princess*. One notable role in the play was that of Koschei the Deathless. Whether some merciless caregiver once again wanted to mock the boy playing Koschei—a scrawny, constantly hungry child who'd originally been nicknamed "Koschei" because of his incurable thinness—or whether the play's organizer had spotted in him some semblance of acting talent, it was decided he would play the role of the Deathless One. By now, nobody even remembered his real name, though the director had his documents—his official name and surname—buried deep in a cabinet. They said his father was in prison for theft, and his mother had drunk herself into oblivion. As far as the staff was concerned, for someone like "Koschei," life in the orphanage was practically paradise.

Among this ragtag crowd of children, who were nobody's responsibility and not much desired by anyone, the caregivers still had their favorites: the most obedient, docile, and pleasant-looking kids. Those chosen few sometimes received sweets from the caregivers or the kitchen staff. But nothing like that was ever said about Koschei—he was rebellious and unattractive, and nobody ever slipped him any extra food. Most people felt not sympathy but aversion toward him. Nevertheless, they made him play the villain on stage, since they couldn't find a better candidate for the part.

Koschei was always hungry. Always. So when he—still up on stage during the final scene—spotted an unfamiliar, richly dressed boy in the audience, sitting next to the orphanage's chief guest— the uniformed officer—and absently chewing on sweet corn and fruit, Koschei heard the loud rumbling in his own stomach and felt his mouth water. Still, he finished the performance to the end as needed, along with the other kids.

After the play, Koschei mustered the courage to approach the wealthy-looking boy, hoping for pity—maybe he'd get an apple or something else to eat. And the boy, Kirill Midiyatdinov—Colonel Midiyatdinov's son did, in fact, take pity on him. He held out to Koschei…the brown, eaten apple core. And nothing more. Meanwhile, Kirill himself went on chewing an orange.

As Kirill and his father left, Koschei watched them for a long time. The face of that boy who had made fun of him etched itself indelibly into his memory.

***

Tashkent, 1975

Alexei Irmanov arrived in Tashkent and, at his father's invitation, stopped by the State Depository.

"Alyosha, I have an important assignment for you," said Vadim Borisovich. "Over the ten years you've spent as director of a diamond-processing plant, and now a diamond-mining plant, you've achieved considerable success. Under your leadership, the enterprise is flourishing, and significant revenues have been pouring into the state's coffers. But you know we're accountable to the state in everything. And I have excellent news today. The Ministry of Finance, which we are a subdivision of, has a crucial task for you. If you handle it as well as you've managed your plant, it's quite possible you'll earn a post as one of the Ministry's senior officials—maybe even Deputy Minister."

"Father, but why shouldn't you rightly take that position yourself?" Alexei asked in surprise. "You have more knowledge and experience."

"I'm not so young anymore, and this job demands a lot of energy. That's why I recommended you. By the way, they've had their eye on you for a while as one of our best managers. In short, take today off, give me all your factory reports, and tomorrow head over to a conference at the Higher Party School. After the sessions there, you'll meet with several people who'll explain their major issues. You'll need to help them resolve these problems. They will be discussing specific investments into large state projects."

"I understand, more or less. All right, I'll go to the Higher Party School tomorrow."

* * *

Such a situation was a first for Alexei. He understood that the woman who introduced herself as Aleksandra was merely his liaison for the event. She just guided him through the corridors and introduced him to the people his father, Vadim Irmanov, had mentioned. And yet he couldn't take his eyes off her.

Should I ask for her phone number? Alexei wondered. *That might seem awkward. She might think I'm frivolous! But if I don't do something now, I could lose her forever—and never see her again. No, no, I can't allow that!*

By chance, the perfect moment arose on its own. After the first sessions of the Finance Ministry conference, Aleksandra told Irmanov it was time for lunch. He invited her—since she was his official escort—to have lunch together. Strangely enough, after a few seconds' hesitation, she agreed.

They went to the staff cafeteria, took almost the same items on their trays, sat at a cozy table by the window, and began to eat. In truth, they spent more time chatting than eating.

"Sashenka, have you worked here long?"

"No, not really. About five years. And how long have you been at your enterprise? I was told you're the director of some large plant. Is that true?"

"Yes, I'm the director…" The younger Irmanov didn't go into detail about the classified facility. "But I'm afraid you'd find it uninteresting. Better tell me about yourself, Sasha," Alexei said. "Perhaps you're one of the rector's or pro-rector's secretaries?"

"No, no, I'm just a lecturer," Aleksandra replied with a modest smile. "I teach economics courses here at the Higher Party School. But I did an internship abroad, in London—specifically, at the University of Essex."

"Wow, that's quite impressive! I've read it's one of the UK's most prestigious universities, and indeed one of Europe's. Good for you!"

"Well, I can't take much credit for having ended up there—my father helped me," Sasha confided, unexpectedly for herself, to someone she was meeting for the first time.

"Really? Who might your father be, if it's not a secret?" Alexei switched on his male charm, hoping to learn the name of someone who might be a useful contact.

"I doubt his name would mean anything to you. His name is Stanislav Zakharovich Levidovsky…"

Alexei nearly choked.

"I'm sorry, what did you say? Levidovsky?!"

"What? Do you know him? But my father's been living for several years now in…"

"London, correct?"

"Yes. Why…?"

"Oh, it's nothing, don't worry about it! No, we're not personally acquainted. But I'd very much like to meet and get to know this remarkable man better!"

Aleksandra thought she detected a faint, barely perceptible smirk beneath Alexei's polite exterior.

"I have a feeling I know what this is about. There was a bit of a stir at one time around my father's name. He was accused— if you can believe it—of murdering some official from the State Depository of Precious Metals. By the way, as far as I know, you also work in that system, correct? That's probably how you came across my father's name. But I assure you, that's all just nasty rumors and gossip. Believe me, my father isn't a killer; he wouldn't hurt a fly! He's achieved everything in his life through hard work and ingenuity. And because the investigation never got to the bottom of that murky business—and they tried to pin that mysterious murder on my father while the real criminal was never found—he had to leave the country for a while. Who wants to go to prison for someone else's crimes, right?"

"Yes, yes, dear Sashenka, you're absolutely right!" Alexei nodded, though he was no longer listening to her, lost in his own thoughts...

The girl had no idea just how closely this case and that name were tied to Alexei Irmanov. Of course, Sasha was Stanislav's daughter; she would defend him no matter what. But what if she was absolutely right, and Levidovsky was not guilty of murdering the former director of his plant, Abdukhalikov? That would leave the question of who was guilty. And where should he look for the missing shipment of diamonds? It might not be in England at all. If Alexei could find them, his career would skyrocket—he could move mountains! There was much to consider...

***

A young specialist from Uzbekistan's Ministry of Culture, Rashid Batyrov, was also invited to the Party School conference—mainly to explain to a successful provincial factory director how he could assist the nation's cultural sector. More precisely, the preservation of state monuments of architecture and ancient building heritage. That was Rashid's current focus. And the factory director turned out to be Alexei Irmanov, of course.

"Do you have a plan for how you intend to spend these funds?" Alexei asked Rashid. "It's a substantial amount. I could spend it on… Well, never mind. Just understand that it's not entirely by my own choice that I'm going to allocate you such…"

"Not to me—to the Ministry of Culture!" Rashid gently corrected him.

"Yes, yes, of course—very well. Such a huge sum—to the Ministry, and specifically, as I understand, your department for the protection of ancient architectural monuments. Right? From what I gather, the money will mostly go to the restoration of old mosques and madrasas?"

"Yes, dear Alexei, you understand correctly. There are historical landmarks—structures, pilgrimage sites visited en masse by both worshipers and tourists—objects tied to the most important historical events in our nation's life, its social and governmental development, as well as science, culture, daily life, and the legacies of notable political, state, and military figures, folk heroes, scholars, and artists. There are also archaeological and artistic monuments, monuments of urban planning and architecture…"

"Wait, Rashid, I don't need all the details—just give me the essentials."

"All right, as you wish. Essentially, there are a number of sites in urgent need of major restoration and preservation—otherwise, they'll have to be demolished, which is, of course, unacceptable. These are objects of cultural and historical value. We study them, assess each one's value, and after a thorough and painstaking analysis of their significance and current state, we carry out the required restoration and conservation. This ensures these cultural sites are preserved and protected."

Rashid handed Alexei a list of top-priority sites that urgently needed preservation at the moment.

"I understand the overall picture. Anything else?"

Rashid hesitated for a few moments, then decided to speak up.

"Yes, there's a major problem. There's a very small yet very ancient monument that I find extremely interesting—the Koi Krylgan Kala fortress in the lower reaches of the Amu Darya. A large construction trust wants to demolish this remarkable fortress—which once hosted our Saka ancestors and the legendary Queen Tomyris—in order to build a big road and a bazaar. That absolutely can't be allowed! Therefore, we need to launch a large campaign to protect this site, and naturally, that will require significant funding. You understand me?"

"Yes, Rashid. Don't worry. I'll do everything in my power to help you."

"Thank you with all my heart, Alexei. Well then—we'll stay in touch."

14

Sakastan, 6th century BCE

King Kavad of the Tigraxauda Sakas summoned his eldest and most beloved son, Rustam, his source of hope and support. Rustam promptly appeared before his father and bowed low. Kavad lifted his son's head, embraced him warmly, and then spoke:

"My boy, sit here with me. Your father needs to discuss a matter of great importance."

"I'm all ears, Father. What's happened? Are enemies attacking? Is there some threat?"

"No, no. Though enemies are always a concern for us nomads, as you know. This isn't about that. It's time for you to marry, my son!"

"Oh, Father, I'm really not—"

"Don't interrupt your king and father! Hear me out. I know all too well what you might say: that you're not ready and don't want to yet, that you're worried about my health and about the security of our people. But know this: I, too, think of these things—along with my dear firstborn's future! Everyone knows that in our lands, the law says a younger son is considered heir to the throne. Which means I'd have to pass the kingdom on to Zogak, not you... But that's absolutely not what I want. Understand?"

"But why, Father? My brother Zogak is a fine young man!"

"I don't fully trust him. He won't be able to keep power firmly in our family's hands. Above all, he won't be a reliable shield for all our people. But you—you can do that. True, you lack the subtlety, cunning, and diplomacy that befit a highborn ruler. Yet in time, life itself will teach you all that! And as for your courage, nobility, and sheer strength, Rustam—nobody matches you. Not here, nor likely anywhere in the wide world! That is why I, King Kavad, wish you— and you alone—to succeed me as King of the Tigraxauda Sakas. Don't argue. For that to happen, you must first get married—and not just to anyone, but to a young woman of very high birth."

"But I'm only eighteen! There's still plenty of time."

"That's exactly it: you're already eighteen, my son, so the time has come. I won't hide anything from you. I plan to visit my old friend Spargapis, King of the Massagetae. We haven't seen each other in a long while. And he has a daughter who's grown up— Tomyris. Everyone says she's exceptionally beautiful, taking after her mother. More importantly, she is a genuine princess in every sense. I know the two of you would make a wonderful pair!"

Rustam had no idea that the lovely maiden who filled his dreams and visions was Tomyris herself. He'd never once seen her in person. Kavad, for his part, knew nothing of his son's secret reveries. Rustam, meanwhile, thought his father was trying to tear him away from the beloved woman of his dreams and force him to marry someone else—someone he neither loved nor wanted.

"Father, forgive me," he began, but didn't know how to continue. If he told his father that he adored some myth or mirage, the king would mock him! Such a famed warrior, a champion, and here he was, spouting nonsense about a spirit from his dreams. He simply wouldn't be taken seriously... Rustam abruptly wilted, looking helpless. In a subdued, dispirited tone, he said, "Very well, Father. Introduce us, if your friend, the King of the Massagetae, doesn't object. Then we'll see. Maybe I won't appeal to this daughter of Spargapis at all. And in that case, grant me the right to choose my own wife. Agreed?"

"Agreed, my boy. Then I'll inquire with my friend about all the details. But first—listen to this. You're still a virgin, even though you're a king's son. You need to learn how to be a strong, skillful seducer."

Rustam blushed—his strength thus far had only truly been tested in battle…

But Kavad went on:

"In our camp—perhaps you've heard, Rustam—there's a very beautiful woman, a bit over thirty, named Azer. She's an expert in the arts of love! She's taught many of our men the proper way to handle women, so that women themselves willingly yield to their husbands and long to please them… Azer will come to you this very night. Wash thoroughly, put on the new clothes the servants have prepared, and wait for her. I ask you, my son: whatever happens, treat her courteously. Don't offend her. First, offer her a generous, tasty meal; after that, do whatever she tells you and learn what she can teach. Understood?"

"As you wish, Father," Rustam answered quietly, bowing his head. He felt deeply distressed by all the king had just said but didn't dare show defiance.

That very night, Azer came to Rustam, just as his father had told him she would.

***

Persia, the same era

A large white dove flew into Cyrus's chambers in the palace of his father, Prince Cambyses, in Pasargadae. Cyrus examined the bird carefully, for he already knew that such doves often carried messages. Indeed, under its left foot there was a letter, written on a piece of sturdy silk. The letter was addressed to Cyrus.

The grandson of Astyages had been bored lately, and this missive piqued his interest.

He unrolled the silk scroll. It read as follows:

"Honorable son of Cambyses and Mandane!

I will reveal a secret to you: even before you were born, King Astyages—bloodthirsty ruler of Media and Persia—dreamed that you would attack him and wrest power from him by force. For that reason, as soon as you were born, he planned to have you killed! But the gods protect you… You survived thanks to one man whose name you know well. He dared to defy your grandfather's cruel will and paid a dreadful price for it—the loss of his beloved wife. She loved you and raised you as her own."

Prince, there are people in Media who are certain you have been spared for a great destiny. Your grandfather is a murderer, a fiend, a tyrant! Persia and all Media groan under his madness. We, the foremost people of great Media, can no longer endure his despotism. You, the prince, legitimate grandson and heir of Astyages, must know you now have many friends in Media. Rouse Persia and march against the vile Astyages—if you do, we will surely help you seize your grandfather's entire realm! If you rise up against him, I will come to you and reveal myself. But if you fear to do so, if you shrink from challenging the king, then let my name remain unknown to you…"

There was no signature on the letter. Having read it, Cyrus was deeply disturbed and agitated.

Who could have written me such a message? thought the grandson of the King of Media and Persia. *And why has he not revealed his name yet? Is he afraid? This is all very strange! And why haven't my parents told me that my own grandfather once wanted me dead?! Perhaps they spared me, not wanting to upset me? Likely so. I need to find out about this right away!*

Without delay, Cyrus set off at a brisk pace to the quarters of Cambyses and Mandane.

* * *

Sakastan, the same era

Tomyris entered her father's tent. He sensed she was troubled by something.

"Has something happened, my daughter?" King Spargapis asked anxiously. "Why do you look so pale? Shall I call the healer for you?"

"No need, Father. I'm fine; I'm not ill."

"Then what is it? Come, be frank with me. You've never hidden anything from your father! Tell me what's going on—don't be afraid to upset me."

"Very well. Is it true, Father, that you intend to marry me off?"

"How did you find that out?" The King of the Massagetae was

surprised. "I haven't exactly decided yet… But… Daughter, I do believe it's time. In a few days, you'll be turning sixteen!"

"But why—to Khaidar, that repulsive old man? Aren't there enough handsome young men on Massagetae soil? Or perhaps I could wed some noble prince from distant lands."

"Child, you know the Saka custom: it's not up to the children but their fathers to choose a spouse for them. I know best who is suited to you and can secure your future."

"But I don't love him. One day—most likely—I'd just kill him…"

"Don't say such things, girl. I myself would have killed him long ago for daring to propose marriage to you. Who is he, after all? Just the leader of some tribe, while you are a king's daughter, the heir to the Saka throne! You know I've never feared for myself; my only worry is for you—your fate when I, your father, am gone from this earth and can no longer protect you from every danger and all our enemies. Then you'll need a strong man who can stand by you."

"But is Khaidar really that man, Father? Can he really be trusted?"

"We have no choice but to trust him. You may not know this yet, but another large portion of the Alans abandoned Bikbulat and Queen Kiana. They returned here to our lands and joined Khaidar. Now he commands the largest army in the steppe—even bigger and stronger than mine. At any moment, he could overthrow me, your rightful king, and seize my throne. But if he marries you, then he'll be only the husband of the queen and won't dare strip away the power I soon plan to pass on to you. So, my daughter, it's safer and more advantageous for us to bring him into the family, keep him close—and, above all, not provoke him. Do you follow me?"

"I understand, Father. But please, come with me right now. I want to show you something! Let's go…"

Tomyris led Spargapis out of his royal tent to a distant, far more modest tent in their camp.

Even before they entered, Spargapis noticed a strong, rather unpleasant smell.

When he and Tomyris went inside, the sight instantly provoked the king's anger and fury.

On the floor, in the arms of nearly naked women, lay Khaidar—flushed red from wine and dead drunk—along with several of his closest companions. They were muttering incoherently in their drunken stupor, their poses among the women leaving no doubt as to what was going on. The tent was drenched in the stench of stale, poor-quality wine, so strong it even wafted outside.

"So these are the people you wanted to entrust with protecting your only daughter?" Tomyris asked her father, very gravely, almost sternly.

Naturally, she didn't tell him that she herself, with the help of loyal friends and servants, had staged this unseemly spectacle—so scandalous in the eyes of the Massagetae ruler! But she believed the gods would forgive her. After all, if she had to marry, it would only be for love.

"No, this will never happen!" King Spargapis answered in angry indignation. "Khaidar is utterly unworthy of you, my dear. He's disgraced himself!"

Fuming, Spargapis stomped out of the reeking tent, while Tomyris followed, quite satisfied. The tent was one of her friend's.

Still, Tomyris knew full well that soon her father would take up the subject of her marriage once again. So she resolved to find herself a far better suitor.

15

When Rustam saw Azer up close—he who had never before paid any attention to Tigraxauda women—he stood there, stunned with amazement.

This woman was indeed nearly twice his age, but never had he seen such astonishing beauty. She was not skinny—on the contrary, Azer had a firm, rosy, clean body, like dough mixed with fresh cream, and she exuded a most pleasing fragrance.

Aromas of the finest local herbs, Rustam guessed. For some reason, he felt drawn to her almost at once, yet he stayed put, unmoving, still seated in his spot.

"I was told, Prince, that you're most generous and hospitable!" the woman began, smiling playfully at the master of the luxurious tent he occupied alone. "But I'm not seeing it yet. Aren't you going to offer me something delicious? Something they only serve on the table of a king and his family?… You must have special treats that we ordinary Sakas have never once tasted—am I right?"

With another dazzling smile, she further stoked a certain desire within the warrior. With an awkward hand gesture, never taking his eyes off her, Rustam indicated the laid-out dishes.

"Please, woman, do sit and help yourself. Allow me to pour you some sweet wine! I sent my servants away so they wouldn't disturb us or make you uncomfortable."

"You did exactly the right thing, Prince! I'm not used to—nor will I ever get used to—servants. For my husband and my children, I always do everything myself."

"Wait!" Rustam started, the meaning of her words beginning to register. "So… you have a husband? Then how—"

"Oh, of course I do!" the woman laughed, revealing straight, gleaming white teeth that made her even more enchanting. "Where else would I have gained such experience in love?… Did you think they'd bring you some promiscuous woman, a courtesan? No, I'm respectable."

"Then I should let you go," Rustam said gloomily, barely restraining the first stirrings of a deep passion he had never felt before. "I fear no one, but I have no right to destroy your family! Nor do I wish to bring disgrace to you or your husband."

"Calm yourself, warrior. Yes, I speak as though I have a husband—out of pride, so no one thinks me alone. But in reality, he's been under the cold earth for several years now—he died in one of these wars. That's why I so despise all your wars! And how I delight whenever a worthy man appears at my side… A man like you!!"

A weight lifted from Rustam's heart; he couldn't hide his relief. Not that he took joy in the poor husband's death, but that she was free, and no one could accuse him of any sin with her.

"And you, I see, are sensitive and gentle!" his guest suddenly praised the king's son. "And a bit childlike too: it's all there on your face—both your sorrows and your joys. Well, right now, with a friend rather than a foe, that might be no bad thing. You know, I'm feeling shy—I just can't make myself pick up that appealing sweet delicacy over there… Might you feed me yourself?"

Rustam silently stood, still gazing at her, took a large, fragrant baked fruit from the table, broke off a piece, and held it to the beautiful woman's lips. Then he sat right next to her, very close. He was so drawn to her that he could no longer stay at a distance.

She took the piece of fruit with her lips, chewing neatly, gracefully, unhurriedly. Only then did the king's son truly notice her lips. They were enchanting—thin, shapely, a bright rosy hue, and all around them a clean, smooth, baby-soft complexion. Suddenly, Rustam felt an irresistible urge to bring his face, his lips, against that enchanting, fragrant woman's face, to gently kiss those captivating lips…

And no sooner had that urge flashed within him than—her lips touched his own. At first, she kissed him gently, cautiously; then, as soon as he tremblingly responded, her kisses turned fierce, insistent, passionate.

With his powerful arms, the man lifted the woman—though Azer was hardly petite, to him she seemed as light as a feather, for he was both strong and thoroughly enraptured by her—and carried her to his bed.

Once he laid her down gently, he began feverishly kissing her—her face, her neck, her hair, her hands, her feet; and when she allowed him to undress her, he kissed her entire body. Suddenly, she reclaimed the initiative, kissing him in turn, her hands caressing his body! Soft yet swift and sure, she used her fingers, her tongue, her lips on every part of him—places he'd have thought forbidden to anyone else…

Oh, how sweet it felt! Never had he experienced anything like it before in his life! For a moment, he even felt that the force of this union between man and woman was mightier than any weapon on the battlefield. The pleasure ran so deep, and his body felt such ease and fulfillment, that along with the storm of passion she stirred in him, he was filled with endless gratitude to her for a bliss he had never known.

All evening and night he did not think of the girl from his

dreams, who resembled an angel or a princess, nor of the Massagetae king's daughter, Tomyris…

Drunk on delight, Rustam fell sound asleep. In the morning, when he awoke, Azer was gone.

Surprised, the prince called for his servants, asking after her.

"She left in the middle of the night," answered the servant who had seen her.

Strange that she left! I was sure she'd stay with me forever… Rustam thought, recalling the long hours of intense pleasure Azer had given him. *And her name suits her perfectly! "Azer"—that's fire! Indeed, she's a living flame!! She scorches body and soul, leaving not even ashes behind!!*

He could hardly wait for the next night.

Azer did not come on her own for some reason, so he had to send servants to fetch her. This time, she refused to eat or drink, and to Rustam she seemed much cooler than she had been the previous evening, and certainly less warm than that first night. This puzzled him greatly. He was certain Azer loved him too, only she was out of sorts for some reason. He did not ask questions, believing that if she found it important, she would tell him herself.

Yet their night was once again turbulent and passionate, more wonderful than before. Azer pleasured and caressed Rustam, and with the intoxication, euphoria, and joy, he felt himself soaring among the clouds.

It went on like that for a few days. Rustam felt he was now an expert in the arts of the bed. Only two things pained him: Azer's persistently subdued mood—her apparent coolness toward him outside of their bed—and the fact that she would not allow him to give her pleasure.

"You've only completed the first lesson, Rustam," she explained.

"I've shown you how beautiful, how delightful intimacy can be… But you didn't know how to reciprocate the same to your partner. It wasn't time yet. Now you must learn to court a woman not haphazardly but skillfully—do you hear me? Skillfully and gracefully. So that she not merely surrenders herself to you and pleasures you, but genuinely loves you and is happy by your side— so she'll never betray you and will stay faithful to you alone her whole life! That's a far more difficult task… Do you see why I'm only allowing it now?"

"Oh yes, my dear teacher!" Rustam exclaimed ardently. "I believe I understand. I'll do my very best."

They lay together once more. Not everything went smoothly for Rustam. Azer showed him where he made mistakes. She saw that Rustam had truly fallen for her. The lessons continued.

Then one day…

"That's enough, Prince—you're ready for married life!" Azer announced. "I won't be coming to you anymore. You need to think carefully about finding a bride. Once you marry, the lessons of happiness I taught you will prove most useful!"

Rustam was dumbfounded.

"Wait, Azer! Why are you leaving? What have I done to offend you, my beloved? Tell me! I'll make it right—I'll do anything for you!! Marry me—today, right now—and please, never leave me!"

The woman looked at her noble student and laughed.

"Marry you?! Are you in your right mind, Prince? What just happened between us wasn't 'love'—it was youthful passion, bodily desire. It'll soon pass. I'm not your equal. The moment your father hears of this, he'll have me killed. Besides, I need none of it—I don't love you."

Rustam was even more shaken and grieved.

"How can that be? Why not? I thought—well, it seemed—"

"Yes, it only seemed that way," the beauty replied with a dazzling smile. "Truth be told… I do feel somewhat fond of you—and that's the problem. You see, men usually pay me to teach either them or their sons about love and how to treat women. Your father Kavad paid me well—and it was certainly not so that you'd invite me to marry you! Oh no, no! You were meant to learn not to lose your composure around a woman, especially a beautiful one."

Rustam listened, entranced, as Azer continued:

"Do you remember how timid and awkward you were at the beginning, at our first meeting? And yet, women appreciate a man's tenderness, but never his timidity or fear of them! Every woman needs an experienced, strong, confident man, someone who can tame and conquer her! Keep that in mind. So once you'd mastered Lesson One, you began on Lesson Two…"

"I did? And what was that?" asked a baffled Rustam, realizing for the first time that all this had been her teaching.

"You started learning how to pleasure a woman, to bring her joy and delight. But you became so taken with me, so enamored, you simply lost your head—and in doing so, you forgot your pride. A woman, like a man, values a fortress that isn't easily taken! You gave yourself to me wholly, with no chance for me to serve you, to please you with my warmth. Forgive me, Prince, but with me, you became like a slave or a servant."

"I'm not angry at you, my dear Azer. Everything you say is important to me. I'm amazed…"

"Everything in moderation, Prince. When you felt me being distant and realized that no matter what you did, you couldn't captivate me or make me love you, you slackened your aggression, regained your self-respect! That made me value you more. That was my third lesson. You didn't turn indifferent or start humiliating me; you still loved me, and I felt it. But then you became so dear to me that I nearly fell under your spell—and that shouldn't happen… So, Rustam, my work here is finished, and I'm leaving. A great destiny awaits you, and I'm sure that someday you'll truly love a beautiful young woman who'll be your wife! Remember my lessons—and from here on, life itself will teach you the rest."

"Thank you for everything, dear Azer! I'll never forget you…"

"And one last thing. Rustam, you have a mighty and very, very beautiful body. Any woman who lays eyes on it will lose her calm. Always remember and appreciate that…"

* * *

Persia, the same era

"Father, Mother—I'm rallying Persia against Astyages!" Cyrus declared, visibly agitated. "I'm going to make his dream come true—but on my terms!"

Cambyses and Mandane exchanged worried glances.

"No, my son, you can't do that," Prince Cambyses responded. "Your grandfather is still powerful, and Media remains strong. That's why we were forced to hide the truth of your childhood from you…"

"And neglected to mention that Astyages gave an order to kill me as soon as I was born!!"

"What else could we do?" His mother, Mandane, was nearly in tears. "For so many years, we ourselves were weighed down by sorrow, not even knowing you were alive. Apparently, some kind souls—"

"Yes, they saved me and raised me!" Cyrus interrupted impatiently. "And recently I learned that my mother, Spaka—who loved me more than anyone in the world—was mercilessly executed! Do you know who's responsible?… King Astyages—your father, Mother!"

"Cyrus, you must calm yourself and try to put all this behind you," Prince Cambyses said, placing a hand on his son's shoulder. "Now that you're finally here with us, we can't risk your life again! That's why we didn't poison your mind against your own grandfather. Mandane and I never wanted to disrupt the family's peace or lose you again, just when we'd found you. There's such hatred burning in your eyes for him! You see? The peace is broken, and we're anxious for your safety… And what's changed for the better? Has evil been punished? Has justice prevailed? No—it's all as it was, only worse for us now, because those who hold power are always in the right… So, my son, quell your anger and accept things as they are!"

"Never! And I promise you, justice will triumph! I'll punish King Astyages for all his evil!"

"But how did you learn that he wanted to—"

"Just now, I received a letter telling me so. And it's my duty—my honor, Father—to liberate your homeland, Persia, from my bloodthirsty grandfather's yoke! If I don't march on Media, Astyages, fearing me because of his dreams, will soon crush Persia himself—and you and I can't allow that! So, dear parents, give me your blessing for this war! May Ahura Mazda protect me."

"Very well, you have our blessing," Cambyses said with a surge of hope, trusting in his son's success.

Mandane, pale and trembling, remained silent, fearing for Cyrus's life…

16

Tashkent, 2012

Saltanat, the daughter of Tamilla Mahkamova and Rashid Batyrov, met with the driver, Shukhrat, and retrieved her mother's phone from him. As an experienced cell phone user, she immediately checked all the recent incoming and outgoing calls and text messages.

"Look, Shukhrat—there's a message here that's probably from the kidnappers! It has the exact address where my mother was supposed to go! See?"

"Yes. Some old hangar at an abandoned factory that's been shut down for ages. All right, Saltanat, say we find your parents there. How do we handle the thugs? They could kill both of us on the spot. We're no use to them, and usually, criminals don't want unnecessary witnesses! I have great respect for my boss and would do a lot for her, but giving my life when it probably won't even save hers… No, forgive me, I'm not sure. And I'm scared. I still think you were right about the police. We'll need a whole squad."

All of a sudden, Saltanat remembered that she had a contact in the police. She sensed that she couldn't manage without his help, because at her local precinct, they wouldn't even accept a missing persons report until "enough" time had passed.

Saltanat first checked her own phone's contact list. Finding nothing, she then (though normally she would never do such a thing unless forced by extreme circumstances) searched through her mother's phone—and located the number she needed.

"Hello? Hello, I need to speak to Colonel Daniyarov, Sharaf Ulugebekovich."

"Good afternoon, that's me. Who's calling? I don't recognize your voice."

"Sharaf Ulugebekovich, I'm the daughter of your good friend Tamilla Mahkamova. My name is Saltanat—maybe you remember me?"

"Ah, Saltanat, my dear! I'm so glad to hear from you. How are you? How's your mother doing? Is everything all right? I haven't heard from her in quite a while—she's forgotten this old man."

"Oh no, she remembers, but she's been so busy with work and a million other things…"

"Yes, last time I saw you, you were just a little girl. You must be all grown up now. Probably married, with children?"

"Yes, all that's in order," Saltanat replied politely, but she was quickly running out of patience. *Oh, these elderly folks…* "Actually, I… have an urgent matter."

"Something happened? To your mother?" the experienced operative guessed right away.

"Yes!! And to my father as well… They're in trouble. But this isn't a conversation for the phone."

"All right, come to my place. Write down the address. Just be warned, I live on the fifth floor, and the elevator's out. Will you be able to manage?"

"Wait, Sharaf Ulugebekovich. You mean… you're no longer on the force?!"

"No, of course not. I've been retired for a long time. But I still want to hear you out. Maybe I can help."

Saltanat had no other options, so she went to see the elderly officer.

"Oh, my dear, I feel for you. Quite a strange story with your parents!" Colonel Daniyarov said, shaking his head after inviting the young woman to sit in his living room. "It does sound like they've been kidnapped and are being held hostage. But who did it and why? That's not clear. Most likely, yes, they're criminal elements. Or, as they're oddly referred to these days, 'serious' people. In my book, they're just the dregs of society, excuse me—riffraff. They call the police 'garbage,' but what about themselves? Right, hold on, let me make a call—to some colleagues. If I understand correctly, this abandoned factory is on the very edge of the city. Just a minute!"

Saltanat nodded gratefully and waited for the phone call to end.

"Well, I spoke to one of the bosses at the local precinct. It's already late today—they have a scheduled meeting, then a roll call. But tomorrow at nine in the morning, he can see you. You'll explain everything to him, and he'll do his best to help! That is, to help your parents."

Saltanat was thankful to the colonel—who, as it turned out, was already retired. She took her leave without letting him see how upset she was: her parents would have to spend the entire night goodness-knows-where!! *What if it's damp or cold or filthy or dangerous?…* The mere thought terrified her.

Her train of thought was interrupted by a call on her cell phone.

"Hello, is this Rashid Kudratovich's daughter?" asked a man's voice, which Saltanat found somewhat familiar. "This is your father's coworker speaking. My name is Isamitdin Valievich. We met once when you visited your father at work! Anyway, Saltanat, my office is next to your father's. Our boss—the Minister of Culture—just told me he can't reach Batyrov since noon. He knows your father went out on some errands, but he should've been back long ago. He hasn't come back, and his cell phone is off. Do you know what's going on? Has something happened?"

"Yes, unfortunately. My father is missing!" Saltanat decided not to tell this almost-stranger all the sensitive details of her parents' dangerous predicament.

"Missing? What do you mean?"

"I don't really know much myself. Sorry. Please apologize to the minister. Goodbye…"

"Wait, don't hang up! There was another call—from Moscow. The girls in reception transferred it to me when I got back to my office. You see, I'd been out all day visiting my own sites. Then…"

Saltanat felt her patience slipping again for the umpteenth time on this neurotic day.

Still, Isamitdin Valievich went on:

"Anyway, someone named Irmanov called. I'm not sure if it was *the* Irmanov or someone else—maybe you know? A woman named Anastasia spoke to me. This Irmanov is also looking for your father, and he seems pretty angry, saying Rashid is letting him down."

Saltanat nearly exploded. In her mind, the idea of "Dad" and "letting someone down" were utterly incompatible. Rashid Batyrov had never, in his life, let anyone down.

"I see, Isamitdin Valievich. Did this Anastasia leave the phone number for their office?"

"Yes, take it down. Might I help you somehow?"

"No, thank you very much. I'll try to work out these issues myself. And I'll speak to Irmanov personally. Thanks again."

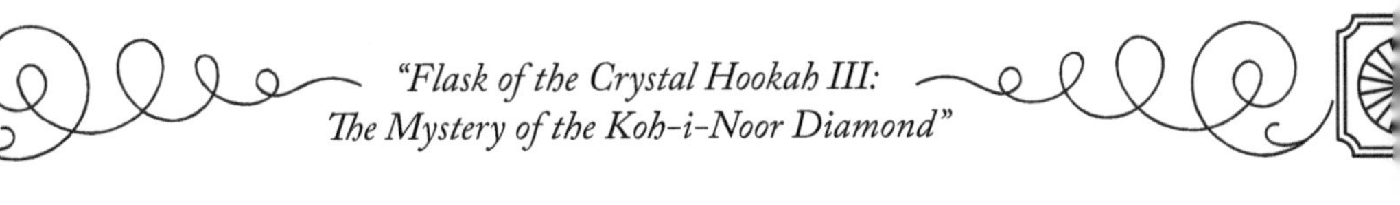

***

In the old hangar, night had brought colder temperatures, and Tamilla Mahkamova was feeling ill. She tried not to show it, to avoid worrying Rashid any further.

But Rashid Batyrov was a sensitive man, especially concerning his family. Right now, he admired his wife's courage more than ever. Her dignity in such an extreme and dangerous situation—where at any moment they both could be killed—inspired in him both awe and determination to behave just as bravely and nobly. He called for Dmitry. The guard came over reluctantly; it was already nighttime, and the easygoing, non-aggressive guard was even sleepier than before.

"What's up? You need a drink? Hang on," Dima mumbled, half-asleep.

"Well, sure, tea wouldn't hurt," Rashid said with a slight smile. "But that's not the main thing. Dmitry, it was hot during the day, but now you see how cold it's gotten! Would you please take my jacket off me and put it on my wife? Can you do that?"

"Yeah, no problem," the guard replied calmly. "That's totally allowed."

He draped Tamilla in her husband's jacket, and she immediately felt much warmer. Still, she worried about Rashid being cold now.

"Why did you do that, my dear? It wasn't necessary!" she said awkwardly. Yet, as a woman, of course, she appreciated her husband's loving care.

"That's enough, my sunshine. Not up for discussion. Another thing… You know, I'm getting the feeling we're here not only because of those diamonds. By now, these thugs have probably checked and seen you didn't bring the Koh-i-Noor stone into Uzbekistan! Obviously, someone set you up, making these creeps think you had that diamond so they'd target you. Yes, it's a big reason, but not the only reason we're detained. I'm almost sure there's something else going on—something equally significant."

"I agree. My intuition tells me it might be related somehow to my students—the gifted kids I sent abroad. If only Konstantin Ivanovich could find us! He's so well-connected, I'm sure he'd help us get free and figure out what happened to those kids, why they haven't responded…"

Tamilla didn't bring up—though she couldn't forget—the incident with one of her students last year. His name was Dilshod Inagamov, an outstanding student at Tashkent Medical Academy. Tamilla, together with Konstantin, had arranged for him, among others, to do an internship in the United States.

Midway through the year, Romanov told Mahkamova some tragic news: Dilshod had died unexpectedly, drowning in Boston Harbor. No one could figure out what he'd been doing there, why he was swimming there. Tamilla recalled that Rashid, upon hearing of the tragedy, asked her if she had informed the boy's parents of his death. Tamilla explained that Inagamov had no relatives at all.

Konstantin Ivanovich had flown to Boston himself, double-checked everything, spoke to the police, and confirmed Dilshod really was dead. As Romanov reported, the young man's body had been found near Nantasket—way down on the southernmost edge of Boston Harbor…

"Anyway, my dear," Rashid broke into his wife's sad reflections as they sat bound together in the hangar, "let's not lose heart. Let's keep faith that things will get better! Everything's going to be all right for us, wife, you hear? We just have to believe. Do you agree?"

"Yes… Everything will be fine…" Tamilla replied, not very convincingly.

"My dear, that story of yours about the ancient Sakas, and your father's stories, and our own youth—it's good for both of us. It distracts us from this ordeal and makes it easier to endure these cramped conditions. So please, if you can, continue!"

"Of course. Listen on…"

***

Tashkent, 1975

Alexei Irmanov was angry. Everything at his diamond-mining operation had been going rather well. He had even managed to finance both the Ministry of Finance and the Ministry of Culture of the republic. He'd formed a strong friendship with Rashid Batyrov, a young specialist involved in safeguarding ancient architectural monuments. But then…

The diamonds in the Gazli mine abruptly ran out. Completely. Certainly, the plant still had small leftover batches of its own diamonds, plus some new shipments of Yakut diamonds. But there were already plenty of places in the vast USSR that processed Yakut stones. So, Alexei's plant—far from the capitals, in a region lacking robust infrastructure—was now deemed unprofitable. The decision was made to shut it down. Alexei, with his managerial talent and expertise, was needed at the Ministry of Finance. Of course, the workers were not abandoned either; they were offered jobs at various other locations.

On one hand, the younger Irmanov was glad to move to

Tashkent—he would be closer to his father, and he'd be able to see Sasha Levidovskaya from the Party School more frequently. He simply couldn't get her out of his mind! On the other hand, Alexei felt guilty over the large Yakut diamonds stolen from his plant ten years earlier: they had never been found, nor had the murderer of the former director been identified. At least Alexei himself hadn't been targeted—he was grateful for that, but found it all strange and puzzling. Who could a harmless old man like Abdukhalikov have crossed? Maybe he knew something he shouldn't have… Or maybe he'd simply been defending state property, the republic's and country's wealth? And for that, he was…

Meeting with Aleksandra in Tashkent was thrilling for them both. As Alexei had anticipated and hoped—especially since they'd spoken on the phone a couple of times after first meeting at the Higher Party School—Aleksandra, too, found him appealing.

It was a Saturday evening. After a romantic dinner at one of the best cafés in the Uzbek capital, where the young man had invited the lady of his heart, he walked her home. He learned she lived with her daughter, but for the moment, she was alone—Nastya, Sasha's young daughter from her first marriage, was visiting her grandmother, Lida, at the family dacha.

Aleksandra softly touched his cheek with her hand. This emboldened him. Alexei, an experienced manager accustomed to decisiveness, now, without overthinking, seized her in a warm, strong embrace and kissed her passionately on the lips. He was afraid she might recoil at this sudden gesture, shove him. But instead, she reciprocated with some pleasure. She did not push her bold suitor away.

All at once, Alexei felt he had power over the girl. That would have been problematic if she didn't also have power over him—but in this, they were equals. Overwhelmed by emotion, he took a step away from her, hinting that it was probably time for him to leave.

"No, wait…" Aleksandra whispered enchantingly. "You haven't said…"

"Said what?" the man asked, not understanding at first. Then suddenly he realized; his heart gave him the answer:

"Ah, you mean that I love you? Sorry—of course, I love you! Sasha, will you be my wife?"

She was over the moon, her spirit rejoicing and singing: He had said it!

Moving gracefully, almost as if dancing, she offered him her hand. He took it and kissed it.

Sasha smiled softly, mysterious in her happiness:

"Come with me. Why hesitate? I can't wait until the wedding—I want you now."

They went up to her apartment. Neither Aleksandra nor Alexei had ever in their lives experienced such bliss…

A month later, the couple got married. Alexei treated little Nastya as if she were his own, raising her and trying to care for her like a father. Yet she insisted on calling him only "Uncle Lyosha," which hurt him.

Throughout that month, Alexei worked at the Ministry of Finance. He didn't become a deputy minister—another promising figure blocked that—but Irmanov was appointed head of the department responsible for liaison with public organizations. From that post, he continued helping Rashid in his good cause however he could.

Meanwhile, Rashid Batyrov was hardly idle. He had become deeply fascinated by the history of the Uzbek people's ancestors—

the Sakas. In particular, he was intrigued by the fate of the legendary Massagetae queen, Tomyris. So Batyrov grew very interested in archaeological excavations. He'd heard that in the lower reaches of the Amu Darya, scholars were searching for a golden turban that had supposedly belonged to Tomyris—a turban rumored to possess magical powers. Rashid didn't believe in magic, but he very much wanted to see that turban one day and touch it—to be close to such a great piece of Uzbekistan's history.

Alexei promised his friend all the help he could give in this matter. He found a talented archaeologist, Pulat Gafarov, and entrusted him with preparations for an expedition to the lower Amu Darya.

A few months later, Gafarov departed for the site. He began painstaking excavations in ancient Sakastan, seeking the splendid golden turban of Queen Tomyris.

* * *

Moscow, 1977

Kirill Midiyatdinov's non-biological aunt Farida arrived to see the fourteen-year-old boy, bringing him a treat: tasty Tatar meat pies.

"I can't eat these, Auntie," Kirill muttered, though he couldn't take his eyes off the mouthwatering pastries.

"Why not?" Farida was puzzled.

"I have to ask my father's permission first. He might get mad if I accept gifts from outsiders without asking."

"What do you mean, 'outsiders'? I'm your aunt! Come on, have some—don't talk nonsense!" With a laugh, she grabbed the boy by the elbow. And then… she noticed something impossible to overlook. How had she not seen it right away?… Kirill's arms were covered in bruises.

"Ah, I see…" Farida gasped. "Poor child! So your father's been beating you, has he? That scoundrel—my own brother, no less. He's so used to being cruel at work, and now he's taking it home, too. And I guess you're not always a perfectly obedient boy, right?"

"It's hard for me," the boy admitted, close to tears at being pitied.

"Sure it is—you're just a kid. And you have reason to be lively."

"So… my dad, when he was little, was he like me?" The boy struggled to phrase his question. "Was he the same way I am?"

"Well, as for your father—I'm not sure. But your mo—" Farida cut herself off, remembering she wasn't allowed to say anything about her sister, Marina, being Kirill's real mother, or Oleg would kill her. She paused, then decided to risk it and share a little with her nephew: "Listen, Kir, I think your father treats you this way because you're not really his. He doesn't love you. He only needs you because… he needs his superiors to praise him, to make him look good in their eyes, understand?"

"N-n-not really his?!" The boy was shocked, trembling on the verge of tears. "How does that…? 'Look good' how?"

At this moment, he clearly didn't understand anything. Farida frowned.

"I'm tired of lying and being scared of my brother! He's not my real brother either; I was taken from an orphanage, and Marina is a stranger to me… I found out by chance when I was a kid, and you should know the truth, too. That's why I'm telling you. But don't breathe a word of this to him or Marina, do you hear me? Maybe you'll get lucky and go back to your real parents."

"Auntie Farida, do you know them—my mom and dad?" Now the boy was bawling outright.

"Shh, quiet, or your nanny will hear and report to your father." She sighed. "I know… No, I don't know them. Why do you ask?"

"When I grow up, I'll kill that evil Oleg! He won't beat me anymore! And I'll find my mother and father. Or they'll come for me themselves. I know they will find me! Do you hear?"

"I hear you, Kiryusha," his aunt nodded. "Yes, indeed. Let's hope that's exactly what happens."

* * *

Tashkent, the same year, 1977

Maryam continued running the Palace of Culture at the Porcelain Factory. She organized various clubs and held many interesting, engaging events. Her daughter, Tamilla, turned out to be every bit as energetic and lively as her mother. She didn't want to be an engineer, as her father, Sardor Mahkamov, had hoped, because she felt a strong creative streak and was eager to develop it.

Tamilla found several talented girls who could sing and formed a vocal group performing modern Soviet and foreign songs. The only initial snag was finding musicians, but Tamilla managed to recruit two capable guys with guitars. That gave them a proper vocal-instrumental ensemble. Tamilla herself didn't sing; she was the group's manager, arranging their shows.

At first, the group performed on an amateur basis, but as their level of professionalism rose, they started getting invitations for paid gigs. Meanwhile, Tamilla also studied English. *It'll always come in handy!* she thought.

At one multi-artist concert, which featured stars of the Uzbek pop scene, Harun Zikirillaev, a well-known singer, noticed Tamilla. He was greatly taken by the pretty, dynamic young woman. They began to see each other and talk on the phone. Tamilla's mother, Maryam Baburovna, didn't miss this, although they never discussed it directly. Maryam wanted her daughter to open up on her own about her feelings and decisions. But for some reason, Tamilla kept silent on the subject.

About a month after Tamilla and Harun met, Maryam asked her husband—just to know what he thought:

"Sardor, how would you feel if our daughter were to get married?"

"Is she already thinking of marriage?!" Mahkamov exclaimed. "Isn't it a bit soon?"

"She's eighteen—I think that's reasonable. Tamilla hasn't said anything definite to me yet, but I've heard from her friends that a young, handsome, and quite well-known musician—Harun Zikirillaev—has started courting her. You know him?"

"I've heard of him," Sardor replied, sounding a bit discontented. "Honestly, I don't have much faith in these musicians and singers— they're usually not very serious, flighty, narcissistic… I wouldn't want my one and only dear daughter to tie her life to that Harun. Even his name is so… old-fashioned. It'd be bad enough if she's already fallen for him. I'll definitely need to talk with our Tamilla!"

17

Sakastan, 6th Century BCE

Neither the Tigraxauda Sakas nor the Massagetae were left in peace for long by their enemies. Kavad, having only just returned home after talking with King Spargapis about a possible marriage between their children—Rustam and Tomyris—faced a sudden invasion into his lands by the Kangju from the banks of the Jaxartes.

"Father, please let me join you and Rustam in battle!" pleaded Kavad's younger son, Zogak, now fourteen years old.

"Are you out of your mind? No, you're not going!" the father snapped at the son he did not favor. "You're too young and too weak. Besides, you're a failure! I'm afraid I'd lose this war if I brought you along, and the stakes are high. You'll stay in camp with the women and children."

For any Saka male—no matter how young—these words stung.

Rustam, who happened to be in the royal tent at that moment, overheard the exchange.

"My father," he spoke up, "if I may say something: every prince needs to be tempered in the fire of war! Zogak may be young, but he's already a brave fighter. I taught him how to battle, and I'll vouch that he won't let us down. Let him go with you and your army to face the Kangju. I will always stay by his side and help him."

"All right, let it be as you say," Kavad relented. He saw no reason to argue over such a trifle with his beloved firstborn—the

Tigraxauda Sakas' main hope in battle.

Zogak, however, was overjoyed at the chance to prove to everyone—especially his father—that he was better than Rustam.

At war, the brothers remained side by side. The gigantic Rustam treated his younger, brave but slight-built brother with touching warmth, never suspecting Zogak's hidden envy and lack of brotherly affection. Zogak skillfully concealed all his jealousy and hatred toward his older brother.

The Tigraxauda Sakas confronted their Kangju foes somewhere in the Seven Rivers region, near the highest burial mounds.

The Kangju leader, Tahmasp, struck so hard that the Saka ranks wavered, turning their horses back in flight. With the tide of battle all but decided, Rustam—sent around the flank with his detachment—struck from behind. Astoundingly quickly, the mighty warrior crossed steep mountain passes and smashed into the Kangju forces in a head-on clash. He emerged in the enemy's rear, and without hesitation, he and hundreds of fearless horsemen attacked the scattered Kangju lines. Rapidly sizing up the situation, cutting down adversaries at every turn, Rustam charged straight for their commander.

Though Tahmasp was seasoned and fought fiercely, he could not withstand Rustam's power. The firstborn son of Kavad skewered him with his sword as if he were a mere hare. The Kangju leader doubled over in the saddle, clutching his bleeding chest. His retinue quickly called for a healer—and on Rustam's orders, carried their wounded leader to Kavad's tent so he might receive treatment. Rustam even provided his own physician to aid him.

Rustam entrusted Tahmasp to the care of his foster brother, Ferid, and surrounded the prisoner with his warriors. This proved wise, as the Kangju—recovering from Rustam's surprise assault—

fought back furiously, desperate to reclaim their chieftain. Rustam's detachment was weakening, but Kavad managed to rally his fleeing forces, hurl them back into the fight, and secure victory for the Tigraxauda Sakas by sword and whip.

Throughout this struggle, Zogak fought valiantly, though it was his first true war. For all his frailty and less-than-mighty constitution, he showed a talent for battle. Wounded by both spear and sword, he managed to save several Tigraxauda warriors. But his father took no notice. Besides, Rustam's new feats once again overshadowed Zogak entirely.

"Won't you at least praise me, Father?" Zogak asked hopefully.

Kavad glanced at his younger son, bloody from combat, with near indifference. He said nothing, then headed for his tent, dismounted, and went inside. There, he saw Tahmasp lying on the ground.

"Well now, warlord, are you dying? Admit you're finished!"

Tahmasp, trying to stem the flow of blood as he occasionally lifted his bandaged chest, answered only with a sullen glare.

King Kavad, triumphant, stood over his fallen enemy, legs apart and hands on his hips. Peacock feathers streamed from his golden helmet. The sight of this gloating foe enraged Tahmasp, who finally spat out:

"What are you so proud of, you petty king? Weren't you the one fleeing from me like a whipped, cowardly dog? If it weren't for your Rustam, you'd be in a shroud right now, and I'd be celebrating my victory atop your back with the brave Kangju! Compared to Rustam, you're a weakling, and you've no right to sit on the Tigraxauda throne. You'd do better to yield it to the one who truly surpassed you in every way!"

"Tahmasp, you've given me a fine idea," Kavad replied calmly.

"Today I'll feast with my brave warriors, riding on your back, celebrating our triumph. You're right: Rustam is indeed greater than I. But you're wrong if you think he has surpassed me… No, he hasn't, because he doesn't have a son like Rustam. And I'll show you the honor befitting a valiant warrior like you. Your wish is your last, and I will fulfill it… Not Zogak, but Rustam shall inherit the Tigraxauda throne! But of course, only after my death."

All this time, Zogak stood beside his father. Noting the younger son's expression—turning pale-green at his father's words—Tahmasp, wanting to sting Kavad further, addressed him again:

"Don't blame the gods, Kavad, for sharing your manly strength only with Rustam. But he's not your younger son, so by our law he cannot become king!"

"I'll do as the kings of Media and Persia do," Kavad shot back. "I'll name my elder son heir—one without flaws! Not a weakling, but a true warrior!"

Hearing these words, Zogak was outraged inside. He had been so hopeful… All his dreams were shattered… No—he didn't dare show anger toward the father he revered!

Zogak walked out of the tent. Catching sight of Rustam, his resentment flared into greater hatred than ever before…

***

Media, the same era

General Dinar, one of Astyages' close associates, burst into the Median king's chambers. He was used to warfare and even loved

it, but the news of the oncoming attack caught him off guard. In his panic, he even forgot to bow before the monarch, as custom demanded:

"My lord, Persia has risen against us!" Dinar blurted breathlessly, having hurried over. "Forgive me, but the rebels are led by… your grandson, Cyrus! What are your orders?"

Astyages laughed haughtily:

"Are you suggesting I should fear some boy? A mere suckling?! And you, a general, trembling at any trivial military disturbance? I order you to march immediately with your retinue into Persia, crush all those rebels in my name, and punish them! And as for that… wretched brat—take him alive and bring him here to Ecbatana! I'll make sure he doesn't escape a second death by my will!!"

Dinar confronted the rebel Persian troops near Pasargadae.

The Persians, as usual, were intimidated by the Medes and fled. No matter how much Cyrus tried to halt his forces, their flight was unstoppable. When Cambyses' and Cyrus's chaotic host reached the Persian capital, they found the gates barred, and the women atop the fortress walls showered their surrendered warriors with mocking jeers.

Cyrus himself narrowly managed to evade Dinar and returned home safe and sound. The young prince rebuked the deserters severely, reminding them that the Medes mercilessly executed any rebels they overpowered. That is, if the Persians gave in to the Medes, the latter would simply kill them on the spot.

"Hey, brave warriors of Persia!" Cyrus exhorted. "You hold yourselves in high esteem, you are the best. I believe, in truth, that we Persians are far stronger and braver than the Medians! We can pull ourselves together and defeat them!"

Shamed by his words, the Persians turned back once more

toward Media. Dinar, however, had no inkling of this; he had already returned to Astyages in Ecbatana.

Astyages ordered Dinar to prepare to storm Pasargadae.

"Now, after your crushing blow, the Persians won't recover for a long time," the Median king told his general. "But gather your army quickly all the same. We will annihilate them all!"

Then suddenly, quite unexpectedly, the Persian army descended upon Dinar's forces. Shocked, the Median general saw that this time there were many more Persians than before, and they were far better armed.

Where did this horde come from?! he thought in horror. *We must retreat!*

But there was no time. Dinar was slain by Cyrus, and Astyages' army was practically destroyed.

Cyrus led his troops deep into Media.

* * *

Sakastan, the same era

Nastaran was the eldest—and, in fact, unwanted—daughter of the wealthiest Tigraxauda Saka, Khoja, son of one of the tribe's elders, Sadyk. Khoja had always wanted only sons, but he believed his wife had let him down during their first union by becoming pregnant with and giving birth to a daughter.

Nastaran was never considered beautiful and, much like Zogak, was ignored by all her relatives. They only tolerated her because she looked after Khoja's younger children—his three sons. Nobody predicted a prosperous future for her, but the young woman herself felt sure that one day she would become happier and more successful than all of her kin.

Having endured endless humiliations from her harsh and boorish father, Nastaran harbored a bitter hatred toward both him and her mother, who never once shielded her from his cruelty and seemed wholly indifferent to her. Nastaran's mother loved only one person in the world—her husband, Khoja.

Thus, Nastaran's chief wish was to grow up, to climb as high as a nomadic woman's life would allow—and to show all her family what she was really worth.

One day, after the Tigraxauda returned from battling the Kangju, Nastaran happened to notice how deeply upset King Kavad's younger son, the heir Zogak, was. She had known him since childhood, but they weren't friends—her father would never have allowed her time for friends. Her entire existence belonged only to him and his sons. Still, she had always sensed that Zogak felt compassion for her, pitied her. And she knew he was every bit as unhappy as she was.

Once, she had asked around among familiar warriors what had happened with the royal family during the campaign, and learned that King Kavad, instead of appointing Zogak heir, had named Rustam to succeed him. Spotting a free moment and summoning her courage, Nastaran came to the younger prince's tent. By now, she was grown, stronger, and even her father could no longer control her as before—he saw she had developed an unprecedented aggression and inner strength. As such, it was much harder for him to subdue her.

In spite of his foul mood, Zogak was glad to see this old acquaintance.

"My prince, I can help you in your sorrow!" Nastaran said confidently. "Just trust me and do everything I say. I promise you, it won't be long before you, not anyone else, become king of the Tigraxauda Sakas! And in time—who knows—perhaps you'll rule all of Sakastan! But I'll need your support too—don't fail me. Remember, my name means 'dog rose'; I can be both a blessing and sharp thorns to a person!"

Though he barely understood, seeing Nastaran's furious, almost frenzied resolve, Zogak agreed at once. He knew he had nothing left to lose.

* * *

Media, the same era

Astyages was at a loss. That youth, Cyrus, was making victorious progress across Media, steadily drawing closer to Ecbatana, having annihilated the forces sent against him and killed Dinar! Yet Astyages still had soldiers, as he had summoned to his army all men from sixteen to fifty years old, and it was vast. But since Dinar was dead, someone else—another experienced commander—needed to be selected.

It didn't take the king long to realize he had just the person: Harpagus, his former general! This warrior had repeatedly proved himself both loyal and dependable. After all, he had long had the chance to avenge the king for ordering the execution of his wife, Spaka, but he had never done so—nor had he even once brought up her name to Astyages. He had shown neither sorrow nor suffering, which meant, clearly, that he had endured it all quite calmly. Only such a steadfast and unflappable man could serve Astyages as commander-in-chief of his army.

"Of course, Your Majesty, my predecessors, including the late

Dinar, have badly weakened and demoralized the Median army with their constant defeats, cowardice, and poor leadership," Harpagus said gravely to Astyages. "But I assure you, while the Persians try to breach the impregnable walls of Ecbatana, our troops will fully recover from their earlier setbacks, and then they will fall upon the Persians and finish off both them and their feeble young leader!"

Astyages had to agree with his commander, placing his faith in him. The Median king did not even recall that Harpagus had once raised Cyrus in his own home as though he were a son.

Meanwhile, through his spies, Cyrus learned of the Median king's plans, and he broke into a joyful grin; he had never anticipated such a blessed turn of events. Leading the Median army now was… Harpagus, whom Cyrus had regarded as a father from birth! Now, despite Media's innumerable host, Persia's victory was assured. After all, someone had greatly aided them when they first entered Media. Some unknown influential ally had dispatched a large force to reinforce Cyrus's army—just when Cyrus's men were fatigued and depleted from the journey.

And suddenly it dawned on him…

Of course! It had been Harpagus all along! His foster father had always supported him, and it must have been Harpagus who had sent him that mysterious letter describing himself and his wife, Spaka, Cyrus's foster mother. How did Cyrus not realize it at once?… Now the young prince was overjoyed.

Cyrus was right. When his troops reached Ecbatana, the capital of Media, the city gates… swung wide open before him. The Median commander, Harpagus, surrendered Ecbatana without a fight to his foster son, personally meeting him at the gates and receiving him in a strong fatherly embrace. Cyrus gratefully thanked Harpagus for all his kindness.

The Persian warriors, who savored the extreme ease of this triumph that cost them nothing, were astonished beyond measure: there was no battle at all with the Medes for Ecbatana! The great city welcomed its occupiers with open arms…

***

Sakastan, the same era

Tomyris was becoming a brave warrior. Yet she still had little experience.

"Father, I'm afraid I won't be able to become a good enough defender of our people one day—a worthy successor to you," she said sadly to Spargapis while he was teaching her to fight at the fortress Koi Krylgan Kala in the lower reaches of the Amu Darya.

"You will, my daughter, you certainly will!" the King of the Massagetae reassured her. "After all, you are my child, my blood. I have never surrendered to anyone, never feared anyone—and I still don't! Besides, there's something I've long wanted to tell you…"

"What is it, Father?"

"When you were just born, a stranger came to our land… He was a little boy from Hindustan. His name was… I don't quite remember—maybe Karna. Who knows, you might meet him sometime in your life. I'd like that. Anyway, this Karna foresaw a grand destiny for you. Know this: you shall be a true queen, Tomyris—a genuine ruler of Sakastan! I believe it with all my heart. You are the best, my child!"

Tomyris was astonished, pondering her father's words deeply…

***

One night, King Kavad of the Tigraxauda Sakas awoke with the urge to relieve himself, sat up, and suddenly exclaimed:

"Hey! Who is that? Who are you, young woman? And where is my wife Balkyz?!"

"Who am I?" the girl chuckled quietly yet brazenly, right in the king's face. "Don't you recognize me in this dim light, my king? I'm the granddaughter of your elder, Sadyk—the daughter of his son Khoja, with whom you lost quite a few gold coins at dice the other day!"

"Aah… yes, I recall now… But what are you doing in my bed, you insolent hussy?! How dare you sneak into the royal tent?! I'll send you back to your father in disgrace!"

"And what if I scream right here and now?" Nastaran (for that's who it was) showed no sign of embarrassment. "Your servants will come running, and both your sons will hear too—their tents stand very close to yours! By the way, don't worry about your wife Balkyz—she's fine, spending the night at one of my friends' tents. If you cast me out, it won't be me who's disgraced, but you, Kavad! But if you'll just hear me out, I can make it so my father forgives your debt—and never brings it up again!"

"You?!" the king snorted, refusing to believe her. Still, he did not immediately throw his uninvited guest out. "Everyone knows your father treats you like a servant and doesn't care for you one bit! Why would he listen to a silly girl like you…?"

Nastaran, however, knew that her father's mischievous sons still needed a nanny. If he refused her demand, she could abandon them anytime—she could easily run off, with or without her parents' permission, with the first stranger who came along! But if he complied, even if she married, Nastaran would still look after and care for those unruly boys.

"You don't realize—things have changed somewhat, and I no longer fear my father," the girl replied. "So he will listen to me. And in return… you, my king, must grant me a wish!"

"And what wish is this?" Kavad asked sourly. He was used to others fulfilling his wishes, not the other way around. The girl was bold indeed!

"Marry me off as soon as possible to your younger son, Zogak," Nastaran demanded, trying to keep her tone gentle so as not to insult the king. "He means nothing to you anyway, right? He's a child of a wife you don't love."

"Why would you want that, girl? Listen: Zogak isn't going to get the throne or a rich inheritance! Then again, I doubt you'd have one either… I can't imagine Khoja paying a big bride-price for a questionable beauty like you!" Kavad added with a smug laugh.

Nastaran smirked to herself: *We'll see about the throne!*

"So what's your decision, King?" she pressed him, serious and persistent.

Kavad paused to think.

"You say you'll settle my debt with Khoja? All right, fine. After all, I lose nothing. Let that weakling Zogak marry whomever—sure, marry you if you want! What do I care?"

Nastaran bowed gratefully before the Tigraxauda king, quickly got dressed, and slipped out of his tent as if she had never been there…

A few days later, Zogak and Nastaran were wed. But before that, the audacious young woman had managed… to visit Rustam's bed. By questioning him, she confirmed that he had no desire for

the throne whatsoever. With her caresses, she persuaded him to tell Kavad that he was forever renouncing the Tigraxauda crown for the sake of his beloved brother Zogak! Indeed, everyone knew Rustam was a mighty hero—why would he need to be king as well?

Rustam gave his word. The very next day, Kavad learned of his beloved elder son's firm resolve never to claim the throne. This greatly saddened the Tigraxauda king, but he dared not thwart his adult son's will.

For Zogak, this news was the best wedding gift from Nastaran.

"My lord," she whispered softly yet beguilingly to her new husband on their wedding night, "see how I keep my promises? All that's left is to wait for your father to die... and the throne of the Tigraxauda Sakas will be yours!!"

18

The struggle for supreme power among the leaders and elders of the Massagetae continued unabated, especially since King Spargapis was far from an angel. To maintain his rule—and sometimes just for entertainment—he often pitted entire armies of different tribes against each other. Spargapis could keep the tribes in check with an iron grip, but silencing all rebellious voices proved difficult even for him.

Thus, the Alan leader, Khaidar, rejected the king's offer to marry Tomyris—who had mercilessly mocked him—in exchange for vast riches, and decided to call a meeting of various chiefs and elders behind Spargapis' back. His goal was to challenge the king's fitness for the throne and his right to continue ruling. Secretly, Khaidar—and not he alone—hoped and believed that sooner or later the Massagetae would choose him as their new king.

At the union gathering, the chief of the Apasiacs, Sher, spoke out sharply against Spargapis:

"Down with Spargapis and his worthless little daughter!" he roared. "That little minx is aiming to become queen! But do you really want to take orders from a weak woman, Massagetae?! And hasn't Spargapis himself worn us all out? He rules only to strengthen his own power. He doesn't care about us nomads—our welfare means nothing to him. Why do we need such a ruler?!"

"We don't! Overthrow Spargapis! Down with him!!" yelled other chiefs.

But at the moment, few in the assembly backed the brazen Sher, as many still feared Spargapis and deferred to him. Hence Sher's cries got lost in the tumult of the crowd.

"Chiefs and elders!" spoke up Kuzybek, the leader of the Karats. "We must think carefully and decide together how to proceed. I hear that a former leader of the Tocharians, and supposedly once 'king' of the Massagetae, Zakir, has returned to our lands—though no one ever officially chose him king. Remember, Spargapis once proclaimed Zakir's rule over the Massagetae. Hardly anyone liked it at the time…"

"Well, well, this is interesting!" murmured and rustled the union members.

"Please, don't interrupt! Let Kuzybek speak!"

"We're listening, Karat chieftain."

"It's said that Zakir is now hiding somewhere, lying low, waiting for his chance to get revenge on Spargapis, who humiliated him! But don't you recall what a terrible 'king' Zakir was? Haven't

you heard that in his brutality he killed my two little children at once?! And so, if we try to depose Spargapis right now, we could be opening the way for Zakir. He's not alone; the entire Tocharian people might come back under him, for after Zakir, they never chose another leader. You all know how strong and dangerous the Tocharians can be. I say: of two evils, we must choose the lesser one! Better to have Spargapis on our side than against us. At least my tribe is safe under him."

At this juncture, an elder named Asror, of the Abii tribe, intervened:

"Saka, you want the Abii in your alliance? Fine, but I give you my word it won't happen if Spargapis remains king! You must choose: it's either us or him!"

"Why do you Abii hate him so?" the others asked Asror.

"He has shed enough of our tribe's blood; many of our warriors died by his sword. Most importantly—wasn't he the one who stole, like a thief, and then slaughtered the daughter of our chieftain, the beautiful Zaryana?..."

"But isn't it an honor for a man to steal away his beloved bride from her kin?" objected Berez, chief of the Guz tribe. In general, he hadn't even wanted to come to this meeting—he was friendly with Spargapis—but the chiefs of neighboring tribes compelled him to attend.

Well then, I'll just share every detail with the King of the Massagetae afterward, and I won't let them disgrace him here—I'll stand up for him in everything! Berez resolved privately.

"You don't yet know our main piece of news…" Asror went on.

Everyone started up again:

"Yes? What news?!"

Asror assumed a weighty air:

"Recently… our honored elder Tursun, father of Zaryana and leader of the Abii—has died!"

"Ay-voi!!" The chiefs and elders stroked their beards. "Oh, dear! May he rest in peace…"

"Now then. The closest heir and relative of Tursun is his nephew Salih, son of Tursun's sister. Although Salih cared for his gravely ill uncle with exceptional devotion, overall—he's useless. He's an inexperienced youth and no warrior; he won't be able to protect our tribe!"

In reality, Asror spoke like this only because he himself greatly coveted the leadership of the Abii, though he could scarcely lift a weapon heavier than a child's whip. Nonetheless, he continued:

"But Salih is a close friend of Spargapis—though the king doesn't know what Salih truly thinks of him. Salih is, in fact, the cousin of the king's daughter, Tomyris. The King of the Massagetae places his complete trust in Salih. If Spargapis remains king, he'll definitely support that underbred whelp in everything. No, elders, we can't allow that!"

No one knew or understood why Asror claimed Salih disliked Spargapis, while the Massagetae king had long considered him a best friend…

In the end, the meeting reached no decisive conclusion; many present either openly or secretly feared Spargapis. Moreover, most of them saw themselves alone as the rightful occupant of the kingly title, each trying to grab the biggest piece of the pie for himself.

What they failed to reckon with was the presence of Berez and a few other supporters of Spargapis at this gathering. Once the ruling king of the Massagetae learned through his friendly, influential neighbors (who had entered lucrative deals with him) what had happened, he swiftly and skillfully reinforced his power.

Suffice it to say, he had a great talent for running state affairs!

Immediately thereafter, Spargapis dispatched a messenger to the Abii with a thousand well-armed guards in escort. The envoy delivered a royal decree admitting no objection: henceforth, Salih was to be installed as chieftain of the tribe in place of Tursun—without delay. If not, so the king declared, he would wipe out every Abii—except for Salih.

That very day, Salih became the new leader of the Abii, and in all significant matters he dutifully consulted his friend, King Spargapis.

***

Media, the same era

King Astyages of Media was in a wild rage—he had never expected such an outcome. He felt he ought to have executed all his fortunetellers, priests, and astrologers. Indeed, some of them—those perpetual upstarts Zartosht, Ardashir, and Faridun—had foretold this disaster, the conquest of Media by the Persians led by his grandson Cyrus, but not that it would be on such a frightening scale! At the time, he hadn't believed them, didn't even want to listen...

Worthless scum, traitor! Astyages fumed inwardly at Harpagus, for now he hated not only his grandson but also the very general he, Astyages, had appointed—who had then betrayed him so thoroughly. *It's completely unclear what I ever did to this Harpagus! How dare he betray me so? For what reason?!*

He did not recall the cruelty he had shown toward Harpagus's wife, Spaka. Instead, a different thought struck him:

There's still something else I don't understand. If that wretched Cyrus wasn't truly born of my daughter Mandane—who by all accounts was never pregnant—and if, consequently, he isn't of my blood, then... why does he so resemble my father, Uvahshatra (Cyaxares)? There's some riddle here...

Meanwhile, Cyrus and his inner circle of Persian commanders, along with Harpagus, entered the palace in Ecbatana.

The luxurious interiors of each of the many rooms that the general showed him left Cyrus stunned. He still moved through these lavish halls like a guest rather than a conqueror—much less as the new master of such splendor. It had never even crossed his mind that all of this might now belong to him, Cyrus!

After touring the palace, they brought in King Astyages himself, hissing with rage, still powerful and ferocious like a beast. The young Persian's hand immediately flew to his dagger.

"No, Prince, wait!" Harpagus called out loudly. "You shouldn't do that."

"Why not?!" Cyrus asked in genuine surprise. "This man tried to have me killed!"

"But he didn't go through with it when he finally saw you again after all those years," the Median general explained calmly. "Moreover, your mother Mandane—this tyrant's daughter—would be deeply distressed and might never forgive you if she learned that her beloved son had killed her own father. Even though he has been cold toward her for many years and abandoned his fatherly affection once she was grown, he doted on her as a child, and she still remembers and appreciates that. I beg you, spare his life."

"Then we should throw him in a dungeon!" Cyrus grumbled, displeased—though on this joyous day of victory, he hardly wanted to dwell on anything grim.

"That won't do either, son, forgive me," Harpagus spoke again. "That, too, would upset your mother. It's best if we assign Astyages a modest room somewhere in the palace, under thorough guard. That way, on one hand, we'll keep a close eye on him, but on the other, we won't upset Princess Mandane."

"Let it be as you say, dear Father!" Cyrus agreed. He could not bring himself to argue with this revered man who had raised him as if he were his own son.

When Astyages—spitting in the direction of both Cyrus and Harpagus—had been led away, the young noble went on:

"This is your day, Harpagus! Without you—without your timely help—I would never have achieved victory over Astyages. I owe you everything, absolutely everything! I'm so grateful… Therefore, I swear that from now on, your every word will be as precious to me as gold! I also swear I will forever honor you as my father and mentor!"

Moved, Harpagus embraced his foster son for the second time that day.

"How sweet it is to be avenged," said Cyrus with a contented smile. "Above all, Media's yoke over Persia is ended once and for all! Right, Father?"

"True, my son. Persia is now a free land… But you're slightly mistaken if you think that's the most important thing."

"Really?" Cyrus exclaimed in amazement. "Then what is?"

"Astounding that you haven't realized!" said Harpagus, daring to be frank with the prince. "I helped you so that you, Cyrus—son of Cambyses and Mandane—would become King of Media and then, if you wish, King of Persia as well! That is what matters most now. Or do you mean to discuss the throne with Cambyses, seeing as he's a Persian prince? Because if so, my tremendous efforts on your behalf will have been almost in vain."

Harpagus's words startled Cyrus.

"Let's do this, Harpagus. My father Cambyses never claimed Media's throne. I could now… Actually, let me put it differently: is there anyone besides me who could take your country's throne? Does Astyages have any close relatives—brothers or nephews I don't know about?"

"Fortunately, no. Astyages once had a younger cousin, but our power-hungry butcher killed him long ago without remorse… So, my son, there's nothing standing in the way of your ascending the Median throne! Come on, have courage—take up the royal crown and rule Media!"

"I'm pleased, no denying that, but… To be honest, I'm also scared because I have no experience and don't know how to rule an entire country."

"I'll teach you everything. It's a pity you don't have that magic stone…"

"Magic stone? What do you mean, Harpagus?"

"Long ago, when you were very small, a boy from Hindustan came with an incredible, very large gem—some kind of diamond— gleaming on his turban like a mountain of light! Our wise men said that the stone grants a person amazing power, riches, dominion, and success… I'm sure that if you had it, you could conquer the whole world! But that boy vanished suddenly back then—no one in these parts has seen him since. If you sent envoys to Hindustan now, maybe they'd find him…"

"I'll consider it. But for now, let's return to what you called 'the main thing.'" Cyrus's eyes sparkled with excitement. "When do I become King of Media? I want it now!"

"I'll take care of everything, my king," Harpagus said, bowing reverentially. "Trust me. I'll gather the people—and as the state's chief minister, I'll proclaim you to them."

…And within two days, Cyrus was crowned King of Media and settled into the grandest, richest hall of the Ecbatana palace.

He was so overjoyed that he even forgot to invite his parents, Cambyses and Mandane, to his coronation. He found it so enthralling to issue commands, to rule over throngs and an entire country, that he soon realized one thing: Media alone was far too small for him. He wanted to possess every land and people under the sun!

Taking part of his fully armed army—and Harpagus with him—Cyrus first traveled to his homeland, Persia, to see his parents. He needed immediately to settle the matter of his reign… over Persia as well!

19

Tashkent, 2012

Saltanat knocked on the deputy chief's office door at the district police department.

"Hello, I'm Saltanat. Yesterday Colonel Sharaf Daniyarov called you about my situation."

"Ah, yes, yes—Sharaf Ulugebekovich did call. Come in, have a seat. So how's our retired old-timer doing? Still busy with investigations, can't sit quietly at home? By now he should be walking the grandkids in the park or reading newspapers, but he keeps telling us how to do our jobs! You know, he won't let us get on with our work. Anyway, what have you got?"

"The thing is, my parents have gone missing. Actually, they've been kidnapped..."

"Kidnapped? Why? What, are their organs made of gold and diamonds?" the police boss joked crudely.

"Of course not. Why are you saying that? This is serious! It must be some gangsters, but I don't know what they want from my mother and father."

"What are your parents' names? Got photos of them, or any other details?"

"Yes, of course."

Saltanat explained everything and handed him the photos.

"They look like pleasant, educated folks. Why would anyone kidnap them?" The policeman was perplexed. "Who'd want that? This isn't the wild '90s anymore—there's no lawlessness, especially not in our country! Here, you see, everything's orderly, practically no crime. Sometimes we just sit around bored. And you're talking about 'kidnapping'? Where do you even get that idea? ... All right, then. Do you have any idea where they might be held? Any location?"

Saltanat mentioned and described the place listed in the text message that came to her mother's phone from the criminals. The officer's face darkened, and suddenly he seemed in a hurry.

"Fine, young lady, leave all that information with me. I'll think about what can be done! Right now, excuse me—I just remembered I have to get to a briefing."

As if I'm going to butt heads with the KIR mafia based in that hangar! The police officer thought to himself after ushering the distressed girl out. *Like I want to get myself killed? No way. Besides, they pay us off regularly! I know they won't kill that girl's parents— these days they're not into murder, from what I hear. Let them manage on their own. Their so-called 'godfather' is just a Moscow crime boss on an extended 'tour' here in Tashkent. People say he's untouchable—he's got strong connections in Russia's MVD and even overseas! Probably he just wants to shake those folks down for something—money or valuables… Let Saltanat's parents handle it themselves… however they can.*

Meanwhile, after leaving the station, Saltanat immediately dialed Anastasia in Moscow. Anastasia told her that her boss, Irmanov, was "livid," searching for Rashid Batyrov because a major event was "imminent," and a significant sum of money had been allocated to Batyrov to organize it.

Knowing that Alexei Vadimovich was a longtime good friend of her father (although she herself had never interacted with him— there had been no need until now), Saltanat asked Anastasia to pass along the serious trouble her parents were in. They needed urgent help; they had to be freed! Anastasia promised to relay everything in detail to Irmanov.

* * *

Tashkent, 1979

The young economist and mining engineer Alexei Irmanov called his friend, historian, and local researcher Rashid Batyrov, suggesting they have lunch together at a café. Rashid agreed, sensing from Alexei's mysterious, upbeat tone that he wanted to share something extremely important. They each ordered a portion of plov, tea, bread, and salads.

"Rashid, I've got fantastic news!"

"I can tell it's something good, my friend. You're absolutely glowing…"

"They're inviting me to Moscow—permanently, to work and live, with my family! Our Ministry of Finance reports go up to the Union ministry there, and can you imagine—they've noticed and appreciated me as a specialist! I'm so pleased. So basically, they offered me either a position in the same department at the USSR Ministry of Finance or a directorship at a glass-packaging factory. I've thought it over and decided on the factory. You know, I've long wanted to handle real, profitable production rather than just papers and figures."

"I'm happy for you, Alyosha. So, you'll leave your father, Vadim Borisovich, here all on his own?"

"No, he's not alone—he still has a young wife! That's all in order. Of course, I'll keep in touch with him by phone, and I'll help however I can. I'm not planning on abandoning him."

"Excellent. Your salary in Moscow will probably be good, right?"

"It'll be high, no doubt! But more importantly, there'll be opportunities and the potential for career growth. So here's the deal: I want to invite you to come with me! I'll talk to the right people, and we'll quickly find you an interesting, well-paying job. You're a valuable talent; such people are needed everywhere! Maybe you could be my deputy at the factory…"

"What?!" Rashid nearly choked. Glass packaging was something he knew nothing about.

"All right, if you're not interested, you're not interested. That's up to you. I could help you get into the Russian or even the Union-level Ministry of Culture! Or an organization directly tied to your passion for archaeology. So, what do you say, Rashid? Did I get you interested?"

"I'm sorry, Alexei, but… no. I love Uzbekistan dearly. And I just can't imagine living in another country. I truly am delighted for you if this invitation makes you happy, but please don't try to persuade me. I'm not going anywhere. Besides, I'm completely absorbed in our ancient history, particularly the fate of Queen Tomyris. She was so… strong, intelligent, brave—truly extraordinary! Probably no one like her exists now."

"Well, maybe someone does—who knows?" Alexei philosophized a bit. "But has that archaeologist Pulat Gafarov found anything significant yet?"

"Yes indeed! Over nearly four years of excavations in the lower reaches of the Amu Darya, in what used to be ancient Sakastan, he's discovered many intriguing artifacts—mainly Saka clothing, utensils, coins, tools, and weapons. After meticulous study and registration, Pulat brings them to Tashkent and hands them over to our Ministry of Culture, which then distributes them to museums. Gafarov says it's quite possible there might be fragments of the Koh-i-Noor—which in antiquity belonged to Tomyris! Can you believe it? Pulat is actively searching for them right now."

"What—the Koh-i-Noor? Come on! You mean that same famous diamond that's been in the British royal crown for centuries?!"

"Yes, that's exactly what I'm talking about. Queen Tomyris wore the diamond on her head—actually, on a magnificent golden turban. There is evidence that some fragments have remained here since ancient times, on Uzbek land!"

"Really? To be honest, that sounds more like legend than historical fact."

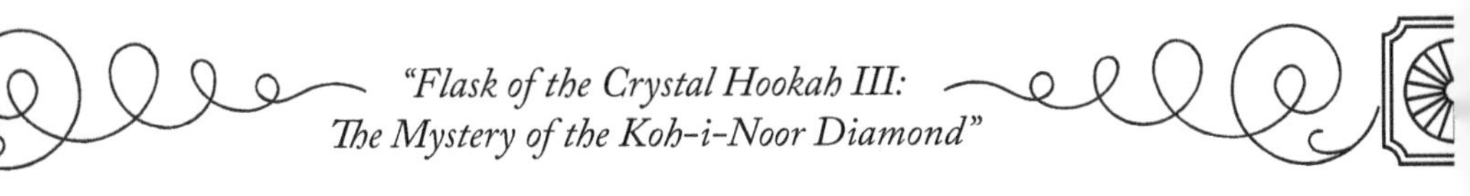

"Possibly. But until the excavations are over, I won't give up hope of witnessing, with my own eyes, at least some fragments of that legendary diamond—or even the queen's golden turban."

"Well then, good luck, my friend! Let's keep in touch. I'll try to call you from Moscow. But I'll be happy to get your calls, telegrams, or letters too."

"Sure, it's a deal. And the best of luck to you, Alexei!"

* * *

Harun Zikirillaev invited Tamilla on a date at a restaurant. She declined, citing that she was too busy. The young woman sensed that he had very serious intentions toward her. Yet, she also knew beyond a doubt that she did not love him. Because of this, she tried her best to keep him at a distance, even though she genuinely enjoyed talking with him about music. Harun truly knew a great deal—and he already had useful contacts with local pop performers from different cities, including Moscow. Tamilla was not greedy or calculating, but she did find it interesting to learn more about famous artists.

Harun's band, which performed modern Uzbek songs, was growing in popularity, whereas he regarded Tamilla's ensemble with a slight smirk, as if it were child's play. His attitude irked her somewhat, though she quickly forgave him, being kind by nature and unable to stay angry for long.

Nonetheless, he found a chance to meet with her.

After one of her vocal-instrumental group's performances, Zikirillaev approached Tamilla with a luxurious bouquet of flowers. Waiting until she'd finished removing her stage makeup, he blurted out, all in one breath:

"My dear Tamilla, please marry me!"

Stressing his respect for her, he addressed her formally, even though he was actually a few years older. Naturally, she also spoke to him using that same formal address.

Tamilla blushed. On one hand, she was very touched—no one had ever proposed to her before, let alone with such deliberate care: dressing up in a costly, elegant suit and spraying expensive imported cologne.

Harun took a small velvet box out of his pocket and held it out to her.

"Please open it!"

Tamilla wanted to flee her dressing room. She did not take the box in her hands.

"I'm sorry, Harun, I…"

At that, he opened the box himself. Inside, of course, was an engagement ring.

"Harun, I have enormous respect and affection for you as a friend," Tamilla said gently, striving not to hurt the feelings of this unexpected would-be fiancé, "and I am thankful for your proposal. But I can't marry without love! Please forgive me."

"Ah, so it's not out of love?" snapped Zikirillaev, indignant at her rejection, certain of his own irresistible virtues. Stung, he asked sarcastically, "What, are you waiting for some prince on horseback?"

"Maybe a prince—or maybe a simple yet truly faithful man who speaks to my heart."

From then on, they no longer met. Harun absolutely did not want to see the woman who had refused him. He refused even to admit to himself that he was still madly in love with her. It felt more like hatred to him.

Suddenly, an anonymous complaint was submitted to the

Central Committee of Uzbekistan's Communist Party against Tamilla's father, Sardor Shakhmuradovich Mahkamov, the director of the Porcelain Factory. Allegedly, he was embezzling public funds and involved in illegal foreign-currency dealings.

A series of inspections followed at the factory. Eventually, investigators found a packet of U.S. dollars—clearly planted—inside Sardor Mahkamov's office, and the police detained him. However, they released the director of the plant soon afterward for lack of evidence. Not a single fingerprint of Sardor's was found on the packet or on any of the bills! Besides that, all his colleagues unanimously testified that Mahkamov would share his last penny with them, describing him as a man of absolute honesty and integrity.

The police no longer had any claims against him. After some delay, Sardor Shakhmuradovich was reinstated in his position as director.

Tamilla immediately guessed that Harun had some hand in the dirty affair involving the anonymous letter. Evidently, she had genuinely offended him so badly that he had decided to take vengeance on her entire family! But Tamilla was not going to let this vile deed by the famous singer slide.

"Papa, please—I'm sure the police should investigate Zikirillaev! I'm almost certain that he set you up… probably because of me."

"Daughter, it's unseemly to accuse anyone without proof… Well, all right, I'll ask the detective who took me in and later released me. He turned out to be decent!"

The police did check on Harun. They found no direct proof of his involvement in the false charges against Sardor or the planted money. The real culprit had skillfully covered his tracks. The person Harun hired to place the foreign cash in Sardor's office had simply disappeared, leaving no leads.

In the end, the authorities did not detain Harun, but the investigator, Shukhrat Yuldashev, made a mental note to keep an eye on him. And in the Mahkamov family's eyes, since they could not recall anyone else who might want to compromise Sardor Shakhmuradovich, Harun remained the prime suspect. At first, Tamilla thought of confronting him, but then—being someone who hated pettiness and could easily forget negativity—she simply went on living her life, deciding only to erase Harun from her life for good.

***

Moscow, 1979

Kirill Midiyatdinov was already sixteen. Although Oleg no longer beat him, he still showed no tenderness or fatherly love toward his adopted son.

Kirill grew up a bitter, hardened young man. On the streets, he befriended a rough crowd. A twenty-year-old hoodlum named Yura taught him how to drink, smoke, mess around with weed, and even steal whenever the opportunity arose.

One day, a very drunk Kirill asked Yura:

"Yuran, can you get… some poison?"

"Are you serious, kid? Are you already tired of life? Isn't it too soon?"

"No, it's not for me—I want to serve it to my old man."

"Wow!!" Yura whistled. "Why would you do that to him? He must've done you real dirty if you're planning to punish him like that! Well, it's not really my business. I can get it—what's the issue? But everything costs money, and poison does too. Especially one strong enough to kill. You'll have to work for it, got it? Tomorrow, you'll come with us to the jeweler. I've already planned everything. You and Vaska will be the foot soldiers."

Kirill was frightened.

"N-no, I won't go! What are you saying? I can't… into a jeweler's. There's security there."

"Why are you freaking out? Don't worry—I'll handle the security! You just take an empty bag with you. Your task is to quickly stuff that bag with jewels."

Yura's small street gang eventually robbed the jeweler's shop, managing to leave no obvious traces; Yura had wisely handed out two pairs of rubber gloves to each participant. Kirill felt both scared and curious—he suddenly felt even more grown-up than when he'd smoked or drunk vodka with the local men.

Yura kept his promise. A couple of days later, he brought Kirill a packet of poison wrapped in three separate bags.

"Listen, be careful—this stuff is very dangerous! Take the poison with a teaspoon, and then don't use that spoon again; immediately put it in a bag and throw it away! Understood? We can't have someone accidentally poisoning themselves. Hide the rest of the poison safely, or return it to me—it's up to you."

Kirill hesitated.

"Nah—I'd rather keep it; who knows, maybe I'll need it someday!"

"Alright, as you wish. Just mix the poison into your old man's tea—he'll fall asleep, and most likely, after that, he won't wake up."

"That's scary, Yurka…" Suddenly, Kirill started doubting his own criminal plan. "Will he die for real? Forever?!"

"What are you, stupid? How long do people die for? An hour, maybe? Of course, it's forever. Now, if you're a complete coward, just say so. Why be shy?"

"N-no, I'm not a coward! I'll go and do it. Besides, my old man isn't my real father…"

"Go ahead then, do it. And later, I'll teach you how to sort out the apartment situation. By the way, do you know if your old man ever wrote a will or not? It'd be best to check that first. His apartment isn't just anywhere—it's in central Moscow!! What if he didn't leave it to you? Then what's the point of killing him? You'd get nothing. And where would you live after his death? Think it through."

Realizing Yura was absolutely right, Kirill phoned his "aunt" Marina.

"Hi. Tell me, do you happen to know if my father wrote a will?"

"And why would you need to know that, sonny… I mean, Kiryusha? What do you want?"

"Just tell me, if you know."

"Yes, he did. He left his apartment to be divided equally among the three of us—between you, Farida, and me. But Farida and I have already decided to decline our shares—in your favor."

"Really?! That's great! And why?"

"Because we already have somewhere to live. What use do we have for these apartments? You, my dear, need it more!"

* * *

Kirill hadn't even expected that later that evening, Farida would show up at their home again. He had already prepared tea for his father… with that very poison. Farida had come to them from the market, carrying Kirill's favorite tomatoes and fruits.

It was quite warm outside, and the woman was very thirsty. Not knowing that a mug had been set out on the table for her brother's arrival, Farida immediately drank all of its contents.

"Kirill, Kirill," she suddenly called to her nephew, who was sitting playing cards in his room. "Do you have any painkillers at home? I'm feeling unwell…"

"What's wrong with you, aunt?" Kirill asked.

Suddenly, he noticed his father's empty mug on the table—and understood immediately.

"Tell me, did you drink from here? You drank?! You fool, aunt! What have you done?!"

She began to lose consciousness. Kirill, shaking with horror, frantically dialed for an ambulance. The crew arrived quickly, and Farida was rushed to the hospital, into intensive care.

* * *

Alexei Irmanov, along with his wife Sasha and her daughter Nastya, successfully relocated to Moscow. Alexei, as he had told Rashid, became a factory director.

Aleksandra's daughter, Nastya, was not a particularly beautiful girl. Moreover, in early childhood, she had fallen awkwardly and since then had developed a slight limp in her right leg. She needed an expensive operation, but neither Sasha Levidovskaya nor Alexei Irmanov had that kind of money at the time.

Unkind schoolchildren often laughed at Nastya and teased her. One day, when she was leaving school, one of the boys from her class began harassing her:

"Hey, you, lame leg! Can you beat me in a sprint? Huh? Come

on!! What, you think you'll be first at the start?! Or maybe we'll even compete in the high jump… What, are you chicken already?"

A passing boy from another class overheard these insults.

"You're only tough against a girl, huh?" he asked the bully. "Don't you know it's not manly to mistreat and mock women? Perhaps you'd like to fight me instead?"

The insolent boy, named Artur, was surprised by the boldness of the unfamiliar boy. But what struck him most was that someone was so determined to defend this plain, lame girl!

"Uh… fine, let's fight…" Artur said uncertainly, noticing that this young stranger looked fit, strong, and athletic.

Then, the boy who had stepped in to defend Nastya approached Artur. He slung his backpack off his shoulder and, with a confident punch, struck Artur. The bully who had made fun of Nastya fell to the ground, writhing in pain, but almost immediately recovered, jumped up, and… ran away at once! As they say, his heels were practically flashing.

Nastya approached the hero and smiled warmly at him. She was very pleased that such a handsome boy—even if a bit younger than her—had so bravely and gracefully come to her defense.

"Thank you so much! You weren't afraid, even though everyone is terrified of Artur. You're very brave!"

"It's nothing. Just let me know if you need anything. And don't be afraid of anyone now, okay?"

"All right, thank you!" she said, extending her hand. "My name's Nastya. And yours?"

"I'm Igor, but everyone calls me Garik. Come on, I'll walk you home. Do you live far?"

"Not really. Mostly, local kids go to school from around here."

"Of course. I live not far either. But honestly, I don't feel like going home at all. I never want to."

"Why?" Nastya asked in surprise. "Home is nice and cozy. You can sleep or watch TV."

"At my place, only my mother and stepfather watch TV—and only whatever he chooses. My mother, having married him, listens to him in everything. And she's completely stopped loving me. She's always nagging, scolding, criticizing me for everything. She loves only her new husband…"

"I've had almost the same story," Nastya observed. "No, my own mother is good and kind. But my stepfather, Uncle Lyosha… He seems to try to replace my real father. But I love my real dad, Dmitry! I don't know why my dad left my mom or why he never visits me. But I believe he loves me just as much as I love him! Someday, I'll visit him and say, 'Dad, here I am—Nastya, your daughter. Look how I've grown—adult, beautiful, and happy!' And he'll surely be overjoyed for me."

"I understand you," Garik nodded, then continued, "The truth is, I'm no longer needed by my own mother; I've become nothing to her. Just two years ago, I was a top student. Teachers said I had great mathematical abilities! And now…?"

"What, you're not a top student anymore? But, Garik, a person's abilities never vanish. They stay with you forever—they just develop, or sometimes they don't."

"Exactly, that's my problem. I feel like I've stopped developing. I have no drive; my energy is sapped. My mother constantly calls me an 'idiot' and a 'fool,' saying I'm worthless, hopeless, and that nothing good will come of me…"

"Ah, now I see!" said clever Nastya. "So you've simply lost faith in yourself—that's what it is. It's called a 'complex of inferiority.' But don't despair, Garik! It's fixable. Want me to help you? If it means even a little to you, I'll tell you now: for me, you're attractive, strong, brave, kind, and smart. And when you grow up, you'll definitely become someone famous!"

"Really, you think so, Nastya?" Garik beamed, his eyes sparkling with joy.

"Of course. I truly believe in you. All that's left is for you to believe in yourself!"

* * *

Oleg Midiyatdinov, by some sixth sense (though he mostly worked in the police headquarters administration, he was also very skilled at deciphering crimes), realized what had transpired in his apartment. Moreover, the doctors at the hospital—where the dying Farida had been taken—had conducted tests and discovered highly concentrated rat poison in her blood.

"It's fortunate, comrade Colonel, that your sister ingested a liquid containing this particular poison rather than a more aggressive one!" commented Farida's attending physician. "Truly, it's a miracle—and thanks to our considerable efforts—that she survived. Now she requires proper care. Please, make the necessary arrangements."

"Of course, I will do everything," promised Oleg. "Don't you worry."

Despite his natural greed, the colonel made a point of generously thanking the doctors for saving his sister's life. Oleg then asked Marina to keep an eye on Farida. Marina readily agreed—she was deeply worried about her elder sister, who was only just beginning to recover.

Later, upon arriving home, Oleg Shamilievich called his "son" in.

"And why did you do that, you little runt?! Why did you put poison in the cup?! What—did you want to get rid of me? Know this: you'll never get this apartment in your life!"

Kirill remained silent, at a loss for words, terrified of his adoptive father's wrath.

"I'm sorry, Dad, I won't do it again..." he stammered.

"Oh, you'll do it again, you little scoundrel—I know you! What sort of villainous creature did you take after, anyway?" Oleg raged.

He recalled that Marina and Denis were perfectly normal, even balanced people. Perhaps some distant genes from their ancient ancestors had awakened in Kirill?

Midiyatdinov mercilessly decided to lock up Kirill. However, without a statement from the victim, Farida (who flatly refused to file a report against her nephew), the case wouldn't be escalated to serious criminal charges—and Kirill could be given merely a suspended sentence. Legally and factually, Oleg was not even considered a victim; the attempted attack on him was unproven.

And everything might have been tolerable for the young man if it weren't for one additional circumstance.

For the first time in his life, as with everyone who comes under investigation, Kirill Midiyatdinov had his fingerprints taken. It turned out that an expert forensic scientist from the investigative team—which had been working on the recent robbery of a jewelry store—had discovered a couple of barely noticeable fingerprints that, so far, hadn't been identified. During the theft of the jewels, as Kirill brushed against dust, his nose began to itch badly. He removed his glove and rubbed his nose with his left hand. In lowering his hand and failing to put the glove back on in time, the boy accidentally touched one of the items in the store.

Kirill's fingerprints were then uploaded into the police database. It turned out that the previously cold case could now be pinned to someone—with full justification! There he was—the jewel thief!

Although Kirill soon handed over his informant and the leader of their little street gang, Yura, as well as a second accomplice, Vasiliy—who had been with him during the robbery—the bulk of the evidence pointed against Kirill himself, while the guilt of the others was still to be proven by the police. And when it was proven, things turned even worse for Kirill: he and his accomplices were charged with having committed a crime as part of a "group of persons" with a "prearranged conspiracy," which considerably increased the severity of their sentence.

In short, the young man was sentenced—indeed, he received an actual prison term of several years. And no matter how much Marina and Denis pleaded with Oleg, no matter how much they begged him to help get Kirill out of jail, he, in his fury at Kirill, was unyielding and unwilling to lift a finger to reduce even a fraction of his prison sentence.

Marina visited Kirill when he was still in pre-trial detention. The woman confessed to him that she was, in fact, his biological mother. She wept and begged Kirill to permanently discard the idea of killing anyone and, at court, to claim that he had simply mistaken poison for sugar! She also urged him to say that he had only turned to robbing the jewelry store because he'd been forced into it by those who overpowered him.

Kirill did not rush to embrace his mother or plant kisses on her. On the contrary, he was very angry with her.

"How could you give me up to that monster?! Why?! Get out! I will never forgive you!"

Devastated with grief, Marina left.

After the trial, Kirill was placed in a cell with other convicts sentenced for "medium-severity" crimes.

"Hey there, young man!" said a skinny, unattractive fellow—one who looked remarkably like a diminutive version of Koschei the Deathless, yet was neatly dressed—addressing Kirill in the cell. In fact, this was none other than that same Koschei, who had once met Kirill at the orphanage and who, on that day, had memorably marked him forever. He knew that Kirill would not recognize him. Of course! Would the son of a colonel ever bother to remember the poor, perpetually hungry, and unlucky orphan? "My name is Konstantin. Everyone here obeys me, and you will too. Got it?"

"And why's that?" Kirill retorted boldly, not yet realizing that such behavior was strictly forbidden in prison—especially speaking to a "daddy," even if he was young. Moreover, Konstantin was a bit older than Kirill. "And what if I don't?!"

Immediately, two thugs—a couple of hulking brutes—approached Kirill and began brutally beating him, leaving him bloodied. Kirill whimpered in excruciating pain.

"I get it, I get it, I'm sorry!" he cried, turning his head toward Konstantin.

"All right, guys, that'll do for the first time!" Konstantin ordered. He decided under no circumstances to reveal his true intentions to Kirill, thinking to himself: *You see, kiddo, now I get a chance to get even with you for that apple core! Rest assured, I will. You'll remember my lessons for good, mark my words!*

"What are you in for?" Konstantin inquired.

Kirill told him everything.

"I see. Listen to me well, and do exactly as I say, and I'll help you out. If you follow my instructions precisely, you'll be out of here quickly, and you'll even get some money. Want a lot of money?"

For some reason, Konstantin burst into a sinister, unpleasant laugh. Naturally, Kirill was eager. Oleg had rarely given him money—only in his early childhood—and Kirill adored money. The young man was a little frightened, but he tried to remain stoic and said little. When required, he nodded and agreed, for his life was still precious.

"You, boy, don't be angry with your mother—perhaps she isn't to blame," Konstantin lectured him. "You know, life can be unpredictable. Maybe that Oleg intimidated or blackmailed her. Or there's some other serious reason she gave you up. But the cruelty of your adoptive father cannot be forgiven! You must take revenge on him, you have to punish him! And I, as I said, will help you in everything."

* * *

Boston, USA, 2012, a few days before the abduction of Tamilla and Rashid

Students Daniil Shevtsov, Aibek Khashimov, and Ekaterina Solovyova were flying to Boston on the same flight, although their internship placements were at different major universities in Massachusetts. Tamilla Mahkamova and Konstantin Romanov had arranged year-long placements for them: future geo-engineer Daniil was headed to Boston University, future programmer Aibek to the Massachusetts Institute of Technology, and future economist Katya to Harvard University in Cambridge, located near Boston.

The young people met each other only at the Tashkent airport, where they were seen off by Tamilla Sardorovna and Konstantin Ivanovich.

Even before disembarking from the plane, the three young people knew that different people would meet them and accompany them to the dormitories of their respective institutions. In a few days, classes were to begin for each of these top students.

Imagine their surprise—Daniil, Aibek, and Katya were greeted by... a single person. He confidently pronounced each of their names and surnames, speaking Russian almost perfectly without any noticeable accent. The students had been expecting to be met by local, Bostonian Americans, which baffled them.

"Hello, my name is John McConnley," the man introduced himself.

John appeared to be just over forty. He wore a rumpled hat and, in general, was dressed rather sloppily. Observant Katya noticed that he wore mismatched socks. His shirt looked stale and un-ironed. The girl and guys, who had been eagerly anticipating the glamour and refined elegance of America, felt both wary and disconcerted by the sight of this stranger.

However, sensing their doubts, John thrust his identification directly before their eyes. It read: "John McConnley, United States Department of Education"—in other words, a credential from that country's Ministry of Education.

The students immediately felt relieved. Everything was as it should be! After all, who knew—perhaps these Americans were indeed as democratic and unpretentious as he appeared, without the usual formalities? They were not in Parliament, after all!

"Mr. McConnley, you could easily speak to us in English!" remarked Aibek. "All three of us, as it happens, are fluent in English."

"Certainly!" Daniil added promptly. "It would be strange if, having been sent abroad on a generous grant as the best students from our universities, we didn't master English perfectly!"

"It's okay, it's okay," John quickly answered. "You'll have plenty of time to talk in English. And it's not hard for me to speak Russian. However, we need to hurry."

John helped the students collect their luggage and then led them to his car.

"Please, get in, everyone, and let's go," he invited the arriving youth.

"Wait, please, sir!" protested Katya. "But aren't we supposed to be going to different universities, to different addresses? Why is there only one car?"

"It's alright," John mumbled quickly, not even meeting her eyes. "But before I drive you to your universities, I've been instructed to settle you all in at one hotel, where you will have lunch in the restaurant and get proper rest. Then, tomorrow morning, you'll enjoy a pleasant tour of the city and its attractions, followed by more rest. And the day after tomorrow, we'll transport you to the dormitories of your respective schools! Agreed?"

The students and Katya nodded. Of course, they agreed and understood everything! Naturally, they were very excited to explore the beauty of Boston—one of America's most gorgeous cities. And after a flight lasting over eighteen hours, they were eager to eat and sleep—there was nothing else to say.

The students from Uzbekistan were happy—their dream was coming true… Everything was like a fairy tale!

20

Sakastan, 6th Century BCE

Unexpectedly, the people of Urartu attacked the Massagetae. Spargapises knew that these Urartians were distinguished by their particular ferocity and cunning military tactics. Even the bravest and most valiant warriors had reason to fear them—and Spargapises was no coward. Yet his strength might not suffice to fight off the Urartians. So, he entreated his friend, King Kavad of the Tigraxauda Sakas, to send the renowned Rustam to his aid.

"And while you're at it, you'll get to meet your bride—Spargapises's daughter!" King Kavad said to his eldest and most beloved son as he sent him off on the long journey to the Massagetae. "But I ask you, my son, to take care of yourself. You know how dear you are to your father. And remember, you are the main hope and support of all the Tigraxauda Sakas!"

Rustam grimaced. He was in no hurry to see Spargapises's daughter, Tomyris, let alone to marry her. For he found himself increasingly haunted by dreams of a beautiful girl—a princess from his visions...

"Aren't you rushing things, dear Father? Have you and Spargapises decided everything for both of us too quickly?" Rustam murmured gloomily. "What if I don't appeal to Tomyris at all? Am I really supposed to force her to be my wife? No—I don't want that. Besides, they say she has quite a headstrong nature, completely like her father!"

"Nothing, my son, for you two are perfectly matched—both royal children, heirs to your lands, and both Saka! You will support the Massagetae in battle and remain close to Spargapises's daughter—and she will surely notice you and come to love you. You, my son, are the finest groom on earth! Just have faith, and all will be well."

…Spargapises, however, categorically refused to allow Tomyris to take part in the battles against the Urartians, so initially, she remained at home. Under her father's orders, Tomyris attempted to govern the remaining Massagetae in the camp. These were mostly women and children, for the men had gone to fight.

But the hot-blooded girl soon grew tired of this. She had long decided that if she were to command, it should be over men. Without asking her father's permission and taking a few of her personal guards with her, she set out to the battlefield where the Massagetae were fighting their enemies.

Rustam struck down many agile and elusive Urartians. He longed to continue fighting on the front lines. Yet when Tomyris arrived at the battlefield, Spargapises, deciding that he could now handle the front on his own with his warriors, entrusted Rustam with his only daughter—whom he had earlier chided for coming to the fight. Now, the primary task of the warrior was to ensure Tomyris's safety.

For some reason, the girl did not immediately take a liking to the young man; his constant shadowing of her curtailed her freedom, and she was fiercely independent. But when Rustam first laid eyes on the Massagetae princess, he was stunned with surprise…

"How can this be? Could it truly be her? The one I have dreamed of for so long, the one I have long been in love with? Oh, Tomyris, if

only you knew how my heart aches for you... Protecting you from our enemies and guarding you is both my honour and my delight!"

In one battle, reinforcements from the enemy arrived unexpectedly and pressed hard. The Massagetae valiantly and boldly repelled the assault.

Tomyris was nearly struck by a sword—after all, she was still an inexperienced fighter. She raised her acinaces to deflect the attack, and before she could even glance around, an enemy, reaching for her life, was instantly bloodied and dead, collapsing to the ground. Tomyris immediately realized that it was Rustam—riding on his warhorse right beside her—who had slain the vicious Urartian.

"Why?!" the princess erupted. "Who asked you, oh Tigraxauda? That Urartian was mine—mine alone to claim! I intended to defeat him myself!"

"Brave lady, fear not; you will vanquish countless enemies yet," the hero replied with a smile, very calmly.

"No need to guard me; I can handle myself," Tomyris muttered indignantly, not quite understanding how Rustam's help might actually benefit her. Then, softer and more conciliatory, she added, "I am grateful for your efforts, Prince. But I beg you—ride to the front! Leave me behind. I'm sure you are needed there much more!"

Rustam did not want to do what she was asking. Yet he dared not disobey Spargapises's daughter, for in this context, he was not the king's son but merely saving the Massagetae...

Still, unease weighed upon him, and Rustam left one of his servants to keep watch over the princess, instructing him to report frequently on whether Tomyris was all right.

Why did she ever go to battle? It's hardly a woman's duty! the son of Kavad thought to himself. *She'd be better off waiting for her father and me at home... She is so beautiful... If only she knew how much I love her! Ever since I first saw her, I've fallen even more deeply in love than before!*

The next morning, early at dawn, a servant roused Rustam. He was extremely agitated:

"My lord, wake up!" the servant gasped, barely catching his breath as he ran. "King Spargapises still doesn't know—I'm telling you first: Princess Tomyris has been abducted! She's nowhere to be found—neither among the living nor the dead! She could not have simply returned to her camp and abandoned everyone. Our night-long searches on the battlefield and in both our camp and the enemy's have, alas, yielded nothing… It hardly seems to be the work of the Urartians…"

"Immediately, saddle the horses!" Rustam shouted, straining to suppress his sorrow and anxiety with all his might. "Someone must cautiously inform Spargapises that we are setting out in search of Princess Tomyris. I swear, I will find her!!"

The servant obediently nodded to his master.

Within moments, Rustam, gathering a band of his most loyal men, set off at a furious pace along the hot sand, pursuing the kidnappers and their captive.

The hero tried to fathom: if it wasn't the Urartians—who were now as easy to see as if laid out on a platter—then who would have a need to abduct the Massagetae princess? And most importantly—why?

***

Media, same era

"See, Harpagus, not all of Media yielded to me as easily as you promised!" Cyrus reproached his adoptive father and commander of the Median army. "In some regions, we had to suppress numerous rebellions. Many nomadic tribes living in the cities and steppes of Persia have not yet submitted to us, and I haven't even taken the capital, Pasargadae… I don't know what I'd do with Media without the help of Armenian King Tigranes and his troops."

Harpagus fell silent. He was not pleased that Cyrus was beginning to forget his contributions.

"Well," the young ruler continued, "I have assumed the title of King of Media, filled my treasury with gold, silver, and all manner of treasures. And now I must soon become ruler of Persia as well!"

"My son," the general finally said, "I advise you simply to send a respectful letter to your father, Prince Cambyses, asking whether he objects to you—his own child and heir—assuming rule over Persia right away…"

"Like hell!" Cyrus interrupted indignantly, with a hint of anger. "Have you forgotten that Persia has always been under the yoke of Media?! And since I am now the legitimate king of this country, it follows naturally that Persia belongs to me by right!"

Harpagus wanted to say that he himself had, not long ago, freed Persia from that eternally hanging, unjustly striking sword of Media's domination! He wanted to say so, but for some reason, he held back—perhaps feeling that the wrong word might now provoke the fiery wrath of his protégé.

Meanwhile, Cyrus went on:

"And I have no intention of asking anyone's permission to rule over Persia too! I will declare it to Cambyses as a fait accompli—either he submits to me and accepts my sovereign will, or…"

"Or what, son?" Harpagus interjected. "Are you really prepared to kill him—your own father? And how will you do that?… Cut off his head? Isn't that too severe a punishment for a parent?"

Cyrus suddenly paused. He realized he had gone too far.

"Well… no, of course not… That's why I won't ask! I'll march into the Persian capital with my army—and your father and mother will have no choice but to submit to me."

"I think, Cyrus, that Cambyses himself will willingly hand over Pasargadae to you!"

"Thinking, from now on, is for me, agreed?" Cyrus snapped sharply at his mentor and guardian. Then, with a touch of merriment, he added, "And we won't humiliate the Medes; let them live and pay me tribute! Let them be counted as equals to us Persians."

"As you wish, my son," Harpagus nodded. "But I still advise you to be a bit more gentle and kind with Mandane and Cambyses…"

"I'll think about it," Cyrus said quickly and impatiently, making it clear that Harpagus should now leave his quarters.

And why does this man always address me so informally, when I am the king and his master?! Cyrus thought in amazement.

***

Sakastan, same era

Nastaran, lying on a warm, cozy reindeer hide and wrapped in a thin sheep's wool blanket, called out to Zogak: "My dear husband, why are you so late? Come to me!" Young and passionately in love with her man, she especially longed—with the onset of night—for him to quickly sate her unbridled natural desires.

Yet now she noticed that Zogak was inebriated.

"Ah—have you been out with your friends again for far too long?" the young woman deduced, her mood plummeting instantly. "Have you not yet realized that all they really want from you is your wealth and the prospects you can bestow upon them in the future?! Truly, only I love you!"

"I was drowning my sorrows in wine," Zogak admitted honestly, without specifying which "sorrow" he meant. Astute as always, Nastaran understood—it was about his relationship with Kavad.

Even half-drunk, he could easily lie to his beloved wife, but now he saw no point.

"And you're mistaken about my friends, Nastaran!" he continued. "I take pleasure in knowing that they love and understand me. Their affection is sincere, from the bottom of their hearts…"

"Then tell me—who pays for your banquets? Who provides the food? Them? Or you?"

"Well, let's say it's me," Zogak replied, seeing no reason to lie again. His head was spinning, and his stomach churned—he had decidedly overindulged that evening. The young man sat down beside his wife on the bed. "And so what? They're far poorer than I am!"

"But if they truly loved you, dear, they would spend on you, sacrifice something for you, do something tangible and noticeable!" she chided, beginning to help her drunken husband undress. "Isn't that so? Otherwise, how clever of them—to always go out at your expense!"

"But one cannot be a greedy man, wife, counting every tanga," he protested.

"Why not?" she sighed. "The way you act around them, you're like the biggest fool…"

"Woman, I'm telling you!" Zogak objected to her unkind criticism.

"After all, you have me," softened Nastaran, "and you know I am always ready both to listen and to understand you completely! Can you clearly tell me what happened this time? Did your father humiliate you again?! And—apparently in public, as usual? Yes?"

Zogak nearly wept; the burning sting of insult and the wine had rendered him feeble.

"Kavad doesn't even consider me a man—he offers not only no parental love but not the slightest respect! He sharply rebukes me in public as if I were a misbehaving pup… And when my mother, Balkyz, hears of it and tries to stand up for me, he punishes her—cursing, shouting, and sometimes even striking her… I pity her so; she suffers terribly because of me—the unloved son in his eyes! It's all unbearable…"

"I understand you. For me, too, I was never needed by my father as a daughter…"

"And Kavad is always like this—loving and valuing only one, Rustam! Even now, while my brother is far away. The King himself sent him to the Massagetae, and every day he anxiously awaits him, having dispatched couriers to King Spargapises several times to learn whether his eldest son is well and prosperous…"

"Yes, it is painful, of course, that only he receives all that paternal warmth."

Deeply distraught, Zogak could not calm himself.

"Sometimes dreadful thoughts come to me, Nastaran. I think: if only this Rustam… were killed in some war already! Then perhaps my father would pay attention to me! For he was told that Rustam had firmly renounced the throne and that, apart from me, there is no heir or contender for the Saka-Tigraxauda throne. And yet my father stubbornly believes and hopes that one day Rustam will succeed him as king. It is so humiliating for me… I have no strength left to endure this!"

"And you must not endure, husband," Nastaran said softly, her voice almost a purr. "Why wait for your brother to truly return? What if he fails with that princess Tomyris—and decides to retreat to his native lands? And what then if he seizes from you your priceless right to the throne?! The people might support him in that, clear as day. And what will you do then? Will you let your life end? No, that cannot be allowed! Understand, we must not wait. We must act—and as soon as possible!"

"What do you mean, wife? You're not suggesting we kill Rustam!"

"Why kill him? Let him remain far from here for now, busy aiding those Massagetae! Someday, in his own time, his turn to die will come… But now—it is time for your father… to depart into eternity, to join the ancestors!"

Zogak was nearly sober now. Horror struck him at his beloved's words.

"No—no, not at all! Under no circumstances! I am no patricide. And I won't allow it! Kavad is my own father!"

"Calm down, Zogak! Be a man already, not a weakling! After all, don't you want to become king of Tigraxauda? Then you must understand that nothing worthwhile comes easily or without sacrifice. Let the sacrifice be him—not you! Trust me completely. Understood?"

Zogak nodded meekly.

"Listen, husband," Nastaran cooed, "do you perhaps regret not being taught about love by that woman?… What was her name? I think—Azer. They say Rustam was crazy about her, and you saw how happy he was in those days… Perhaps you desired the same?"

Zogak swallowed hard. Of course, he would not have refused… but he was intimidated by his wife.

"No—no, dear! How could you even suggest such a thing? Why would I need any woman past her prime? After all, I'm lucky—I have you, so young and beautiful!"

"Well, well, smooth talker," Nastaran nearly relented. "We shall see. But if you truly desire her, then I ask you—just tell me outright, all right? I won't be offended, and I promise I will let you be with her—say, for a couple of nights…"

"You are the best wife ever!" Zogak beamed. "But I wouldn't want to—I love you."

Of course, I will allow it! thought Nastaran. *I need you to sample pleasures—so that, once and for all, you choose me! But I will never let you seriously fancy anyone else!! Don't even dream of it, my dear… I will swiftly obliterate any rival! I, and I alone, must become the queen of the Saka-Tigraxauda!!*

***

Persia, same era

Afshin, a servant of Queen Mandane in the palace at Pasargadae, knocked softly and measuredly on the door to his mistress's private chambers before entering and bowing low.

"Madam, that woman… she comes again… or rather, she demands your presence!"

"Who? Ah—oh, I understand. Is it her again? What does she want this time?!"

"I dare not presume to know, my lady!" Afshin bowed once more.

"Send her away at once!"

"Forgive me, my lady, but I'm afraid that cannot be done: she continually threatens to expose some secret of yours to the world… No matter how I have urged her to keep silent, or how our guards have tried to intimidate her, it is all in vain. This Artosta, it seems, fears nothing nor anyone. She claims that we cannot even execute her, for Prince Cambyses and all of Persia would learn of it immediately."

"I don't understand—who supports her, and where do these connections come from?" Mandane asked in astonishment. "Perhaps I've been a fool all along. I've long known to expect nothing but mischief from that woman! Once, I was careless myself—and now, for many years, she has been blackmailing me… Well then, Afshin, there is no alternative. Bring her here!"

"At once, my most exalted princess," the servant intoned repeatedly before departing into the corridor.

Within moments, a woman just over thirty burst into Mandane's chambers—a woman bearing a striking resemblance to Mandane herself, though slightly younger. Her attire was bold and fashionable, albeit excessively garish and affected, and her shoes matched the ensemble. A scent of expensive, sharp floral perfumes, which did not suit her at all and in which, judging by her overall appearance, she clearly had no expertise, surrounded her.

"Well, greetings, princess!" Artosta chirped brightly and confidently as she entered. Without waiting for an invitation and showing not the slightest hint of modesty—as if she were at home—she flopped onto the soft divan. "Can you imagine? I've missed you terribly, my dear sister!"

"Do not call me that!" Mandane retorted irritably. "Remember, though you strut about as a noble lady at court, I know full well that you are nothing—merely a former goat herder and once my maid, now dependent on me!"

"Oh, come now, sister, why be so choleric?" Artosta laughed in her face. "After all, you yourself do not wish for our secret to become common knowledge throughout Persia, do you? So you'd best speak to me more kindly, with sweeter words!"

Unlike Mandane—who had been deprived of natural beauty—Artosta was herself strikingly attractive with a robust, healthy figure honed on freshly mown meadows, fed on mutton fat tail and goat cheese. She exuded a vigour that Mandane, the legitimate daughter of King Astyages, had never possessed, always remaining timid and insecure. In contrast, Artosta—King Astyages' illegitimate daughter, born of one of his many slave concubines whom he had long forgotten—always knew precisely what she wanted from life and from people, and invariably got it.

"What is it that you want from me?" Mandane asked with

rising irritation. "I believe I have already told you that I have no personal wealth left; you have wrung every last coin from me."

"And do not be insolent with me, dear sister!" Artosta replied coolly. "You always found a way to pay me tribute! And now I very much need to expand and fortify my household, to renew my roof—winter is nearly upon us. I heard, Mandane, that my son, Cyrus, is coming here…"

"That is my son!!" Mandane exploded, her anger flaring. "Do not you dare call him yours!"

"Very well, let him be yours," Artosta answered calmly, "after all, you paid a handsome sum to buy Cyrus from me at his birth! And you even gifted me a night with your husband—the charming Prince Cambyses! You remember that, don't you?"

"Silence!" Mandane cried, thoroughly incensed—her usual gentle nature completely lost.

"Listen, sister, you haven't let me finish. I long to speak candidly with Cyrus, for he and I are not strangers. Isn't that so? And according to reliable whispers, he has become not just anyone, but the King of Media! He commands both the Persian and Median armies. It is only a matter of time before he ascends to rule over all of Persia. Then why would you allow him to learn everything? And what of Prince Cambyses? You claimed he does not care for me? Or shall I reveal everything to both of them… That you, not I, bore Cyrus? After all, Cambyses never suspected a thing—you lied to him after that night, saying I had been unable to conceive from him. But what if he learns the whole truth—that his son was not carried and born by you? I can make it so!"

"You are no mere herder nor a refined lady; you are a true queen of blackmail!" Mandane nearly wept at the audacity of her unbidden visitor. "Fine—I will secure a sum for you, a great sum.

But only give me your word that this will be the last time."

"Well, perhaps… We shall see how you behave, dear sister! I expect your money or expensive trinkets within two days—and no more. I advise you not to delay!" Artosta laughed, clearly pleased and satisfied with the outcome of her visit.

After Mandane's younger half-sister—born a slave—departed from her chambers, the wife of Prince Cambyses ordered Afshin to ascertain who was continually allowing this Artosta access to the palace and who might be supporting her.

As soon as the servant returned and peeked into his mistress's room, he said:

"Princess, I am at fault, but… your insignificant slave Afshin… has lost track of that treacherous woman! She vanished as if swallowed by the earth. I don't even know where she has gone…"

"Perhaps," Mandane said hopefully, "some kind soul, moved by pity for my bitter fate, has finally… done away with her? For this Artosta is a real bloodsucker! She wouldn't hesitate to send anyone who stands in her way to the next world! I know it sounds harsh, but I confess… I might even be glad to see her dead. May the gods forgive me! How am I ever to continue furnishing her with golden coins and jewels?! Oh…"

"Do not worry, princess. Your faithful Afshin will surely contrive something! Now, please, rest and do not trouble your mind with such thoughts. I will do all I can to help you…"

21

Unknown Land, 6th Century BCE

Tomyris opened her eyes—she had just come to her senses after a severe faint. In the dim half-light, she looked around and shuddered from both horror and cold. They had placed her in a damp, foul-smelling basement that resembled a prison dungeon. With winter approaching—when it was still fairly warm during the day under the open sky and only cool at night—this cellar, with its frozen floor and damp stone walls, was unbearably frigid. She was overcome by thirst and hunger. But above all, Tomyris now needed to understand what had happened to her and whether there was any way to escape.

Enemies! Only the cruellest of enemies could have done this, she deduced. And what if they kill me? Well, so be it—I am the daughter of a proud nomadic king and the finest of warriors. I, too, am a warrior; if fate decrees my end, I shall meet it with honour!

She began to recall the events. After a battle with the Urartians, Tomyris had headed to her campaign tent to rest when, suddenly, someone had seized her with great force. A cloth was thrust into her mouth to silence her screams, and her hands and feet were swiftly bound. Then, as if gathering a bundle of kindling, the abductor had thrown her upon himself, mounted a powerful horse, and galloped away. She had not been able to discern his face, for it was hidden behind a mask of thick black cloth. She hadn't even managed to draw her acinaces from its sheath at her belt to defend herself against the robber.

The kidnapper did not kill me immediately, the daughter of Spargapis mused. *That means I am of use to these enemies somehow. In short, there is still hope for me to live…*

Tomyris did not fear death. To her, death was merely a transition—or perhaps the flight of the soul to another, as yet unknown, mysterious, and more perfect realm. Yet she fretted for her father—for he might not survive her demise!

So many questions crowded her mind. Where had they taken her? For what purpose? And who were they? The princess was lost in conjecture, still bereft of any answers.

Suddenly, the cell door creaked open, and a lamp was lit. A man in black entered—the very same type of black cloth bandage covering his face that she had seen on her captor! Now, in the light, she could make out his figure; he was of stately bearing. Perhaps he was handsome—she allowed herself a fleeting thought.

So this is him, she thought. *Yes, yes—the scent is the same. It smells of river wormwood that grows along the banks of the Oxus—or, as others call it, the Amu! Could it be that this young man hails from there? But what does he want from me…?*

"Take this, princess, and eat; you must keep your strength," he said in a nearly gentle tone. His voice betrayed a firmness—though he was robust, there was a clear youthfulness about him.

"Tell me, who are you and what do you want from me?" Tomyris demanded, not even deigning to rise for greeting, as befits a royal lady—even now, when her very life depended on this man's actions. "If you seek gold or silver, I swear that if you let me go, I will procure it for you! My father is a king, and his wealth is vast…"

"We know who your father is!" the youth interrupted, his tone now sharper and more brusque. "Had it not been for him, perhaps no one would have even thought of abducting you. The king of the Massagetae owes much to my master—and my master promised me, not money, but something far more esteemed and valuable, for you! But I've talked to you enough already… You are too beautiful, princess, and—truth be told—I pity you."

"Then release me, stranger!" Tomyris pleaded. "You are a good man, not a murderer—I can see it. Besides, you like me…"

She could not tell whether he was younger than her or only slightly older, yet that did not stop her from engaging him with a hint of coquettish charm.

"No, Tomyris, do not try to seduce me with your feminine wiles—I will not yield!" the young jailer declared, a note of nervous uncertainty in his voice. "If my master learns that I have let you go, he will kill me on the spot! And if I complete his orders, he will make me his right hand! And someday, when he is gone, perhaps his title will pass to me, and I will assume his honoured position!"

"Ah, to be the leader of bandits and brigands—what an honour!" Tomyris laughed, no longer afraid of him, and she even began to eat slowly.

"We are not brigands!" the young man retorted, slightly offended. Suddenly, they both heard heavy footsteps approaching. "Listen, Tomyris, I beg you: be quiet, so that my master does not kill you but merely takes a ransom from your father—what he needs. And I must go now. Otherwise, if my master finds out that I am conversing with you as if we were friends, I am doomed! I am young and hands… well, it does not matter. I still want to live! I know you are strong and brave. But now, please—do not rebel, do not anger the master! He despises that above all else…"

"And who is your master? Am I to know him?" Tomyris called

out loudly after the door, as the man swiftly closed it and departed. But he gave her no answer.

No, I cannot allow my father to suffer because of me! the girl thought anxiously. *Anything but that! Better yet—perish!*

Meanwhile, she checked the door—it would not budge, locked fast as if it had never been opened before.

I must escape at all costs, Tomyris resolved. *But how? This coward left no door even half-open for me... Oh, where is my acinaces? Where and how could I have lost it?! It would be most useful right now! And also... No, what a foolish thought! And why did I even think of it—of that clumsy, brutish giant, the Saka-Tigraxauda? I drove him away, repelled him. Yet he looked at me so... No man has ever gazed at me with such devotion and adoration... Perhaps, for one like him, I would even consent to marriage... Of course, it is absurd to dream such things, especially now, on the brink of death... Oh, gods, what is this?! It seems above me—there is a sudden noise and a crash! What could that be? Perhaps something terrible and dangerous... Who knows—maybe the earth shakes often in these lands, and the house will collapse at any moment? Well then... There is no escape. Farewell, beloved father! I must now prepare my soul for its passage to another world...*

* * *

Persia, same era

Artosta laughed and flirted in his embrace like a coquettish girl.

"Prince, are you sure you've securely locked the doors to your chambers and that no one will intrude?"

"Absolutely, my beauty!" Cambyses replied with a merry laugh as he kissed Artosta. "I trust that not even a soul in the corridor witnessed your entrance?"

"That sly little Afshin—your wife's servant—is always tailing me like a hound guarding a sheepfold, sniffing around for something. Yet every time, I manage to outsmart him. Your loyal attendants even help me, distracting him this way and that while I outwit that foolish simpleton! But really, what can one expect? He's all too much like his dim, gullible mistress…"

"Do not speak so of Mandane, I beg you! She is, after all, your own sister—and incidentally, my wife. Though she failed to bear me any children, Cyrus still thinks she…"

"Oh, our son Cyrus still considers his own beloved mother to be… nothing but a dog! How dreadful—to know that your son was nursed by an animal! It would have been better if he'd been entrusted to me—I had the milk back then. If not for my cruel father, Astyages…"

"A dog?! Oh—ah! I think I understand you now. Are you referring to the wife of Harpagus, the general who raised Cyrus? No, Spaka is a human name, though among the Medians it means 'dog.' But she was merely an ordinary woman, I assure you! She is gone now, and there is no reason for jealousy over her. Cyrus treats Mandane—and me—with the utmost respect, consulting us in everything. It is no accident that I named him after my father, King Cyrus the First! He is a worthy scion of our lineage."

"Forgive me, King of Anshan…" she murmured, recoiling slightly from him.

"Better address me as 'Your Highness'!" Cambyses declared, not allowing her to break free of his strong embrace.

"Your Highness, I fear you are embellishing a rather unpleasant reality. The current young king of Media holds both of you in such high esteem that, in the several months he's been there, he hasn't once invited you to visit—not even to the ceremony in which he assumed his royal title! Forget about me—he knows nothing about me. But you!"

"And yet—Cyrus the Second is coming here! That means he wishes to pay homage to me, his father. Perhaps he needs to consult with both me and Mandane about something… Come on, do not be angry that I mention her name in your presence! Though, I must say, she was far more distraught than you when, many years ago, she learned that the newborn Cyrus was gone. You, on the other hand, hardly seemed to care."

"That is because I knew I would scarcely ever be recognized as his mother! Yet you know that I am a good mother to our little girl… It's fitting that we named her Shenez—'the king's pride'! She is already five years old… I thank you for never abandoning us!"

"Of course—how could I? Both of you are my dearest and most beloved in the world! And of course—my son Cyrus. I eagerly await his return to us… But there's something I've been meaning to ask: tell me, my dear, why do you visit my wife so often? What is it that you need from her?"

Artosta evaded the question, drawing Cambyses away with tender caresses and fervent kisses.

* * *

Sakastan, same era

A messenger on horseback arrived to the king of the Massagets with a letter. Its contents read:

"Spargapis! Your daughter Tomyris is in our custody. If you wish her to remain alive, you must immediately comply with all our conditions:

First, issue a royal decree declaring that the throne and title of King of the Massagets shall never fall to your daughter Tomyris;

Second, assemble the chieftains and elders of all the Massaget tribes and, for all to hear, proclaim that you forever renounce the title of king along with all its honours, prerogatives, and riches;

Third, command your physician—or one of your warriors—to excise your liver in its entirety, and have your friends send it in a sack to the destination we specify here… To prove that it is indeed your liver, include with it the finger of your right hand bearing your royal signet!

Decide quickly: either now you lose your liver and die, in which case, by all the gods, we swear we will immediately release your daughter alive and unharmed; or, within three days, we will send you, one by one, all the organs of your Tomyris!"

Ever strong and brave, Spargapis roared like a wild beast caught in a trap! He initially wished to execute the messenger—this vile courier sent by his enemies—but then resolved to postpone the envoy's death penalty until he could ascertain who had dispatched him. Besides, Spargapis was no fool; he reasoned that if the messenger failed to return by the appointed time—with or without a reply from the king of the Massagets—then they would surely kill Tomyris at once. He could not risk the life of his only, beloved daughter. Yet the messenger remained silent, revealing nothing about his masters. Under heavy torture, he might have eventually confessed, but in the end the envoy proved utterly mute—the man's tongue had been cut out by someone.

Spargapis recalled that, according to his friend, the chieftain of the Guz, Berez, during the last assembly of chieftains and elders, the leader of the Karats, Kuzybek, had declared: "Chieftain of the Tocharians, Zakir, is somewhere nearby; he hides and bides his time, waiting for the opportune moment to exact vengeance on the king of the Massagets…"

"So it is Zakir—the contemptible scoundrel—who has abducted my daughter?!" Spargapis fumed aloud. "He plans to take revenge on me? Fat chance! Or has he forgotten who is the mightiest in the steppe? I will find that jackal and personally flay him!"

The king summoned his closest and most trusted aides—brave warriors ready to do anything for him.

"Friends, now more than ever, I need your wise counsel," he said confidingly. "Tell me what to do, and I will heed your advice…"

A respectful silence fell over the royal tent. Then, suddenly, the thundering voice of Spargapis broke the stillness:

"Massagets! The enemies of your ruler demand his immediate and agonizing death! They wish for the light in our camp to be forever extinguished, for darkness to reign!"

At these words, the warriors erupted in a burst of indignation and fervour, and the tent filled with clamour. No matter how ruthless Spargapis might be, there were men he valued and loved with all his heart—and they responded in kind, pledging their undying loyalty and vowing never to let him fall.

"We shall not allow it! Your enemies are our enemies too—let them all fall! King, if need be, take our lives instead!"

For a moment, Spargapis's face lit up with unexpected support; he had not foreseen such backing.

"Now, my king, if you will permit," proposed Aramezd—one of the king's closest aides, regarded as the shrewdest and wisest of them all—"let us thoroughly examine the messenger. Perhaps something in his appearance will reveal from which land he comes and who might have sent him."

Aramezd's suggestion pleased everyone, especially Spargapis.

Shortly thereafter, the messenger—bound hand and foot—was brought into the royal tent. Spargapis's aides began to inspect him very carefully.

There was no doubt: the man was a Saka. Yet they all began to speculate about his tribe. His head, a little like a pumpkin—as seen among the Alans—suggested one thing, yet atop his head he wore a pointed cap, the kind often worn by the Saki-Tigraxauda of the lowlands of Oxus.

The investigators grew perplexed. Then, suddenly:

"Wait a moment—look at the waist belt tied over his kaftan! It resembles the waist belt of the new chieftain of the Alans, Haidar!" Aramezd observed abruptly. "Could it be that the great king himself sent you this messenger? Although Haidar is a Massaget, we all know how furious he is with you after being denied the hand of your daughter—the beautiful princess Tomyris! Surely you know, my king, that this is his token?"

"Yes, it does look very much like it," agreed Spargapis. "Perhaps it is indeed Haidar?"

"But… notice the bow slung over his back," objected another friend of Spargapis, the grey-bearded Olim, "and its scent of silk and thuja. As we know, those grow on the border with the western land of Zhou. Moreover, the arrowheads of this messenger's arrows are made of fine copper—mined only in those regions. And there, as we know, live…"

"Oh, calamity! They live among the Guz!" Spargapis cried out in anger. "But that cannot be—I refuse to believe it! My friend

Berez, chieftain of the Guz, would never betray me, never!"

For a brief moment, all fell silent. It was painful to see the king so distraught.

"After all," Spargapis finally said, "do you not understand that such an expensive bow could have simply been given as a gift to the messenger?" He was still hoping that his old friends did not want him dead. "Or that this youth might have taken it from his foes in some skirmish, as a trophy? No—I think we're on the wrong track. If we keep going, we might end up accusing, say, my friend and brother Salih—kinsman of my beloved wife Zaryana—of being my fiercest enemy… What nonsense these Massagets spout!"

Once more, Aramezd fixed a piercing gaze on the messenger, then on King Spargapis—and suddenly fell silent, visibly shaken.

"Mighty king," the sage said in a soft, cautious tone—so as not to incur the wrath of the lord of the steppes—"you well know that the Abii are nearly identical to our most detested foes, the Sarmatians, or as we more commonly call them, the Sauromatians! For those dwelling near the Black Mountains, the Abii are the closest neighbors of the Sarmatians. Beyond that come the Bosporus and the Greeks… And although your friend Salih, the new chieftain of the Abii, is the cousin of your daughter, and he is not a Sarmatian but, like us, a Massaget, we must not forget that in his day he was not indifferent to your wife, Zaryana…"

"Silence, you lying cur!" roared Spargapis in furious wrath, cutting him off. "I have granted no one the right to even utter the sacred name of my beloved and chaste wife—let alone to slander or defile her or any of her kin!"

"Forgive me, great king," Aramezd bowed humbly. "They were merely idle rumors, repeated by your servant in vile gossip. I am at fault and ready to accept punishment."

"You said it yourself!" the king thundered, still seething. "Begone from my sight!"

Utterly dismayed and incensed by the fruitless council, the king of the Massagets resolved to dismiss the rest of his attendants for a while. Yet he chose not to execute Aramezd—for the wise man was still needed by the entire camp.

Meanwhile, the king suddenly recalled what his friends had told him: that the elder of the Abii, Asror, on the day of the council, for some reason, had laid blame on Salih—hinting at his complicated attitude toward Spargapis! As if Spargapis knew nothing of Salih's true opinion of him! Allegedly, Salih, in truth, harbored some undisclosed enmity toward Spargapis…

To the king of the Massagets, this was inconceivable, unacceptable, and strange; for he had always regarded Salih as his best friend! And only recently had he appointed Salih as the leader of the great Abii tribe—not just anyone, but his very own Salih! How could Salih suddenly become a traitor?… And why so?

Could it be that what Aramezd had just said—and what sounded like deceitful slander—namely, that Salih was in love with Tomyris's mother, Zaryana, might be true? Salih had never hinted at such a thing to Spargapis! Such resolve, such determination!

Or perhaps Salih, because of this very matter, wished to avoid a quarrel with his friend? Or is Spargapis now vainly attempting to justify an old comrade? What, then, if the chieftain of the Abii had been waiting for a more opportune moment to sting the lord of the Massagets more grievously?!

Spargapis could hardly bring himself to believe it—this was a crushing blow. Could it really be that it wasn't the Sauromatians, who openly hated him, nor the former leader of the Alans, Bikbulat, nor Haidar, embittered by Tomyris's actions, nor even Zakir, mortally offended by the king, who had secretly kidnapped the Saka princess and were now blackmailing her unfortunate father? Could Salih have done it? His dear brother, his closest friend!! Could it be true?!

Spargapis sank down onto a soft hide, determined to ponder all these matters deeply…

He sat there, sleepless, until dawn. He could not bear the thought of dying—of surrendering his body even to a friend who had turned out to be a scoundrel. Yet his beloved daughter was worth more than life itself! What choice did he have? He would have to sacrifice himself for her salvation. He saw no alternative.

And then, as the golden rays of an early, once-joyful sun began to touch the royal tent and the weary king—mired in grim and sorrowful thoughts—a loud pounding of hooves was heard nearby, within the camp. Soon followed shouts of exclamation, expressions of delight, and unrestrained, raucous joy from a throng of people!

Spargapis was astonished: how could his own people dare act thus in such a bitter hour for him?…

"My lord, the hero Rustam has arrived," a servant of the king burst into the tent without invitation. "He has brought our princess with him!! Praise the gods—Tomyris is alive and unharmed!!"

Spargapis immediately leapt to his feet and rushed out to meet the arrivals, barely holding back tears of joy—a joy he had not yet fully recognized nor believed possible.

Tomyris threw herself into her father's arms, drenching him in warm, filial kisses.

"Father, father, do not worry—I am all right! I do not know who abducted me, for my chief captor managed to escape. And his accomplice—the one who brought me to that dungeon—was wounded and lost consciousness. But I know who rescued me and carried me away from there. It was Rustam! He has come here with

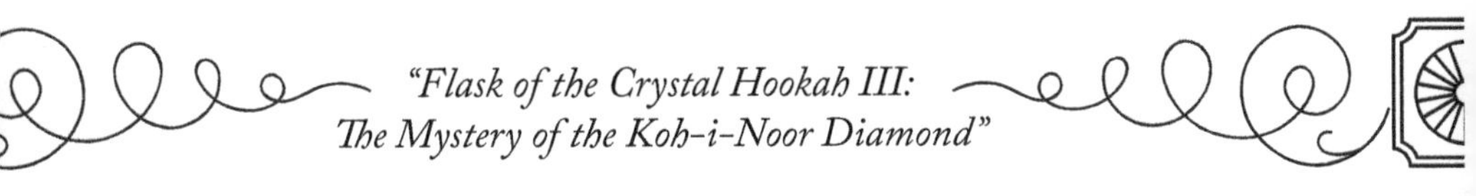

me. Father, he is brave and valiant, fearing neither man nor beast! Rustam is the finest of all men. And he loves me—oh, how he loves me, I can see it. If you will allow it, great king of the Massagets, I… I shall marry him!"

Spargapis, usually headstrong, independent, and authoritative, on this occasion allowed not a single word or thought to run counter to his daughter's desire.

"Let it be as you say, my dear," he answered quietly, holding Tomyris tightly in his embrace. Yet at that very moment, a burning jealousy toward Rustam crept into his heart.

***

The king of the Saka-Tigraxauda, Kavad, had long since ceased to share any intimate bond with his second wife, Balkyz—the mother of Zogak. He made no secret of his utter dislike for that plain, unrefined wench. And since he was still a relatively young man, both his spirit and his body frequently craved fresh, vivid sensations—adventures and diversions. Consequently, he spent much of his time with his concubines, never managing to fully sate his lust with any one of them. Perhaps this was because the women of his tribe were far from corrupt; they had never been trained in the art of deliberate and skillful seduction.

In the entire tribe, there was only one person capable of doing absolutely anything for her future happiness—and that was none other than Zogak's wife, Nastaran. She had promised her husband that, come what may, she would make him king—and she intended to pursue her goal at all costs.

As for Azer, she never employed her charms for sordid, deceitful ends. Moreover, Nastaran would never have turned to Azer for help; therefore, the young enchantress resolved to act on her own. She discovered some very ancient writings in which the secrets and reliable techniques of seducing both men and women were immortalized.

Thereafter, Nastaran struck a deal with Kavad's favored concubine—one who was accustomed to visiting him on certain nights—and paid her handsomely. On one such night, by a twist of fate unbeknownst to Kavad, Nastaran found herself in the concubine's place, once again lying next to the king of the Saka-Tigraxauda.

Nastaran already knew that behaving seductively did not mean being overtly provocative. A man craves mystery in a woman; thus, it is better to enclose one's body in thin, tight fabric than to expose it entirely. And yet there was one part of her body—her one redeeming feature in lieu of a striking face—that Nastaran deliberately left bare: her breasts. Moreover, she had come to understand the art of fragrances well; before going to see the king, she anointed herself all over with divinely scented, delightfully intoxicating balms.

At first, Kavad was quite taken aback by this substitution and sought to put an end to it.

"What are you doing, shameless harlot?" he shrieked in indignation. "Why are you here again? Get away immediately! After all, you have a husband—my son, Zogak—and I have a wife! Have you no shame?"

"Remembering his wife, that old, despicable sinner!" thought Nastaran. She offered him no reply; instead, while lying with him, she began to caress his body—gently stroking his hair and his neck. She already knew that a man's neck was an erogenous zone, and

that when a woman caresses it while lightly nibbling at his ears, he quickly becomes aroused.

And so it happened. Suddenly, overcome by wine and maddened by passionate lust, King Kavad greedily attacked Nastaran's lips and every inch of her body—her soft, rosy, enticing breasts and her slender waist. He kissed her continuously, unable to stop.

Nastaran responded with restrained yet pleasing embraces and kisses, and when Kavad grew tired, she treated him to her special, cool, tart, and delicious drink.

This went on until dawn—and the next night the same cycle repeated.

King Kavad was utterly enchanted by Nastaran.

Yet, a few days later, he fell gravely ill. Soon he could no longer rise from his bed. Kavad was convinced that his old battle wounds—sustained in countless fights—were finally betraying him, and the notion that his fatal illness might be connected to the arrival of his charming daughter-in-law—the wife of his younger, disfavored son—never occurred to him…

On his final day, Kavad eagerly awaited his dearest heir, Rustam. A messenger had been dispatched with news of the sudden illness of the king of the Saka-Tigraxauda and a personal plea urging Rustam to come and visit him as quickly as possible.

But despite his overwhelming desire, Rustam could not make it to his father—he was busy with his wedding to his beloved Tomyris. To forgo such an important and splendid celebration would have deeply insulted both his adored bride and her powerful father, the king of the Massagets.

Nevertheless, Rustam resolved that immediately after the wedding, after informing his wife, he would set out at once for a brief visit to his father. He hoped and believed that Kavad's condition was not truly perilous—that the gods would aid him and his father would soon rise again.

But it did not come to pass… The fated curses of Kavad's brother, Sakesfar, were fulfilled!

Rustam and Tomyris celebrated a magnificent wedding, and on the very same day Kavad died. Nastaran's prophecies were realized: without delay, Zogak—her husband—became the new king of the Saka-Tigraxauda. Soon thereafter, he himself sent a messenger to Rustam bearing a royal decree: remain in the land of the Massagets and never return to your native land again.

22

Tashkent, 1979

"Sweetheart, I don't know about you, but we will definitely celebrate your twentieth birthday at a restaurant!" Sardar Mahkamov, Tamilla's father, embraced her. "After all, isn't it true that I, the director of a major factory, can afford to throw a proper party for my family on my hard-earned money? Haven't I earned that? And don't you deserve it as well?"

"Perhaps I don't deserve it yet," Tamilla replied modestly.

"You're such a good girl! You're excelling at the institute, and you even formed your own band! At your age, very few can claim such achievements. Though I'd much prefer it if you, my beloved daughter, followed in my footsteps…"

"Don't worry—I started with my mother's path, and when the time comes, I'll follow yours too, dear Daddy," Tamilla winked playfully.

She hadn't yet explained that while she wasn't opposed to someday engaging in something like production, it would have to be on a different economic platform—not a factory. Truth be told, she wasn't entirely sure herself yet; she was simply musing and searching for her own way.

"In any case, it's decided: the day after tomorrow, on your birthday, our whole family is going to the best restaurant in our capital, 'Uzbekistan,' where they serve the world's finest pilaf and Kyiv-style cutlets! Of course, you may invite your closest friends and companions to join you for the evening!"

* * *

Young, fair-haired Lena, an accountant at the Ministry of Culture, knocked on the door of Rashid Batyrov—the head of the Department for the Protection of Monuments of Archaeology and Ancient Civilizations—and, not waiting for his reply, confidently stepped into his office.

"Yes, Lenochka?" he greeted her with a smile. "Is something important the matter? How can I hel—"

"Again with the formal 'you'?" she interrupted sharply. "Since when did we go back to using the formal 'you'? Rashid, are you ill? Can't you recognize me anymore?!"

"Forgive me, Lena—I do recognize you. And I'm perfectly healthy. It's just that we're at work, and people might see us! I find it rather awkward to make our relationship public."

"And what's wrong with that?! Are you such a scaredy-cat?

Afraid of other people's opinions?"

"I'm not scared at all! It's just that I worry about you. I'm a man, and no one will judge me for my… ahem… affections and, shall we say, my courtship! But if it comes to you, gossip will fly. They'll whisper behind your back that you've taken yourself a lov— someone you meet openly—and yet he refuses to marry you."

"Well, then why don't you marry me, darling?"

"Lena! Is that some kind of joke? I thought I made it clear from the start that nothing serious could come between us—and I never promised to take you to the registry! Forgive me."

"All right, all right! But will you at least come over tonight? I'm baking chicken with vegetables in the oven."

"Unfortunately, I can't tonight. A friend is arriving, and we're heading out to a restaurant. He hasn't had a proper meal in months—eating nothing but potatoes with stewed meat, pasta, and even dunking rusks in tea. I must urgently rescue his poor, emaciated stomach!"

"What kind of friend is that? Does he live in the desert?"

"Almost. He's an archaeologist who's just returned from a trip down south on an assignment. He'll be here for a few days before heading off again—to those underground ruins."

"Is he excavating there? How fascinating! Has he already found something valuable? Perhaps some ancient ornaments?"

"I'm not sure yet. He always finds something interesting, and in my work, I oversee his discoveries. In fact, we were just about to meet—he was going to explain everything in detail! It's very important to me. Whenever he comes, we immediately go to a restaurant. Then he slowly readjusts to home-cooked food."

"Clearly, your friend must be a bachelor too, since there's no one to properly care for him. And why is it that you grown men never get married?"

"Perhaps because neither he nor I have yet found our one true other half—someone for a lifetime. You know that song by Pugacheva, *All Can Be Kings*? Well, my friend Pulat and I—we're far from kings, and we'd rather marry for love! Fortunately, we have the right to do so. In any case, Lena, tonight I'm sorry, but I won't be able to come."

"Alright, I got that already. Fine, please send my regards to your archaeologist!"

* * *

Moscow, 1979

The doorbell rang at the Persievs' apartment. Denis, not even bothering to look through the peephole, opened the door immediately. He knew that hardly anyone unfamiliar would come—climbing five flights on foot was a real hassle.

"Farida, is that you?" he greeted her with mild surprise. "Come on in. Marina isn't home; she's gone to the market. You didn't call to say you were coming—has something happened?"

"No, nothing's wrong. I just missed you and my sister and decided to drop by on a day off. Is that so wrong? Oh, and I brought you your beer. And salty crackers—everything just the way you like it!"

"Thanks!" Denis immediately popped open a bottle of beer and fetched two glasses, preparing to pour the frothy drink for both of them. "Such care—what's the occasion?"

"No, no, I won't have any," Farida waved him off. "Drink it up. What do you mean—'what's the occasion?' We're family, aren't we?"

"Maybe I should make you some coffee?"

"No, thank you, don't trouble yourself. After all, if I want coffee, I'll make it myself. I'm not exactly a guest here, am I? This is my dear sister's home—even if she isn't blood-related!"

"Whatever you say... Farida, have you heard anything about Kirill?"

"Wow! And you ask me about him, his real father?! Shouldn't I be the one getting all the news about your son?"

"You know full well that I never raised Kirill as a father! He's been nothing more than that scoundrel Oleg's son his whole life! And now you're telling me this. Are you mocking me?"

"It's all because you've always been a wimp instead of a real man! You couldn't even stand up for your own child! Sure, Oleg pressured both you and Marina. But he's that kind of man. Long ago, you could have found some clever way to win your son back!"

"And how's that? I never meant to harm Marina. Have you forgotten that she was dying? That her heart wasn't worth a damn at the time?! Marina needed an operation urgently. And Oleg financed that surgery and saved your sister's life! Let me remind you: my wife owes her very life not only to the famous cardiologist, but to Oleg himself! And you act as if that doesn't matter."

"Of course she does—if you must know, she curses herself for having agreed to it all back then!"

"What were we supposed to do? We had no other choice! And if Marina hadn't survived... I can't even bear to think of it! Who would have ever imagined that one day Kirill might—God forbid—kill Oleg, his adoptive father!"

"Yeah, and that Oleg would find out about it so quickly..." Farida faltered, suddenly realizing she'd said too much. Now, the reproaches were about to start...

"It's all your fault!" Denis snapped without delay. "If you hadn't come by then and drunk that stupid tea…"

"Ah! I nearly died in intensive care—I was barely saved, and now I'm being blamed too?! I must say, what a great relative you are! I suppose the apple doesn't fall far from the tree! And our little Kirill—he's all you! Just as treacherous. Aren't you ashamed to lay such accusations at my feet? Fine, I don't pity you. But Oleg? So, you wouldn't have minded if he had kicked the bucket back then, huh?"

"What expressions are these, Farida?… No, I didn't mean that at all," Denis began to defend himself, his mind clearly muddled by the situation. "Forgive me. Of course, I wish no harm on either of you! I just thought that if Oleg had drunk that poisoned tea himself, perhaps he'd have been too weak afterward to pick a fight. And then our boy wouldn't have ended up in jail. Though maybe I'm mistaken… But I know one thing: if Marina and I had raised Kirill, he would have turned out a completely different person. It pains me… The kid's only sixteen, and his whole life is already derailed."

"That's exactly it," Farida nodded. "And if you and I had our own little boy, he would've been even better!"

Denis's eyes widened in shock at Farida's remark.

"Have you lost your mind? What do you mean 'our own little boy'?"

"Oh, have you completely forgotten? Don't you remember that eighteen years ago—before you met Marina—you were my fiancé? You swore your love to me back then. And when I became pregnant, you forced me to have an abortion—you didn't want any children from me. And after the army, without marrying me, you immediately left—as soon as you saw my little sister. You fell head over heels for her and completely forgot about me. You even acted as if I wasn't there when we met! You've forgotten it all, haven't you?"

"Farida, well… I haven't forgotten. But that's all in the past. Let's not talk about it anymore."

She rose from the table and moved closer to Persiev. Wrapping one arm around his neck, she stroked his hair.

"Maybe now we should continue, hmm? You and Marina don't have any children—Kirill doesn't count; he's long since not truly yours. So you have nothing to lose. You can always divorce her!"

"What nonsense are you spouting?" Denis blushed. "I love only my wife! Please, let's forget this conversation forever, and I won't mention it to Marina."

Farida forced Persiev to stand, clinging even tighter to him, and, embracing him passionately, tried to kiss him on the lips. Denis turned away, refusing.

"No, Farida, I can't. Please, don't be offended. Leave, alright? Marina will be here any moment, and she certainly won't take kindly to your advances!"

"Oh, my! I'm so frightened of my so-called 'sister'! Men— you're such spineless, gutless cowards. Alright then, live freely for now! We'll see what happens. I'll let you know if there's any news about Kirill. I hear he's due to be 'moved along' somewhere. And anyway—he'll be sitting in jail for a few more years yet… Goodbye, Denis! Give my regards to Marina!"

***

Tashkent, 1979

"Why did your parents leave so quickly—just congratulate you and then vanish?" asked Tamilla's friend, Mavluda.

"My mom told my dad that my birthday should be celebrated with my peers, with my own friends!" explained Tamilla. "And they decided to continue the celebration of my twentieth at home by themselves! Later in the evening, my father's driver will pick us up and drop us off at our respective homes. We'll even swing by and drop you off in your district."

"Really? How nice—thank you! You have such wonderful parents!"

"That's true," Tamilla beamed.

…The birthday girl and her guests spent the evening in high spirits. Toward the end of the party, when Tamilla's friends—including the musicians from her small band—had all become rather tipsy, an unfamiliar man unexpectedly approached their table. He was also clearly drunk, with a disreputable, almost thug-like appearance: unshaven, expensively yet disheveled, his shirt heavily wrinkled.

"Hey, beautiful, get up—come dan… dan… dance with me!" he slurred, his words stumbling drunkenly as he addressed Tamilla.

Startled, the girl recoiled from him.

"Get away from me!" she said, her voice quiet but firm, though without panicking.

"That's definitely a criminal!" Mavluda whispered confidently into Tamilla's ear. "Maybe we should get out of here soon?"

But they didn't manage to leave in time. The repulsive man roughly grabbed Tamilla by the hand and dragged her—not toward the restaurant's dance floor, but to his own table. She struggled valiantly, using all her strength to break free from him, yet refrained from calling out for help; it was simply too awkward to scream in front of the guests she had invited.

"Bahrom, leave that ice maiden alone! What do you need her for?" two other rough-looking guys, who were mingling with the loathsome fellow, jeered.

"Shut up, you moooorons!" Bahrom bellowed harshly at his cronies. "I like h… her—and that's that! She's a young beauty, and she'll be mine—ri… right now, understand?"

He intended to haul her onto the table and, in his drunken state, violate her. In response, she struck him sharply on the cheek; yet the vile man did not relent. Instead, the girly slap only fanned his fury and brazenness further.

"Ah, so… so that's how it is?! Hold on tight! I'm going to punish you!"

Suddenly, strong, masculine arms gripped the man, twisting him up and swiftly escorting him outto the street. Instantly, the restaurant fell into complete silence, and within seconds the subdued murmur of dozens of voices and the familiar soft strains of restaurant music resumed.

Tamilla, still in shock from the ordeal, remained silent. Her two friends, Mavluda and Nazira, quickly came to her side, gently taking her by the arm and leading her back to their table. In principle, it might have been possible to settle in for the rest of the evening peacefully—no one else was spoiling the celebration—but Nazira nonetheless suggested that Tamilla leave.

"Of course," Tamilla agreed without argument. Still trembling slightly, she spoke slowly, "Let's wait for my rescuer—I want to thank him, and then we'll leave immediately."

At last, the brave "knight" of Tamilla's night returned to the room. A handsome young man of about twenty-five, he approached her table without delay.

"Good evening," he began politely, nodding in turn to each of the young ladies. Then, turning directly to Tamilla, he said, "Miss, you are very courageous—I am simply in awe of you! Truly. You never shrieked, nor did you call out for help! I apologize for not coming to your rescue sooner; I was seated here, chatting with my friend, and only gradually realized that something was amiss in the room."

"Not at all. The important thing is that you arrived in time," Tamilla replied with a gentle smile, still not fully recovered from the shock. "Thank you so very much!"

"I must confess, I have never met a woman like you before!" continued the young man, lavishing further compliments. "And rest assured—the man who harassed you will trouble you no more. I took him to a car; he left immediately. He was simply too drunk and utterly uncouth."

"Just a real lout and scoundrel!" interjected Mavluda. "You're a hero."

"Not at all—what heroism is there? I merely felt it was right to help a defenseless girl," he replied modestly.

"Tamilla, shall we go now?" asked Nazira once more, convinced that her friend had had enough male attention for the evening.

"Wait—so your name is Tamilla?" the young man suddenly interjected with lively energy, his face brightening like a freshly minted coin. "I'm Rashid Batyrov. I'll let you in on a little secret: I work for the Ministry of Culture. If you ever need anything, do not hesitate to reach out!"

"Understood. Once again, thank you," Tamilla said, managing a composed smile.

She felt a warm sense of pleasure in conversing with this courteous and evidently kind gentleman—though she was simply exhausted and not in the mood.

Little did she know the profound impression she had made on him! Rashid returned home later, intoxicated, enchanted, and uplifted—unable to fall asleep. The image of the young Eastern beauty he had met, Tamilla, danced before his eyes.

Before retiring for the night, he called his friend:

"Pulat, how did your journey go? All right? I'm glad. And no—don't apologize for not helping me with that scuffle with the scoundrel! Of course, I'm not mad at you at all. You were worn out after that trip. And truly, what you've told me is astounding! You found a bowl bearing the image of Karna—the Son of the Sun—with a golden turban atop his head! For it was that very turban that Karna presented to Queen Tamyris! This means we're on the right track, and soon you'll find the golden turban itself— and perhaps even the remnants of the Koh-i-Noor diamond! Isn't that wonderful... And there's something else I wanted to share with you—imagine, I believe I've fallen in love! Yes, for the first time in my life. The moment I saw her—when she was seated at her table—I noticed her immediately, and, you know, felt such a warm glow in my heart! An incredible sensation, as if she were my own kindred spirit... But what a fool I am, Pulat! I completely forgot to ask for her telephone number! I stood there, utterly spellbound, admiring her beauty, and lost all sense. I didn't even realize she was about to leave—and now I might never see her again!"

"I think, Rashid, that if she truly is your person, you will certainly meet again someday! Remember my words—everything will work out well."

***

The outskirts of Boston, USA, 2012 — during a city tour for students to see its landmarks, three days before the abduction of Tamilla and Rashid…

"Wow, what an unusual place!" exclaimed Daniil Shevtsov, the future geotechnical engineer, as he gripped the bus's front seat handle. "A dense forest, a narrow path… It's very exotic! But this route isn't on our itinerary! Where exactly are we?"

"Oh, we're heading to a one-of-a-kind site," replied their guide, John McConnley, mysteriously. "I am absolutely convinced, young fine folk, that it will leave an indelible impression on you—one that will last for the rest of your lives."

"You're scaring us, Mr. McConnley!" shrieked Ekaterina Solovyova, a future professional economist, with a shudder. "You're keeping secrets. Honestly, nothing like this appears in our program. What's with these strange improvisations during the act?"

"Keep in mind, dear sir, that if, heaven forbid, something were to happen to us in your country, our parents would be worried, and so would the project leaders—Tamilla Sardorovna and Konstantin Ivanovich—who'd raise the alarm," interjected Aibek Khashimov, a soon-to-be certified programmer.

"I'm absolutely terrified—I'm shaking!" quipped the Russian-speaking McConnley in a gloomy, ironic tone. "Did you say… Konstantin Ivanovich?"

For some inexplicable reason, he let out a snicker that the others found utterly baffling.

"Yes. He's a businessman from Moscow who generously supports our students with grants."

"Right. No, I was just asking. By the way, we're almost there. And there's nothing to fear, youngsters."

In a low murmur to himself, McConnley added,

"You'll have something to fear later... But me—I'm not scary at all."

They drove through towering metallic gates that swung open before them. The minibus then trundled along a paved path cutting through a pristine lawn and came to a halt.

"Everyone out!" McConnley commanded.

The students followed him, their eyes meeting an enormous mound reminiscent of a Scythian burial kurgan. A little way off, directly opposite, stood another set of massive metal gates—or rather, a set of colossal doors, the kind one might see on hangars or bunkers. McConnley gestured for them to follow him inside. Eagerly, they proceeded, still hopeful that this was merely an extension of the city tour.

"What's this? A former military base?" Aibek inquired impatiently. "I think I saw something similar in that film about Edward Snowden—he was a secret system administrator at a National Security Agency base in Hawaii."

"It'd be so interesting to see what's inside!" Daniil added in admiration. "The soil here is fascinating; we'll have to study it later."

However, Katya did not share the boys' enthusiasm, though she joined them nonetheless.

This time, McConnley remained silent, offering no further explanation. Gone was his overly courteous manner; his face had grown stern, his gaze businesslike and tense. It was evident that something troubled him.

McConnley then rang a code bell by the bunker's door. The door swung open.

After entering, they proceeded for several more minutes along a long, dim corridor. The students had many questions, but a sudden, inexplicable anxiety overwhelmed both the boys and the girl. They were gripped by an attack of claustrophobia intertwined with an acute fear of being alone, rendering them incapable of uttering a single word. Each of them came to understand one thing: this was no excursion!

Where exactly had they been brought? And why? What purpose could they possibly serve here?

At last, they reached a foyer decorated in a fairly modern style—one common to office spaces anywhere in the world. McConnley confidently located a door marked "Head of the Laboratory" and entered it, turning back to address the students:

"Ladies and gentlemen, please come in! Do not be shy."

In an instant, their fear vanished as if it had never existed. And as quickly as the terror disappeared, John McConnley himself seemed to evaporate with it.

Standing before the students from Tashkent was a respectable, stout American with a beaming, kindly smile. He practically threw open his arms in a friendly embrace:

"Ah! My dear guests from Uzbekistan!" he exclaimed in English. "How delighted I am—delighted beyond words! I'm sure you're a little surprised about why you've been invited here. Please, have a seat! Behold, the most comfortable chairs in my office are at your disposal!"

After exchanging polite greetings, the students settled into the soft armchairs.

"Are you, by any chance, a scientist?" Katya ventured, addressing the rotund man. "And is our internship going to take place here at the end of the academic year?"

Solovyova was immediately struck by her own absurd question, thinking, *What am I saying? How do the end of the academic year and these September days relate? And what kind of internship could be held in a single location—for all of us, students of different majors? That's some sort of nonsense. Still, he does look every bit the scientist. What does he do here? What exactly is this laboratory...?*

"Indeed, of course, my dear lady, you've guessed correctly! I am a scientist. Allow me to explain the purpose of your visit. You see, your supervisors neglected to mention that a scientific and cultural exchange is currently underway between the USA and Uzbekistan. Some of our resources are being sent to your country, and in return, we receive some of yours..."

For some reason, he coughed and then paused, as if deliberating how best to explain everything.

"Excuse me, sir..." began Daniil.

"Oh, I nearly forgot to introduce myself! I'm Dr. George Moran—at your service!"

"But, Mr. Moran, you must understand that we aren't exactly the titans of modern science—we're just ordinary students..."

"Ah, we know all about you!" George retorted with hearty laughter. "Daniil Shevtsov studies geotechnical engineering, Aibek Khashimov is learning programming, and you, Lady Ekaterina Solovyova, are pursuing economics. Am I right?" He burst into another robust laugh. "And you aren't ordinary at all—you are the finest representatives of your generation! The most brilliant and talented among your peers! That's exactly why you're my guests!"

He smiled broadly, his teeth gleaming in his radiant grin.

"But where did you…?" Daniil stared at Moran in disbelief. "Tamilla Sardorovna and Konstantin Ivanovich never mentioned anything about you!"

"I didn't understand anything either," Aibek admitted, clearly confused.

"My friends, don't rush to conclusions," Moran said warmly. "Soon, you will be treated to a delicious, hearty lunch, and after that, you will learn about our further plans."

"And when do we head to our universities, to study on grants?" Khashimov inquired. This thought had been subconsciously circling in his mind for hours, refusing to let go. At last, he had processed it enough to speak. Besides, his head was pounding terribly.

"By the way, yes!" Daniil interjected. "Our bus is waiting for us back there. Would you tell us, Dr. Moran, when we'll finish viewing this attraction and resume the tour? There seem to be discrepancies in the schedule!"

The young man, like Katya, began to feel that something was utterly nonsensical.

"In short, dear sir, when will we be free?" Katya summed up in strangely self-directed words, her head spinning as if she were short of air in this underground bunker.

"Never!" Moran answered cheerfully and good-naturedly. "Forget about that. Now, you are our guests, and you will live here—forever, until your final days!"

"What?!" the students cried out in unison.

"What do you mean—forever?!" Daniil protested. "What do you mean by 'until your final days'?!"

"Don't worry; you won't be bored here! There will be plenty of interesting work for you. For now, relax. You will be shown your rooms. After lunch, get some sleep and gather your strength. Your bright minds will be needed not only by you but, more importantly, by us."

* * *

Tashkent, 1981

Rashid Batyrov stepped out of his office in the Ministry of Culture and into the corridor to attend to one of his many errands. Suddenly, he noticed a beautiful young woman a short distance away, standing by the door of the Head of the Department for State Support of the Arts and Folk Creativity. Her face was sorrowful—undoubtedly troubled—and she was wiping her eyes with a handkerchief. He recognized her immediately. Rushing over, he called out,

"Tamilla! It can't be—what a coincidence!"

Batyrov was sure she would ask, *Do we know each other?*

But Tamilla Mahkamova merely smiled and replied,

"Oh, hello, valiant knight! Rashid, right?"

"What a memory! You haven't forgotten me, then? After all, we met just once, and it has been two years already," he said.

"Such a meeting is unforgettable. Besides, our encounter took place on my 'jubilee'—my twentieth birthday. That's why it stayed with me."

She withheld the thought of how often she recalled his kind eyes filled with genuine admiration and tenderness. But he hadn't sought her out again, and she didn't dare visit his workplace on her own—such an act would have seemed improper.

"You're so forthright! Aren't you afraid now that I know your age? Yet, if truth be told, you still look every bit seventeen!" Rashid teased.

Tamilla's smile deepened at his compliment.

"Thank you! You always know how to lift my spirits—even in the darkest of moments."

"Has something happened to you? Did you visit Nematov's office? Please, tell me."

"Oh, yes. But I'm afraid I might distract you from your work!"

"From the moment I saw you, no matter what else demands my attention, nothing could be more important than you!" Rashid declared in a tone both earnest and devoid of any impropriety. In that instant, his heart filled once more with the same intoxicating thrill he had felt in that restaurant. How he adored this girl—even in tears. Now, two years later, she seemed to have blossomed even further, unfurling like a fragrant, resplendent flower.

"Thank you. I do, actually, have a major problem,"

"Tamilla, it's almost lunchtime. I suggest you come down to our dining room with me. We'll have a bite to eat, and you can tell me about all your sorrows and worries. Okay?"

She agreed. Right now, she really needed assistance. Or at least consolation and friendly support.

This is what Tamilla told Rashid over lunch:

"My vocal and instrumental ensemble took part in an international charity event. There, we were noticed and highly appreciated by guests from Morocco. And one of the leaders in the Moroccan pop scene, Mr. Abbad, invited our band on a short tour of his country. It was very flattering for us to be recognized. Mr. Abbad said he would fully pay for our accommodation in hotels in Rabat, Marrakesh, and other cities in Morocco. But we must cover the cost of round-trip air tickets ourselves. However, we don't have

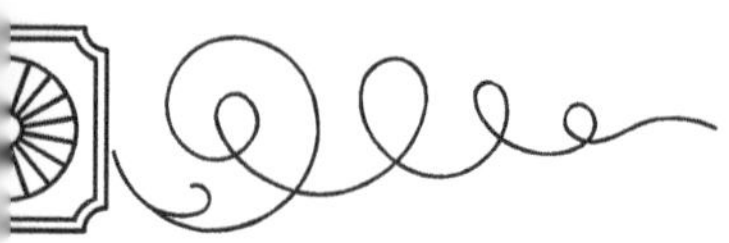

such funds. I have asked the ministry for help, but they refused. And our entire team is already so eager to go!"

"And you will go," Rashid said reassuringly. "Well, obviously I can't promise miracles, but I will do my utmost to help. You see, there is also the head of another unit at the ministry, the Department of International Cooperation. As it happens, Agzam Sadykov is an old friend of mine. I'm certain he can arrange everything for you. But after I help you, don't disappear again for so long, alright? Perhaps we should exchange phone numbers, just in case?"

Two weeks later, Tamilla and her vocal-instrumental ensemble departed for Morocco.

At first, Tamilla called her parents several times to report that everything was going splendidly, that the ensemble was being received with great enthusiasm everywhere. Then, all the calls abruptly ceased. Two weeks passed without a word from her.

Sardor Shakhmuradovich and Maryam Baburovna were thrown into a panic. Where was their daughter? Was she alright? They could not imagine that she had abandoned her family and homeland to emigrate—Tamilla was not that sort of person.

Once again, her parents turned to the Ministry of Culture, yet no one seemed to have any details. Then, the following day after their visit to Aziz Nematov, a telephone call rang out in the Mahkamov household. The parents' hearts leaped. Could it be, at last, that their beloved daughter was calling?

But the voice on the other end was unfamiliar and masculine.

"Hello, good day. Am I speaking with Sardor Shakhmuradovich?"

"Yes, I'm listening. Who is this?"

"My name is Rashid Kudratovich Batyrov. I also work at the Ministry of Culture. I happened to overhear that you visited our area yesterday—while I was away on assignment at a venue. You may not know me, and I understand you might not have bothered to come by, but I am acquainted with Tamilla. Has something happened, Sardor Shakhmuradovich?"

"Yes. Tamilla still hasn't returned—it's been a month since the tour began! It's high time she came home. And she hasn't called at all. Her mother and I are terribly worried."

"I understand your concern. I assisted Tamilla with her departure, though I was unaware of the current situation… I simply don't have any contacts in Morocco. But I will try to figure something out—find out what has become of your daughter. I hope nothing serious has befallen her. And if it has, we will resolve it! I promise to fly to Rabat at the earliest opportunity, locate Tamilla and her ensemble, and do my best to bring them all back home."

"I would be deeply grateful! Thank you so much, young man."

"Not at all. All the best!"

The next day, after finishing his urgent work, Batyrov set off, as promised to Tamilla's parents, for Morocco's capital—driven by thoughts of the young woman he could no longer imagine his life without.

*****

Tashkent, 2012

Saltanat could hardly sit still. It had been several days since her parents were abducted and taken hostage. For some reason, Alexei Irmanov hadn't returned her call—clearly, he was extremely busy. The young woman understood that without a power of attorney from her father, she couldn't withdraw money from his bank account to fund the festival and return everything to Irmanov.

Determined, she decided to call Alexei Vadimovich once more. As usual, the phone in his office was answered by Irmanov's stepdaughter, Anastasia.

"Yes, I've passed your request on to Alexei Vadimovich," Anastasia replied in a clipped tone. "No, I'm sorry, he can't come to the phone right now; he's very busy. What is it you want me to tell him? Ah, that you want him to finance the festival again and send someone to Tashkent to oversee the event? Very well. And then, when your father is released, he'll repay Irmanov all the money? Yes, yes—I understand everything. I'll be sure to let him know. But, Saltanat, what if your father doesn't come out of there alive?... Oh, I'm sorry! Alright, I'll remind Dad—that is, Alexei Vadimovich— once more to try to help Rashid Kudratovich."

Saltanat couldn't simply sit back and wait for "the tide to turn." She resolved to take matters into her own hands, to seek any possible means to rescue her parents.

One acquaintance suggested something out of the ordinary— shocking, even:

"Why not seek help from… some gangsters? They may be fearsome—or, as they say nowadays, 'serious' people—but they're reliable. If they say they'll do something, they get it done, without fail—as long as you pay them on time and don't mess around. They'll get your parents out quickly. There's no hope with the police or the prosecutor's office—none of them want to get involved. But perhaps the gangsters will agree!"

After making rounds through the contacts of her fifth and tenth acquaintances, Saltanat finally got hold of the phone number of a former convict. She had to go meet him in person; he refused to discuss her case over the phone.

"No, I don't know who might have tied up your parents," said the ex-con, Timofey Karaev. "But listen, girl. Perhaps there's no one in this whole city who can help you except 'KIR'! You know, it's a criminal syndicate. Though they're dangerous, ruthless thugs. You're not scared, are you?"

"Not when it comes to my mother and father—I'd go to the ends of the earth for them. I'm not afraid."

"Good for you, I respect that! Here's a number for one of them. Write it down! I've heard that their boss is truly formidable. I'm not sure what his exact name is, but since the gang is called 'KIR', I figure their leader must be named Kirill. That's usually how it goes—a gang takes on the name of its chief. And parents are sacred. You got my utmost respect for fighting for them and trying to save them. Good luck!"

"Thank you. I'll never forget your help," Saltanat said.

"Don't thank me just yet. Now go, and act. I truly believe that only this 'KIR'—or rather, its all-powerful boss—can free your parents!"

23

Persia, the 6th century BCE

The servant of Princess Mandane was making his way to his room in the palace at Pasargadae for a brief nap when, suddenly, someone yanked his sleeve.

"Greetings, magnificent Afshin—the most capable and clever of all your mistress's servants!" came a lilting voice. Even in the dim glow of the evening, Afshin immediately recognized the speaker as Artosta, the former maid of Mandane. He knew that Artosta had once tended goats and now often visited his mistress, resorting to blackmail. Beyond that, however, he knew little else about her.

"What do you want from me, you madwoman?" he asked, puzzled, for he had not expected such an abrupt encounter in the dark corridor of the palace.

"Now, now, mind your manners, dear!" chided the illegitimate half-sister of Mandane. "Don't speak so rudely, for I am vindictive and bear grudges. But know this: I am ever grateful to those who help me and serve me faithfully!"

"Who are you to expect me, an attendant of the princess of all Persia, to obey your commands?" Afshin retorted.

"Who am I?!" Artosta's eyes gleamed cunningly, and she let out a soft, conspiratorial laugh—so low that only Afshin could hear. "I am the mother of the king of Media, Persia, and all the world! Rest assured, you will soon see it for yourself when the son I bore—Cyrus—comes here and ascends the throne at Pasargadae!"

Afshin was dumbfounded, his mouth agape in astonishment. "Who?! Mother of the king?!"

He had not expected such a fateful twist. Yet after a moment's thought, he decided that this impudent trickster was merely playing a joke.

"Don't believe me, do you?" Artosta teased. "Then you may ask Cambyses, and he will confirm that Cyrus is indeed our son!"

Oh my gods! She dares to call the prince of Persia himself by his first name—as if he were her brother or her husband! What on earth is happening? thought the perplexed Afshin.

"So, what is it that you desire, my lady?" he inquired, feigning respect with a slightly sarcastic tone, still hoping he was merely the victim of a playful prank.

"Here's what I want. I have a small gift for your mistress," Artosta whispered close to his ear. "You must find a pretext to present it to her—ensuring she never suspects that it was I who delivered it! And it won't do simply to hand her the object; Mandane must actually make use of it! Do you understand?… Hold on! Take it very carefully, through the fabric: it carries a contagion…"

Cautiously, yet with a spark of curiosity, Afshin accepted the gift—swathed in thick cloth—destined for the mistress of the palace.

"And this is for you, keep it!" Artosta then quickly slipped a small pouch, tightly filled with gold coins, into Afshin's other hand. "When I become the honoured mother of King Cyrus the Second, I shall make you my favoured servant—the chief above all others. I give you my word. Do you desire that?"

Greed sparked in Afshin's eyes; the promise of true wealth swayed his reason. Swiftly, he concealed the hefty, though not bulky, reward in his pocket and, bowing low to his new mistress, silently departed.

***

Sakastan, same era

Although Rustam was no stranger to matters of the heart and relationships with the opposite sex, the prospect of lying with a man was entirely new for Tomyris—exciting, nerve-racking, and deeply significant. She hadn't allowed her husband to approach her immediately after their wedding; instead, she took several days to prepare meticulously for their first night together, "freshening up" in her own way.

In a tender tone, she said to him:

"Darling, I beg you… get yourself properly ready."

At first, the mighty warrior didn't understand what the beauty meant.

"What does that mean? I'm always in perfect shape!" he wondered in surprise.

Then it suddenly struck him: he needed a thorough wash—perhaps even more than once—and to apply fragrant balms and oils so that he would smell delightful.

And so he did. When the long-awaited night finally arrived, and Rustam lay beside his beloved, every aspect of him pleased her. His powerful, finely built body exuded a heady fragrance that drew her irresistibly.

Tomyris felt exquisite as she saw how desired she was by her chosen one and how tenderly he regarded her! And how happy Rustam was himself! He savoured every inch of her presence and the intoxicating, mesmerizing scent of his beloved. Her statuesque, flawless figure, her ample, soft bosom, her doe-like black eyes, and the cascade of golden hair—all drove him wild. And her scent! What a divine aroma it was! It bewitched Rustam, and Tomyris could see his unrestrained, passionate desire for her.

This idyllic phase lasted for several nights. The young woman devised clever ways to prolong the anticipation of physical ecstasy in her man's soul, transforming him into a restless stallion or a ravenous wild beast! She revelled in the feeling—the illusion of absolute power over a man…

Then, however, things began to change. At times, Tomyris deliberately interrupted his pleasure in possessing her body, holding him back for a while. She was a little afraid that it might provoke

Rustam's anger. Yet, in reality, her playful teasing tormented him terribly. But like a subjugated slave, he dared not show anger or demand anything from her; instead, he pleaded with her to continue their union.

More than anything, he thought only of one thing: that she would always be by his side, that she would never abandon or cast him out—for to him, that would be death. And after such playful games, Tomyris almost always eventually allowed him back into her embrace, keeping him close until he cried out like a falcon diving for its coveted prey.

But one morning… Rustam awoke and found that Tomyris was no longer beside him.

"Wife, my love!" he called out loudly, but there was no reply.

He looked around; his wife was nowhere to be seen in their tent.

Rustam's heart sank. Had she been taken away again? Abducted right from under his nose?!

He quickly dressed and dashed out of the tent. To his immense relief and joy, his beloved was seated a short distance away on a large stone, gazing off into the distance.

Rustam approached her and draped a warm garment over her shoulders—since it was very chilly, and she had dressed rather lightly.

"My dear, I was so worried… What made you get up so early and leave without a word? Did I somehow offend you last night? Was something amiss?"

Tomyris remained silent, and for some reason, she looked at him with a touch of disdain. Had she been an ordinary Saka woman rather than the daughter of the Massagetean king, and had he been any other Saka warrior instead of the noblest of heroes, he would have torn her to pieces on the spot for such disrespect towards a man—and especially toward her husband!

Yet Rustam couldn't hide how deeply he adored her. All his life he was ready—not to strike or scold—but to carry her in his arms! If only she would let him, if only she would allow it… For Tomyris firmly believed that men—except, perhaps, her father, King Spargapis the First—were made primarily to be the slaves of women.

Rustam sat down beside her, at the edge of the same stone, and waited patiently for her answer.

"You shall never touch me again, mighty warrior," the Massagetean princess finally declared, "and you will never lie beside me again. Never."

Rustam was stunned. For so many days and nights, everything between them had been so wonderful! He had believed they were both completely happy—even when she, with a severity unbefitting a young woman, tormented and teased him. What could have suddenly changed?

"Do you… no longer love me, Tomyris?" he asked sadly.

"Why? I do love you. Well… perhaps. I don't know. But that's not the point, Rustam—understand!"

"And what is it then, my dear?"

"I can't quite figure it out yet, let alone explain it. You just have to wait. Perhaps things will eventually get better… At least, when I understand it fully, I'll let you know."

"Alright. But… will we still see each other, still live together?"

"Yes, of course. Like brother and sister. But you mustn't mention a word of this to my father!"

"As you wish, my lady," her husband replied obediently, without a hint of protest.

* * *

Persia, same era

Princess Mandana had not seen the son she always considered her very own for many months, and she missed him dearly. Her eager anticipation for his arrival had even touched her husband, Cambyses. The Prince of Persia already imagined wrapping his strong arms around his beloved son—the very one destined to free his country from the long oppression of the cruel Medes.

At last, the much-anticipated day of Cyrus the Second's arrival at Pasargadae had come. However, spies brought word of a most astonishing development to Cambyses: King Cyrus was returning not with a retinue—or even merely with a Persian force—but with a vast Median-Persian army!

This could mean only one thing: a violent seizure of power.

Deep down, the Prince of Persia was both outraged and deeply insulted by his son's actions.

Nevertheless, Cambyses and Mandana welcomed Cyrus warmly—as loving parents should—without reproach or admonition. Yet, when they were alone with Cyrus, Cambyses was the first to propose:

"Tell me, my dear, would you like us to arrange your coronation in Persia as soon as tomorrow?"

Cyrus looked carefully at his father, wary of any hidden catch or trap. But Cambyses regarded his son with sincere kindness, his gaze open and honest. Still, to put any lingering doubts to rest, Cambyses explained further:

"It seems you're surprised? But, my dear son, you are my

whole life—my very reason for being! I have ordered the very best chambers in this palace for you, far superior to any you've known before! Your mother and I have long awaited your return. However—pardon me—we did not expect such a colossal host to arrive with you… So, you'll have to see to their comfort yourself. Most likely, your many warriors will have to camp outside for now!"

Cyrus flushed with embarrassment, realizing that by returning to his homeland and his parents' home as an invader, he had indeed overstepped all bounds.

Yet, shortly afterward, as he left Cambyses' private chambers, he mused, *On the other hand, who really knows this prince? He is practically a stranger to me—I did not even grow up before his eyes.*

The new king of Media was so eager to swiftly claim both Media and Persia that he eventually accepted Cambyses's proposal for his immediate coronation. And the very next day, Cyrus the Second was proclaimed King of Media and Persia.

A month later, a cholera epidemic broke out in Persia, claiming many lives. The palace, however, was rigorously guarded against any contagion—few were allowed inside, and nearly no one was permitted to leave—while every item brought into the palace, from food and clothing to utensils, was scrutinized with the utmost care. Meanwhile, Cyrus began considering a permanent move to Ekbatana, where he believed he'd be safer.

Then another shock swept through all of Persia, astonishing both Cambyses and Cyrus: another victim of the cholera outbreak was… Princess Mandana.

Afshin, the poor, devoted servant of the princess, wept bitterly by her bedside—hesitant even to touch the carrier of such a deadly infection. Clutched in Mandane's hand was a bright, beautiful handkerchief embroidered with silk threads—a piece that seemed entirely new to Cambyses, for he had never seen it on his wife before.

Yet the greatest mystery was not the handkerchief itself, but rather the question: how could the princess have contracted the infection? After all, she had not left the palace for months, had not mingled with the sick, nor touched those who had died in the epidemic—although she always pitied those unfortunate souls. Instead, she had helped them from a distance by sending supplies and food to the ill, but she had never come into direct contact with them. It was all so strange… so very strange.

"Increase the palace's security measures!" ordered King Cyrus. "We must investigate to discover how and why Mand—my mother—died."

That very day, as planned, Cyrus departed for Media with his army. His grandfather, Astyages—no longer residing in the luxurious palace of Ekbatana but confined to a dungeon—had attempted, through one of his former servants, to poison the new king of Media and Persia. On Cyrus's orders, Astyages was immediately put to death. Astyages' prophetic dream about Cyrus had come true. The former king was buried with honours in the royal tombs of Ekbatana.

Cambyses and his new wife, Artosta, did not love Mandane enough to investigate the causes of her death. And poor Afshin—who possessed no such rights or authority and had little time left for mourning—was soon absorbed by his duties. No sooner had the days of mourning for Mandane ended than Afshin began to serve his new mistress faithfully—her late sister, who now, as she had instructed, was to be called Princess Artosta.

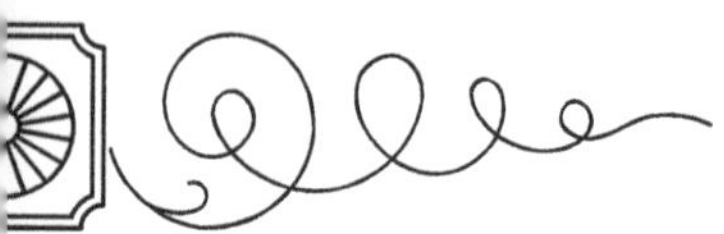

***

In the months and years that followed, Cyrus, overcoming resistance from the local populace, seized the lands that had once belonged to the former Median state—Parthia, Armenia, and others—as well as Cilicia and Lydia. Hyrcania submitted to him voluntarily. During those same years, his Persian-Median army captured the entire territory of Elam, and later, Ionia, Caria, and Lycia.

Cyrus's general, Harpagus, began building high earthworks against the walled Greek cities, then took them by storm. The inhabitants of Phocaea, the largest Greek city in Asia Minor after Miletus, refused to submit to the Persians. They fled by ship first to the island of Cyrnus, and then to Italy, to the city of Rhegion, where they founded a colony.

The people of Teos followed the example of the Phocaeans and relocated to Abdera in Thrace. The remaining Ionian cities—except for Miletus, which had earlier forged an alliance with Cyrus—tried to resist Harpagus. However, defeated, they were subjugated and subjected to tribute. After Harpagus subdued the Ionians on the mainland, the Ionian islanders, fearing the same fate, surrendered to Cyrus without a fight.

Because he needed the Greeks as seafarers, Cyrus did not worsen their conditions compared to those they had endured under Croesus, the former king of Lydia.

Having subdued Ionia, Cyrus and Harpagus marched against the Carians, the Kaunians, and the Lycians, taking along with them the Ionians and Aeolians. The people of Caria surrendered to the Persians without a fight, offering no acts of self-defence against the occupiers. Indeed, the inhabitants of Knidos, situated on a peninsula, attempted to dig through the very narrow isthmus separating them from the mainland to turn their land into an island. Yet they encountered solid granite, halted their efforts, and were forced to surrender without resistance. Only one tribe of the Carians—the Pedasians—offered some measure of resistance to Cyrus. They fortified themselves on Mount Lide and caused Harpagus considerable trouble. In the end, however, they too were subdued.

Only the Lycians and the Kaunians in Asia Minor put up fierce resistance against the numerous Persian forces, meeting them in open battle. Cyrus and Harpagus drove the Lycians back to their city of Xanthos, where, gathering their wives, children, and servants in the acropolis, they set it on fire. The Lycian warriors themselves perished in combat with the Persians. The Kaunians resisted just as stubbornly, but these small peoples could not halt the advance of the large and heavily armed Persian-Median army.

All of Asia Minor thus fell under Persian rule. In reward for his loyalty, Harpagus received Lydia from King Cyrus as a hereditary domain. But Cyrus completely forgot that he had once called this man his father. He treated him like a servant—a slave.

***

Sakastan, the Same Period

Spargapis kept racking his brain: who could have played such a cruel trick on him and his beloved daughter? Who had dared abduct her?... He did not want to believe that all the clues pointed to Salih... Yet the king of the Massagetae nonetheless ordered the new chieftain of the Abii to be brought before him for judgment.

"Bring him here with full honours, so that this mangy dog does not suspect my wrath too soon!" Spargapis commanded the servants who went to fetch his late wife's kinsman.

When Salih arrived at the royal encampment, Spargapis himself came out to greet him, skilfully feigning the customary hospitality and warmth with which he had always welcomed his best friend. They embraced firmly.

The king invited his guest into his tent, where a lavish feast awaited.

"Summon Tomyris in my name!" Spargapis ordered his servants. "It will do her good to hear our conversation with her great-uncle. And I believe he will also be glad to see her!"

Ordinarily, women did not attend men's feasts, but Tomyris was a princess, and everything was permissible for her. Besides, her father himself had invited her, and in his presence no one would dare cast an improper gaze at his daughter, especially since she was a married woman.

Spargapis decided that Tomyris had the right to learn firsthand the motives and circumstances of her harrowing imprisonment— to look the villain straight in the eye.

He strove to appear relaxed, doing his best to hide his tension and anger.

When a special dish was placed before the guest, covered by a deep clay plate, Spargapis's eyes gleamed with malicious satisfaction for some reason.

Meanwhile, Salih was in high spirits from the sweet, heady haoma, and the reunion with dear friends had further lifted his mood. But when he uncovered the dish by removing the clay plate, he was left perplexed, astonished, and furious. Lying before him…

was a raw human liver, still bloody, and a severed finger bearing a ring.

"Go on—have a taste, my dear friend!" Spargapis said loudly and mockingly. "Here you have what you wanted from me! Forgive me, though, for not cutting out my own liver or slicing off my own finger with the royal signet! This is from one of our Massagetae warriors who died in a recent battle. But what's the difference for a jackal that feeds on carrion—am I right? Look, the liver is still full of human blood! Go on and drink it, murderer! And don't you dare ever lay a hand on me or my daughter again! You will die this very day!"

Salih leapt to his feet and instinctively reached for the hilt of his acinaces. But the dagger was missing. He suddenly remembered that, upon entering the royal tent, as was customary, the doorkeepers had taken his weapons—no one was permitted to enter the king's quarters armed. Crestfallen, Salih sank back down to his seat.

Tomyris stopped eating; in such an atmosphere, not a single morsel could be swallowed.

"I don't understand, my king, what you mean by all this..." the Massagetae guest said in bewilderment. "What did your loyal friend Salih do to deserve such offensive treatment? How have I wronged you or Tomyris?... When your men came to invite me here, their sugary tone indeed put me on my guard. But at the time, I paid no special attention to that strange feeling, for I do not recall any wrongdoing toward either of you! This liver, this finger—they're horrors, as if I were some kind of monster or cannibal. What were you implying by that? I'm your friend and the friend of your—"

"Yes, I know what you're about to say!" Spargapis flared up. "That you were once a close friend of my wife, Zaryana! Isn't that right? But remember, chieftain of the Abii, out of the two of us,

Zaryana chose only me! She rejected you, despite having known you all her life. As for the recent threats against me—don't play the fool or pretend it had nothing to do with you, you treacherous serpent! Go on, claim that it wasn't your people who recently orchestrated my daughter's kidnapping!"

"What?! Tomyris… was kidnapped by someone?!" Salih exclaimed, genuinely astonished and indignant. "Who dared? If I find that villain, I'll strangle him myself for harming our dear little girl. Tomyris, tell your uncle Salih what happened to you!"

Tomyris disliked this entire scene her father was staging. She had no wish to recall such distressing events, much less recount them to a beloved relative she knew had once been a faithful friend to her mother.

"Uncle, forgive me, I don't…" She cast her eyes down, ashamed of her father, and fell silent.

"Those villains kept my beloved child in a dank prison for many days, where she went hungry and slept among rats! And in exchange for Tomyris, they demanded… my life! How dare they? And you say you had nothing to do with all this?!"

"I fear, mighty king," Salih sighed sadly, "that you have forgotten what true friendship is… And I suspect you judge other people by yourself! You've taken me for a monster, a serpent? Was it not you who once killed this dear girl's mother—beautiful Zaryana—by your own hand? Perhaps you've hidden that truth all these years from your daughter so she wouldn't condemn you?…"

Tomyris felt a lump form in her throat; her heart nearly stopped. What she heard horrified her. The Massagetae princess looked questioningly at her father. Spargapis, enraged at Salih, flushed red and turned away from his daughter, at a loss for words.

"Uncle, what are you saying?! My own father… killed my…"

She could not bear the thought.

Tomyris dashed out of the royal tent and ran, not even knowing where she was heading. Soon, exhausted, she collapsed onto the frozen ground and burst into desperate sobs…

24

Marrakesh, Morocco, 1981

Tamilla opened her eyes. Sunlight was already streaming insistently through the windows of her hotel room, which, in order to save money, she was sharing with her ensemble's lead vocalist, Irina. But Irina's bed was empty—that surprised Tamilla.

"Probably, as usual, Irka went down to the bar to chat with someone," thought the leader of the band.

Tamilla got up and immediately made her bed neatly. Still, something felt off. Right! Normally, Irina's belongings were scattered all over the room—a habit that had often annoyed the tidy Tamilla. Now, though… there wasn't a single one of her friend's things here. Where could they have gone? Tamilla opened the wardrobe—only her own clothes were inside.

She stepped out of the room and knocked on the doors of two other rooms occupied by her musicians. No answer. No one opened. This was all very strange. They simply could not have left—or even gone anywhere—without her!

Tamilla returned to her room and tried calling reception right away. The line was busy. She decided not to waste time and went straight downstairs to speak with the hotel staff.

"Ah! One moment, please, let me check," said a polite young Moroccan woman in a hotel uniform bearing the establishment's logo. "Yes, ma'am, it's correct. All those people you just named left the hotel early this morning."

Tamilla was in shock. How could that be? It was beyond comprehension!

How could these shallow, barely educated people—so dependent on her in every way—just up and abandon her, betray her, ditch her? Unthinkable!

Tamilla went back to her room.

Just in case, she checked the drawers in her nightstand. Luckily, her documents and her cell phone were still there, but her money… all the money was gone. Vanished! She searched the entire room, looked everywhere, turned her suitcase inside out several times— no sign of the funds she had set aside for the group's upcoming tour (and it was no small sum). She now understood everything.

"Not only did they run off like traitors, they robbed me as well!" Tamilla thought, outraged.

She decided to call Mr. Abbad's office—the man who had invited her ensemble to Morocco. Yet, to her great surprise, the esteemed gentleman, according to his secretary, did not wish to speak on the phone or, much less, meet with Miss Mahkamoff. Let the lady forgive him, but no, he couldn't help her.

Only a couple of days earlier, after their concert in Rabat, they had been getting along splendidly—everything had been simply wonderful! Now… all of it was very, very strange.

***

Casablanca, Morocco, the Next Day

Tamilla's now "headless" musical band—without Tamilla herself—finished giving its first independent concert, organized by Mustafa Abbad and led onstage by vocalist Irina. Afterward, the group headed to a city hotel in one of the jeeps that Abbad had generously provided for the Tashkent musicians during the entire tour.

"Still, Irka, I think we did a bad thing to Tamilla," began Sasha the guitarist timidly. He had always been fond of the group's founder and, until recently, its director.

"Yeah, I agree with Sanya!" nodded Andrei the bass player. "I've got a nasty feeling about this. And what stories we spun for that Abbad about poor Tamillka."

"It wasn't *we*—Irka's the one who spun those stories!" Alexander corrected him. "Pure lies! Telling him Miss Mahkamoff supposedly called him a 'stupid, fat turkey.' Naturally, he's furious at her now! And in reality, she never said anything of the sort."

Misha the keyboardist remained silent for the moment.

"Everything's fine, guys," Irina responded coolly. "What are you fussing about? It's only fair. Tamilla got what she deserved. She never treated us—or rather, you men—as actual people! We do all the work, and she collects the percentages. Don't you get it? She's pocketing our money! She signed all the contracts by herself. She barely consulted us on the routes or the schedule—always decided everything on her own! Where and when we needed to go, what time we'd perform, how many concerts to do, or not do. Like we're total idiots who don't understand anything."

"Well, that was normal," Andrei objected. "She was our finance manager, producer, boss. Besides, Tamilla's a real strategist—she plans everything ahead, down to the last detail. She's the only one who can handle negotiations in a 'commercial language' with foreigners and push them to pay a proper, decent fee… She always somehow knows what kind of audience will be in each venue, and which songs will work for one crowd or another. She's the reason we succeeded."

"Exactly! She knows so much—way more than us rookies!" Sasha burst out, more upset than anyone. "Tamilla speaks multiple languages and understands the customs and traditions of each country we visit. She's a very gifted person, even though she's not a musician. You dealt with her harshly, Irka, and we're going to have a tough time without our… well…"

"Without your beloved Tamillochka, is that what you mean?" Irina sneered. "I know you've been in love with her for ages. But she never let you get close, because to that spoiled daughter of a rich factory director, you're just not on her level!"

"We've arrived, guys. Let's calm down and go get some sleep," interjected Mikhail for the first time since they got in the jeep. "Tomorrow we've got a long trip to another city and, in the evening, a big concert. We need some proper rest. We can decide tomorrow if we'll go back to Tamilla or not. But generally, I'm with Irina. It's high time we had our freedom and independence. We're musicians, not soldiers in an army. I'm going to my room. Good night, all."

"Still, we really ought to bring Tamilla back into the group!" Sasha insisted as he got out of the vehicle.

He felt a particular guilt toward the founder and, until recently, head of the band—both for himself and for the others. Yes, she had turned down the idea of a relationship with him, politely brushing him aside. But even so… he shouldn't have betrayed her.

"Besides," Sasha added, "we have no idea about the customs and mentality of Moroccans, but Tamilla does. You'll see—it'll be impossible to handle this tour without her… Honestly, I shouldn't have gone along with you guys in the first place. This whole thing is just wrong."

* * *

Moscow, that same 1981

"Denis, what are you doing—getting up? Are you leaving again?"

"Yes, it's already two in the morning. I really need to get home. Marina will worry."

Lying beside Farida, Denis wrapped one arm around her body and used his other hand to stroke her silky hair. But Farida was in no mood for tenderness now. Her face took on a look of anger, and to Denis it seemed even more captivating that way.

"Marina, Marina!! It's been the same story for a whole year. When are you finally going to tell her about us and move in with me for good?"

"Farida, darling, I can't… I'm sorry. And don't tempt me, like some ancient serpent."

"If it hadn't been for me, you and my so-called 'adopted sister' would've split up long ago!"

"Don't say that. You know I lov—"

"Yes, I've heard it a hundred times already!!" Farida shouted, cutting off the words she didn't want to hear. "But have you

forgotten one little 'detail'—that because of her artificial valve, she hasn't been able to have real sex for a few years now? You were furious about that a year ago, and she was upset with you too!"

"Everything was fine between us!"

"Oh sure, right! Notice you said 'was.' It's been a long time since it was fine. You two were always fighting—over her endless refusals, how she just lay there like a plastic doll, and over Kirill, too!"

This time, he said nothing—he really had no comeback.

"Basically, I've been a fool," continued Marina's 'sister.' "I should have waited until you completely stopped loving her and dumped her! I shouldn't have gotten involved with you so soon. By comforting you, I've only solidified myself as the third wheel. But, you know the saying: 'The night cuckoo always outcalls the day cuckoo.' Sooner or later, you're going to be mine, Denis—only mine! After all, we're both under forty; we're not old."

"Faridka, forgive me. I was the fool for leaving you so many years ago. And why didn't I see your beauty sooner?! But I really do love Marina… She and I have so much in common. She's smart, educated, reliable, faithful. She loves me deeply. I'm used to her. And I feel sorry for her. She's helpless—she'd be lost without me. With you… you see… I don't think it's love. It's more like an animal passion, a sickness. You attract me, mesmerize me, intoxicate me! When I don't see you, I'm a normal, healthy man. But the moment I lay eyes on you—especially if you're naked—I become like a drunken tomcat, chasing only after you, wanting only you!"

"What will you do if she finds out about us?"

At those words, Denis flared up, got nervous, jumped up, and began to dress hurriedly.

"I hope, Farida, you're not so stupid as to tell Marina

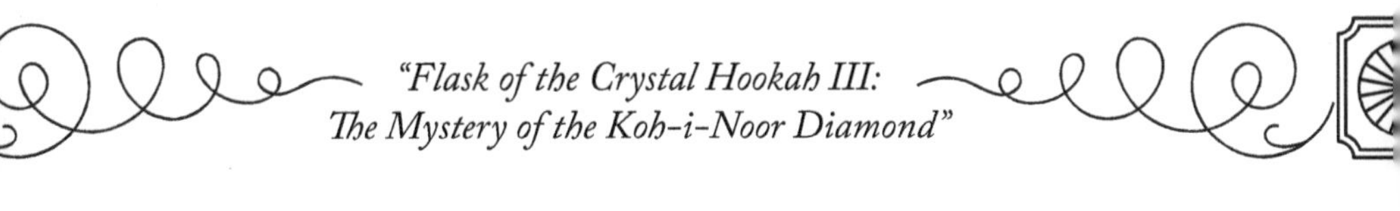

everything?!"

"Of course not, darling, not that stupid. Just make sure you don't give yourself away! I don't want her, with that weak heart of hers, having a second heart attack! So go on—keep lying and squirming. You men love to do that!"

* * *

Morocco, 1981

No sooner had Rashid Batyrov arrived in the country than, after dropping his things off in his hotel room, he decided to contact the organization that, as he'd found out, had invited Tamilla Mahkamova and her pop group on tour. Mr. Abbad wasn't there— he had left on a business trip for several days. But his assistant indicated to "Mister Batiroff from Uzbekistan" where the ensemble touring Morocco could be found. That same day, Rashid took a commuter bus to Casablanca.

Tracking down the Tashkent musicians wasn't difficult. There weren't many Uzbek performers giving concerts in that fine city at the time—or in the country, for that matter. Rashid waited for them at the exit of the concert hall.

Everyone in the group was in low spirits—the concert had been lacklustre. On top of that, rumours were spreading throughout the country, tarnishing their reputation. Unaware of Moroccan customs, the guys had made a major blunder after their previous two concerts: they showed up to banquets held in their honour... empty-handed, without bringing any gifts. They had assumed their music alone would be enough. But around here, you just didn't do that.

Their troubles, however, were of little interest to Rashid. He immediately started asking the members of the band about Tamilla—where she was, why she wasn't with them, what was going on.

"How could you abandon your leader like that?!" Rashid exclaimed indignantly when he heard what had gone on between them. "I understand that people can disagree, that sometimes creative groups fall apart. But to leave a girl in a foreign country without even enough money for a plane ticket home? That's too much, sorry—even for the worst of scoundrels! And not once in all these days did you call her to see where she is or how she's doing! Maybe she's starving somewhere…"

"To be honest, I did call her—many times," Sasha tried to defend himself. "But she won't pick up. Maybe her phone's turned off."

"Of course it's off!" Rashid raged. The musicians listened in silence, not interrupting or arguing, because deep down they each felt guilty. "Did it ever occur to you she might have run out of money? Her parents in Tashkent are going out of their minds because she hasn't phoned in so long. Obviously she can't—who knows where she's even sleeping, how she's eating, now that she's broke?"

"You don't know Tamilla very well," Mikhail, usually the calmest, tried objecting. "Tamilla is smart and has a strong spirit; she won't just vanish. She'll cope."

"I'd like to believe that," Rashid sighed wearily. "But tell me what to do now? Unlike you all, I actually need her—and I care about her! How can I find her and bring her home?"

"Why don't you go back to Marrakesh," suggested Alexander. "Here, take this flyer from the hotel where we stayed. Maybe she's still there. If not, maybe someone there knows something. And I promise I'll do my best through concert channels to see if anyone's heard of Tamilla Mahkamova from Uzbekistan. Too bad she's not a singer or musician—it'd be easier to track her down. Anyway, here's my contact info. If you hear anything, call me anytime. That's your number? All right. If I learn anything, I'll call you right away! Goodbye, Rashid."

Irina, who had been silent the whole time, gave Sasha a disgruntled look—she didn't like how hard he was trying on Tamilla's behalf, nor the fact that he just couldn't (or wouldn't) forget her…

* * *

Moscow, that same 1981

Thanks to the connections of Konstantin—respected in the criminal underworld—Kirill Midiyatdinov was spared from being sent to the Siberian lumber camps. Instead, along with Kostya, he ended up in one of Moscow's more lenient prisons. And given the large sums of money this young "godfather" possessed, he, Konstantin, and a couple of other gangsters were living there almost like they were in a luxury hotel suite.

Kirill practically worshiped Kostya, regarded him as a teacher and mentor, obeyed him in everything, and tried to be just like him. Whatever Konstantin said or ordered, Kirill carried out without question, barely even thinking about it. In this way, Kirill grew in stature—he became someone the other inmates feared more and more.

One day, Konstantin ordered Kirill to frame one of their fellow gang members and have that man, "using his own hands," stab to death an inmate named Dmitry Bobrov, with whom Koschei-Kostyan had a personal score to settle. Dmitry was an authority figure in his own right and had refused to bow to Koschei or pay him tribute. No matter how Koschei tried to force "Dimon the Defiant" to kneel, it never worked. This offended and enraged Konstantin to the point where he decided it was time for Dima to leave this mortal coil. And he needed to "set up" yet another "disobedient" inmate—Vladislav Petrenko—to take the fall as the scapegoat.

Young Midiyatdinov deftly carried out everything Koschei ordered. Everyone knew the truth—or at least suspected it—but kept their mouths shut. Vladislav received a sizable sentence extension for murder, while Konstantin and Kirill emerged, so to speak, with clean hands. After that, people feared them both even more.

* * *

Marrakesh, Morocco, that same year

On his way back from Casablanca to Marrakesh, Rashid marveled at himself: in a short time, Tamilla had come to mean so much to him—far more than two years before. Now she was constantly on his mind; she had become a treasure for his soul, a precious diamond.

Rashid already understood that he wasn't searching for her simply because her parents worried about her and he had promised to find her. He felt that if he didn't see her soon, didn't hold her tightly in his arms, he would go insane. And suddenly, he realized his concern for her had a peculiar nature: on the one hand, it was genuine worry for a girl dear to his heart. On the other hand, his heart was free of panic or anxiety—there was no sense of hopeless despair. For some reason, he had a bright certainty that some invisible higher power was protecting his beloved, preventing any misfortune.

The lover's instinct did not mislead him. When he inquired about Tamilla Mahkamova at the hotel where she had been staying with her musicians, it turned out that not only was she still living there (albeit now in a much more modest room), but she was also… working there!

"Rashid, what brings you to Morocco?" Tamilla asked, surprised, when they met and shared a warm, friendly hug. "And how did you find me?"

"Tamilla, hello! I bring you greetings from your parents. They're worried about you. And truth be told, I came here just for you, to take you home."

"That's wonderful!" The young woman smiled, but Rashid could sense tears behind that smile. She noticed his concern. "No, no, my friend, don't worry. I'm all right! The hotel management kindly agreed to give me temporary work—no formal papers, just cash wages. It's true I'm longing to go home, but I can't yet afford a return ticket."

"I can help you with that, if you'll allow me. But may I ask what kind of work you're doing here?"

Rashid posed the question, fearing the reply would be "cleaning staff," since he knew that in situations like Tamilla's, there usually weren't many other options. If it was that, it would still be better than nothing. He imagined how little she might be earning.

"Because I speak several languages, they offered me a job as an interpreter with tour guides. The hotel has many guests—tourists from all over the world—and most of the local guides don't know English, French, or let alone Russian. Though Russian tourists rarely come here anyway. The guides explain the sights in Arabic or Tamazight (one of the Berber dialects), and I go along on the excursions, translating for the foreign tourists."

"Tamilla, you are so—"

"So what?" she asked with a mischievous laugh, noticing the admiration and enchantment in this man's eyes—eyes so appealing to her—and guessing what he wanted to say.

"You're brilliant! And besides that—a real beauty, and… you have no idea how wonderful you are!"

"Oh, enough, dear Rashid, don't make me blush," she smiled. "So when can we fly to Tashkent?"

"Anytime you like—tomorrow morning on the earliest flight," beamed the man who was head over heels in love.

Rashid felt completely happy in this young woman's presence—especially now that she'd been found and he could see that she was safe and sound. He thrilled at the thought that she would fly home to her family—with him!

* * *

Tashkent, 1982

"Sasha, I'm asking you to leave. Why did you even come here?"

"You know why, Tamilla. We need to talk!"

"Rashid will be here soon, and he won't like another man being in his fiancée's home, even if my parents are here."

"Yes, I know about your wedding. That's precisely why I came. Listen, you can't go through with this!"

"I beg your pardon—can't do what?"

"You know exactly what I mean. I'm begging you—not to marry him! He isn't worthy of you!"

"And who is worthy?" she asked with a smirk. "Could it be you? The guy who swore he'd love me forever, then, in a single moment, abandoned me and ran off for money or some other dubious temptation?"

"But you wouldn't be my girlfriend back then. You turned me down."

She smirked again.

"You could have fought for my attention, tried to win me over, instead of giving up straight away. Where are your actions, not just words?

Rashid, for example…"

"I wasn't thinking about that. And… yes, yes, Tamilla, I know—I'm guilty of betraying you! I'm a fool and a scoundrel. Irka engineered it all so cleverly back then, persuaded all of us. I was an idiot to give in to her plan for us all to become 'free and independent.' And that freedom and independence led to the group breaking up. We haven't had any decent tours in a long time. Without you, it's like we've lost our breath of life—our creativity, our inspiration! Come on, please come back to us, okay? Bring us all back together—minus that fox Irka. You could easily find a different vocalist here in Tashkent; there are lots of good singers now! But there's only one of you, Tamilla. You're unique. We've realized you were the true soul of our group—our muse!!"

From the faint smell of alcohol on his breath, she could tell there was more he wanted to say, something else he meant.

"I see, Sanya, why you're inviting me. You're also hoping to rekindle things between us. Right?"

"Well, yes—that too," Sasha admitted. And then, weakly and without much conviction, he added, "Tamilla, you know I love you."

"Sanya, understand this: real love doesn't vanish in a heartbeat at the first sign of betrayal. What you felt was infatuation, euphoria, maybe the illusion of true emotion—but not actual love. Besides, don't you get it? I don't love you. I love another man, one who's decent and faithful. I'm sorry."

* * *

Moscow, that same year

The police had to break down the apartment door.

They found Farida Midiyatdinova lying dead, covered in blood, her body already cold, on the floor of her bedroom. According to the forensic expert, she had died that morning—sometime between nine and ten o'clock—from a severe blow to the back of the head with a blunt object.

Neighbors of Farida testified that they had repeatedly seen a good-looking, fair-haired man of about forty (maybe a bit younger) visiting her. One witness claimed to have heard Farida, on that very morning, loudly arguing with him—or perhaps with some other middle-aged man.

Whoever she had been quarreling with was obviously the one who finished her off, concluded Investigator Evgeny Volobuyev, without spending too much time or effort on the case.

Several days later, after the funeral, the victim's relatives were questioned. Her grief-stricken and unsuspecting sister, Marina

Persieva, said that she and Farida had always loved each other dearly, that from childhood onward they had been close.

"My husband?" repeated Marina Shamilyevna. "Ah, his name is Denis. No, he wasn't at home at eight o'clock in the morning—he'd already gone out somewhere."

"Did he tell you where?"

"No, no, he didn't. Why would he? You see, my husband and I have complete mutual trust! We never interrogate each other or suspect each other of anything. We think it's best not to share absolutely everything with our better half—sometimes it can hurt them. But, Comrade Investigator, do you suspect us of something?!"

The investigator remained silent.

"Well, good if you don't. In any event, I think—no, I'm certain—that Denis was already at work by then. You know, he's a well-educated man, a geography teacher at a school. The kids adore him, especially the girls; he's very handsome. My husband works hard; he takes on two shifts. I'm mostly at home because of my health, tending the family hearth!"

...The investigation, however, established that Denis Persiev had not been at school during that hour—he had taken off the first two lessons for some personal matter.

Volobuyev's inquiries also revealed that Persiev had been involved in a secret intimate relationship with the deceased Farida Midiyatdinova. It was clear that he absolutely did not want his wife to find out. The neighbors said that—based on what they could hear through walls and open windows—the argument on that fateful morning was about exactly that. Farida had been quarreling with her suitor, and it was he who was shouting.

That was an obvious and serious motive. Acting on a warrant from the investigator, officers arrested Denis Persiev and took him to a pretrial detention center.

"I didn't kill her! It wasn't me!" Persiev kept protesting, looking terrified.

The case, backed by various pieces of evidence, was sent to trial. The defendant's wife, Marina Persieva, could neither believe nor accept what she was hearing: her beloved husband—together with her beloved sister—had cheated on her! How could that be?!

Shattered by the sudden revelation, poor Marina suffered a cardiac episode. In tears, distraught and humiliated by her own family, the poor soul was taken by ambulance to the hospital.

Persiev was sentenced to ten years in a high-security penal colony for murder. Colonel Oleg Midiyatdinov of the Ministry of Internal Affairs, though he felt some regret for his murdered half-sister Farida, chose not to interfere in the case. He was expecting a prosecutorial review and was busy preparing for it in every possible way: buying delicacies, wines, and cognacs to treat the visiting inspectors.

* * *

Tashkent, still 1982

"Rashid, my dear…" began Tamilla slowly, as though weighing each word. "I agreed to marry you on one condition: that you cut ties forever with all the women from your past!"

"My love, you talk as if I were some Casanova with a whole string of women," Rashid Batyrov laughed, stroking her gentle hands and kissing her cheeks.

"Doesn't matter how many—even if it was just one—forget her, got it? Otherwise… I'll kill you both!"

Of course, Rashid understood that this kind-hearted woman was speaking figuratively, only threatening in jest. But he decided to play along a little.

"I'm terrified of you, my mistress and lady, my fierce and warlike Queen Tomyris! In order to stay alive, I wouldn't dare even think of disobeying!"

"There you go, joking again," said Batyrov's fiancée with a slight frown. "Meanwhile, I've made a big decision for you and for our future family: I'm not going back to the pop stage anymore, and I've broken off all contact with my former admirers. You know I do research, and I've already defended my PhD in the arts."

"Yes, you've done great things! I'm sure success awaits you in anything you do. And by the way, I really appreciate all your sacrifices for my sake, oh ruler of my heart!"

Rashid laughed cheerfully.

"So now you're being sarcastic about my success too? You don't believe in me? You're mocking me, huh?"

"Not at all! I'm being perfectly serious about that. It's just that… well, Tamilla… Honestly, it pleases me that you're jealous and that you value our relationship so much!"

"Then let's agree, Rashid, that we'll never keep any secrets from each other and will always speak only the truth, okay?"

"Of course! I'll do my best. But if I realize that the truth might hurt you terribly, then… For instance…"

Rashid paused, wondering whether or not to tell Tamilla about Lena, the coworker at the Ministry of Culture. After all, Lena meant nothing to him—he wasn't to blame that she'd gotten strange ideas in her head.

He decided to start gently, carefully:

"Tamilla… well, there was a girl who loved me—or rather, used to love me… Her name is Lena; she and I—"

"Oh, darling, I don't need the details! Please spare me. If you want to be my husband, forget all these Lenas forever. Agreed?"

"Of course, I understand. It'll be done, as you command, my lady!!"

After the wedding, Tamilla Mahkamova, who kept her father's surname, moved into the apartment of her husband, Rashid Batyrov—an apartment newly furnished with beautiful furniture.

Their honeymoon was like a fairy tale. The newlyweds went off to the Maldives, where they blissfully revelled in each other's company.

A few months later, Tamilla became pregnant. Rashid, not so young anymore, was overjoyed.

25

Sakastan, 6th Century BCE

About a year had passed since the last events.

The young king of the Saka Tigraxauda, Zogak, already knew that his uncle Sakesfar and his son Skun continued to dream of the throne. Zogak had heard that both of them were currently hiding among the Haomovarga, with whom neither Kavad nor Zogak maintained any contact. And though Skun's father had failed to seize the Tigraxauda throne from his elder brother Kavad, Skun, now grown, was certain that, with his father's help, he would not miss the chance to appear suddenly among his kin, harboring the most aggressive intentions.

Zogak realized he needed to properly prepare for a meeting with his dear relatives and not lose face before them—especially because there were concerns he might lose the throne. Many of the Saka Tigraxauda were dissatisfied with Zogak's rule. Only with the cunning assistance of his wife, Nastaran, had he managed to keep them in check and prevent any rebellion.

"And this Skun—he's handsome, is he?" Nastaran once asked her husband, without the slightest hint of embarrassment.

"He's all right," replied the king of the Saka Tigraxauda. "But why do you ask?"

Like I'd tell you! his "beloved" thought to herself. *If Skun were to become king here instead of Zogak, I would do anything to make him my husband! And Zogak can go wherever he pleases then—provided he isn't killed before that… Too bad our king, my husband, isn't the hero Rustam. Rustam is so splendid, strong, and brave—and I like him so much! He chose a wife from another tribe, that Massagetean woman, Tomyris. And how am I any worse than she is?! I'm stuck with this foolish runt, Zogak… I have to be ready for any turn of events, and I won't yield my place to any other woman!!*

"Oh, no reason, darling," she quickly lied to Zogak.

And while he pondered how to neutralize his dangerous blood relatives, placing extra guards wherever possible to protect his precious self, the restless Sakesfar and the languid but no less ambitious Skun—having received a firm refusal of military support from the Haomovarga (who did not wish to go to war against the far stronger Tigraxauda warriors)—began persuading various forces to ally with them.

First, Sakesfar paid a visit to his "most beloved nephew in all the world," Rustam. But Rustam refused to take up arms against his own younger brother—even though that brother had betrayed him and effectively driven him from his homeland. Rustam wanted neither plots nor thrones; he had decided to remain forever with the Massagetae, not out of fear of the far weaker Zogak, but because of his deep love for Tomyris and his desire to protect and support her and her father, Spargapis.

Then Sakesfar appealed for help from the Bactrians, then begged the king of Khwarezm, and after that turned to Parman, the ruler of Sogd… All in vain. Each one firmly refused to support two people with no reliable prospects, no army of their own, and no riches.

In the end, Sakesfar made a bold decision: together with his son, he set out—no less—to see the king of Media and Persia, who by that time had already conquered several lands: Cyrus the Second!

***

Persia, same century

The cholera epidemic in Persia had ended; only in the distant reaches of the country did isolated outbreaks of that deadly scourge still appear. But all of this was now far removed from the royal palace. Cyrus began coming more frequently to Pasargadae to check on how well his regent—Prince Cambyses—was governing his land.

Cambyses had already introduced Cyrus to his new wife and to Cyrus's own mother, Artosta, as well as to their little daughter,

Shenez. Her elder brother Cyrus treated the girl very warmly, so Artosta's fear that he might resent his parents' devotion to Shenez proved unfounded.

As for the relationship between Artosta herself and Cyrus—since the two barely knew each other—it was not particularly close or heartfelt. Cyrus still felt the absence of Mandane, but he missed Spaka far more—his mother in every sense but blood, who had nursed and raised him, only to be cruelly murdered by his grandfather, Astyages.

One day, the young King of Media and Persia was awakened by a strange commotion.

The outcry came from Artosta: her daughter, now a young girl, was missing—not in her quarters nor anywhere else in the palace! And the princess's nurse was nowhere to be seen either. The child's mother fell into a panic. After a long search, they finally found the girl—she was lying on the grass at the far end of the palace gardens. Her nurse, Atefeh, lay next to her… with a knife in her heart. Shenez herself was uninjured, though her clothes were badly soiled—apparently, she had had to run quickly from someone. Although the little girl had just recently learned to speak a bit, she was now so frightened that she could only make wordless sounds. She was unable to explain the strange incident that had shaken the entire palace.

Everyone was at a loss: Had the girl been chased by her nurse, Atefeh? But why? Or had Atefeh been hastily taking the child away to protect her from some danger?

Summoning all the palace residents and staff at Pasargadae, Cyrus nevertheless ordered them not to spread alarm, so as not to frighten the rest of his subjects.

"Why such a fuss?" the king chided them. "The main thing—

praise the gods—is that my little sister is alive! As for the nurse's death—yes, it's sad, and unfortunately, we don't know the reason or who committed it. But our era is full of deaths—they're everywhere! Is it worth giving this too much importance, especially when it concerns some minor servant? Besides, that nurse must have been incompetent if she let the princess fall into danger! I've brought to Pasargadae an entire sea of servants and slaves—men and women—from Media and the lands I've conquered. Tomorrow, my aides shall find and propose to me several top candidates to care for Shenez. I myself will choose the most suitable. Tonight, let the girl sleep in her parents' chambers!"

The king's decision was neither lacking in wisdom nor fairness. Everyone soon reconciled themselves to what had happened and obeyed him without protest.

"Long live our king!" everyone at the palace exclaimed in delight.

The very next day, Kimiya, an Arab servant, was appointed Shenez's nurse. Everyone liked her: it was clear that Kimiya loved children, that she was gentle and compliant. She never contradicted her mistress—Artosta—and always followed her instructions. Artosta was very pleased by her son's selection and thanked him warmly.

"Think nothing of it, it's a trifle, Artosta," he said, still not calling this woman "Mother."

Several more months passed.

But still—who killed that poor nurse Atefeh, and why? What was her crime? Maybe she was only trying to save my child? Artosta once wondered.

These thoughts plunged the new wife of Prince Cambyses into anxiety and sorrow. But no matter how much she brooded over what had taken place, she couldn't find an answer. Seeing Kimiya outside the palace windows, playing with her daughter—watching them run around among the splendid garden flowers, laughing together—Artosta calmed down once again.

***

Sakastan, the Same Century

Tomyris hated her father. She was certain this was something one could never forgive—not even if you loved that person. How could he have done such a thing? How could he have raised his hand against a woman—her own mother—who was not some slave but his lawful wife, no less?!

There was no excuse for it. Unbearable pain squeezed her heart and tormented her.

The only outlet Tomyris found was in warfare—among the Massagetae, battles almost never ceased. If they themselves were not attacking someone to take spoils (the nomads most of all needed good food, especially in cold weather), then someone else was attacking them: the Sarmatians, the Haomovarga, the Khwarezmians…

Land, pastures for livestock, gold, and weapons—these were the main goals and the essence of most wars. As well as people: if captured, they inevitably became slaves of the victors.

Now Tomyris fought on her own, no longer alongside her father. Rustam, however, served under her command—although he often made independent decisions about attack or defence plans.

Spargapis—until recently a powerful, unshakable, and invincible leader of all the Massagetae chieftains and tribes, the most esteemed of all the Saka kings, who could at times crush entire hordes without difficulty—had suddenly weakened, lost heart, defeated by his guilt before the people dearest to him: his wife and daughter. He could not endure the cold, merciless, and unkind looks of his daughter—who had so recently been attached to him, so thoroughly dependent on him…

But Spargapis was a warrior and a king, not a gentle girl. He did not know how to ask for forgiveness.

Moreover, he was used to being possessive. Now he was jealous of his daughter—for everyone and everything, but most of all for her husband, Rustam. Spargapis pictured Rustam embracing his precious child, his one and only treasured daughter.

Despite all of Tomyris's orders that Rustam curb his displays of affection toward her, her father proved right.

After yet another battle—in which Rustam, just like in their very first encounter, once again seized the initiative from his beloved wife and bested the enemy—Tomyris flew into a rage at the hero.

"Why?! Why did you wipe out that squad?!" she roared at Rustam like a lioness. "One more moment, and my cavalry and I would certainly have struck them all down with our spears and swords! You robbed me of my triumph!!"

"I was afraid for your life," the giant tried to justify himself. "The enemy crept up on you without warning; they were so close they could have killed you! I could never bear that…"

In that very instant, she realized why, just a short while earlier, she had refused Rustam's intimate advances. So that was it! She had not wanted to be a mere woman who lived solely for her husband and children, dependent on them…

Tomyris believed her mission was grand—that she was a protector of the people, a hero! Perhaps she would become a true

Amazon—a warrior woman smashing her enemies. That was a glorious life's goal indeed!

Hence, in her relationship with her husband—beloved though he might be—and in bed with him, she wanted to lead, to dominate. Everyone must bow to her alone! Everywhere, always, in everything, she must be on top, firmly in the saddle, commanding all!

But Rustam did not give her such an opportunity—he was used to being in charge, to leading.

Moreover, Tomyris expected him to kindle in her some greater, more powerful feeling—one she lacked. She began to understand that everything she felt when she saw her husband still did not bring that deep rapture of a woman's soul—the heady natural elation a female ought to experience in a male's embrace. She derived physical pleasure, bodily delight, but not the delight of her soul. Rustam had not yet succeeded in awakening in her the real woman, unique and incomparable. Nor did she see in him a man without peer.

Yet—if only to spite her father, sensing as a woman that he was jealous of Rustam even without knowing for certain—Tomyris allowed Rustam to come to her at night, and sometimes by day, to lie with her. But she never admitted to her husband how much her body needed it, especially after battles.

As a married woman, the princess could not simply sate her desires with just anyone—that would be unseemly, impermissible for her. And while her father lived, even with all the love and guilt he bore her, he would still be obliged to punish her for such behaviour: in camp, everyone, including kings and their children, had to obey tribal law. Men could have women on the side, but women—no, never! That was a crime punishable by death.

But it was not the written laws of the tribe that frightened this wilful, headstrong Saka princess. She honoured the unspoken, higher laws of conscience and honour that forbade a person from debasing themselves with vice. In everything—absolutely everything—Tomyris strove to act rightly, honestly, purely, and devoutly, convinced that her mother, too, had always conducted herself that way. From rumours, Tomyris knew that Zaryana, despite noticing her husband's affairs, had never once in her life reproached him and had never cheated on him, not even in thought. And Tomyris had always wanted to follow her mother's example, striving to be just as virtuous and worthy as a true princess should be.

Moreover, Tomyris understood that she did, in some measure—though not as strongly as Rustam—love him. And so, though she had told her husband that henceforth he should not touch her, she herself broke her own word. He was unspeakably happy about it.

And so, when Rustam—still hot from battle, after all the warriors had gone to their homes—threw her down onto a bed of grass, Tomyris melted with carnal pleasure. She knew that even amid combat, in the thick of aggression and war, the sight of her stirred in Rustam a passion he could scarcely contain. There was no other woman in the world who drew him so powerfully. His teacher Azar had been correct: back at the dawn of his manhood, his first nights with a woman had been boyishly naïve, almost frivolous. But now his passion for his wife burned so hot and deep that it might engulf an entire camp. He could caress and kiss her tender body for hours on end, unable to stop.

Thus, on a certain day… Tomyris conceived a child by her husband. But for the time being, she told no one about her pregnancy.

Meanwhile, a thought still tormented Spargapis: *Who, after all—who—posed the greatest threat to him and his daughter?* Tomyris had prevented him from executing Salih; besides, the king had realized that his friend had nothing to do with the kidnapping of the Massagetae princess. Soon, he simply let Salih return to his Abii—without so much as an apology for the wrongful accusations, but with a friendly pat on the shoulder. Salih was happy enough just to be alive. He valued his life, knowing it still had much to accomplish, that as the Abians' chieftain, he could still be useful.

But now the king of the Massagetae had to find out: was the Alan leader Haidar guilty of those crimes?

Spargapis reflected for a long time, recalling what his wise man Aremezd had said: *the messenger carrying the letter from the one who ordered Tomyris's kidnapping wore a distinctive waist belt, very similar to Haidar's sash, and it could very well have been his.*

It was common knowledge how badly Haidar craved the throne, and only Tomyris's cleverness and Spargapis's own might had kept him from unseating the king. But Haidar was cunning, no simpleton; they couldn't just corner him like some lowly messenger, or even like Salih. This wealthy Alan still managed to keep Lord Spargapis in his debt—and a debtor, as is known, is virtually a slave to his creditor.

Spargapis knew these problems had to be solved quickly. Yet the strain of it all unexpectedly undermined his already waning health.

The Massagetae king became bedridden. A month later, barely able to move his lips from weakness, he told his senior servant:

"Summon my daughter Tomyris. The king wishes to see her."

"At once, Your Majesty."

The servant went to the princess's tent and conveyed the king's words.

"Tell my... tell the king I won't come to him! May he forgive me," she said.

"Princess, I beg you, come!" pleaded Spargapis's senior servant. "The king is in terrible shape. It's in the hands of the gods, but it's plain he has little time left... He wants to speak with you about something important..."

Tomyris hesitated. Suddenly she remembered all the good her father had done for her...

And then—though it was already late evening—her tent was bathed in a bright, sunny light. On its threshold appeared a very swarthy, handsome boy with a turban on his head. In that turban was a large diamond, from which came this strange and marvellous glow.

"Tomyris, noble princess," he addressed her, "I implore you: learn to forgive, even your enemies—do not harbour resentment toward anyone!"

"Who are you, dear stranger?" the princess asked, amazed.

"I am Karna, son of the Sun. I've been sent from on high to give you this turban with a precious diamond, granting great, magical power to whoever wears it... But remember: this magnificent diamond helps only those who are fair to their offenders, who can forgive and do not hold hatred in their hearts! Yet it can bring harm to anyone filled with ill intent or treachery. You deserve the very best—so be the best, the most splendid princess in all the world! Wear this turban with honour. May it make you even better, and bring you good fortune and happiness!"

And Karna vanished as suddenly as he had appeared. Yet upon Tomyris's head remained a turban set with a jewel shining like the sun. She hadn't even had the chance to thank young Karna for such an extraordinary and lavish gift.

At once, Tomyris felt her heart contract with pain—not for her mother or herself, but for her father. Without hesitation, the young woman went to visit her dying, now helpless parent.

"I forgive you for everything, Father," she said gently. "You know—I love you..."

It was very hard for him to speak. With gratitude and fatherly love, as warmly as his limited strength allowed, he simply squeezed her hand in his emaciated one and pressed it to his parched lips. He wept in silence.

"It's all right, Father... all right. Everything will be fine," the princess murmured, barely holding back her own tears, which threatened to choke her. She truly did not want to lose him. "As proof of my daughterly love, I'll make you happy: soon I will bear a child—your grandchild. I feel it will be a boy. I promise, dear Father, that I will name him after you."

Spargapis smiled blissfully and closed his eyes—this brief visit had exhausted him. Lying before the princess was no longer a king, but just a man—the closest, dearest man to her...

Shortly thereafter, King Spargapis died. And a few months later, Tomyris and the hero Rustam had a son—Prince Spargapis II.

26

Media, same century

Several more months passed before Sakesfar and his son Skun finally arrived in Ecbatana, and before Cyrus granted an audience to these two rootless wanderers who longed for power in their homeland. Cyrus had heard little about the Saka, so he was quite curious to learn as much as possible about these nomadic tribes. The King of Media and Persia graciously allowed Sakesfar to sit near him; Skun stood quietly at his father's side, listening to their conversation without a word.

"I had no idea that certain nomad-kings—lacking lavish palaces, large retinues of servants, and wearing nearly the same clothes their whole lives—could wield such formidable power and be so adept in war and battle!" Cyrus remarked in astonishment. Then, with mocking confidence, he added, "Still, I doubt any of them would be capable of defeating so serious an opponent as me!"

Sakesfar did not argue. He realized that despite Cyrus's youth, this was a man of enormous power and considerable authority. The brother of Kavad understood that if his nephew Zogak won over Rustam—who loved him no matter what—and if Rustam, in turn, brought in the Massagetae, then even Cyrus might struggle to overcome all these allies of Sakesfar and Skun.

"Tell me, venerable elder," the master of the palace in Ecbatana continued in a polite, measured tone, "what do I gain if I install you or your son as king of your tribe? How do I personally profit? My splendid warriors, in fighting your Tigraxauda Saka—and of course defeating them—will nonetheless suffer losses. Some might die. Who will compensate me for that? I'm used to valuing my property—meaning my resources, my army."

Sakesfar did not know how to answer; he had nothing of substance to offer the self-interested Persian. He had assumed that, if he merely asked, the king might benevolently grant his request.

"If my son Skun becomes king," Sakesfar ventured at last, "then I'll find a way to reward you, my lord—and reward you handsomely."

"You think you can give me wealth beyond what I already possess?" Cyrus laughed heartily. "All right, all right—don't trouble yourself. I've come up with something: here's my proposal. I help you—or your son, that's for you two to decide—become king, and all the people of the Tigraxauda tribe become my subjects forever. Your land will pay me tribute for all time. Agreed?"

At first, Sakesfar was taken aback, but then he nodded submissively. Cyrus went on:

"Moreover, you'll persuade all the Saka kings to do the same. Deal?"

"Forgive me, Cyrus, but I'm afraid the Haomovarga—and especially King Spargapis, his daughter Princess Tomyris, and the Massagetae—won't agree to that. I doubt I can convince them…"

"Not a problem! Then I'll simply… annihilate them—wipe them from the face of the earth. That's all, old man—you may go. Let some time pass; I can't deal with this right now. I'm planning to march on Babylon and a few other lands. After that, I'll slowly move toward your side of the world. What did you say is the name of that pathetic little king who keeps all the Saka in awe? Spargapis, yes? Well then, I promise you: he and his daughter will bathe in

their own blood!"

Sakesfar grinned and nodded—why should he care about Tomyris? Who was she to him? Let Cyrus do whatever he pleased with her!

"By the way," Cyrus asked suddenly, "haven't you heard rumours in your parts about a certain wondrous precious stone? A diamond, I believe. If I'm not mistaken, it was brought there from Hindustan by a boy I've been searching for. Do you know anything about that?"

"No, my lord. I've heard nothing about diamonds, nor about this wealthy boy," Sakesfar confessed guiltily.

"A pity. One ought to keep track of such things," said the young King of Media and Persia, already accustomed to lecturing others. "Our conversation is over."

Sakesfar and Skun bowed humbly—almost like slaves—and left Cyrus's chambers.

* * *

Sakastan, same century

Just as the most ambitious and power-hungry chieftains of the Massagetae tribes were about to divvy up the throne left vacant after Spargapis's death—each imagining how he might elbow aside his rivals—a fresh onslaught of dangerous enemies descended upon the Massagetae.

At such a moment, even the most unyielding among them— men like Haidar, chieftain of the Alans; Parviz, chieftain of the Sakaravaks; Sher, chieftain of the Apasiaks; and Kuzybek, chieftain of the Karats—understood the need to unite. And they saw that without the cunning of Tomyris, and above all the mighty strength and vast battle experience of her faithful husband—the stalwart hero Rustam, who served all Massagetae—they could not win a war that promised to be extremely difficult. Without Rustam and Tomyris, all the Saka would be doomed.

Hence, these very scheming and restless chieftains agreed to allow the daughter of the late king—Tomyris—to ascend the throne for the time being. They decided this would be temporary, until things calmed down and stabilized.

Tomyris began preparing for the solemn ceremony of her coronation.

Suddenly… commotion broke out in the main camp. A large, swift cavalry detachment galloped in, led by a richly attired, powerfully built, grey-bearded rider. Beside him rode another older warrior, towering and strong.

"Hey, Massagetae!" the mighty warrior shouted. "Assemble the entire tribe at once! We know all your chieftains are gathered here. Let them come immediately. We shall crown our new king—the Tocharian leader Zakir! King Spargapis himself appointed him ruler over all the Massagetae tribes. He is your sovereign now!"

"All right, that's enough, Aidar. Everyone here already fears us. They'll obey us without argument," said the lead horseman calmly, yet with great authority.

Everyone was aghast. Zakir?… *What* Zakir? Was it really *that* Zakir—the one who had fled in disgrace years ago, disappearing to avoid facing the people? The one who had killed the young children of his close friend, Kuzybek of the Karats, and plundered his settlement? The same Zakir who had once ruled like a king, cruelly executing dozens—hundreds—of Massagetae? Zakir, who had vanished for so many years without a trace? He's alive? *Is that him right there?* And now he's demanding nothing less than to reclaim the throne?

The people were stunned. News that Zakir had arrived with an entire armed cavalry instantly reached all the chieftains who had come for Tomyris's coronation.

Kuzybek rode up to Zakir on his horse, drew his sword, and roared:

"You filthy steppe dog! You plan to become king, Zakir?! That will never happen! I'll tear the hide from your old bones myself, right now! You think we'll all cower just because you've come with an army? That we'll hide in some hole or surrender to you? Don't count on it!"

Aidar wanted to answer Kuzybek by running him through with a spear, but Zakir stopped him.

"We are an entire army here," Kuzybek continued. "You're nobody—you were nobody, and you remain nobody, because the Massagetae do not respect you. Tomyris, daughter of the glorious Spargapis, is our true queen! Or do you want to dispute that? Then fight our Rustam, the worthiest hero in the land! But fight him in single combat—if you're not a coward, but a real man. Surely you've heard of Rustam, even in those distant lands where you've been hiding all this time? Tales of his strength, valour, and bravery have spread across the world. What's wrong, Zakir—scared? I thought so! Get out of here; you're a stranger to us!"

"Why dirty our hands on him, Kuzybek?" said Berez, chieftain of the Guz and a friend of Spargapis, in a calm tone. "We need to conserve our strength—the Sarmatians are already at our borders."

Everyone agreed, meanwhile hurling insults—and handfuls of earth—at Zakir and his retinue. Among the Saka, throwing dirt was a gesture of contempt and insult.

Realizing that a whole swarm of warriors was indeed gathering around his cavalry—some on horseback, some on foot—Zakir's eyes flashed. He bared his teeth, yanked his reins, and shouted to those with him:

"Hey, my Tocharians! After me! I think we'll be back here again…"

***

Persia, the Same Century

Time passed, and Shenez, daughter of Cambyses and Artosta, grew older.

One day, in a palace corridor, she happened to overhear the servants talking:

"Did you know, apparently there are lands ruled by a woman? An elderly Saka nomad, visiting King Cyrus, mentioned that somewhere far from our borders lives a beautiful, valiant, and powerful Queen Tomyris, feared and respected by all her enemies! They say her rule is more merciful and just than a man's. So, if the stars align favourably and the gods are kind to us Persians, perhaps one day our lovely young Shenez will become Queen of all Persia!"

Shenez was enchanted by these words. From that moment on, she began to imagine herself as the fairest and mightiest queen of Persia.

Sometime later, Cyrus travelled to visit his parents—people he had never truly grown close to in spirit, yet whom he honoured for the sake of his own good standing and reputation among his people.

After dining with this family that, to him, felt largely like strangers, Cyrus began to play with his little sister, Shenez. He genuinely liked the girl—she resembled him in both appearance and temperament. She was single-minded, fascinated with all sorts of weaponry, and had a keen, sincere interest in the various kingdoms of the world (not for nothing did her name mean "the king's pride"!). She was also intrigued by wars and conquests.

Moreover, Shenez simply adored her older brother—still young, yet already ruling over all—and always rushed toward him with eager devotion. She treasured every moment spent by Cyrus's side. She was curious about his entire life, peppering him with questions that sometimes wore out the son of Cambyses and Artosta, since he had to explain things in detail. Yet he never became angry with her.

On one such day, Shenez asked Cyrus:

"My dear, beloved brother! I've heard there are not only kings in this world, but also queens. Is it true that one day, when I'm grown, I could be a queen? A queen of Persia—and of the whole world! I want it so much! Of course, it would only happen after your death."

For a moment, a deathly silence fell over the grand, luxurious hall where they sat with their parents and closest retinue. Everyone present had heard Shenez's words and stood frozen, fearing for her. Obviously, the girl had spoken pure foolishness. Some servants even thought they glimpsed a terrifying flash in the king's eyes. But then all exhaled in relief, for King Cyrus gazed intently at his young, beloved sister, stroked her hair affectionately, and laughed in good humour.

"Why, yes, of course it's true, my darling!" he said. "You certainly shall become queen of Persia—and of the entire world! After all, your mighty brother Cyrus won't live forever. And you will succeed him! But for now—go and play with your nanny. Your brother is tired and wishes to rest."

With that, Cyrus rose and hurried out of the hall.

That same night, Prince Cambyses came into his chambers and said to his wife:

"Perhaps it would be best if you and our daughter left here for a while?"

"Where to?" asked Artosta, puzzled.

"To the mountains—your parents' home, for instance," he insisted more firmly.

"But why?" Artosta seemed genuinely surprised. "How strange you are… Right now, the entire family is here! Even our son Cyrus has come. It's wonderful for us to be all together!"

"As you wish," Cambyses replied. "But I sense it's getting dangerous here…"

"Nonsense! I see no reason at all to leave," said Artosta, shaking her head—the woman was never considered particularly clever. "We'll stay in the palace."

"Very well—I warned you," mumbled Cambyses, drifting off to sleep.

And as he dozed, he recalled that his previous wife, Mandane, had been far wiser.

***

Sakastan, same century

A moment came that King Spargapis's daughter would remember for the rest of her life.

In the presence of a huge crowd, the chieftains and elders of all the Massagetae tribes lifted high a rug made of camel felt, upon which Tomyris sat proudly, and they acclaimed her their queen and ruler!

She knew, however, that this coronation was not a temporary appointment—it was for life, so long as the gods did not call her from this earth.

Inside the royal tent, Rustam approached. He looked at his beloved wife with warmth in his eyes, though he seemed worried.

"What is it now?" Tomyris asked, her voice edged with irritation.

She had spent much time lately pondering how to save her people from their enemies, trying to determine the best strategy. She had studied the art of war in detail, for the situation around them was tense and complex.

"Tell me, dear," said the husband of the Massagetae's first queen, "do you plan to use your father's tactics in the war against the Sarmatians? We know King Spargapis mainly employed light cavalry, which was highly manoeuvrable. Such troops could travel great distances and carry out a wide range of strategic tasks—breakthroughs, flanking and rear attacks, feints, raids deep behind enemy lines, pursuit, and so on, by day or night, in any season. And if things went badly, they could retreat swiftly from their pursuers, with archers on horseback. Mobility and agility—or cunning—were the basis of Spargapis's tactics. Is that the foundation you'll rely on?"

"You've studied warfare well," Tomyris responded, softening slightly. "But let me be frank: I believe my father's tactics are now outdated. They were suited to internal feuds among Massagetae clans and the limited forces King Spargapis commanded. The diversity of my large army, drawn from all the Massagetae tribes, calls for a restructuring of both tactics and strategy. I need to decide how we'll fight in a new way."

"All right. Maybe so. Then adopt my strategy! It has served the Saka Tigraxauda well in battle. If I may, I'll explain the basics?"

"No need; I already know them. I've fought at your side—both as an ordinary warrior and as a commander alongside another commander. You, Rustam, are unique as both a warrior and a leader. I hold your fighting talent in high esteem, and I'm constantly learning from you on the battlefield! You excel at mustering the entire army and delivering a strike at the enemy's most vulnerable point, scattering fragile lines and shattering their ranks. You have a keen intuition for the shifting tides of conflict and always strike precisely at your opponent's weakest spots. Panic seizes them when they suddenly see a tightly packed mass of armoured cavalry with spears and shields riding down on them—led by you, a mighty hero! Every charge you make is like a gust of powerful wind sweeping away dry tinder and road dust."

The hero listened quietly, careful not to interrupt. He sensed there would be more to this speech than simple praise—otherwise, his wife would not have begun it at all.

Tomyris went on:

"All that is fine. But the key to your success lies, above all, in you yourself! Understand? Your unparalleled talent in battle and your extraordinary strength allow you to break through the toughest enemy defences. Even so, remember that in one of our earlier battles against the Sarmatians, their iron ranks, though battered, did withstand your assault! They would have remained intact if not for my small reserve, which I personally led into the fray. Only after I intervened did we defeat the enemy! Or will you deny it?"

Rustam let his mighty head fall forward. He could not help but concede his wife's point: his tactics alone did not always suffice—particularly against the experienced and dangerous Sarmatians.

Only a month after this conversation, the Sarmatians suffered a defeat at the hands of Queen Tomyris's army. While many male warlords would have scorned adopting anything from their beaten enemies, Tomyris—free of prejudice and guided by a woman's intuition—borrowed from them everything she deemed most useful.

Disregarding the chieftains' grumblings, she introduced a form of heavy cavalry akin to that of the Sarmatians and Khwarezmians, outfitting not just the riders but also their horses with armour, and replacing the short, light Saka spears with heavier, longer ones. Not the slightest detail escaped Tomyris's watchful gaze. In the art of war, she considered nothing a trifle—everything mattered, everything was factored in, and everything was used to glean a lesson.

The Sarmatian war also led Tomyris to appreciate the fighting qualities of female warriors. Her best unit now consisted of fearless, one-breasted girls.

The Massagetae queen decided to revive the martial traditions of her ancestors and asked her milk sister, Sodia, to form a five-thousand-strong detachment of the finest Amazons. Tomyris didn't just serve as their commander—she was the boldest and bravest among them!

"My darling, please, don't overdo it," Rustam once pleaded. "Keep yourself safe. Our son, Prince Spargapis, needs his mother alive! And his father needs you no less. At least leave me the hardest parts of battle."

Tomyris smiled at her husband, grateful for his concern. Yet she continued to fight the Massagetae's enemies fiercely, passionately, and recklessly, setting an example of courage, heroism, and military wisdom. She shattered the Sarmatians, personally felling their Queen Kiana with a well-aimed arrow through the heart, as well as Bikbulat, the former Alan chieftain who had fought shoulder to shoulder with Kiana and taken refuge in her lands for many years.

Tomyris would face many more wars and win many more victories, always aided by her loyal companion and devoted husband—the heroic warrior Rustam.

***

Persia, same century

"Get the physician! At once! Look what you've done, you wretch!" Cyrus roared, furiously slashing the young nurse of his little sister Shenez with his whip.

Nanny Kimiya lay sprawled on the cold, mosaic-tiled palace floor in Pasargadae. He kept striking her, until her entire body—even her face—was covered in bleeding welts and bruises.

"My lord, but you yourself…" the girl tried to speak.

"What?!" Cyrus cut her off. "How dare you lie to me, you worthless nothing?!"

By this time, many people had gathered—Cyrus's parents and members of the court.

"Forgive us, Your Majesty, if we may ask—what has happened?" they inquired fearfully, drawn by the commotion.

"Quickly, call the physician to my dear sister Shenez's chambers!" Cyrus barked at everyone present, without addressing anyone in particular. "The door is open. This foolish, miserable nanny gave the child fish without removing the bones, and the girl choked! She's in a bad way!"

When the physician finally arrived (he seemed in no great hurry), poor Shenez was already dead: a sharp fish bone had lodged in her throat, cutting off her air. No one had managed to help her in time. It had been impossible to save her.

Everyone in the Persian kingdom was stunned by the sudden tragedy.

The nanny Kimiya, deemed responsible for the death of the king's younger sister and the daughter of Persian Prince Cambyses, was executed by Cyrus's order the following morning—hanged upside down.

Artosta wept bitterly for her daughter. She could not fathom why this had happened to the princess, her dear sweet girl, rather than to some servant…

"Oh, wife," Cambyses chided her in a whisper, so that no one would overhear, "I had a feeling. I warned you… Now there's no point in tearing our hair. We can't bring our daughter back."

King Cyrus proclaimed a month of mourning throughout the land for his beloved sister. The entire populace welcomed their ruler's decree, praising the young "lord of the world" for such attentiveness and respect toward his family—toward those closest to his heart.

27

Tashkent, 2012

"Still, Rashid, I don't think it was some small-time crooks who brought us here, hoping for cash or maybe women's jewellery," noted the brave Tamilla. She was exhausted, yet thanks to the toughness forged by life's difficulties, she never whined or complained about hardship. "I'm convinced that whoever 'commissioned' Bahrom, Dima, and their crew to kidnap us is some 'big fish'—a criminal kingpin, undoubtedly tied to the disappearance of my students!"

"So then, you really believe your kids have gone missing?" asked Rashid, also enduring the ordeal stoically, despite his own fatigue. "And that their radio silence for several days is no coincidence?"

"With bright, disciplined people—even if they are young—there simply aren't such 'coincidences' raising all these red flags," Tamilla sighed heavily.

Throughout her life, this honourable woman had never been afraid for herself; what frightened her was any threat to those dear to her, especially defenceless children. And her students were like children to her, too.

"Rashid, I'm worried about my kids and blame myself for letting them go abroad! Their parents must be cursing me for it right now…"

"My love, you are not at fault," her husband reassured her, striving to offer comfort. "Let's trust that the truth will come to light! And that everything will turn out all right—for them, and for us."

***

Secret Bunker, Outskirts of Boston, USA, Around the Same Time

Within their first few days in the secret bunker, the three Uzbek students—programmer Aibek Khashimov, geoengineer Daniil Shevtsov, and economist Ekaterina Solovyova—were subjected to the powerful hypnosis of Greg Darkness. He had completely locked down their will and capacity for independent decision-making.

Nevertheless, they were decently fed, because for experiments on living people—more precisely, on the minds of these young visitors from distant Uzbekistan with high IQs—physical strength and overall good health were essential.

The American researchers in the bunker could hardly use their own compatriots with similarly exceptional abilities for such illegal experiments! Of course, they could have used homeless individuals with no relatives, or the terminally ill, but neither group was suitable for studying the capabilities of the human brain.

If only these young people from Tashkent had known in advance—or at least suspected—what kind of godless experiment they were being lured into by these unknown fiends who knew so much about them! In that case, the clever trio would surely have devised a way out—or better yet, avoided getting involved in the first place. But due to a certain youthful naivety and lack of worldly experience, they were not sufficiently on guard against the looming threat.

On the second day after their arrival in the U.S., John McConnley, who spoke Russian, brought them to that ill-fated location. As he led them through the bunker's first tunnel corridor, he neglected to mention that he himself was protected by a special antidote against the electromagnetic radiation to which the young people would be exposed. It was precisely this radiation that caused them headaches and various inexplicable phobias.

"Listen, Trabs," the owner of the bunker, George Moran, said privately to his chief lab scientist, "I trust you followed my instructions and didn't overdo the electromagnetic field during that initial procedure with the kids?"

"Certainly, boss, everything stayed within the norm!" Henry Trabs replied with a smile. "After all, we couldn't risk giving our young guests here at our secret base any serious damage to the heart—or especially the brain and central nervous system! Now they're as obedient as puppets or robots, free for you, Mr. Moran, to use however you please. And their grey matter is perfect for our experiments!"

It must be said that Moran had grand ambitions. The wealthy and ambitious American wanted nothing less than a Nobel Prize for discovering untapped potential in the human brain—and then to sell his findings to the U.S. Army or intelligence services, or perhaps to the British.

The first step was to insert electrodes about a millimetre thick into the cerebral cortex of each student—a monstrous size compared to their delicate nerve cells. These electrodes were sufficient to pick up the electrical signals from several thousand, or at least several hundred, neurons. Techniques had also been developed that allowed the team to filter out the activity of a single brain cell from the surrounding noise.

The second step was a follow-up experiment. Under Moran's direction, Trabs measured neuronal activity. On his laptop screen, he

showed the subjects a series of well-known visual images—famous personalities, pop-culture icons, renowned architectural landmarks.

As these images were shown, distinct electrical activity arose in individual neurons of the test subjects; different pictures "activated" different nerve cells. Thus, the so-called "Jennifer Aniston neuron," discovered earlier by other scientists—and once referred to as the "grandmother neuron" half a century ago—was confirmed.

This neuron fired whenever a picture of actress Jennifer Aniston appeared on screen. Regardless of which photo was shown to each subject, the "Aniston neuron" rarely failed. It even fired when a clip from a TV series she had starred in came on screen—even if she wasn't visibly present in the frame.

But when the image featured women who merely resembled Jennifer Aniston, the neuron remained silent.

Apparently, this particular brain cell was attuned to the holistic image of that specific actress—not to isolated features of her appearance or outfit. This revelation offered, if not a definitive key, then at least a promising hint about how long-term memories are stored in the human brain.

Where other researchers were hindered by conventional moral and legal boundaries, nothing of the sort slowed down Moran and Trabs! All other scientists in the world were restricted to placing electrodes only in regions of the brain undergoing preoperative study—and even then, only within the limited timeframe of a justified medical procedure.

This severely complicated any effort to determine whether the "Jennifer Aniston neuron," or a Brad Pitt neuron, or an Eiffel Tower neuron truly existed—or whether scientists had simply stumbled upon one cell within a broad, interconnected network responsible for storing or recognizing a particular image.

Moran and Trabs pushed the boundaries even further. They began studying neuronal properties not only in the white matter but—through surgical procedures placing the subjects on an operating table—also deep within the grey matter of the brain.

Trabs produced a photo of Jennifer Aniston and showed it to each test subject. In the young men's brains, that specific neuron promptly lit up, activating regardless of how the actress appeared. Then, when shown only her printed name—"Jennifer Aniston"—the same neuron fired again!

The results were staggering, and the elated Trabs gave a triumphant shout.

Katya, however, was barely familiar with Jennifer Aniston or her work, so her neurons didn't react to those photos. That posed no problem; once they began showing Tom Cruise, her neurons responded vividly to his likeness instead.

After experiments like these, the "patients" might well have ended up severely brain-damaged... But, fortunately for the researchers, that didn't happen. True, the young people retained no memory of what had been done to them—but nor were they supposed to. Darkness the hypnotist ensured that. During the procedures, the three remained conscious and answered the researchers' questions. Yet because neurons in the human brain do not register pain, they felt no sharp pricks from the electrodes and had no awareness of how morally repugnant the experiments truly were...

Summoned by Professor Moran—who was fully aware of the methods used in his bunker and both issued orders and gave recommendations—Trabs reported:

"Boss, we've obtained incredible results! We discovered that neuronal excitation changes at the precise moment new memories form. Initially, the neuron fired only in response to any mention of Jennifer Aniston. But once an association was created between the actress and certain architectural sites in a famous city—say, New York—the neuron fired just at the symbol for that city! What's more, we observed these changes after only a single exposure."

"Excellent, Trabs," Moran concluded. "This is crucial for understanding the neural processes behind memory formation. Existing memories are reactivated, and new associative connections emerge because no real-life event is remembered until it's imprinted in the brain. Our findings could shed light on the mechanisms of episodic memory formation. But there's another, more dangerous experiment I want to conduct…"

"I'm listening, Professor," the mad scientist replied, holding his breath.

"We need to see what happens in a healthy young brain with a high IQ when we implant… cells from someone else's brain! Even better—foreign neurons we've been studying. That would be the experiment of the millennium!"

"Understood, Boss. I'll start preparing our young guests for the procedure."

***

Tashkent, 1985

"Hello, Tamilla, hello, my dear daughter!"

"Hello, Mom! How are you? Feeling all right?"

"Yes, thank you, my dear. I'm still working at my Palace of Culture. It's a shame you can't help me with the events there anymore—it's harder without you. But I understand you're very busy. I just wanted to ask: will you be coming for my birthday?"

Tamilla paused for a few moments. Ever since she had begun living on her own with her husband and little daughter, Saltanat, she hadn't been able to visit her parents often—especially now that she was one of the first in the country to open her own cooperative. But there was another reason that made her hesitant to return to her childhood home.

"I'd love to, Mom, but I'm worried Dad's still mad at me…"

"It's fine, dear, it's fine. I already spoke with him, and I'll talk to him again. It'll be all right! Just come—I'll set the table. We can all sit together and talk."

So Tamilla did come, bringing her child. Rashid said that if he didn't end up working late, he'd drop by later—basically, if circumstances allowed.

Sardor Shakhmuradovich greeted his daughter with a dour expression. After they had tea and sweets, Tamilla herself began the delicate conversation with her father.

"Papa, you're angry with me, aren't you?" she asked softly but bravely—gently, yet directly.

Sardor Mahkamov remained silent, took another sip of tea, and turned his face away from his daughter.

"I understand," Tamilla continued. "I didn't go work at your factory or help with your production. Instead, I opened my own cooperative… I brought you shame by becoming an entrepreneur…"

Sardor Shakhmuradovich stayed silent a moment longer, then lifted his head and looked at his beloved daughter.

"Tamilla, my dear, you have to understand that I've always been—and always will be—proud of your success. It's not just that so-called shameful label of 'entrepreneur' that upset me. Something else was bothering me…"

He paused again and slowly took another sip of tea.

Tamilla let him speak without interruption, wanting to hear him out fully.

Sardor continued:

"When you started your own business, you never consulted me. I have a lot of experience, daughter. I could live without giving advice—but why didn't you say a single word about it?!"

"I'm sorry, Dad! I was so caught up in the new venture. I was anxious. Getting approval for something like that wasn't easy, and I didn't want to use your name for leverage. I was also afraid you wouldn't support me—that you'd be against it. I wasn't sure how you, a professional, would feel about a folk craft cooperative…"

Sighing, Sardor Shakhmuradovich stood up, walked over to Tamilla, and with his firm paternal hand—yet as gently as he could—patted her head.

"My little girl, silly thing! Didn't you know that whatever you do in life, your father would understand and support you? If you make mistakes, I'll let you make them first—and then I'll definitely help you fix them. The only person who never makes mistakes is the one who never does anything. And you've always been a hard worker, doing great things! As for local craftspeople, I respect them very much for their painstaking and often talented work."

Tamilla stood up, tears in her eyes, and embraced her father.

"Thank you, Papa dear."

He beamed.

"By the way, what did you name your cooperative?"

"I named it *Silk Road*! We work in partnership with the Society for Friendship and Cultural Relations with Foreign Countries. We find it really interesting."

"I'm glad for you and your colleagues! Things haven't been

going as well at my factory as I'd like," said Sardor Mahkamov with a sly smile. "If it comes to that, you'll hire your old dad to work with you, right?"

Tamilla realized he was joking, trying to lift her spirits.

"Of course, Dad! I'd be thrilled to have you!" she said, laughing.

Just then, Rashid arrived—carrying a huge, magnificent bouquet for his mother-in-law.

"Oh my, thank you! What a wonderful surprise!" exclaimed Maryam Baburovna. "The flowers are gorgeous! And they smell delightful! Rashid, my boy, come into the living room. I'll feed you in a minute."

"Mom, please forgive us," Rashid said, standing in the hallway. "Tamilla and I need to leave right away. I just got a call from Pulat Gafarov. He has some important news about Karna's turban and also… I'll tell you later. Shall we go?"

"Yes, of course!"

Tamilla quickly got herself ready, apologized to her parents, and left with her husband. She was relieved to have made up with her father and cleared the air between them. Now, there were no lingering tensions or unspoken resentments. But at the moment, something else occupied her thoughts: had Rashid's friend, the archaeologist Pulat, finally located the golden turban—and the remains of the precious Koh-i-Noor diamond?

* * *

Moscow suburbs – Ryazan, 1985–1987

Despite all his sly caution, Kirill Midiyatdinov's crimes in prison eventually came to light. His sentence was extended. Not even his reliable friend and "older brother," Konstantin Koscheyev, could help him—though he tried. By then, Kostya had already been released and had promised Kirill he'd hire a good lawyer to arrange for an early release if possible.

Marina Persieva, who visited her son periodically, also learned that his sentence had been extended. Unaware of Koschei's promise, she hired a lawyer for Kirill herself.

Like many who endure severe ordeals and fall into emotional instability, Kirill couldn't see the situation clearly. He didn't believe it was actually his mother, Marina, who had sent the lawyer—and not Konstantin, the man who had so deftly and elegantly set him up, relentlessly driving the younger Midiyatdinov "down to the bottom." Koschei's thirst for revenge over that apple core in the orphanage had never left his hardened heart.

But Kirill trusted him implicitly. So, upon leaving prison, he didn't go to his mother, but headed straight to Ryazan to see his "friend," who was already waiting.

Konstantin welcomed Kirill warmly, putting him up in his luxurious home and treating him to all sorts of delicacies. Kirill began to relax. He was happy.

After resting for a couple of days, Kirill resumed his old role—just as in prison—carrying out criminal and other assorted errands for Konstantin, running around at his beck and call. Then, after saving up some money, Kirill bought himself a nice apartment, and later he got married—to Veronika, a pretty dancer from a nightclub—naturally, one of Konstantin's establishments.

***

Moscow, 1989

Alexei Irmanov's wife, Aleksandra, did not approve of her daughter Anastasia's choice of fiancé. Anastasia wanted to marry Garik, a mathematician.

Yes, Garik was a clever, decent guy who sincerely loved their Nastya. That was all well and good. But with his candidate-of-sciences salary and limited prospects—even if he soon defended his doctoral dissertation and maybe secured a stable position at his institute—could he possibly meet the limitless needs of her still-young daughter, who was used to comfort? Sure, she and Alexei would help Nastya with anything, but a husband also has to provide for his wife!

Oddly enough, Nastya's stepfather, Alexei Irmanov, actually supported her choice of Igor.

"It's no big deal," he reassured Sasha. "Over all the years Garik and Nastya have been together, I've seen that he's a fine young man. So if he proves himself to be a good husband to Nastya, I'll try to help him find a promising job."

They held the wedding, and Irmanov covered practically all the expenses. As for Nastya's biological father, Dmitry—not only did he fail to give her any wedding gift or financial assistance, such as buying furniture for the newlyweds or paying for the dress—he didn't even bother to attend the celebration, despite having been invited. He never even called. When Nastya finally reached him by phone, he said he was feeling ill and wouldn't be coming.

Alexei, on the other hand, had more than enough funds to host a lavish affair. Over the past few years, Aleksandra Levidovskaya's husband had become a highly capable manager with solid footing. Intelligent, organized, and hardworking, Alexei Vadimovich had raised his glass factory to a level of profitability most directors in the entire Union could only dream of.

Alexei always tried to do everything by the book. He had stumbled only once—guilty of a minor theft of state property. He ended up "under an article of the law," served a brief sentence, and learned a major life lesson. While many ex-convicts struggled to find even a street-sweeper's job after prison, Irmanov not only regained his moral standing but climbed to new heights.

Upon his release, he worked as a shop foreman at a Moscow plastics factory. At the same time, he completed his degree at MGIMO in international law, after which he was offered the position of deputy director at a telecommunications equipment plant.

In short, his career continued to develop steadily.

His father, Vadim Borisovich, an elderly retiree, still harboured past resentments toward Aleksandra's father, Stanislav Levidovsky—the man who had once threatened him for refusing to seat Levidovsky in a "cozy" director's chair at a diamond plant near Gazli. He was staunchly opposed to Alexei having any contact with the man he considered a corrupt figure hiding out in England with the country's stolen diamonds.

So Alexei, not wanting to upset his father, avoided associating with his father-in-law. He would merely say hello if Stanislav called Aleksandra. This arrangement posed no hardship for Alexei, as Stanislav Zakharovich likewise showed no desire to speak with Vadim's son. Moreover, Alexei was angry with his wife's father. He had no need for Levidovsky's money—even if in recent years the man had been earning his fortune honestly and painstakingly. That wasn't the point.

Alexei believed that Levidovsky was a poor excuse for a father and grandfather who gave his daughter and granddaughter far too little attention.

Before long, part of the reason behind the English oligarch's attitude came to light.

Alexei returned home from a foreign business trip and handed his wife a fresh copy of *The Daily Telegraph*. The paper carried an article stating that millionaire Stanislav Levidovsky had gone bankrupt—he had placed all his funds in a bank that had just "gone under." Above the article was a photo of Levidovsky captioned: *"Stanislav Levidovsky with his son and heir, Stepan."*

"Sasha," Alexei asked his wife directly, "why didn't you tell me that your unfaithful daddy—sorry, I mean your father—has an illegitimate son?"

Aleksandra grew uneasy; she clearly hated discussing the matter.

"He's not illegitimate," she admitted sourly, having known for a long time, of course. "Lesh, I just don't want to talk about it."

"What do you mean he's not illegitimate?" Alexei asked, perplexed. "You always said your father spent his life loving only your late mother!"

"Well… not exactly," Aleksandra said, shaking her head. "I just couldn't bring myself to tell you that he… left us. A long time ago, when I was still a girl. Not long after, he married his mistress. And she gave him a son."

"And after all that, you forgave him?!"

"What could I do? Mama died, and he's my father."

"Sashulya, how was he able to just up and leave for abroad so easily? How did they even let him go? You visited him in London—did he tell you anything?"

"A bit. He has an old army friend he once served with—General Oleg Midiyatdinov from the Ministry of Internal Affairs. That friend made all the necessary arrangements for him to leave smoothly, so he wouldn't be hassled at the airport. And even though Oleg was just a colonel at the time, he already had quite a bit of clout."

"Really! Well, everything sure worked out nicely for your dad back then," Alexei remarked. "I'm sorry he's apparently in big trouble now. Who knows? Maybe he'll return home to Tashkent or come see us here in Moscow?"

"I don't know—he never mentioned anything. But... anything is possible!"

* * *

Tashkent, 2012

Saltanat was nervous; she had never dealt with criminals before and had no idea how to go about it. Moreover, this man was now her only chance to save her parents—she needed to avoid angering him to keep that chance alive. And Saltanat had no doubt it would be all too easy to anger someone from the underworld.

Having braced herself, she was just about to call this Artyom—whose phone number had been given to her by ex-convict Timofey Karaev—when her cell phone suddenly rang.

"Hello, Saltanat? Good day, my dear. This is Alexei Irmanov speaking."

"Oh, hello, Alexei Vadimovich! I wasn't even hoping for your call anymore."

"I'm sorry, I've been tied up. Nastya told me everything you said. We'll handle the festival ourselves—don't worry about the funding; that's already being taken care of. But, of course, I'm most concerned about your parents' situation. Any news?"

"No, unfortunately, I haven't made any progress at all."

"But… forgive me, they're at least alive?"

"I don't even know, though I hope so… I feel they are alive—they must be alive! My father and mother are brave, strong people—never ones to give up easily or lose heart under any circumstances. So I believe that even if bandits took them hostage, they won't be broken… and they won't be killed."

"I can't wrap my head around why some gangsters would want anything from your peaceful parents… It's strange."

"Yes. Honestly, I keep racking my brains and still can't figure it out."

"Saltanat, I'd like to give you the phone number of a contact of mine. I think this man, Artur, can help you, because he… well, he's experienced with situations like the one your parents are in. Would you be open to his assistance?"

"Certainly—I'd welcome it! Please give me the number. Okay, I've got it. You know, someone else gave me a name too, but it's better if I call your contact first, since you say he's competent in handling such serious matters."

"Exactly. If anything happens, keep me posted. I'll help however I can."

28

Moscow, 1990

Marina Persieva couldn't believe her eyes—standing on her apartment threshold was… her own son, Kirill! How many letters and phone calls she had sent after he was released from prison—yet he never came. Could it be that now he had come to his senses and remembered his mother?

"Kiryusha!" she exclaimed. "My dear son! Come in, come in!"

He stepped inside while she struggled to hold back tears.

"Why haven't you shown up here even once in the three years since you got out?"

"I couldn't," Kirill answered curtly, almost coldly.

"I see. Let's go to the kitchen. Sit down at the table, I'll fix you something to eat. My son, my Kiryushenka!"

"Don't call me that, Aunt Marina! Got it?"

"Of course, of course, dear boy. But I *am* your real mother—you know that by now. And Denis—my husband—is your father. And Oleg is your uncle, though he raised you like a son."

"Yes, I know!" Kirill snapped irritably. "Actually, it's about him—Oleg—that I wanted to ask you. How's he doing, anyway? Still alive?"

"That's a strange way of putting it, son. Why wouldn't he be? Of course he's alive and well. He helps me out from time to time—with groceries, with money. He's a general now!"

"What a bastard," Kirill spat out angrily.

"What? Why talk like that?"

"No, Aunt Marina, forget it. I just said it in the heat of the moment. That scum locked me up, you know? If not for him… But never mind, it's all for the best. I'm rich now, so don't worry—I'm not holding a grudge. Is he still in his old house, or did he move?"

"He hasn't moved—he's got a great two-story place with all the conveniences. No reason to leave it. Even though it's on the outskirts of Moscow, my brother has a car and a personal driver, as befits a general! So whenever he needs to go somewhere—even into the city centre—he just goes."

Suddenly, Kirill Midiyatdinov became impatient to leave.

"Why are you in such a rush, son? You haven't even had a proper meal!"

"Sorry, I just remembered something urgent."

He left in his own car—one he drove himself—promising "Aunt Marina" that he'd drop by again sometime.

He didn't say a word about his work or even mention his wife—he saw no need to.

He looks so much like Denis, Marina thought, *and more so with each passing year!* She shuddered involuntarily as she remembered her unfortunate husband. *How is he doing now, behind bars? Surely, for an intellectual like him, it must be brutal…*

* * *

Moscow suburbs, same period

Although Denis was serving time for a "serious" offense, he hadn't been sent too far away. After the betrayal that pinned a murder charge on him, his luck had finally turned. His polite restraint and sincere kindness toward everyone—without grovelling or flattery—earned him respect from both fellow inmates and various levels of the prison administration. Thus, though sentenced to twelve years, Persiev was granted early parole and was soon to be released.

He remained calm and self-possessed for one simple reason: deep down, he knew perfectly well he had never laid a finger on his wife's "sister" and his "partner," Farida, in that affair. And he knew—or at least had deduced—who had settled the score with Farida, and why.

It had been his own lawfully wedded wife, Marina. No one else could have done it. She was the one who slandered him in her testimony before the investigator and again at trial. She was the one who ensured a tape recording of Denis's words reached Farida right on schedule—when Denis was nowhere near her.

Denis knew it all, but out of true masculine nobility, he refused to expose his wife—the mother of his son, Kirill.

There was only one thing he didn't know: should he return to this woman after his sentence—a woman he still loved in his own way, someone he had grown used to and deeply attached to over the years? Or should he never, ever forgive her? Forgiveness *might* be possible, considering that Marina—looking guilty as a beaten dog—had visited him in prison more than once, bringing groceries and cigarettes (which he didn't smoke, but shared with cellmates). He spoke little to her, used only vague and general phrases—implying that he knew everything, but wouldn't expose her. That he would remain silent forever, and serve the time on her behalf—if only for the sake of their son.

But should he return to her now?... For eight years, he had wrestled with the question.

In the end, he decided: in his heart, he would forgive Marina and hold no malice against her—but he would not return to her. He would try to begin his life anew, with a clean slate.

* * *

Tashkent, 1990

The Soviet system was collapsing, and the vast country was on the verge of splitting into separate, sovereign "independent" parts. Tamilla and her cooperative were having their "oxygen cut off." Moreover, certain officials felt that the festivals organized by Maryam Baburovna with Tamilla's help were no longer appropriate.

"Can you imagine, Rashid," Tamilla told her husband, "they openly warned my mom to stop putting on the Navruz show… You remember, I used to help her with that—and now they've shut down my cooperative too… What do I do now?!"

Rashid wasn't particularly concerned. Still a fairly young man, all he wanted after coming home was to leave his work troubles behind and relax—making love to his wife, who was still so young, beautiful, and alluring.

Late at night, Batyrov tried to entice Tamilla, coaxing her into intimacy. He embraced her, kissed her, caressed her, whispered tender words of love. But Tamilla felt tense and on edge—her future was being decided at that very moment, and ideas raced through her mind, not allowing her to relax or feel like just a woman, not even for a second…

In the coming days, she needed to write the charter for her new project—a project in partnership with none other than the global fashion and perfume icon Yves Saint Laurent! It so happened that

at an international event, someone had introduced the energetic and intelligent Uzbek woman to the famous French designer, and he had become interested in her ideas, offering Tamilla a long-term collaboration.

"Just think," Tamilla nearly cried as she told her husband, "my friend Nazima said the other day that I look sick. That I'm overestimating my abilities—and, most of all, my capacity! And others, for some reason, also think this endeavour is too big and too difficult for me, that I won't succeed…"

"My dear," Rashid reassured her, "don't you realize your so-called 'friend' and all those people are just jealous? They couldn't possibly do what you can. You're a talented person, and you, my love, will pull it off!"

"Do you really think so?" Tamilla asked, brightening.

Those words gave her strength and renewed her faith in eventual success.

"I'm absolutely sure," Rashid said confidently.

He was genuinely happy to support his wife in every way. Still, deep down, he was a stranger to commerce of any kind.

What worried Batyrov more was the lack of any word from Pulat Gafarov.

Back in '85, his archaeologist friend had miraculously discovered… a fragment of the Koh-i-Noor diamond and a small piece of the golden covering from Karna's turban! But that wasn't enough. Where was the turban itself? It still hadn't been found…

Rashid continued to back the excavation, managing to secure funding through his Ministry of Culture, though it grew harder each year as little progress was made. And now, Pulat hadn't made contact in a couple of weeks.

What might have happened to him? a worried Batyrov wondered. *Could he be seriously ill?*

"Darling, maybe your Pulat found the diamonds and disappeared somewhere no one can find him?" Tamilla suggested, though half-heartedly—she usually tried to think the best of people. "Maybe he's sunning himself in Cyprus right now?"

"How can you say that, honey?" Rashid exclaimed disapprovingly. "That's definitely not Pulat! You know how honest he is—my friend of a hundred years. No, no. Something else must be going on."

"Like what? Do you have any theories?"

"Not yet. But I already called the district administration in the area where Pulat recently moved his research. One of the officials promised to contact the police and find out what's going on. He also told me this right away: apparently, the site I mentioned has long been considered abandoned, almost inaccessible, and not very hospitable—hardly suitable for tourist visits or travel by regular vehicles!"

Tamilla saw her husband's face darken. She was worried about Gafarov too.

"You know, dear," Rashid said, clearly alarmed, "I have a bad feeling something happened to my friend out there at the excavation site!"

* * *

Moscow, 1990

For another couple of years, Stanislav Zakharovich Levidovsky tried to pull himself out of a hole and get his business back on its feet in England. But when that failed, he packed up and headed to Russia.

Levidovsky, along with his wife Lyudmila and his son Stepan Kunitsin—who had decided to take his mother's surname—arrived in Moscow.

"Hello? Kirill? Pleased to speak with you!" said Levidovsky. "This is Stanislav Zakharovich—I wrote to you from England. Yes, I'm in Moscow now, I've been looking for you. Really? You don't mind meeting up? That's excellent, thank you so much!"

Here's how it had happened.

Staying in touch by phone and letters with Oleg Midiyatdinov, Levidovsky learned quite a bit about Oleg's adoptive son Kirill. The shrewd émigré realized that the interior ministry general's son now had more clout, money, and opportunities than the adoptive father. So he reached out to Kirill—who was by then living in the capital—in an attempt to establish, if not a friendship, at least a cordial acquaintance. There were many such letters.

In their correspondence with his army buddy's son, Stanislav Zakharovich came across as paternal in tone, yet also respectfully deferential toward Kirill as a potential patron. Kirill—who deep down was delighted at the attention from this Russian-speaking capitalist—grew fond of Levidovsky back when the latter was still in London. And when they finally met in Moscow, Kirill offered him both help and support.

This was a stroke of luck for Levidovsky.

No surprise, Stanislav Zakharovich had not gone to Oleg Shamilyevich Midiyatdinov—who in recent years had exasperated him with brazen blackmail over those diamonds they had once stolen together from the plant near Gazli and smuggled to England. Indeed, Oleg had been the one to mastermind the heist, but he cunningly pinned all the blame on Levidovsky. The wily industrialist was sick and tired of such treatment.

Levidovsky—now broke—turned up at wealthy Kirill's place and even lived in his home for several days until, with Kirill's help, he rented a solid apartment in one of the capital's prestigious areas. Unlike his adoptive father, the younger Midiyatdinov never pressured Levidovsky but simply welcomed him with no conditions attached.

Naturally, since coming to Moscow, Stanislav Zakharovich had sometimes met with his daughter Sasha, but without much pleasure—he had long been unable to stand her husband, Alexei Irmanov, and Alexei's father, Vadim Borisovich.

Even at Alexei's birthday celebration in a restaurant—where Sasha had invited Levidovsky—the once English oligarch cornered a visiting Rashid Batyrov, an important cultural figure from Uzbekistan who had come for the occasion, and tried to persuade Rashid to frame Alexei for a fee somehow:

"You see, dear Rashid, I think my dearest son-in-law is getting far too big for his britches. Perhaps it's time we put him in his place, don't you agree?"

At this, the honest and honourable Rashid nearly lost his temper and almost threw his old friend's father-in-law out of the restaurant.

Had Sasha not intervened, that's exactly what Irmanov's loyal companion, Rashid, would have done. Once she learned why her guest from Tashkent was so furious, she scolded her father herself:

"Papa, forgive me, but you really ought to go home now."

"You know, daughter," Levidovsky retorted accusatorily, "somehow my real home isn't where you and your husband live, but with another man who's become closer to me and dearer than any blood relative! And I have no wish to deal with you, Sasha, or your entire family anymore!"

"But you hardly ever dealt with us, Daddy," Sasha said calmly, leading her father to a taxi. "For years, I never even knew what you were up to in London!"

…Before long, Kirill helped Stanislav find work, and the older man slowly began to recover after the traumatic bankruptcy and impoverishment he had experienced abroad.

With Konstantin's approval, Kirill appointed Levidovsky as overseer of one of the largest jewellery factories in Moscow. Now Stanislav Zakharovich was in high spirits—he smiled and joked more often. Until one sad event darkened his face…

At his country home in Moscow, Levidovsky's close friend, General Oleg Shamilyevich Midiyatdinov, suddenly died of a heart attack.

The doctors, summoned by the deceased's son Kirill Midiyatdinov, wrote an official report attributing the general's death to acute heart failure. Police experts from the local precinct arrived at the late general's house and found no sign of foul play—such as rapidly dissolving poison. Nothing of the sort.

Kirill and Stanislav Zakharovich, along with the deceased man's sister Marina—and many of the general's acquaintances (though apart from Levidovsky, Oleg hadn't really had close friends)—arranged a proper funeral for him, complete with a respectable wake at a Moscow restaurant.

All the guests marvelled at what a wonderful, generous, and caring son Oleg Shamilyevich had raised! Only Marina eyed little Kiryushenka with suspicion, as though guessing something no outsider would suspect. For instance, she thought it odd that her brother—unlike herself, who had always complained of heart trouble—could just drop dead from heart failure. She also knew who might have harboured lethal hatred for Oleg…

It would be a stretch to say Marina had adored her brother, but she still felt sorry for him… And if she truly loved anyone fiercely, it was Kirill. Therefore, she gave no outward sign and didn't let a single muscle twitch to betray that she had guessed the truth behind Oleg's death.

* * *

Tashkent, same period

Despite her exhausted, depleted condition, Tamilla was stunned. In the abandoned hangar where she and her husband Rashid were held captive, Bahrom—the bandit who liked to present himself as the ringleader—had just brought in… Konstantin Romanov, Tamilla Mahkamova's colleague from international student projects, tied up and gagged!

And Tamilla had so hoped he would be the one to help them and get them out!

So much for that hope… the woman thought desperately. *Who's going to save us now?*

"You monsters, at least take the gag out so he can breathe properly!" Tamilla shouted indignantly at Bahrom. But Bahrom didn't lift a finger.

Dmitry, the guard, glanced at Bahrom, then quickly looked away. He approached the unfortunate Romanov—whose shirt was just as torn and dirty as Rashid's—and pulled a grimy, crumpled rag from his mouth.

"Hello, Tamilla Sardorovna," Romanov managed to say, coughing and rasping. "Please forgive me for my foolishness! It took all I had to find where they're holding you. Then I came with my assistants to free you and your husband…"

Out of courtesy, Romanov would have extended a hand to Rashid, but both of his hands were bound, so he merely nodded politely to Batyrov, who nodded back.

Frightened out of his wits, the Russian intellectual went on:

"But these vile bandits killed my assistants! Can you imagine? It's a nightmare! What do I tell their families?! And as you can see, Tamilla Sardorovna, they've grabbed me, tied me up, and dragged me here to you. So now we're all prisoners together…"

"Indeed, dear Konstantin Ivanovich," Tamilla sighed. "It's like some terrible dream, as if this isn't actually happening to us!"

"They're probably expecting me to persuade you of something," Romanov guessed, groaning and rasping from thirst.

Turning to Dmitry, who seemed more humane than Bahrom (who had just stepped out again), he said:

"Please… may I have some water?"

"We're low on water," Dmitry replied honestly. "But if your friends don't mind, I'll let you have what's left, and I'll bring more in about two hours or so, when someone comes to relieve me. Alright?"

The kind-hearted spouses immediately agreed that their friend should have a drink!

Romanov didn't refuse. He gulped down every drop the guard gave him, without stopping to think that if Dmitry didn't bring more water for another two or three hours, Tamilla and her husband—stuck in this stifling heat—might faint from thirst…

Poor man… he's at his limit, Tamilla thought sympathetically.

"Anyway, as I was saying!" Romanov recollected. "They picked the wrong guy! I'll never betray you, rest assured! We're colleagues, Tamilla Sardorovna—and, no offense to your husband, we're good friends too. So you both can rely on me completely. But if there's something I don't know—a secret you've been keeping—it'd be wiser to tell me now. You know? So I'll know what to be ready for… Because there's something that prompted them to keep you here! And now me too."

He gave a sad, cryptic smirk.

"Believe me, Konstantin Ivanovich, we have no secret," Tamilla Sardorovna assured her international partner. "Bahrom kept demanding information about the Koh-i-Noor diamond, believing some priceless gem from the British crown ended up with me… But let's be honest, that is total nonsense!"

"Seriously?" Romanov marvelled. "They really think that? Pardon me, but that's idiotic. Of all people, they chose you to ask for diamonds… Although…" He paused, then said, meaningfully, "Rashid Kudratovich, dear sir, I heard you once immersed yourself in that subject and supposedly know something special about the Koh-i-Noor! Isn't that right?"

Batyrov froze, recalling his late friend Pulat Gafarov, who had spent his life searching for the golden turban of the Indian boy Karna, once presented to the Massagetae queen Tomyris—and the fragments of that ancient diamond that once adorned it.

But Rashid had no desire to discuss this now. What did some ancient past have to do with their situation? And Gafarov, who had found a few diamond shards, was gone… They needed to get out of here; that was all that mattered to Batyrov.

"All right, perhaps you'll tell me later," Romanov relented, noticing how Tamilla Mahkamova's husband frowned. "And I found out another crucial bit of info: apparently, Bahrom isn't really the top dog here. These Cerberuses are just pawns. Their real boss is named Kirill Denisovich. We need to find a way to see him personally! I'm sure that once we explain we have nothing worth taking, he'll let us go. Although I must warn you—I've heard (and it is my duty to let you know this) that Kirill is extremely cruel and vicious, with blood on his hands! So I beg you, friends: if you do have any hidden treasure—diamonds, gems—for heaven's sake, hand them over to these monsters! That's our only hope of simply surviving and getting out of here in one piece! Promise me you'll consider my humble plea... I don't want to spend the rest of my life here..."

Tamilla felt very sorry that, however unwittingly, her colleague was suffering alongside her and Rashid.

She mulled it over, then looked seriously at her lifelong companion.

"Rashid, maybe you should tell us everything you know about those diamond shards," she ventured. "Then we can decide together whether we should let the bandits in on it..."

"All right, if you insist—and if it's necessary now—I'll tell you," Rashid agreed, seeing no point in arguing with his wife. "My friend, the archaeologist Pulat Gafarov, who was excavating the heritage of the great Queen Tomyris, suddenly vanished..."

29

Sakastan, 6th Century BCE

Several more years passed.

The son of Tomyris and Rustam, Prince Spargapis II, had grown up. Now a striking young man, he began taking part in battles alongside his parents. No matter how hard his mother tried to keep him out of harm's way, danger for the Saka still lurked everywhere. They were never left in peace. As a result, every man—even one so young, and certainly the queen's son—had to arm himself and quickly become a real warrior, a bold and courageous defender of his people.

As a woman and a mother, Tomyris loathed warfare, and under her rule, the Massagetae rarely invaded others' lands first. At every opportunity, she halted hostilities. Yet as the queen of nomads who, after all, drew a major part of their livelihood and wealth from war—second only to raising livestock—she had to reckon with their interests and occasionally carry out military raids on neighbouring territories. As fate would have it, Tomyris's reign was beset by numerous and especially bloody wars—more so than any the Saka had fought before—because they endured frequent attacks from without: from the Sarmatians, the Gurgsars and Caspians, the Khwarezmians, the Sogdians…

Amid all this, Queen Tomyris became a brilliant military commander, a true Amazon in her own right.

Of course, in the countless battles and unending perils, the Massagetae—who now adored and protected their incomparable queen—knew she needed a personal bodyguard. Out of her many warriors, Tomyris herself chose a young, strong, agile, and handsome man named Bakhtiyar for that role.

Months rolled by, and Bakhtiyar diligently carried out his duties, protecting the Massagetae's most precious treasure—their unrivalled queen.

For all her courage and prowess as a leader in war, Tomyris remained, at heart, a true woman. For so many years, she had been not just a warrior but the military leader of her people. Yet she was still quite young and beautiful, and as such—attractive and desirable in the eyes of many of the men surrounding her.

Despite the fact that Bakhtiyar was a bit younger than the queen, he could not help falling under her spell. The imposing bodyguard fell passionately, fervently in love with his queen.

Tomyris, being a woman, could not fail to notice. She saw how he grew flustered in her presence, how ardently and meaningfully he gazed at her. She noted the happiness radiating from him whenever she appeared.

At some point, it even seemed to her that he exuded a certain fragrance—oddly familiar, reminiscent of freshly cut herbs. But she could not recall where she might have smelled it before.

One night, Tomyris had a dream. She dreamed she returned alone to her tent after a battle, exhausted. Except in the dream, the tent seemed extraordinary, lavishly adorned like a Persian palace. As always, she washed and changed into clean nightclothes.

Suddenly, Bakhtiyar entered the tent—where ordinarily, no one but Rustam and young Spargapis could enter uninvited. Yet in Tomyris's dream, Bakhtiyar walked in of his own accord, silently, gracefully like a panther. He was brimming with fiery passion, more than ever before. The young man took his beloved queen by the shoulders. He began kissing them, baring her skin, then kissed her neck, her ears, her forehead, her shining golden hair, as though he were drowning in it.

"Don't, Bakhtiyar, my dear, don't," was all she managed to say. Wearied from the day's trials and caught in the strong arms of this attentive, handsome man, she was utterly relaxed—without the strength to resist him.

A moment later, Bakhtiyar lifted the queen of his heart in his arms and gently laid her upon her bed. He did not dare violate her—he could not force any intimacy she did not desire. Instead, he simply caressed, embraced, and kissed her—sweetly and ardently, yet delicately, with tender caution, so that his powerful body would do her no harm. Bakhtiyar was gentleness itself toward Tomyris.

And then she realized, in her heart… that she actually wanted this. She took the lead, commanding their union as the absolute mistress.

Now she clasped his body with all her strength, swiftly undressing him while kissing his lips. She pushed him back so that he lay fully beneath her. It was no longer he who possessed her, but she who possessed him. Naturally, she allowed him that final motion of entering her, yet she herself dictated their every posture.

Here, at last, was the very thing she had yearned for all these years.

A thought flashed through her mind: it had never been like this with Rustam. Not once in her life with Rustam had she experienced such powerful fulfilment, such profound rapture. Intimacy with her husband had never stirred such a rush of blissful sensations—both physical and emotional—as this splendid young bodyguard had given her in mere minutes.

Bakhtiyar did not dominate or overshadow her; not a part of him tried to rule over her. He belonged to her entirely, like a slave. With him, she felt total ecstasy.

All wet, as though it had truly happened rather than merely a dream, Tomyris awoke.

"No!" she cried into the darkness, as if someone might hear her (indeed, the servants guarding her tent outside might well have heard). Then, more quietly, she told herself, "No, I shall never cheat on my husband, even if I no longer love him at all. I am the great Saka queen! And let my entire people—and all our descendants— know that Tomyris is unblemished, ever faithful to her lawful spouse."

Meanwhile, Bakhtiyar, wholly unaware and unsuspecting of Tomyris's dream, continued hovering around her, showering her with every possible attention and kindness his modest resources and limited wit allowed. Tomyris considered sending him away to remove the temptation. But he served her too well—as both defender and aide—ever obedient and loyal to his queen. So she kept postponing his transfer to one or another of the Massagetae battalions.

Alongside her Amazons, Tomyris also had a personal guard made up of the fiercest, bravest male warriors—whom the tribe dubbed "the Fierce Ones." Her plan was to place Bakhtiyar in command of them.

As for Rustam, even after all these years, he adored his wife with undiminished devotion.

"My dear," he grumbled one day, "I don't like how that… hm… that young warrior looks at you! It's as if he's kissing you with his eyes! What does he want? Do you think he's in love with you?

For the sake of our son, Tomyris, tell me honestly—has he been pestering you? Has he forgotten who you are—the queen—and who he is?"

"No, never fear, my beloved," the queen replied with a smile. "There's no cause for jealousy or worry. That young man—his name is Bakhtiyar—is merely my guard. He's more like a brother to me. A younger brother. So don't fret, Rustam. Everything's fine."

"I hope so. But if I find out that he's bothering you in any way, then be warned: I'll kill him on the spot, without hesitation!"

***

Persia, the Same Century

King Cyrus II now deemed himself utterly invincible. After all, so many lands and cities—most notably the once-impregnable Babylon—had submitted to him. Moreover, both the Babylonian oligarchy and Cyrus himself had skilfully concealed any hint of conquest, blaming the coup on Nabonidus, the last king of the Neo-Babylonian dynasty.

Into Cyrus's chambers came his favourite, still young but already ambitious Cambyses II, named after the father of the conqueror of much of the world.

"Father, I've seen the now-famous Cyrus Cylinder with your manifesto," the young prince began in a displeased tone. "I gather you want everyone in this country to see you not as a conqueror, but as a 'father' and 'liberator.' Right?"

Cyrus smirked smugly, not bothering to deny it.

"I don't see what's so funny!" Cambyses the Younger continued. "All right, I can accept that you promised peace and safety to the people of Babylon's cities. But how am I to understand that you first appoint me—your eldest son and heir—as King of Babylon, and then, barely a couple of months later, you, King of Media and Persia, name yourself King of Babylon and All Lands? Isn't that a bit much for you alone?"

"Son, you know nothing of politics yet," Cyrus retorted. "That's how it must be."

"'It must be!'" the young prince mimicked his father. "Must be for whom?"

"Your time will come, believe me. Formally, I'll preserve Babylon's kingdom and won't change its system. Babylon will become one of my royal seats, and Babylonians will hold a dominant place in my realm. Understand, I want no one in Babylon to see my rule as foreign oppression."

"Yes, yes, I know!" Cambyses broke in. "Everyone says you received this kingdom 'from the hands of the god Marduk' after fulfilling some ancient sacred rites in the Esagil temple. And the Babylonian priesthood is restoring old cults—under your patronage! Nicely arranged, I must say."

"Naturally. And you should learn from your father while you can! By the way, you still don't realize that Babylon, once a sovereign kingdom, will soon, in fact, become just a satrapy of my Achaemenid Empire, stripped of all independence in foreign policy. I've already taken steps to make it so. And after the capture of Babylonia, all the western lands to Egypt's borders—Syria, Palestine, Phoenicia—have voluntarily bowed to the Persians as well. The Phoenician trading cities, just like those in Babylonia or Asia Minor, have an interest in building a vast state with safe roads. Achieving all this, dear Cambyses, is beyond your power for now. Incidentally, within Babylon itself, supreme military and administrative authority will belong to my governor—the head of the Babylonian region and the entire Neo-Babylonian Empire."

"But I hope, Father, that at least you've appointed me as that governor?"

"No, apologies. I've assigned my loyal and capable commander Gubaru—whom the Greeks call Gobryas—to that post."

"But why?!" Cambyses the Younger exclaimed.

"For now, he's more experienced than you. As for Harpagus…" Cyrus paused to think for a moment. "It's time for Harpagus to fall on someone's sword—he's grown far too old. And his shameless insolence is intolerable: he still considers me, the great divine ruler, as his son! It might be forgivable if he kept quiet more often, but he's so used to being the warlord under my grandfather Astyages and under me—always sticking his nose into every campaign. When will my subordinates finally grasp that I—and I alone—am the supreme leader and military commander? I personally lead my armies into battle and always emerge victorious! And as for the Saka—naturally, I myself will lead my soldiers against them!"

"The Saka? Who are they, Father? Those savages from a distant land you once spoke of—the ones whose kings have neither palaces nor even proper houses?"

"Yes, them—the nomads. But they occupy a large—no, enormous—territory, with plenty of valiant warriors and gold! Precisely what we need. I'm told there's a certain wondrous queen there, a Massagetaean Amazon of dazzling beauty, who, with sword and spear, strikes down hundreds and thousands of the bravest male warriors and fears no one! But I'll crack that proud mare-herder like a nut. I've already sent an embassy to her. Understand, my son: it's a matter of principle for me to subjugate her and her boundless country. And at the same time, seize for myself a certain large precious stone—most likely in her possession…"

"You really think you can do it, Father?" Cambyses asked, twisting his mouth.

"Meaning?" Cyrus the Second asked in bewilderment.

"What I mean is this. I'm just wondering—can any single man forever lay claim to absolutely everything he wants in life? Would the heavens allow that to anyone?"

"They certainly allow it to me! I am the Great King of the universe, and everything is permitted to me, for I stand on earth like a god," Cyrus replied haughtily. "Besides, I needn't rely on mere weaponry… I have trickery and deceit, yes? And who is there to stop me?…"

And the king laughed boldly.

Cambyses the Younger thought he could probably never think like that himself.

***

Sakastan, 6th Century BCE

Rustam burst into Tomyris's presence while she was eating her midday meal. He was furious, but held his tongue.

"Care for some roast lamb with fresh onion and vegetables?" his wife asked coolly, continuing her meal without pausing.

If it had been anyone else in Rustam's place, Tomyris would have had him thrown out—or even killed. No one was allowed to disturb the queen's enjoyment of her food. Even in wartime, if she chose to dine (which was not always the case—affairs of state, most of all the conduct of war, took precedence over any meal), once she began, no one dared intrude.

"How delicious these suckling lambs are, raised on our innocent mountain pastures, where no human blood has ever been spilled," she said, chewing each expertly roasted morsel prepared by her personal cook. "Husband, please, don't stand there in my face. Better to sit and eat with me."

"I don't feel like eating now—can't you understand?!" Rustam suddenly exploded.

"Have you forgotten your place?!" snapped Tomyris, knitting her brow and regarding her spouse as a mighty queen would glare at a wayward slave.

"Forgive me, my queen," Rustam said, shaking his slightly greying head as he sat down at the low table across from her. But he did not so much as glance at the food. "I lost control... You know I'm no alarmist. Never have been in my entire life. I've never feared anyone or anything—I've bested entire armies. But now I am afraid—of course, not for myself! I worry for you and for our son... We've got serious problems, Tomyris, and I doubt I can solve them all on my own. And yet I see how calm you seem... Are you truly unaware, or just pretending not to notice? Sorry—maybe this unflappable mask is your secret weapon?"

"Explain to me what's happened that should give me cause to fret. If it's war—those are constant here, and you and I are used to that... If it's a shortage of food among our tribes—well, as always, we'll remedy that with raids or hunting..."

"That's not it!" Rustam grew agitated again. "Why did you agree to receive that sinister brute, that torturer?"

"What brute?" Tomyris asked, settling herself comfortably against soft cushions.

"Don't pretend," Rustam grumbled. "I mean King Cyrus. Why didn't you send his ambassador from Pasargadae packing—back to his own land? You even accepted that ivory Persian throne from him as a gift—welcomed him with honours, served him food!"

"Do you think we have none to spare?"

"You know I'm no miser—you know that perfectly well. Though it wouldn't hurt to keep more provisions… for the common warriors and their families."

"Oh, come on, that's too much! Next you'll accuse me of robbing my own people of their wealth and food! You know perfectly well it isn't so. I'd sooner go hungry myself than let my people suffer. But as for the envoy and his master—we need them. This is politics, something you—"

"Something I, a common soldier and rough brute, don't understand in the slightest!" Rustam finished for her, trying to hide his frustration. "Is that it?"

"Yes. Don't be offended. Simply put, Rustam… the point is to avoid war with a prosperous and powerful conqueror! Cyrus's name is feared everywhere as the bloodiest of kings. We might not survive such a war—his army is vast and strong. It's better for us to receive Cyrus as a guest, a kindly friend and ally."

"And you, my dear, truly believe that a murderous man would travel here from worlds away just to share a cup of sweet *haoma* with you?… And yet you claim *I'm* the one who lacks political savvy. At least I'm not as naïve and soft-hearted as my wonderful wife! Forgive my bluntness, but Cyrus is a wolf who thirsts for blood. He should be killed on the spot before he slaughters the entire flock! I'd rather do battle with him and trust in fate and the mercy of the gods. Cyrus never leaves anyone alone until he's torn them to pieces, devoured them, and drained their blood. His envoy spent a whole month here—riding our horses, snooping and asking questions—and our trusting tribe poured out everything he wanted, showed and explained every last detail. Why? Because you gave no instructions to keep important matters secret, nor did you prevent him from visiting any critical location! All thanks to your boundless kindness, my queen. One day, it'll be our downfall—yours and the rest of us with you. When Cyrus arrives, not with a modest retinue but with his vast Persian-Median host, you'll see I was right about him! By then, it may be too late."

"You're exaggerating. Everything will be fine. I can protect you and all the Saka!" Tomyris laughed, seemingly pleased with her own jest. "Is that everything you wanted to say?"

"No, not everything…"

Rustam paused, trying to find the right words. He was no master of eloquence, and it pained him to speak diplomatically. Yet he loved Tomyris dearly and wanted, at all costs, to shield her from distress and danger.

"The thing is… I feel, dear wife, that we were unwise to let Zakir remain among the Tocharians and reclaim his position as their chieftain."

"Not 'we allowed it,' but *I* allowed it," Tomyris corrected him. "I alone have the authority for that—did you forget? And once again you're reproaching me…"

"No, that's not what I mean! The point is, from reliable sources, I know that scoundrel Zakir, together with the Alan leader Haidar—your old foe, by the way—are plotting a terrible conspiracy against you. They might be ready to do anything, including killing you, Tomyris, convinced that one of them will take your place on the throne. I'm just a warrior, strong only on the battlefield. I'm clueless about treacherous plotting and intrigue. So please, let me strengthen your personal guard!"

"All right, if you like. But only temporarily—and only if I don't have to see or hear them. I don't want them treading at my heels or tailing me everywhere!"

"As you wish, my queen. By the way, where is your bodyguard Bakhtiyar? He hasn't been seen in days—right when tensions are running high…"

"He asked permission to go home for a while, to see his ailing mother. Of course, I let him go. You know I'm merciful and always think of my lo—my people."

"Especially *him*, yes?" Rustam grumbled. "Tomyris, do you still trust that scoundrel? Again I warn you—he's not nearly as noble as you think. You can't trust him at all, let alone set him over your royal guard!"

"Ah, so that's it—Bakhtiyar! You're just jealous! I assure you there's no cause for that, my dear. I've never been intimate with him. I am not, and I won't be."

"Listen—our spies recently spotted Bakhtiyar… *at Zakir's camp*! Why was he there? Do you know? I don't! But it's very suspicious. He's lying to you about traveling to see a sick old mother, yet behind your back, he's working with your enemies! Haven't you had enough traitors in the tribes? Do you really want to house a repulsive, sneaky rat inside your own home?"

"Enough!! That's too much, Rustam. Later you'll be ashamed of these words, because Bakhtiyar is loyal and devoted to me—and he's… never mind. Did you consider that he might have gone there on reconnaissance, to learn our foes' plans against me—his queen and mistress—and then report back?"

"Well then, when he shows up, ask him yourself. Maybe you'll see that I was right."

"Husband, your foolish, groundless jealousy is making you lose your mind! Possibly my fault too, since I haven't shared my bed with you in so long..."

"Yes, ever since your father died, it's like you've come to hate all men—taking vengeance on us for something. You've grown cold toward me; your passion has faded. Only that Bakhtiyar do you greet with favour. But I—I still love you fiercely! Tomyris, my dear, I beg you, for our son's sake if nothing else: please listen to me! You've known me all these years. I could never wish harm upon you!"

* * *

Their Sarmatian danger had subsided for the time being, thanks to Amage, the new and wiser queen of the Sarmatians, unlike her predecessor Kiana. Amage respected, and slightly feared, Rustam and took Tomyris seriously.

Seeing this lull, Zakir, chieftain of the Tocharians, and Haidar, chieftain of the Alans, decided it was the perfect time to act. They devised a plan to strike at Tomyris. Haidar convinced Zakir that he, the Alan leader, had a stronger claim to the Massagetae throne than Zakir—who had lost the respect of most Massagetae tribes and was no longer young. Zakir would serve as "Chief Advisor" to the new king. Unhappy about it but seeing no better option, Zakir agreed.

"We can undermine our queen in two ways," Haidar proposed at a secret council of conspirators. "First, we must drive a wedge between Tomyris and Rustam. Without his backing, she'll be far more vulnerable and weak!"

"Indeed, no one can argue with that," Zakir nodded. "But is it even possible? Everyone knows that even if the queen seems indifferent and harsh toward him, he follows her like a loyal dog on a chain, ready to tear apart anyone who approaches with bad intentions! I suspect we'll need my naïve nephew, who's besotted with Tomyris. Both my troops and yours, Haidar, are on full combat alert. It's all up to Bakhtiyar. He has to seduce Tomyris and keep her occupied, and we'll make sure Rustam hears of his wife's 'betrayal!' Then Rustam will surely leave her—at least for a while. That's all the time we'll need to kill the queen."

"What makes you so sure your nephew will go along with this scheme?"

"That fool already agreed!" boasted the Tocharian chieftain.

"Tell me, what did you promise him?" The Alan leader couldn't contain his curiosity. "Did you lie and tell him that after you die, he'll inherit the Tocharian tribe?"

"You're perceptive, Haidar," Zakir laughed, pleased with himself for how easily he duped people. "Of course the tribe will pass to my son, no one else! My little sister's son, Bakhtiyar, won't even get my daughter—that lovely young Behnaz, whom I promised him as a bride. But I needed to lure that clueless pup and force him to do my bidding! So I promised that if he brought me the turban of Tomyris with its precious diamond, once he 'becomes Tocharian chieftain' and 'my lawful son-in-law,' I'd give it to him. The idiot believes me, Haidar!"

"I trust, Zakir, you haven't forgotten that you actually promised me your Behnaz?" growled the fat, homely Alan chieftain. "A deal is worth more than gold!"

"I remember, of course. And that's why I agreed to make you—not someone else—king of the Massagetae. I know you're an ambitious, wealthy man, and only with you can my daughter become a true queen! She dreams of a throne more than I do. At the same time, we will together take revenge on the entire family of Spargapises the Elder. We only need that nephew of mine not to fail."

30

Media – Sakastan, 6th Century BCE

Uncle to Rustam and Zogak, Sakesfar ventured to carefully remind the King of Persia of his earlier request. Thus, King Cyrus began preparing to march against the Saka.

After passing through Gedrosia, a satrapy of the Achaemenid Empire—sustaining some army losses along the way—and accompanied by his general Gubaru, Cyrus arrived at Tomyris's encampment.

The Queen of the Massagetae received her illustrious visitor in her own tent, instructing her servants to leave its entrance flung wide open so that all her people might see and hear everything that transpired between her and Cyrus.

Standing behind her was Rustam, his right hand resting conspicuously on the hilt of the most formidable and keen-edged of his swords.

In and around the tent, throngs of Massagetae chieftains—fully armed—milled about, as did the dense ranks of her personal guard, the "Fierce Ones." Had the entrance not been open, the crush of people alone would have made it impossible to breathe inside.

The queen herself was in her field battle attire, as though she were not seated on a throne, but astride a warhorse, ready to charge at the first flick of her riding whip. Her pure-gold armor gleamed, reflecting the light. At her belt hung a jewel-encrusted scabbard in which, seemingly at peace, rested a razor-sharp acinaces with a carved tiger-bone hilt.

Over her glorious, long, golden hair she wore a red turban embroidered with golden thread, atop which shone a gigantic diamond, radiant as the sun.

Cyrus, for his part, betrayed no sign that he grasped the meaning of such a setting: the queen clearly stood ready for war against him. Inwardly, though, he scoffed. *How could this delicate woman be any sort of warrior?* Meanwhile, Tomyris treated Cyrus with the warmest courtesy.

He could not take his eyes off her. Though Cyrus was well past his youth, married for many years, and had numerous concubines (with whom, in truth, he rarely spent time, being constantly on military campaigns), he now found himself utterly smitten by the beauty of this "savage" Saka queen. Her ambassador had never told him anything like that!

"Allow me to express my admiration for your beauty, O Queen!" Cyrus began, gazing at Tomyris without looking away. "I am completely enchanted and humbled before you!"

Tomyris gave a measured yet polite smile.

"I thank you, Your Majesty," she replied calmly. "But I feel certain that you, the King of Persia, have not journeyed so far into my great domain merely so that the two of us might sit here discussing my beauty. Am I right?"

Shrewd as he was, Cyrus instantly caught the nuance in that brief response to his flattery, where each word was carefully weighed and considered. She had called him "King of Persia."... Was it only Persia? Was he not also the conqueror of half the world? Some would consider that nearly an insult. Yet Cyrus swallowed it in silence, chalking it up to the ignorance or lack of refinement of his hostess. He also overlooked her pointed hint that all these Saka lands belonged to her and her alone.

"Permit me first, O Queen, to present you with my gifts!" Cyrus said with practiced sweetness. He clapped his hands, and Persian slaves laid the offerings at Tomyris's feet. At a nod from Cyrus, they opened the chests and boxes. They contained all manner of treasures—lavish ornaments, brilliantly hued fabrics in every shade, clothing and scarves, wooden and metal wares, fruits and dried fruit, nuts, jugs of wine and honey…

"To what do we owe such generosity, Your Majesty? What have we done to deserve all this?" Tomyris asked in slightly ironic tones, not so much as batting an eye at the splendid bounty.

Proudly drawing himself up, Cyrus fixed his gaze on the queen and began:

"I am the Aryan Kurush—in another tongue, Cyrus II! I say to you, Queen of the Massagetae, that the bird of fortune, Humayun, has alighted upon your shoulder, for I, the mighty and great king—ruler of all four corners of the earth, lord of every land, son of Cambyses, grandson of Astyages and Cyrus I, descendant of Achaemenes and heir to an eternal kingdom—have chosen that you shall be my wife!"

All in the tent fell silent, tensely awaiting the queen's response.

Tomyris looked at Cyrus solemnly, then broke into a smile. Finally, she burst out laughing—loud, unrestrained, and merry— and her people took up her laughter in chorus.

"What? You want me to be your wife? And why has your envoy never said a word about that to me? Nor did you, who came to court me in person—towing your entire army along! Is that how one asks for a beloved's hand—at sword point?… And need I point out, King, that I am already lawfully married?… Is a Massagetae queen permitted two husbands—both of royal blood?"

Cyrus's envoy had mentioned a "hero named Rustam," but he had assumed Rustam was merely Tomyris's protector and commander-in-chief. He had not known that Rustam was, in fact, her husband—let alone a prince in his own right—and thus he had told Cyrus nothing of the sort.

The king did not like the queen's laughter, finding it offensive. But once again, the Persian forgave the Massagetae, telling himself she must be flustered by such unexpected good fortune.

"Your beauty shines like a bright star, Tomyris. And a star should not remain the companion of a dingy lamp," Cyrus said, deliberately insulting the formidable Rustam with a direct glance at him, "when she might accept the alliance of the Sun itself!"

Enraged, Rustam drew his sword from its scabbard in a single fluid motion. Yet Cyrus showed no fear, standing proudly and confidently. In his mind, no "unworthy barbarian resembling a bear" could frighten the king of a mighty empire ruling half the world.

With a commanding gesture, Tomyris held Rustam back. Addressing Cyrus, she said:

"I will not accept your gifts, King Cyrus. No offense intended. I acknowledge that you are strong, powerful, and in full possession of your authority. I do respect such men; I sometimes take lessons from them. But I, Tomyris—the free-born daughter of the steppe— love the wide-open sky, my native boundless lands, and my own people! I have no wish to exchange them for the bright, wealthy, and stifling prison of your harem. I am the daughter of the great Massagetae lord Spargapis—not a slave or concubine meant to cater to some master's whims! I was born a queen and have ruled, and I shall die as one. And besides, I do not love you. Furthermore, when you prepared for this campaign, you had no inkling of my beauty at all!"

Cyrus tried to interrupt, but the queen raised her hand to show she had not finished. In that moment, she realized Rustam had been entirely correct in warning her of the Persian's cunning.

"All this, King Cyrus, tells me clearly: it isn't me you want, but my kingdom—my large, bountiful domain! I ask you to guard your own borders and not trespass upon mine! In other words, I advise you to rule your own land; if you so desire, call yourself king of the entire world. I've heard you promised your subjects you would bathe me in my own blood! Well, here's my reply: do not even think of waging war against me! Or I swear by my acinaces and the spirit of my father that I shall make you drink your own blood!"

"You will regret those words, Tomyris—there will be no forgiveness for them!" Cyrus flared, ripping off a glove and casting it at her feet. "I declare war on you!! You are nothing but a cheap woman, not a queen! Even the diamond on your turban isn't real—worth no more than a single copper coin!"

With that, seething with anger, Cyrus wheeled around and stormed out of Tomyris's tent, his retinue trailing after him. At a flick of Tomyris's hand, all the Massagetae chieftains likewise followed them outside, leaving only her inner circle in the tent.

"My queen, though that man is a scoundrel, perhaps you needn't have spoken so bluntly?" said Tomyris's great-uncle, Salih, the white-bearded chieftain of the Abii, shaking his head. "We know you can be diplomatic when it serves, and yet you lost your temper today... Now it's certain—war will come swiftly, maybe immediately! You might as well count it begun."

"Were we not prepared for it, Uncle?" Tomyris answered serenely. "I have made my decision. I saw through Cyrus's treacherous plan! Yielding to his vile wiles would have signalled weakness; accepting gifts from an alien who wants to enslave us all would have made us look timid and cowardly. But neither I nor my people are weak or fearful—am I correct?"

All those present confirmed her words. Rustam lifted his mighty sword.

"The strong are respected and feared," the queen went on, "while the weak are subjugated, beaten, and robbed. Yes, I obviously appealed to King Cyrus—everyone saw that. But to have some sordid affair with him behind my lawful husband's back? I would never stoop to that! And anyway, his fleeting fancy would soon pass. What then? I assure you, he came here to make himself lord over all of us—and to make us his slaves. Is that what you all want?"

Salih and Berez shook their heads, recognizing the truth in Tomyris's words.

I will kill Cyrus on the battlefield, thought Spargapis II—her son—but he said nothing aloud. *No one is allowed to insult my father or defile my mother like this!*

"Where is Bakhtiyar, by the way?" the queen asked. "Even now, he's still not here?! At such a critical time! I want to understand, Rustam—what did Cyrus mean when he said the diamond was not genuine? That's impossible! The Son of the Sun, Karna, could never have deceived me—he was a sacred being, incapable of lying. For so many years, I've seen how that diamond shone and glowed, how it helped me by some miracle, saving me from many dangers! That can only mean one thing…"

"It likely means that, not long ago, someone stole your true royal turban and replaced the genuine gemstone with a counterfeit,"

Rustam suggested. "Forgive me for saying so, but… might it have been Bakhtiyar?"

Tomyris frowned. She wanted to retort, *"You're at it again?!"* but this time she held her tongue. After all, Bakhtiyar really had been away from her side for quite a while.

* * *

A few days later, toward evening, Tomyris sat alone in her tent.

Bakhtiyar slipped in without an announcement, then dropped to his knees before her.

"I'll have you executed!" she said angrily, lightning in her eyes. "Where have you been all this time, Bakhtiyar? Don't you dare lie to me and say you were visiting your ailing mother! You know a queen has her own secret intelligence network. My reliable people informed me you were having a long consultation with my enemies—Zakir and Haidar, who've wanted for ages to depose me and seize my place on the Massagetae throne! How could you? And how dare you, after that, come crawling back here to me?"

"O my love!…"

"Do not call me—your queen—by that name!"

"Forgive me, my radiant sovereign, light of my eyes!" he exclaimed, prostrating himself and feverishly kissing the hem of her robe. "When you're angry, you grow even more beautiful. Well… yes, I'll hide it no longer. I was there. But believe me, it was all by necessity—for your sake, my fortune, to protect you from those vile, hateful men! The best way to gather intelligence is right in the enemy's den, feasting at his table, letting him think you're a close friend! There, I learned a great deal on your behalf. These treacherous chieftains you yourself named truly want you dead.

They plan to attack you… tomorrow at dawn!"

"It might be so… But still, you deceived me, Bakhtiyar. Spinning tales of your mother. Why?"

"I didn't want to worry you needlessly, my queen! I feared I might fail—that I'd return in shame, having achieved nothing… Tomyris, let me tell you: the conspirators, knowing how kind and generous you are to me—your unworthy servant—ordered that tomorrow at daybreak, I lead your guard, the 'Fierce Ones,' away from you… the same group you were thinking of placing under my command!"

"What?! My finest warriors? How dare they!"

"Please, hear me out. The chieftains Haidar and Zakir, along with Sher, chieftain of the Apasiaks, and Parviz, chieftain of the Sakaravaks, intend to exploit that chance to slip into camp easily and kill you. They're not afraid of Rustam, either—they plan to murder him first, from hiding, so he won't have time to protect you. I flatly refused to do their bidding and fled before they could drive an acinaces into me. I rode back at breakneck speed to warn you. Without my cooperation, they can't succeed."

The queen fell silent, studying her subordinate carefully: was he speaking the truth, or might he still betray her? What truly drove him—devotion to his mistress, or some motive she had yet to discern?

She thought his eyes brimmed with tender passion and loyalty.

"All of this is so ill-timed! Cyrus could strike us with his powerful army at any moment—the war has, for all intents and purposes, already begun. And now these traitorous chieftains— who can scarcely be called Massagetae—are worse than foreigners themselves… Very well, Bakhtiyar, we'll do this: I don't want those wretches, Haidar and Zakir, to murder you for disobeying them!

So at dawn tomorrow, you truly will… lead my 'Fierce Ones' away from here."

"But my queen!! How can I abandon you?!"

"You misunderstand. You and the 'Fierce Ones,' my best heroes, will lie in wait, hidden among thick brush, ready to ambush these rebels when they approach our camp. At that moment, you'll strike them unexpectedly from behind and destroy them! Now get up. You must prepare to leave. Try to execute this exactly—do not be late. This is crucial."

"I obey, my lady," answered her bodyguard, bowing his head humbly.

"Still, don't worry overmuch for me, Bakhtiyar. Right now, go find Rustam and tell him to come here—if need be, he can protect me. I am no frail, helpless maiden. But… no, not tonight. Let my husband not venture here either! He should come… also in the early morning. I don't think anyone will dare attack under cover of darkness—it's too black in our camp."

"As you wish, Queen!"

"And another thing. Someone has had the brazen audacity to steal my embroidered golden turban with its diamond! Do you know who? That gem always brought me luck…"

Bakhtiyar, dismayed by this, appeared genuinely troubled.

"Forgive me, Tomyris, I don't know the thief's identity. But if I learn anything… I did hear that Zakir wanted a turban like yours. The diamond is so beautiful—it would entice anyone!"

"I see. That's all—go now. If I truly am dear to you, do exactly as I've said!!"

Bakhtiyar kissed her hand, bowed low once more, and left the tent.

** * **

The rebels were already nearing Queen Tomyris's camp.

Late at night, Bakhtiyar stormed into the Tocharian chieftain Zakir's quarters, rousing him from bed.

"Uncle, get up! There's something important to discuss!"

Reluctantly, Zakir rose. He had been lying with his eyes closed, unable to sleep from worry, gnawed by a nagging sense of unease he couldn't quite pinpoint.

"You keep lying to me, Uncle!" Bakhtiyar shouted, outraged.

"Quiet, or you'll wake everyone," Zakir tried to hush his younger brother's son. "No need to yell. Speak calmly—my head's already pounding. Why come in the middle of the night? Couldn't it wait until morning? We've agreed on everything already… Where am I deceiving you?"

"As if you don't know!" barked Bakhtiyar, though lowering his voice now. "Time and again, you promise me mountains of gold, and then deliver nothing! Years ago—remember?—when I kidnapped Princess Tomyris for you, you swore you'd make me your chief lieutenant, that I would succeed you as chieftain of the Tocharians. Under threat of certain death, I dragged Spargapis's daughter into a grim prison so you could blackmail her royal father! And you—"

"Yes, you were just a lad then, but already strong enough to seize and bind her, throw her onto a horse, and bring her to me. A real hero! And now you've grown into a man…"

"And how do you reward this hero? With empty promises! You swore I'd inherit the tribe and that you'd give me Behnaz as my wife! Because I know I can never marry the woman I truly love—Tomyris. As for Behnaz, who does love me—young, fresh, and lovely—I didn't mind marrying her. But behind my back, you're cheating me again. Turns out Haidar has asked for Behnaz's hand, and you promised your daughter to him! That's not how we do things among the Saka. On top of that, you said you'd give me Tomyris's turban with its precious gem as soon as I 'become chieftain' and 'your son-in-law.' Yet it looks like someone stole the queen's turban without telling me, and you're keeping it hidden. How am I to interpret all this?!"

"It's still early, Bakhtiyar! The time will come—you'll certainly receive the turban and the diamond as your inheritance. You'll have Behnaz too. Why be so anxious? First, do everything I ordered you to do!"

"I don't trust you anymore, Uncle. You twist everything around to suit yourself! My whole life, you've lied to me. How long am I supposed to serve you for free? Let me inform you: this time, I'll make sure Queen Tomyris lives, and I won't let you kill her or her son Spargapis! As for Rustam—do with him whatever you please. I don't care."

"Oh? Very well, my friend, so be it. Then this very morning, Tomyris will learn of your 'exploits' against her. I have no doubt she'll order you hanged on the spot as a traitor! And I'll add that you covet Behnaz—which will certainly make her jealous."

"You wouldn't dare!"

"I would dare, dear nephew—indeed, I shall. What could stop me?"

"What?" Bakhtiyar retorted with a laugh. "Tomyris's death. Wasn't it you who planned to kill her…?"

31

Tashkent, 2012

Artur wasn't answering for some reason. Saltanat had called him many times, but no one ever picked up.

Strange, Saltanat thought. However, she decided not to trouble Irmanov about it. Instead, she called the "gangster" Artyom, whom Timofey Karaev had recommended.

Another oddity, she mused. *Their names are so similar… Though why am I even thinking that? There are countless people in the world with similar or even identical names! It's just that in a dire situation like this, everything seems suspicious!*

Artyom did answer the phone.

"Yeah? Who is this? What do you need?" he barked gruffly. "Ah, got it. Listen, lady—not over the phone! Write down this address—we'll talk in person."

* * *

Artyom proposed meeting Saltanat in a third-rate, grimy eatery, a place buzzing with flies on the outskirts of the city.

So are gangsters really so poor? Saltanat wondered, somewhat perplexed. *Couldn't he have asked me to meet him in a more decent place? Or maybe it's just for secrecy, so no one sees us… All right, that makes sense…*

They sat down at a table. Artyom ordered a single pot of black tea for both of them.

"So, young lady," he asked glumly, "what do you want from me?"

Saltanat, as politely as etiquette allowed, studied him closely. He was a tall, lean man of about thirty—or a little older—with features that were definitely not Slavic, and, to her surprise, he didn't look like a criminal at all.

She told him in detail what had happened to her parents.

"Timofey Karaev told me you belong to a gang with the odd name 'KIR,'" Saltanat admitted candidly.

"Oh, keep it down, you!!" Artyom hissed at her. "Why are you yelling 'gang' this and 'gang' that for everyone to hear? There's not even such a concept, officially. But saying it out loud like that could get both of us nabbed by the cops right now! Is that what you want?"

"No, no, I'm so sorry, please forgive me!" Saltanat shook her head fearfully. "So basically, you're… from there, right?"

"Is that really so important to you?" Artyom asked, slightly puzzled.

"Well, Timofey assured me that only that particular—ga… sorry, *organization*—can actually help me! That you can get my parents out of captivity."

"All right, look. How about this: you wait, I'll meet with my buddies and see what they know about this kidnapping, then figure out what can be done. Okay? After that, I'll get in touch with you. Fair enough?"

"You think I can just sit around doing nothing to save the people closest to me—just wait for you to call?" Saltanat protested, trying to stay polite but teetering on the edge of hysteria.

She was disheartened. The daughter of Tamilla and Rashid had assumed that as soon as she spoke with Artyom, he would act swiftly—like criminals supposedly do—and immediately solve her problem.

Instead, though he wasn't refusing her, all he said was, "Just wait."

No one to rely on, Saltanat thought. *All right, I'll just keep looking for other options.*

* * *

Moscow, 1993

"Kiryusha, are you really thinking of inviting that scoundrel Levidovsky to your birthday?" Koscheyev asked with a sneer.

"And why not?" Midiyatdinov responded, surprised. "After all, he's cleverly handling that jewellery factory business for us and bringing profits into our pockets! So what's the problem? By the way, Kostya, you were spot-on about putting him in the ministry as curator, not as director or deputy director of the factory!"

"He was a crook and still is," noted the "perfectly honest" thief Koscheyev. "If you'd put him in charge of the plant, he would've quietly embezzled everything and ruined us all. But as it is—his knowledge and experience in the jewellery trade suit our needs just fine."

That much was obvious to Kirill, and he nodded in agreement.

"But let me, my precious friend, invite whoever I like into my home—friends or otherwise—anyone I choose!" Kirill declared with a slightly haughty tone, sounding a bit irritated.

"Of course, my friend, of course," Koscheyev replied conciliatorily, though in a commanding tone, like a boss addressing a lesser boss.

He noticed the daring note in his younger "friend" and partner.

…After dinner, which they had ordered from a restaurant (Kirill's gorgeous wife Veronika still hadn't learned to cook), they began drinking tea. Kirill Midiyatdinov launched into his favourite subject: wealth.

"Money should be so abundant that you don't have to think about it or depend on it!" Kirill declared. In truth, he had little real expertise—he was hardly a true "financier." "Why should I break my back my whole life, while some Mister Twister in America lounges on a fancy couch, smoking a pipe, taking it easy, and indulging in whatever he pleases?"

"Well, presumably he didn't spend his entire life on that couch," Stanislav Zakharovich remarked with a knowing smile, sensing an opportunity to reinforce Kirill's line of thinking. "What that capitalist has is known as 'passive income.' But to reach that stage, you have to manage your active income wisely during the first half of your life! It's a long explanation. The key point is this: people who don't know how to handle money—no matter how big their fortune—end up poor in the long run."

"Why would that happen?!" Kirill asked, clearly perplexed.

Koscheyev and Veronika stayed quiet, both listening intently.

"Ah, you ignorant kids! One must know how to manage finances!" barked Levidovsky, loud as a boiling kettle, thrilled to be the centre of attention. "What's the point of searching for treasure and finding diamonds and gold? How does that help anyone, I ask you, if no one in this country properly understands what to do with those diamonds? Except me, of course!"

At that final conceited remark, the entire group froze. None of them even noticed his self-important flourish. They had all heard something else…

"Who's finding them? And what are they finding?" Konstantin was the first to speak, his eyes gleaming with renewed interest. "You said diamonds…? Are you talking about something specific?"

"I didn't mean anything by it!" Stanislav Zakharovich snapped, realizing he'd let something slip.

However, after a moment, he felt overwhelmed by a contradictory but powerful desire to finally reveal—at least to someone, even to these ignorant fools—a secret that had fallen into his hands by chance. A secret he had kept to himself for two years, turning it over in his mind now and then, never quite sure how to act on it.

"Well?" the owner of the house pressed his guest impatiently.

"All right. A couple of years back, I attended a function—it was a wedd… never mind. And I happened to overhear my son-in-law talking with a friend. That's how I found out that for the past few years, there've been major excavations in northern Uzbekistan searching for gold and diamonds. I even managed to find out exactly where. The incompetent archaeologists there have already dug up something extremely valuable, I'm sure of it! But the leader of that expedition is far too honest—a real scholarly stiff. Once they wrap up, he'll go back to Tashkent and hand over every last bit to the Ministry of Culture that sent him. Then, after some evaluation, the ministry will pass everything on to… Uzbekistan's state museums! How do you like that scenario? Isn't it absurd? Doesn't it just make any genuine businessman—or an expert diamond cutter—boil with frustration? It certainly does me, friends. No end!"

"Bah, nonsense," Koscheyev retorted coldly, openly sceptical.

"You really think anyone in Uzbekistan these days could find something genuinely precious?… I haven't read a word about it in the press!"

"Oh, you don't believe me?" Stanislav Zakharovich asked, nettled. "Fine! Tomorrow I'll bring you a tiny clipping from a Moscow newspaper—one with correspondents all over the CIS, reporting on cultural and scientific news—and you can see for yourself!"

The next day, when Koscheyev dropped by Stanislav Zakharovich's ministry "on business," ready to scoff at the ex-English industrialist's supposed tall tale, Levidovsky handed him a tattered newspaper. Sure enough, there was a short article about an excavation near the lower reaches of the Amu Darya River, in the ancient land of Sakastan—known to the public thanks to the legendary Queen Tomyris.

Koscheyev whistled, oblivious to the respectable atmosphere around him.

"Well, Stanislav Zakharovich, I was wrong. I take back what I said! But I'm still not interested in the slightest. Actually, I came to discuss our business at the jewellery factory. Did you prepare that quarterly report I asked for?"

"Of course, Konstantin. Here it is. Please excuse me—I've got a lot on my plate right now."

* * *

Tashkent, 2012

"How are you feeling, Konstantin Ivanovich?" asked the compassionate Tamilla, who always had a habit of thinking of others before herself. All the more so in this case, since Romanov had been her reliable partner in international public programs since 2000 and a respected friend she trusted completely. They had met at a business seminar, struck up a conversation—and soon forged a close relationship.

"So-so, thank you," Romanov replied—not exactly grim, but without much cheer. "I've noticed that bandit Dmitry is a lot kinder than the others! When he's on guard, at least we can talk normally and breathe a bit more freely. Unlike that other one—what's his name? Bahrom?"

"Yes, you could say I've been 'lucky' with various Bahroms my whole life," Tamilla Mahkamova said with a weary smile. "They keep causing trouble for me! Remember, Rashid, how we first met at that restaurant on my birthday? You saved me from the crude harassment of some jerk."

"No, sorry, it's been so many years—I don't remember it very well. I mean, of course I haven't forgotten meeting you—how could I? It's just that the moment I laid eyes on you, I fell head over heels in love! I didn't see anyone else around, as if everything else faded into a fog. I was young back then… but even now, when I'm practically an old man, I still get shy and nervous like a boy whenever you're near. Listen, I may never get another chance, so even in front of Konstantin Ivanovich and Dmitry, I'll say it anyway: Tamilla, you are the best thing in my life—the most faithful, noble woman on Earth! I've always loved you deeply and loyally, and I still love you with mad, boundless passion!"

Tears welled up in Tamilla's eyes; she was deeply moved by his words.

"Thank you, my love! To me, you—my Rashid—our daughter, and our grandchildren are the dearest and most important people in the world. You, my family, are more precious than any diamond!"

Rashid couldn't get close enough to kiss his wife, so he sent her a kiss through the air.

"Wait—so you're saying that on that night in the restaurant, a Bahrom tried to court you?"

"No, you couldn't call it 'courtship' at all. He was totally drunk and clearly not in his right mind. And from his behaviour, he definitely wasn't well-mannered or shy. I got the impression he was from some southern province. He kept professing his love and wouldn't leave me alone. But what I really remember were those swarthy, thick hands—and it still gives me the creeps."

"And this bandit Bahrom holding us here, pretending to be the big boss—could he be the same guy who harassed you back then?" Konstantin asked.

"No, definitely not! This man—within their little criminal crew—is relatively young. The Bahrom at the restaurant was also young at the time, but many years have passed since then. By now he should be roughly our age. Or maybe older—like, for example…"

Here Tamilla Sardorovna fell silent. A memory seemed to surface.

"Hold on!" she exclaimed suddenly. "My father told me a story a few years ago about a Bahrom, too! I think it happened back in '93…"

* * *

Tashkent, 1993

At his workplace, Sardor Shakhmuradovich Mahkamov was given a respectful and heartfelt sendoff into retirement.

Technically, he had reached retirement age several years earlier.

But because Mahkamov was so energetic and his experience so valuable, none of his superiors had wanted to remove him from his role as director of the porcelain factory.

Eventually, however, his health began to decline, and he was finally forced to step down—to enjoy a well-deserved rest.

His colleagues spoke warmly of his many achievements and contributions. But most of all, they thanked him for being a sensitive, responsive, and understanding boss—a true friend. The tributes moved the elderly gentleman to tears.

When he returned home, he shared his impressions with his wife.

Maryam Baburovna warmly supported her life partner:

"You've always been a true professional, Sardor! I'm so proud of you. It's wonderful that our daughter Tamilla is so much like you—just as hardworking and talented."

"Yes, that's exactly it—'was,'" Mahkamov said with a rueful smile. "And now I've grown old—nobody needs me anymore."

"Enough of that talk, please! You're still very much needed by our family. I'm lucky to have you."

Hearing this, Sardor remembered his friend Zakhar Khaev's wife, Viktoria, who wasn't so fortunate... *How is she now?* Always on her own—never remarried, no children all these years... Compassionate Sardor felt deep pity for her. The next day, without telling his wife—so she wouldn't worry—he went to the market, bought groceries, and visited Viktoria.

Over the years, Viktoria had "let herself go." Crying so often had damaged her eyesight. She had loved Zakhar so deeply that she wouldn't risk betraying him with anyone else. She simply kept waiting for him, her only husband, with whom she'd never officially divorced.

"Vika, there's still no sign of Zakhar?" Sardor asked, as always, without much hope.

Viktoria's reply took him by surprise.

"No, but about a year ago, somebody rang the doorbell of my—well, mine and Zakhar's—apartment. I opened it because he said, through the peephole, that he'd come 'from Zakhar.' Once inside, I offered him tea, and we talked. The man said that in fact, he wasn't from Zakhar, that he hadn't seen him in a long time but was searching for him. 'What for?' I asked. 'Why do you need my husband?' To which the guest replied: 'You see, I'm an old friend from Karshi. My name is Bahrom. Several years ago, Zakhar borrowed a large sum of money from me and never returned it. I've looked for him everywhere but can't find him. I thought maybe he'd come back here, to his home?' Sardor, I was so outraged by this dark-skinned man's words. As far as I know, Zakhar hates borrowing money—whether large sums or small! Of course, a lot can change in so many years. And I know nothing of Zakhar—whether he's alive or where he might be. I only hope he's alive, because money still arrives for me—rarely now and from various parts of the CIS, but it does come. I've long suspected it's from him, my dear Zakhar, who still loves me and cares about me!"

"That makes sense, Viktoria. But that stranger coming to see you—that's peculiar," Sardor said, shaking his head. "Zakhar never had any old friends from Karshi!! If he did, I'd know about it. Whoever showed up at your place was probably some con man. Or maybe it's the very person Zakhar has been hiding from all these years, all over the world? But why? What could have happened to him? I wish I knew!"

"I understand, Sardor. So do I, even more so."

"Maybe that photo of us—the one Zakhar sent me—was his

way of telling me that no matter what, no matter what happened or how fate scattered him, he would forever remain my true, loyal friend?... But maybe Zakhar's life is still in danger from someone or something? Almost certainly from that Bahrom. There's some mystery here, Vika—maybe even a dangerous one."

* * *

Outskirts of Boston, USA, 2012

John McConnley couldn't sleep. That very day, he had once again visited the secret bunker where Professor Moran and his assistants were forcibly holding those young Uzbek students. John had seen what these monsters were doing to the youths, and it left him deeply uneasy. But he knew almost nothing about the severe, brutal manipulations! Nor had he ever agreed to such Fascist-style experiments, which amounted to barbaric killings!

Surely someone must be looking for these kids by now... Perhaps their parents and loved ones had been searching for a long time but couldn't find them? So far from home, and imprisoned!

Oh, why had John done his boss's bidding by bringing these unfortunate souls to that wretched bunker?... No, no—he couldn't have disobeyed! They would have killed him for that.

It was all on account of his debt to that predatory Moscovite, Konstantin Koscheyev, who had shady dealings with Moran! And the debt was tremendous...

Just three years ago, John McConnley had been an ordinary Russian citizen named Ivan Makonin, living in Moscow and working as a waiter in a small restaurant. A certain top criminal figure, who had recently moved from Ryazan to Moscow, started showing up there frequently. His name was Konstantin Koscheyev—a gaunt man in his fifties with an unpleasant face that inspired neither sympathy nor trust.

At some point, while Makonin was serving Koscheyev's table, the latter noticed that the Russian waiter, whose attentive and courteous service he liked, seemed depressed.

"My friend, I see you're upset about something. Care to tell me?" Konstantin asked sympathetically.

"Who could possibly care about my problems?" Ivan replied in despair.

"I do! I care a great deal. If you keep working with that miserable look on your face, your boss might fire you—even my pal, who owns this place, might not help you then. I'd hate to lose such a capable, considerate waiter, one who always suggests the dishes I like best!"

Koscheyev had a knack—ever since his time in prison—for finding the right angle with each person.

"The thing is, no matter how I try, I just can't pay off the big mortgage on our house!" Ivan Makonin confessed to the restaurant patron. "Because of that, my family's falling apart—my wife is threatening to leave me and take our ten-year-old daughter, Katya. I love my child so much, you understand?"

"I do understand, absolutely. I have two kids of my own, both grown," Konstantin lied smoothly and without batting an eye. In truth, he'd never had a wife or children—only lovers, most of them hired "night ladies."

"My salary's nowhere near enough to cover the loan," Ivan continued. "And if my wife strips me of the right to help raise our daughter, I'll probably die from the heartbreak!"

"You won't die—I won't let you!" his VIP customer assured him optimistically. "Give me a couple of days. I'll think about what can be done. All right?"

Makonin, forcing a sad smile and suspecting only empty promises and flimsy comfort, agreed without much enthusiasm.

To his surprise, exactly two days later, the crime boss Koscheyev not only returned to the restaurant but specifically chose Ivan's section again. As soon as the waiter approached, Konstantin initiated their conversation:

"My friend, I've figured out what you need to do!" Koscheyev announced with a self-satisfied grin.

Ivan listened carefully, unsure whether to expect good or bad news—whether to continue despairing or let hope buoy him. Meanwhile, Koscheyev, like a mentor with his protégé, shifted into an informal form of address.

"Right, so remember I told you the owner of this modest establishment, Yury Mikhailovich Trukhin, is a friend of mine? Well, I exaggerated. We're more like old acquaintances from the '90s. He had his crew of thugs, I had mine; he had his turf, I had mine. You get the drift?"

Makonin nodded. He did. This was clearly about gang feuds. Koscheyev had been head of the Ryazan gang, while Trukhin led the Moscow gang. After neutralizing him and killing several of Trukhin's people, Koscheyev had moved to Moscow. But since Trukhin escaped, not buying his way out, Konstantin decided at some later stage that Trukhin had to be pinned down and finished off once and for all! Yet for a while, Koscheyev couldn't pull it off— he was waiting for the right moment to strike.

Like an eel, wily Yury Trukhin had managed to slip away repeatedly, and even upon meeting Koscheyev, he always dodged harm and slithered out of reach. Then the 2000s arrived.

Ultimately, after many years, Koscheyev tracked down his old adversary and debtor in that man's private restaurant. Hence, he started frequenting Trukhin's place.

Now, Koscheyev had formed a plan to punish the delinquent who'd refused to pay him "the rightful tribute."

"So, Vanechka, you memorized the safe's combination, right? Great job! No, they won't catch you—don't worry. My men will cover you if anything goes wrong once you're in your boss's office. Just act boldly. The money belonging to Yury Mikhailovich will pay your mortgage! You want your daughter Katya to stay with you, correct?"

Makonin's daughter's name was the hook by which Koscheyev reeled him in. In his anxiety, Ivan failed to grasp that he was about to commit a crime—he risked being caught by the restaurant's security, maybe even going to prison!

In short, it was a trap for both Trukhin and, especially, Makonin, whom Koscheyev planned to recruit for his own ends. The crime boss naturally concealed from the naïve Ivan that just days earlier, accompanied by his gang of gorilla-like enforcers, he had visited Trukhin in the latter's private home (not the restaurant) and clarified the situation:

"Yurik, you know you lost our old duel. You owe me. There can be no questions in this matter—I think you know! But here's what we'll do. You let this man I name open your restaurant's safe and take out a tidy sum. Then, as if by chance, the cops will show up and nab him. I'll get him off the hook—using part of your money you owe me. But I'll also tell that clueless clown that now he owes me loads of cash—so he'll be working for me forever. Meanwhile, in return for your cooperation, I'll forgive most of your debt. You'll end up paying me a lot less than you really owe. That good?"

Terrified at the sight of Koscheyev's goons, Yury Trukhin agreed.

Thus, Ivan Makonin, unaware of the catastrophic turn events would soon take, obediently carried out Koscheyev's directives to the letter—and became Koscheyev's eternal debtor. How could he pay him back? He not only failed to get the desired money, but he also never paid off the bank mortgage on his house. As he'd feared, he also lost his wife and daughter. His wife divorced him, and because Ivan was arrested by the police for theft, the court forbade him from seeing his daughter more than once a month. Now, Koscheyev subjugated Makonin, using him much like he used Kirill Midiyatdinov—exploiting him for vile criminal exploits.

A few years later, seeing that Ivan Makonin knew some English, Koscheyev sent him to America as his courier to George Moran. The courier was to deliver secret documents and materials that no standard mail service could be trusted with. Thus, Makonin—given a forged ID claiming he worked for the U.S. Department of Education—would become John McConnley each time he entered the country.

How he longed to escape, to break free of captivity! But he could not. Both Moran and, especially, Koscheyev kept a close eye on his every move. The shrewd, nimble young man was too valuable to Koscheyev, who even promised to reunite Ivan with his daughter.

But this time, after McConnley again arrived "on business" at the bunker outside Boston, he learned—quite by chance—just how horrifying the trials inflicted on his Russian-speaking near-compatriots from Uzbekistan really were…

And in some odd twist of fate, which Makonin noticed right away (when he had no idea how cruelly Moran and Trabs would treat their young "guests"), among these "guests" was… a girl named

Katya! The same name as Ivan's own daughter!

True, the student Katya Solovyova was significantly older than his little girl. But still… Torn from his beloved daughter, the wretched father thought he would never survive if his own Katya fell into the hands of such scientific monsters—her brain used for these inhuman experiments, her life in mortal danger…

Hence, upon discovering just how grave the peril for the Uzbek youths truly was, Makonin tossed and turned all night, unable to sleep. He weighed the pros and cons. After all, Koscheyev had promised to reunite him with his daughter! But could one trust that monster? Ivan brooded deeply. He tried to figure out: could he rescue those poor young captives from that dreadful bunker without sacrificing his own life…?

32

Kungrad–Tashkent, 1993

The phone rang in Tamilla and Rashid's house—it was clearly a long-distance call.

"Hello, Rashid? Greetings, my friend!"

"Pulat? Hey, buddy! Finally! Where are you calling from?" Batyrov was as delighted as a child.

"I stopped in Kungrad specifically so I could call you. You must've been worried about me…"

"Tamilla and I were so anxious—we couldn't get through to

you at all! Where have you been, my friend?”

“Forgive me, Rashid—I’ve been off where there’s no connection at all. And no normal living conditions either. It’s the edge of civilization, although in ancient times, the civilization here was quite advanced! And how’s Tamilla Sardorovna doing?”

“All is well. She’s home, right here with me, sending her best regards.” Rashid added proudly, “She’s doing great. She became Chair of the Peace Fund and also a UN Goodwill Ambassador. We were about to start searching for you through Interpol and various international NGOs!”

Pulat gave a short, manly laugh at his friend’s joke and decided to play along a bit.

“Right—I see. As if I’d run off abroad with precious artifacts?… Never! You know there’s nothing dearer to me than our native Uzbekistan. Give your wife my regards and my thanks—both of you—for worrying about a vagabond like Pulat. It means a lot. But listen, Rashid—I’m actually calling for a reason. I’ve got important news!”

The cultural official perked up, all ears now:

“Go ahead, Pulat—I’m hanging on every word!”

“You remember how I told you about Koi Krylgan Kala, the fortress down in the Amu Darya delta, where the Saka once lived, and where Queen Tomyris herself was said to have been? That site your friend Alexei Irmanov helped preserve from the authorities…?”

“Yes, of course I remember. By the way, did I mention that Alexei’s now the director of a telecommunications equipment plant? He’s constantly moving up!”

“No, you didn’t say, but I’m very glad for your Irmanov! Pass along my regards. But about our work—so, over in Koi Krylgan Kala, I managed—finally—to locate the nearly intact golden turban of Karna…"

"Wow!"

"Yes, exactly. But there are no diamonds on it; they haven't survived. We do have the turban itself, made of ancient dense fabric, and on top of it—pure gold plating."

"That's terrific news, Pulat! Congratulations to all of us, and especially you. You're our hero! So when are you coming to Tashkent with this find?"

"No, Rashid, I can't come. We've started a dig on these burial mounds, and the work is in full swing—we have to finish before the autumn rains set in. I barely got away long enough to phone you from the city. There's a good friend of mine passing through here from the Nukus Savitsky Museum of Art, on his way to Tashkent—specifically to your ministry. I'll send the artifact along with him. It's absolutely safe, trust me."

"Well, if you say so, then fine—hand it over to him. But don't disappear on us for so long next time, all right? Try to stay in touch. You're really important to us."

"I know, and I'll try to call. But there's no connection out where we're digging. I told you—there aren't even normal living conditions there. But we archaeologists are used to the 'comforts' of fieldwork! Only—there's something else…"

Rashid thought the line had cut out. But it was just Pulat pausing.

"You see, Rashid," he went on, sounding strangely sombre, "these mounds aren't straightforward. Based on my calculations, there must be diamonds there—the fragments of the Koh-i-Noor we're seeking. But… these places are scary, let me tell you. There are about a hundred ancient burial mounds. 'Kurgan,' from old Russian, can mean 'fortress,' but also 'burial mound,' or a 'tomb.'

And you know how ancient peoples buried their dead—as you're well versed in history and art. We can find not just everyday objects or the deceased's treasure, but also all sorts of eerie magical or sorcerous stuff."

"You believe in that, Pulat?" Rashid teased mildly.

He was somewhat uneasy—they had already been speaking for three minutes, and Gafarov was probably racking up charges. It would've been better if Rashid had called him back from the ministry phone. Except that those phone lines were now under tighter scrutiny—this was no longer a vast, wealthy Soviet state, but an emerging independent republic with its own budget.

Meanwhile, the archaeologist continued:

"Here, local folklore includes the same sort of legends found in many cultures—that graves, especially royal ones, must never be disturbed! At first, I dismissed all that as purely pagan superstition. What do ignorant folks know, right? But when we opened more of these mounds, suddenly… everyone on our team started having severe headaches. Many got nosebleeds. Two diggers suffered major injuries and nearly died. And that's not the half of it. There might be dangerous disease spores, maybe pockets of poison vapours. Bottom line: it's risky work."

"Then, you know, maybe you should leave that place and come back," Rashid said, truly worried. "Or try digging somewhere else—some site less treacherous and deadly!"

"I can't. I have to see this through—you know me. Every line of inquiry regarding the fragments of our diamond leads to these Saka mounds. Because that's precisely where Tomyris and her closest circle travelled…"

"Well, good luck, my friend. And please be careful. No job's worth your life."

***

Tashkent, 2012

Still battling her shyness—she had always been uneasy about bothering busy people—Saltanat called her father's friend in Moscow. He answered.

"Hello, Alexei Vadimovich! It's Rashid Batyrov's daughter speaking."

"Ah, Saltanat! Hello, my dear. What's the news? Any progress on your parents' situation?"

"No, alas. That's why I dared to call. Your acquaintance, Artur—he hasn't been picking up the phone at all! He might be my last hope now."

"Don't say that, child. Forgive my advice, but I'm sure hope must stay alive in your heart always, even in the toughest, most critical, seemingly hopeless times. As for Artur—strangely enough, I can't reach him either. Maybe he's been sent on some special assignment. But you know, I did tell him about you once, and he promised to help!"

The older man's words confirmed Saltanat's suspicion that Artur was some sort of national security agent. Yet if he was off on some unknown mission, how could he help her? And if not him—then who? She didn't hold out much hope for the underworld figure Artyom from "KIR."

"Sorry, Saltanat, I have a call coming in from the ministry. If I learn anything, I'll call you right away, okay?"

They said their goodbyes. Suddenly Saltanat's phone started ringing—someone was calling her now.

"Hello, miss? It's Artyom. Still remember me? Good. All right, listen: my pals and I thought over your problem. Bottom line—we can fix it! Got it? And you can hold off on talking about rewards! We don't need anything from you. We've got our own interest in this matter. But you got to promise me one thing—don't butt in yourself. No meddling, no action on your part, period! Understand? That's good. Because otherwise, I can't guarantee your parents' lives. But if you don't get in our way, then there's a chance we'll save them. You do want them alive and well, right?"

Of course, Saltanat wanted that desperately! She had no choice but to agree to these odd conditions. *I'll do anything, if only they free Mom and Dad soon—please let them still be alive!*

Artyom did not tell her what he knew perfectly well: the gang holding her parents hostage was none other than the criminal organization known as "KIR."

* * *

Moscow, 1998

From childhood, Kirill Midiyatdinov had loved money and dreamed of growing up to be truly wealthy. Fortunately for him, the Soviet era had passed, and he could easily shrug off all that communist talk of levelling social classes.

Neither Kirill's first attempt on the life of his adoptive father, Oleg Shamilyevich, nor the murder of that "parent" was ever formally proven. And so, Kirill inherited two large properties in Moscow: Oleg's luxurious house (technically on the city's outskirts, though on paper it was within city limits) and the apartment belonging to his grandparents. That apartment was where the late

Farida had lived for a long time and, by rights, could also have gone to both Midiyatdinov sisters and their brother, Oleg. Meanwhile, Marina remained in the small apartment that belonged to Denis—the one he had permanently left to her.

Thus, in 1992, Kirill had already become a rather wealthy heir. But in order to hold on to that fortune, he couldn't squander it on frivolities. From his dealings with Konstantin Koscheyev—going back to the mid-1980s—Kirill had tried to understand the nature of business, entrepreneurship, and how to make other people work for him with minimal effort on his part, thereby swiftly multiplying his capital.

By the late 1990s, he realized he could earn handsomely, for example, by producing "bootleg vodka"—the repugnant swill without which, he believed, the vast majority of Russian men couldn't live. This was a goldmine for "businessmen" like Kirill.

First, he found out where and how to get large quantities of cheap ethanol and who could transport it. Next, he hired people to collect empty vodka bottles. Then he rented a storage barn to hold and wash them. They soon amassed thousands of bottles. Kirill arranged for a small printing press at a large Moscow enterprise to make a stamp matrix from a new liquor plant and to print a huge run of brand labels for his counterfeit vodka. As for manufacturing the product itself, he hired former factory workers—people used to small wages but who knew the process inside and out. They also forged tax stamps for the bottles.

Business picked up from there.

His biggest challenge was finding good "spirit men"—the people supplying bulk ethanol in giant tank cars. Sought after by many, these alcohol suppliers quickly gained money and influence, and therefore began making demands on Kirill, trying to flex their newfound power.

But Kirill was becoming ever more like his stepfather—pragmatic, ruthless, and unyielding. Very soon, he announced to the ethanol haulers:

"Well, boys, now I am your 'protection.' Got it? On the days I specify, you'll cough up a share of your business to me. That's my cut!"

They had only two choices: submit to Kirill and regularly pay him hefty percentages from selling spirit to various entrepreneurs, or get out of his way altogether—maybe take up… some handicraft, like cross-stitching. In this manner, Kirill subjugated all the "spirit men" in his part of Moscow. Indeed, he managed to bring many traders under his control, skilfully bending them to his will.

Kirill handled business competitors simply and radically: by eliminating them or any rival protection racket that tried to challenge him. But few people dared cross him now that he was rich and brazen. Kirill formed his own criminal gang. People feared him even more than in his jail days, back when he—on Koschei's orders—had taken out fellow inmates.

Now there were no higher bosses over Kirill. He was his own master, his own "little tsar." Even Koscheyev, who was part of the same gang, recognized his sway and called him his "brother." Konstantin even went so far as to invent a thieves' nickname for Kirill—"Tsar Kir"—explaining:

"Bro, for some reason you remind me of that fearsome King Cyrus the Second, who once conquered half the world! And look at that name of yours—Kirill! See, everyone's scared of you like they're scared of a real tsar, and they have to respect you. Just be careful… Stay away from those strong, freedom-loving women like Queen Tomyris!"

With that, Konstantin laughed, pleased with himself for knowing a bit of world history so well.

* * *

Tashkent, 2012

Rashid Batyrov continued his story pensively. At last, Dmitry had brought water for him and Tamilla, and now speaking had become significantly easier.

Romanov, who had also quenched his thirst, was listening very attentively to Batyrov.

"Several months passed after my phone call with my friend Pulat Gafarov—when he himself called us at home. Just as promised, Pulat sent, via an acquaintance, a carefully packed golden turban in a special case. We attribute that turban to the legendary Indian boy Karna. According to ancient sources, Karna secretly visited Queen Tomyris in her tent and presented her with this magnificent turban."

"And one evening," spoke up Tamilla Sardorovna, who had been silent for a long time, "when I was all alone in a room, sadly remembering my late parents, that same Karna came to me! Before, I thought he was merely a figment of people's imagination, but now I know for certain that he exists. Karna is like a symbol of Good on Earth and love for humanity! He strengthens and comforts those whose hearts are heavy with sorrow, giving them joy and hope. By the way, although he is from India, he disavows any idea of reincarnation that might be associated with his name. He says a person comes to this Earth only once—not to get rich or become famous, not to make others serve him—but to serve others and do as much good as possible for the whole world. That is why Karna himself is eternal—he brings only goodness and peace to humankind. He was surprised when I asked about his golden turban. It turns out he has given out many such turbans to people in different corners of the Earth, so they could use the power he bestowed on them to perform more just and humane deeds. As for me, he said, 'Tamilla, you don't need such a turban anymore, because you have already learned how to do good for people…' My meeting with Karna filled my soul with light, joy, and hope—hope that my life is not in vain!"

"And what happened to the golden turban your Gafarov found during the excavations?" asked Romanov, a little too curious, it seemed—he just couldn't let it go.

"It disappeared," Rashid replied. "Just like the diamonds Pulat discovered. But I'm absolutely convinced my friend had nothing to do with it. Tamilla and I both know he himself suffered—he died a senseless death because of the treasure he had found!"

"Is that so? And what exactly happened?" Romanov asked, attempting to sound sympathetic.

"Well, it all went like this. First, Pulat's colleague from Nukus did indeed bring the turban to our ministry and handed it over to me. In other words, I saw it with my very own eyes! I have to say, it was a marvellous, indescribable spectacle—a genuine work of art. But maybe my wife Tamilla is right in thinking that its greatest value is not material, but spiritual. I don't know—each person has their own view of that. However, my dear, if you say you saw the mysterious Karna—that he himself appeared to you—I personally have no doubt in your words. I believe you! And I think only someone with a pure and noble heart can see him—this symbol of light and goodness, as you called him, or, as Coelho wrote, 'the

Warrior of Light'… In any case, as required, I immediately turned this precious turban over to the state repository of rare historical valuables. How and when it disappeared from there remains a complete mystery to me. To this day, scholars are still searching for it, but so far, nothing has been found. Such a shame…"

"And what about the diamonds?" Romanov was relentless. "You said, Rashid Kudratovich, that they disappeared as well? How so?"

"I'll tell you. In 1994, I received a letter from my friend Pulat. Many years have passed since then, but I remember every word of it by heart. Here is what it said:

'My dear Rashid!

Most likely, if you are reading this message, I am no longer in this world—otherwise, I would have come to you in person and told you all of this. As I mentioned on the phone, the area of our current excavations at the Saka kurgans is extremely dangerous—pathological, even. I've lost several members of my team—not because they left or betrayed our shared cause. They simply… died under the strangest and most mysterious circumstances! I must say, the cause of death remained unclear to all of us. But that is not the worst of it. We began to find shards of a diamond! So far, I don't know whether these are all the fragments that exist or just a portion of them. But there is no doubt that the structure of the stone indicates it is the wondrous Koh-i-Noor—pure as a child's tear, radiating a "mountain of light." Such a treasure must never fall into the hands of bandits and criminals! However, just such people have recently appeared in our area and are often loitering around our base camp at the kurgans. They pose as travellers, as tourists. But everything about them—their appearance, their behaviour—suggests a direct link to organized crime. It alarms and worries me. Of course, I'm not afraid for myself—what's so important about an old fossil like me, nearly as ancient as the relics I dig up? No, I'm worried for the lives of the people still in my group. Meanwhile, we are closer than ever to finding the principal object of our search! And we cannot allow these diamonds—small though they may be, yet undeniably real and an absolute national treasure of our republic—to slip abroad into the hands of crooks. I asked an educated local woman, a schoolteacher from a nearby village, to mail you this letter—addressed to you—in the event she learns of my death. That would mean I was unable to save myself from these bandits while trying to protect the diamonds. I don't know why I'm telling you all this, but it struck me as remarkable that the head of their gang is called "Koschei" by his accomplices. He really is somewhat Koschei-like—skinny, malicious, and frightening! Only this isn't a fairy tale, but a sad reality. I can't call the police here, because the bandits haven't openly attacked us even once—they are clever, elusive, and cautious. Our valiant authorities would just laugh at me. But I feel certain—utterly convinced— that these robbers are specifically hunting for our diamonds, and that the lives of everyone on this expedition are in serious danger. I'm even considering disbanding the crew to save my colleagues' lives… Also, I'm trying to figure out how to get the diamonds we've already found into your hands—or, more precisely, into the hands of our government, through you. Without doubt, they would benefit the economic and cultural development of an independent Uzbekistan! I myself cannot travel—I have no one I can entrust with the equipment and historical artifacts we've unearthed. At the time I write this letter, I am still alive—so I will do my best to protect these treasures… Farewell, my best friend in the whole world! Please give my regards to your charming wife…

Always yours, Pulat Gafarov.'

"To be honest, my friends," continued Rashid Kudratovich, still being held captive in the hangar, "this message from someone so dear to me—someone who had already departed this life—shook me to the core. Why is fate so cruel to the best among us? Could things really be that bad at the excavation site, among those ancient Saka kurgans? Would I never again see my dear and faithful friend Pulat?… And after reading this detailed letter, I realized one thing: the diamonds discovered by Pulat and his crew—the fruit of so many years of work, countless sleepless nights, and days spent under the scorching sun—had vanished without a trace. And since neither I nor any of the surviving members of Pulat's team ever heard anything more about those fragments of the Koh-i-Noor diamond, Pulat's worst fears may have come true: perhaps the treasure was indeed sold off to some wealthy foreign buyer…"

Tamilla was moved by the story but chose not to interrupt; she simply listened.

"Certainly to foreigners, I've no doubt about it!" Romanov declared, smiling for some reason. "Otherwise, by now… But that's not important. And how do you know what Gafarov's archaeological crew thought about all this? Did you see them?"

"Only one of them came to see me—Leonid Belozerov. And even then, he didn't come openly to the ministry. He called me at home and asked to meet in the park that evening. We spoke on a park bench, and he kept nervously glancing around, worried that someone might be following him. He was very afraid of Koschei's gang. Lenya told me he'd heard a lot about me from Pulat."

"'He gave me your phone number just in case,' Belozerov explained, 'in case I ever found myself in Tashkent and needed help. But I don't need any help right now. I just want one thing: to get away from here—somewhere far off—and lie low for a while so that Koschei and his men can't find me…'"

"Koschei?" Romanov interrupted Batyrov's narrative. "Where did I recently hear that name? Ah yes, you quoted your late friend's letter mentioning someone called Koschei. So, was he really that dangerous?"

"Apparently so," Batyrov replied. "The police investigating Pulat Gafarov's mysterious murder—knowing only the gang leader's nickname—never managed to find him. Unfortunately, no one could do anything, and every lead in that terrible crime vanished without a trace. If you're interested, when I spoke with the investigator on Gafarov's case, I was told that Pulat supposedly ran into a sharp metal beam late at night near his tent—at the spot where the archaeologists had pitched camp. Unfortunately, they found no fingerprints on the beam. But I couldn't fathom how a beam ended up there, among ancient kurgans… And I certainly still don't believe it was an 'accident'!"

"So you think it was those bandits?" Romanov guessed.

"I'm sure of it. And by the way, the rest of Pulat's crew—simple labourers he hired for digging—scattered in all directions. The police managed to locate only one of them, and the poor guy couldn't say anything coherent. He claimed, 'I didn't see anything, didn't hear anything. I don't even know when they killed the expedition leader—it was night, and I was asleep.' So, for lack of evidence, the case was closed. But it was all very strange… I suppose the only small consolation is that Pulat's body was promptly brought here, to Tashkent, and Tamilla and I, along with several mutual friends, were able to give him a proper funeral."

At those words, Tamilla suddenly remembered one of her former students—a medical student named Dilshod Inagamov, who had died the previous year in Boston. Moved by the memory, she turned to the Muscovite:

"Konstantin Ivanovich, in all this turmoil I forgot to ask you again about something that really worries me: you said our students who were awarded grants should be all right? Are you certain? It's just that they haven't been in touch for several days now… You're sure nothing bad will happen to them? That they won't meet the same fate as poor Dilshod?"

"Oh, come on, stop panicking, my most honourable lady!" Konstantin responded dryly, with some irritation. "They're young, active, and curious! Probably just off enjoying themselves in wealthy America—on my dime, I should add. I'm not worried—so why should you be?"

"Yes, yes, of course. If you say so, then let's hope they truly are fine. And that once we get out of this cursed place, I'll be able to reach them by phone!"

"Oh, you'll get through to them," Romanov muttered, even more peevishly, adding in a sharper tone, "Why ask silly questions?… What I'm really interested in right now is something else: what about those diamonds Gafarov's crew found? Did that worker, Belozerov, bring you any of them? I mean, did your Pulat manage to hand over even a part of those diamonds to you through Leonid? It's impossible that Leonid took such a big risk just to pay his respects and tell you how afraid he was of those thugs! So where, where are those diamonds?!"

It was clear that the Moscow businessman was deeply intrigued by this subject.

Tamilla Sardorovna looked at her business partner in surprise—she had never seen Romanov so fervently engaged before…

33

Sakastan, 6th century BCE

The conspirator chieftains, along with their armed detachments, had moved right up to Tomyris's encampment. Bakhtiyar, knowing this and having already led the queen's "Fierce Ones" out of the camp, was afraid of Zakir's threats and failed to bring Tomyris's guard back at the crucial hour.

Tomyris was left virtually defenceless. The oldest and most experienced among the "Fierce Ones" questioned Bakhtiyar: What was going on? Why had they all abandoned the camp and their queen? In response, Bakhtiyar claimed it was on Tomyris's own orders—they were supposedly to be the first to intercept Cyrus's forces and repel his attacks, while waiting for Rustam's detachment to join them later. No more questions were asked.

Hardly had the sun begun to illuminate the vast steppe when Tomyris's encampment was surrounded by the rebels, armed to the teeth. Tomyris took up arms and stood ready.

Suddenly—surprising everyone but the queen herself—Rustam appeared on horseback, accompanied by a band of ordinary Massagetae warriors and Tigraxauda fighters. They were few in number, only about two hundred, yet they courageously and valiantly defended their queen and her entire camp!

An enraged Zakir, unprepared for so many to rise in defence of his rival to the throne—and not fully grasping Rustam's strength, military skill, and combat prowess—began insulting and provoking him. He aimed his spear at the hero, only to fall dead on the spot from a powerful sword blow. Rustam remained as invincible as ever!

In the end, Tomyris and Rustam achieved a complete victory. According to steppe law and with the people's consent, all the conspirators were executed that same day. Tomyris had wanted to spare them and merely take them prisoner, but with a difficult war against the Persians looming, there was no way to guard captives. Together with the Council of Elders, Tomyris appointed new, loyal chieftains to replace those who had been overthrown.

The queen's red turban, adorned with the precious diamond taken from Zakir's head, was removed and returned to Tomyris. The queen was glad that Karna's gift had rightfully found its way back to her.

Suddenly, a day after the battle ended, Bakhtiyar appeared—bringing along the "Fierce Ones."

"How timely you are—barely a day late!" Rustam remarked with biting sarcasm. He was about to strike Bakhtiyar with his fist, knock him down, and grind him into the earth when he noticed Bakhtiyar was wounded.

Tomyris gave him a somewhat angry yet compassionate look.

"What happened this time, Bakhtiyar? Why didn't you come in time to help, as I commanded? If not for Rustam, I might have been killed!"

Bakhtiyar fell before her, bowing his head—and she saw that it was covered in blood.

"Forgive me, forgive me, my queen! Someone came up behind me early in the morning and must have struck me hard. I lost consciousness—probably for a long while. The moment I came to, I made my way straight to you… I'm so sorry I was late…"

Tomyris helped him up and gently smoothed his hair.

"Bring a healer, now!" she ordered her servants. "Rustam, you could have been a bit gentler. Don't you see the man is injured? It's obvious he really was attacked. At least he managed to warn you about the plot—and you got here in time!"

"No one warned me about anything," Rustam said testily. "I simply felt worried about you and got my detachment ready—just in case. Turns out I was right. A turbulent day indeed! But the important thing is that you are alive."

* * *

The war between the nomads and the Persians began under difficult circumstances. The Massagetae cavalry, riding at full gallop, loosed their well-aimed, razor-sharp arrows at Cyrus's forces, inflicting heavy losses: tens of thousands of Persian foot soldiers were killed. Many Persians also died during the harsh marches across desert terrain. Enemies of the Massagetae perished not only by their weapons but also from thirst and from brackish, foul water. Diseases took a further toll on Cyrus's uninvited army on Saka lands. Usually ruthless, Cyrus this time tried to restrain himself, preferring not to subject his own soldiers to further misery or executions—enough of them were dying already, and he needed every man he could keep. He knew he could not win a war against the Massagetae with a small army.

The Persians grew wary of the Massagetae and their repeated, successful raids. Cyrus and his men were accustomed to victories and the spoils of war. Here, they saw no gold, no rich cities, no slaves—only sands and desert thistles. Only Cyrus's name and the unshakeable faith of the Persians in their leader kept the army in check.

Cyrus's loyal servant, Afshin, entered the king's campaign tent with a deep bow.

"Forgive me, Your Majesty, but there is a young Saka pleading for an audience. He begs for mercy and claims to have important information for the mighty ruler of the entire world!"

"Why wasn't he killed on the spot, given that he's one of our enemies?"

"He says he's not merely a servant, but a close confidant of Queen Tomyris—her personal guard—and that she trusts him. He claims he knows better than anyone how to defeat the Massagetae."

"Better than I?" Cyrus sneered. "Fine, let him in."

Afshin bowed low again and left.

"So, you miserable wretch, why do you betray your queen?" Cyrus asked as the newcomer entered, not even acknowledging his greeting. "What is your name, Queen Tomyris's guard?"

"Bakhtiyar, Your Highness."

"You must say 'Your Majesty'! Surely, you stupid scarecrow, you know who stands before you?!"

"Forgive me, my lord—Your Majesty. It won't happen again."

"So, why are you here? Speak quickly—I have little time. I need my rest before the next battle."

"That's precisely why I came. I know that because of the Massagetae's sudden raids from behind the hills—which they know like the backs of their hands—you are losing many men. I suggest that instead of confronting your enemies in an open field, you use cunning, for in war all means are fair. Queen Tomyris has moved close to the foot of the Black Mountains. Near our ancestors' burial sites, she has set up a large fortified encampment. I overheard her say at a war council that the Persian army must be harassed with arrows and spears—so the camp by the tombs would be unassailable. I asked her to keep me in charge of her personal guard, the 'Fierce Ones.' She agreed—she trusts me. And I will help you. I'll do everything I can so you'll prevail. You'll see. But in return, I need you to do me a favour!"

"You're naming conditions for me?" Cyrus let out a booming laugh. "That's amusing. Aren't you afraid I might just skewer you right here?"

"You might still find me useful! As I said, Queen Tomyris trusts me greatly. And I have something that will definitely interest you."

"Really? And what might that be?" Cyrus asked, expecting the visitor to offer some trivial item or another tactical suggestion.

"I speak of the most magnificent of stones—one that glitters even at night, like the sun!"

"Wait!!" Cyrus exclaimed. "You know where the true diamond of the Indian boy Karna is?"

"Yes, it's once again in Tomyris's possession. But I know how to get you that diamond very soon! Even if you don't win the war— if you're forced to withdraw—you'll at least leave with the royal turban bearing Karna's diamond. Yours forever."

"What do you want in return... and also for your trea—well, let's call it your help?"

"Gold, of course. A great deal of gold... Then I will go with you to Persia."

"Very well. You shall have your gold, guard. We have an agreement."

* * *

Tomyris convened a war council. They discussed strategy and tactics for attacking the Persians, deliberating and arguing at length.

"What's the use of bickering now, when we don't even know the exact—or let's be honest, not even the approximate—size of the enemy's army?" the queen said. "We need that information as soon as possible. One of my trusted people must head out with a few warriors to scout Cyrus's camp. Who isn't afraid?"

Bakhtiyar volunteered. Tomyris hesitated, pitying him because he had recently been wounded.

"Better I should go," Rustam said darkly, casting a glance at Bakhtiyar. "Give me permission, my queen."

"My queen, let me go!" said the young warrior Spargapis the Younger—always eager, like his father, to be first—as he turned to his mother.

"No, absolutely not!" Tomyris gasped. "Not you, my son. Not any of you three."

"Listen, I'm already fully recovered!" Bakhtiyar insisted. "Besides, I'll be most useful there, since I know a bit of Persian. I'll be able to make out what the Persian guards are saying. If I'm lucky, maybe I'll even overhear the commanders talking!"

Tomyris deliberated for a moment, then reached her decision.

"All right, Bakhtiyar, you've convinced us. You shall go. But please—I beg you—be extremely careful. I'll assign you several of my warriors from the 'Fierce Ones' to accompany you."

* * *

Three days later, Bakhtiyar returned. He was wounded again, though not badly and not in the head.

"Why are you alone?" Tomyris asked in confusion. "What happened to the others?"

Bakhtiyar did not reveal the truth—that, luring his companions

407

from the 'Fierce Ones' into a treacherous trap, he had slain them one by one.

"It was the dastardly enemy!" he lied to the queen he was sworn to protect. "They spotted us, chased us down, and started killing everyone. By some miracle, I alone escaped—barely got away from the Persians. I lost my horse, and I come to you now on foot…"

"Why did you not defend your tribesmen?!" Tomyris exclaimed in shock. "Why did you not stand up for my warriors, leaving them in peril?!"

It pained her to lose her best, most loyal fighters—her friends in all but name.

"But I had to bring you the report you so desperately needed, Tomyris! What right did I have to risk it all? Then you would have had to dispatch another scouting group, with no guarantee they wouldn't also be slain. Isn't that so? And who's to say they would have brought you the information your loyal servant Bakhtiyar managed to obtain?"

"Speak—what have you learned?" Tomyris asked, trying to come to terms with these bitter circumstances. "What is the size of Cyrus's army, and where are its various contingents stationed?"

"I was fortunate enough to eavesdrop on two of his generals," Bakhtiyar declared proudly. "Turns out most of the Persian army… is already gone! Of the troops that remain, the largest detachment is currently heading for a certain camp… I know where it is and can lead you there! Cyrus himself is commanding only a small, weakened band. I don't yet know where he is, but I'll certainly find out! I suggest we march at once to that Persian camp. We must hurry—before they move on!"

* * *

Tomyris led the Massagetae horsemen to surround the Persian camp.

With a crushing blow, the Massagetae destroyed the entire Persian detachment. By evening, exhausted, they began searching the camp for any remaining provisions.

"Hurray, my queen, there's plenty of food here!" the warriors and servants joyfully reported to Tomyris. "There's even wine! It seems these foolish Persians, setting out on campaign, dragged along too many supplies from home—way too much food and baggage! Obviously, they found it hard hauling all that weight across our steppes and deserts! We have it easier—we're on our home turf and travel light most of the time. Shall we distribute the food to all the warriors? We're so tired… we could really use a meal!"

"Wait," Rustam suddenly said in a very serious tone. "Something feels off here. I sense something strange in this camp… Didn't you notice there were only wounded and sick Persians left here? Where, then, is the main body of their army—their real strength?"

"Perhaps their strength is all spent!" Tomyris said a bit irritably, weary of the protracted war with the Persians. "You're always imagining something, Rustam. Another one of your 'hunches'— this time, quite unfounded!"

"Let us hope so," Rustam replied, choosing not to argue.

"Then there's no need to stir up worries… You there—come here!" the queen commanded one of the low-ranking servants. "Taste a little of this roasted meat from that cauldron, and take a sip of the Persian wine! We'll see if their food and wine are fit to eat—and whether we can share them with everyone."

"Tomyris, please, at least don't allow them to drink the wine," Rustam implored.

But the servant, having tasted the food and drunk the wine, showed no signs of poisoning and felt perfectly fine. The wine even seemed to cheer him up, bringing colour to his cheeks.

Thus, the queen permitted them all to settle in comfortably until morning, enjoying the provisions and indulging in the free wine. Such spoils were common enough for the Saka.

"Everyone eat and rest!" commanded Tomyris. "Tomorrow, we'll set out at midday, find the remaining Persians, and crush them. I've had more than enough of them already!"

"My queen, allow me to take your 'Fierce Ones' and stand watch behind the camp to guard your peace," Bakhtiyar proposed. "One never knows… And we—we won't drink any wine."

Tomyris thought for a moment, then granted permission, thanking Bakhtiyar for his devotion.

* * *

Morning came… and the Massagetae could not rise. They were alive, but… almost all were incredibly weak from a sleeping potion the Persians had mixed into the wine. This had been Bakhtiyar's treacherous plan.

Like a hurricane, the Persians fell upon the Massagetae, unleashing a brutal massacre on Tomyris's army. The Massagetae— mounted or on foot—resisted valiantly with what little strength they had, but the spell of Morpheus held them in a cruel grip.

Only in the very centre of the camp—where Rustam was stationed with his small detachment, along with his son Spargapis, neither of whom had drunk any of the wine—did the Persians meet fierce resistance. Rustam would not allow Tomyris herself to enter the fray, though she longed to. For now, she remained in her tent, giving orders to her warriors as the commanding leader. The queen was shaken by what was happening—she could not fathom how or why events had unfolded like this.

"Bring me my son!" she ordered her servants.

"Forgive us, Your Majesty, but that's impossible right now. Spargapis is in the thick of the fight!"

Tomyris's heart sank with sorrow. It was not the first time her son had faced grave and dangerous combat, but she had never feared for him this intensely.

"And where is Bakhtiyar?" she demanded of the servants at her side—those who, like the queen, had not partaken of the sweet and soporific Persian wine and so remained alert. "And where are my 'Fierce Ones' once again?! What on earth is going on?!"

No one could answer. The servants did not know where Bakhtiyar had gone or why he had not joined the others by morning with the still-missing 'Fierce Ones' to help their kinsmen trapped by the Persian attackers. At Tomyris's command, a warrior scout—still able to stand—was sent to find Bakhtiyar.

He returned before long with bad news: Bakhtiyar was nowhere to be found. As for the heroic, daredevil fighters of the 'Fierce Ones,' he found them sprawled on the ground—dead drunk. He tried everything to rouse them but failed; they slept on soundly. He came back to the queen with nothing.

So Bakhtiyar is indeed a traitor! Tomyris finally realized. *So Rustam was right yet again? And to think how Bakhtiyar swore he loved me! If I find him, he'll die by my own hand...*

Meanwhile, several of Tomyris's friends arrived at her tent, having shaken off the effects of the potion: Salih, chieftain of the

Abii, and Berez, chieftain of the Guz.

"What are your orders for the war, Tomyris?" her uncle asked.

"Wait," she said. "I need time to think. Does anyone know if Cyrus is taking part in this battle?" she asked the chieftains.

"No, we haven't seen him," Berez replied. "I found out that leading the battle on the Persian side is their general Gubaru, said to be a fearsome, merciless man."

Meanwhile, Rustam's fight with his detachment was growing ever fiercer. At the queen's command, Salih and Berez attacked the enemy from the right and left flanks.

Yet the most desperate, bloody clash remained at the centre of the camp. Rustam no longer felt his arms or legs, nor the burning pain of his many wounds. He fought on, valiantly holding his ground and striking down one foe after another. The Persians, both admiring his indomitable courage and fearing him, kept up the assault.

Spargapis fought heroically, fending off the enemy's attacks with all his might. But he lacked his father's experience, so he was in grave danger. Rustam, striking down numerous Persians, did his utmost to protect his son.

Just as Salih was about to ride over and help Rustam, over the clash of swords and the cries of the wounded, he heard a sudden, terrible shout from afar.

"No, no!! Not you—never you!!"

The typically calm, composed Rustam had cried out. The Persian general Gubaru had driven his razor-sharp sabre straight into Spargapis's heart. The young warrior let out a brief cry. Rustam, seeing this, galloped up to Gubaru and, mustering some newfound heroic strength, killed him with a single sword blow—Gubaru never even realized what was happening.

Rustam hastened to Spargapis. The youth was barely breathing, gazing up at the sky.

"Father, I… I'm proud… of you… I love you…"

Those were the young man's last words. Rustam tried to reply—

"I love you so very much too, my son!"—

but he was too late. The prince was gone…

When word of this tragedy reached all the Massagetae, and it was relayed to Tomyris, the queen howled like a steppe she-wolf. She refused to believe it; she tore at her hair, moaned, and wept bitterly.

"Oh, Spargapis! Why, why did you go into that fight? Why didn't you stay by my side? My beloved son, my own flesh and blood! Forgive your sinful mother! I… I will never forgive myself for your death. And know this: all our enemies will pay for it. I will avenge you!"

Soon the battle ended; the Persians were defeated. All the Massagetae who had drunk the wine finally woke up. Overcome by shame and guilt, they dared not look their queen in the eyes.

A healer tended to Rustam. The Tigraxauda prince angrily shooed him away.

"What do I need a healer for now?" he said heavily and grimly. "My wife does not love me—she rejects me. My only son, my heir, the joy of my heart… is no more. I—I couldn't save him! For what purpose should I go on living? Healer, better you bring me jars of haoma, as much as they can. I shall drink myself into oblivion and die. Life has lost all meaning for me."

* * *

Tomyris ordered the establishment of a new Massagetae camp—she refused to remain in the Persians' camp, where so many of her people had fallen. All the dead were buried at once, and the royal son, young Prince Spargapis, was interred with special honours.

Tomyris understood that somewhere nearby, Cyrus himself still had a detachment left. Contrary to Bakhtiyar's false reports, it might in fact be a large, formidable force—the remaining portion of the Persian army that the Massagetae had nearly destroyed. But whatever it was, it still posed a threat to Tomyris's land and her people.

The Massagetae queen realized that the current lull in the fighting was only temporary and that a new storm would soon erupt.

It was hard for her to think or plan because her every thought kept returning to her fallen son. Grief and tears choked her.

I swore—and I will punish our enemies, avenge you, my son Spargapis! she vowed silently.

In her own homeland, she had kept in reserve a splendid, dazzling, irreplaceable unit—an incomparable force of warrior women, the Amazon fighters. Now Tomyris summoned them without delay to reinforce the remainder of the Massagetae army's new camp. When these warriors arrived, the rest of the Massagetae also readied themselves in proper military form. Tomyris gathered the entire army, even the simplest farmers among her people. Everyone was prepared for the likely decisive clash with Cyrus— everyone except Rustam.

Tomyris went to see Rustam, to visit him. She found him in his tent, silent, grim, unkempt, and unwashed, dressed more like a vagrant than a warrior. He was drinking.

She did not scold or lecture him. She simply stepped up quietly from behind, sat down beside him on a bench, and gently wrapped her arms around his powerful, heroic back. Then she rested her golden-haired head there.

An hour passed before Rustam noticed he had drifted off in her firm yet tender embrace. At last, he woke up. Now his wife sat facing him, still holding him close.

"Why, Tomyris?… Why did it happen to him instead of me?!" Rustam cried out in despair, as if she might have an answer to that impossible question. "And why did you wait so long to come to me? Didn't you know how much I've been suffering?…"

Tomyris had not really thought of him in that way. She was so consumed by her own grief over the tragedy—and so preoccupied with the ongoing war, where the Persians had exacted a terrible toll and the threat remained unvanquished—that she had scarcely paused to think of her husband.

But the moment she remembered, and someone reported how deeply he was grieving, she went to him at once. Not as a queen, but as a wife.

"Forgive me, Rustam. Forgive me…" Tomyris said humbly, without excuses.

The next day she sent a healer to force him into some kind of treatment. Then she came to him again, this time bringing two of her servants. Rustam was drunk once more—worse than before. But he was not raging; he was almost asleep.

Tomyris ordered the servants to undress him carefully, wash him thoroughly, and clothe him in fresh garments. When they had done so, she dismissed them to stand guard outside Rustam's tent. Then she lay down beside her husband and started to caress him, embracing and kissing him. He could not wake up.

In the morning, when Rustam opened his eyes and saw his beloved wife, already awake, lying in his arms, he was nearly struck dumb by happiness! He hugged her with his strong arms and kissed her fervently, repeating:

"Tomyris! My dearest! Oh, Tomyris… how wonderful this is…"

Suddenly, Rustam saw in her eyes the gaze of his son, Spargapis, who had so resembled his mother. Overwhelmed by heartbreak, he let out a wail and began to weep like a child.

Tomyris understood. Gathering all the willpower she had, she forced back her own bitter tears and comforted her husband with more kisses.

In a rush of shared grief and emotion, for the first time in a long while, they were intimate. They surrendered to each other.

Rustam felt somewhat consoled, returning at last to good fighting form in preparation for the looming battle with Cyrus's detachment. This was precisely what Queen Tomyris needed. And she realized, too, that she… loved Rustam and needed him—as a woman needs a man.

* * *

Day after day passed, yet Cyrus made no move to launch a new offensive. It puzzled Tomyris and made her uneasy.

Suddenly, a Persian messenger galloped up—sent by Cyrus— bearing a letter. It read:

"To Queen of the Massagetae and all the Saka lands, Tomyris!

The Great King of the world, Cyrus II himself, has deigned to honour you with this message. My offer of marriage still stands. Will you accept it? If not, then prepare for the crows to drink your blood, the blood of your husband, and the blood of all your subjects! Your friend and bodyguard Bakhtiyar languishes in my captivity, in dire torment. We have also taken prisoner a daughter of your people, the young beauty Behnaz. If you still wish to see them alive, then come at once to the place my messenger will name! And bring the true turban, woven with gold threads and adorned with Karna's diamond, which shines like the sun! Then, I give you my word that we shall spare the lives of our prisoners—and yours. I have spoken. Cyrus."

"Don't believe them!" Rustam warned his wife urgently. "He acts like he's doing you a favour by sparing your life! Who is he to talk that way to the fearless Saka queen?! And haven't you realized by now it's a trap—and that your Bakhtiyar is a traitor?"

"He's certainly not mine," Tomyris replied. "But who is Behnaz? I've never heard of her!"

"I think there's a girl by that name among the Massagetae," one of her warriors said.

The queen sent her servants to ask around the camp to find out who Behnaz was.

"I know her," reported Kuzybek, chieftain of the Karats. "She's the daughter of my onetime friend—later mortal enemy—Zakir. She's betrothed to Bakhtiyar..."

Tomyris was shocked to hear this. But Bakhtiyar had sworn eternal love to her!

Through the Persian messenger, she swiftly sent Cyrus her response:

"You may kill these traitors; I would not pay even a copper coin for them! All the more so, I would never surrender my magnificent royal turban adorned with Karna's diamond! Cyrus, do not be a coward—stop trying to win this war with sly tricks and deceit! Come out and face the Massagetae in an honest fight on open ground, if you are indeed still a man and a warrior!"

Upon receiving this reply, Cyrus began preparing at once for battle with Tomyris.

* * *

That night, King Cyrus dreamed a strange dream. In it, the son of his nobleman Hystaspes, a young Persian named Darius, appeared alongside his lover and introduced her to Cyrus. Then the young man asked: "Does your wife, Cassandane, know that you, too, have a mistress? Her name is Death, for Death is a warrior's mistress! He rushes to meet her time and again! Don't deceive her this time, King! My own mistress is named Persia! And with her, I shall live a long life…"

Cyrus awoke, drenched in sweat and suddenly afraid, tormented by dire forebodings. But then he remembered his childhood and his foster parents, the kindly Spaka and Harpagus. For a moment, he felt relief… then came a flash of shame that he had ordered the death of his foster father, General Harpagus. He thought: In what way was he better than his cruel grandfather Astyages?

However, Cyrus banished these sombre thoughts as unworthy of his attention. He was king of the mightiest realm and a formidable warrior—why should he fear his own subjects, or, for that matter, those rough-hewn nomads of the steppe? Nonsense!

…The following day, the decisive battle took place. Tomyris commanded the Massagetae to throw every last resource into meeting the enemy face-to-face, prepared to die for their homeland but never to yield. Anyone who was frightened could remain in the camp—but henceforth, such a person would be labelled not a warrior but a feeble, cowardly crone. No one agreed to that. She also gave orders to take no prisoners, to kill all enemies—except Cyrus, who was to fall only by the queen's own hand.

And so it happened. The battle was unimaginably gruelling for both sides—one of the harshest the battle-seasoned Massagetae had ever fought. The nomads defended their steppe fiercely, and Queen Tomyris thirsted for righteous vengeance upon the killers of her only son. Cyrus knew that, eagerly executing their ruler's will, the Massagetae would fight to the death rather than concede anything to the Persians. In all his campaigns against many peoples, never had Cyrus faced adversaries as formidable as Tomyris and her tightly united people. Even sustaining heavy losses, the Massagetae refused to fall back, holding their ground to the last.

When the Massagetae's position began to falter, Tomyris unleashed her hidden reserve—the gallant, fearless Amazon-like detachment, unmatched in combat. She herself charged forward with them at full gallop. A triumphant battle cry rang out over the field—these warriors had yearned for real, perilous combat. Their blows against the Persians struck with terrifying might, cowing their foes into awe. Gaps opened wide in the Persian ranks, and Cyrus's army not only grew thin, it melted away. Roused by Tomyris and her Amazon fighters, the rest of the Massagetae took fresh heart and crushed the enemy with even greater determination. The Persians, caught off guard by the appearance of these new forces, found their fighting spirit fading with each passing hour.

The Persian army was routed. Nearly all of it perished under the Massagetae assault of spears, swords, and acinaces. Those few who survived barely managed to escape, eventually fleeing home.

The "Iron Ruler" Tomyris galloped up to the now-exhausted Cyrus, then felled him with two or three mighty blows. She kept her vow to her son: their enemy, King Cyrus, died by her fearless hand.

"Let him lie there on the field," Tomyris ordered, "and let the crows peck at him."

…Sometime later, Cambyses II—Cyrus's elder son—became King of Persia. After him, for a very brief period, it was Gaumata, or the False Bardiya, who ruled. But soon after, the throne passed to Darius I. Thus, in the end, Cyrus's final dream proved prophetic.

* * *

After the gruelling, bloody battle that had brought the Massagetae their momentous victory, someone unexpected appeared in Tomyris's camp—Bakhtiyar. He burst into her tent.

"O, greetings, my love, queen of my soul!" he cried, throwing himself flat before her and kissing the hem of her garment, sweet-talking the bravest leader of the Massagetae—her former charge and, as she once believed, her friend.

"Weren't you in captivity?" Tomyris responded, unmoved by his flattery yet with a smile masking a hint of derision. "Cyrus wrote to me that you were being tortured and killed in his camp. Together with your fiancée, Behnaz."

Suddenly, the queen's gaze grew stern. The diamond on her turban flashed with blinding brilliance.

"Don't be angry, sun of my life, my queen!" Bakhtiyar pleaded, clueless to her ire. "Zakir and Haidar forced me to marry that girl! But I don't love her; I adore only you, and you alone are all I need!"

"I have my beloved husband. Did you not know?" Tomyris said coldly. "Oh, and by the way, Bakhtiyar, I've recently recalled why you seemed familiar. The scent of the herbs along the Oxus, and your voice! You're the one who abducted me years ago from my father and brought me to that horrible, dark dungeon! True, I remember you fed me there and confessed your love—but you never freed me! And why? Because you've spent your whole life fearing your uncle—Zakir. I realized you're his nephew, forever running from me to him like a spy, reporting all my secrets!"

"I'll kill that lying uncle of mine and that vile chieftain Haidar too," Bakhtiyar said heatedly. "They gave me none of what they promised! They're scoundrels—snakes—vermin!"

"There is no one left to kill—they were executed long ago, while you were busy betraying both them and us, running off to Cyrus. And did Cyrus promise you a fortune for delivering my life, hmm? But the moment you heard the Persians were defeated, you came running back to me again. Unbelievable! What, should I praise you, my friend? Maybe even reward you?! Especially after the death of my only son, Spargapis, who perished because of you, because of your treachery!!"

"Forgive me, Queen, I didn't know," Bakhtiyar tried to defend himself. "I'm innocent! Besides, I'm the one who slew your enemy, Cyrus, and brought you his head in this sack!"

"Pardon me... who killed Cyrus?" Tomyris looked at the brazen liar in surprise. "You killed him?! And I suppose I—what—mistakenly believed that I did... Well done, what a hero you are!"

She laughed until tears came. Then she called to her servants:

"Cut off this vile traitor's head and place it in a leather sack along with Cyrus's, the one he's just brought me! Let the blood of these two wicked foes mingle! Toss the sack onto the battlefield!

"So, Cyrus, you yearned for blood—then have your fill!" the queen declared proudly. "You craved blood—now bathe in it yourself! Justice has been served on you."

Her servants carried out the queen's order immediately; Bakhtiyar did not even have time to protest or beg for mercy. There can be no mercy for the treacherous. He had no idea that Cyrus, had he emerged triumphant from the battle safe and sound, also intended to dispose of him. Even that tyrant could not abide traitors…

That same day, an unexpected visitor appeared in Tomyris's tent once again—the boy Karna!

He looked no different from before: time held no sway over him at all.

"Queen of the Saka, the magic turban with the diamond has more than once granted you strength against your foes. Yet while wearing it, you have shed blood—even if it was the blood of a cruel murderer. Remember what I said to you? You must not harbour hatred toward your enemies—you must forgive everyone! Defending your homeland is essential, yes, but without a trace of malice, with a kind and merciful heart. Those destined to die will die regardless; those fated to survive will survive. Now the shining diamond… is no longer as pure as it once was, for it is stained with human blood. To prevent it from being further defiled by blood, forgive me—but I must take it away."

And just as suddenly as he had appeared, Karna vanished. From that day on, Tomyris never again saw her remarkable red turban with its sun-like, radiant diamond. Who received it next? Some king, or perhaps simple folk? Where could it be now?

* * *

…In time, Queen Tomyris of the Massagetae realized she was pregnant by Rustam. They lived on for many years in harmony and happiness with all their children—united by deep love and abiding loyalty!

Brave, valiant, and just, Tomyris and Rustam went on to win many more victories. Yet they never forgot that grueling but unparalleled triumph over Cyrus, King of the Persians, and they constantly remembered their courageous firstborn son, Prince Spargapis… The two of them—Tomyris and Rustam—forever became a stirring legend for future generations the world over, who likewise dream of love, heroic deeds, and glorious victories…

34

Tashkent, 2006

A now-aged Viktoria Khaeva, moving with difficulty around her apartment, headed toward the front door in response to a ring. Peering through the peephole, she saw a figure she didn't recognize. Yet he looked harmless enough, so she opened the door.

The silver-haired, stooped stranger stood there silently, not saying a word.

"Hello," the apartment's mistress began politely. "How can I help you? Who are you looking for? You must be from the local Society for the Blind?"

"No… Vika, hello! Don't you recognize me? I'm your long-lost husband, Zakhar."

The middle-aged woman nearly fainted, but the elderly man—who indeed was Khaev—steadied her just in time, gently guiding her into one of the rooms.

Viktoria Sergeevna wept as she looked at him.

"So you've finally come back! My dear…" she murmured, scarcely believing the joy she had awaited for—what—nearly forty years. She had waited for him, loyally and steadfastly.

He moved closer and embraced her. It was nearly impossible to reconcile this woman in his arms with the one he had once known; she had changed beyond measure, in ways that could never be undone. But the moment he gathered her into his embrace, he felt how deeply familiar she still was to him.

"Forgive me, Vikulya. I'm so very much to blame!" Zakhar Ilyich said, trembling as he bowed his grey head. "But believe me, I had a serious reason for staying hidden so long."

When Viktoria Sergeevna had calmed down, they sat drinking tea, and she asked:

"What on earth happened to you, Zakharyushka? Tell me everything!"

"All right. You know that back then, in the late sixties, I was renting out my late aunt's apartment. You never interfered in my financial affairs because you knew I would never leave you without material support. I've always been grateful for that.

"So here's what happened. One day, in response to my ad about renting that apartment, a swarthy man came to me—he could barely speak Russian. When he learned the rental price, he managed in broken Russian to say he was fine with it and wanted to move in. Naturally, I asked to see his passport—I couldn't just rent to the first person who happened by! But as it turned out, he was not merely some random individual… he was, in fact, a repeat criminal offender. Of course, I didn't know that at the time. He very calmly and confidently showed me his passport. This was before photocopiers, so I couldn't make a copy. But I did note down his details on a slip of paper, just in case. Never in my wildest dreams did I imagine that "case" would end up sealing my fate, shattering my life… Forgive me, Vika—it ended up shattering yours too, since you never forgot me all those years."

Viktoria Khaeva poured him more tea, pushing a plate of slightly stale cookies closer. She thought about telling him that the same Bahrom had come to see her twelve years ago! But she decided to hear him out first.

Zakhar Ilyich went on:

"Some time passed, and Bahrom moved out of my aunt's place—apparently, he'd found something better, fancier. Well, his choice. I didn't mind in the least, as I had other prospective tenants lined up.

"But then something else happened. I was putting together documents for a director's position at the porcelain factory—oh, how I wanted to outdo my friend Sardor Makhkamov! One night, I stayed late at work, until well into the evening. Exhausted, I just wanted a drink to unwind. I felt awkward about doing it at home. Later, I replayed the whole situation in my mind dozens of times, always thinking, *If only I'd done it at home!* Even if you'd scolded me, even if we had quarrelled, we could have avoided the tragedy that befell us later…

"So instead, I went to a café near our plant that stayed open late. At that hour, there were hardly any customers—maybe seven people total, counting me. I took a seat, ordered alcohol and a snack, and had to wait quite a while, since the waitress was busy chatting with someone. Bored, I looked around. Behind me, though not at the next table but the one after, two men were talking quietly. One of them, who was turned away from me so I only saw the back of his head, I definitely didn't recognize—he was a stout man in his fifties with a big bald patch on top. The only surprising thing was why such a well-dressed, respectable individual, who looked like the director of some large enterprise, would be in a café so late at night. Then I shrugged it off—who knows, maybe it was a business meeting. I had no idea what those two, so different in appearance, might be discussing. Possibly the man facing him was trying to sell him something. At that point, the bald guy no longer held my interest."

"But the one across from him certainly did! Because it was… Bahrom Avazov, my former tenant from Kashkadarya!

"Bahrom hadn't noticed me—really, he wasn't paying attention. Then something unexpected happened: the heavyset man got up and left, probably to use the restroom. Meanwhile, Bahrom poured some kind of white powder into the man's tea. I stared at him, stunned, and that gave me away. Bahrom saw me! He didn't say anything or come over, just winked and gave me a horrifying grin. Right then, I realized I had to get out fast. I jumped up, abandoning my untouched drink and food, and dashed off.

"I knew he could easily kill me—just like he was about to kill that bald fellow. How do I know he did kill him? Because barely a day later, the newspapers reported that Davron Abdukhalikov, director of a classified provincial enterprise, had been found dead in his office. They included a photo of the same bald, heavyset man. Apparently, it was all very mysterious because that morning, when he was found lifeless, he'd returned by bus from the capital to his city, then walked into his office as if nothing was amiss. And then he never came out—they carried him out.

"I suspected the cause was a slow-acting, lethal poison that Bahrom Avazov had slipped into his tea. I also felt guilty for the man's death: I had witnessed the attempt on his life! Yet I was so terrified of Bahrom that I did nothing to save that unfortunate man… The newspapers also reported that a highly valuable consignment of goods had been stolen from that factory. They didn't say exactly what, since it was a secret enterprise, but I could guess—most likely diamonds.

"To jump ahead, I'll tell you what I learned much later: Avazov had stolen those diamonds at the request of a certain Stanislav Levidovsky, who later fled with them to Great Britain, where he started his own diamond-processing business. But did Levidovsky specifically instruct Bahrom to kill the industrialist Abdukhalikov? I suspect probably not. Likely it was Avazov's own initiative—he was ruthless that way.

"I kept quiet at the time, dear, so as not to alarm you, and I really hoped Bahrom wouldn't try to track me down—or at least, wouldn't be able to find me. My assumptions there were extremely naïve.

"A few days later, I caught a glimpse of him… in the corridor of our plant! Panic seized me. That was the day I left my home, my family, my job, all my friends…"

"I see… But why, in all these years, did you never call, never write a single letter, not even a telegram? You knew I was waiting for them! Why, Zakhar?"

"Vikulya, I did send you money orders!"

"Yes, I know. But if you really think that's all I needed from you, then you and I have nothing else—"

"Forgive me, my dear! No, I don't think that. It's just that I was truly afraid Bahrom would trace my calls or letters. If he found me, he'd kill me for being a witness to his face and real name. And he must have feared something too: that I'd turn him in to the police! He didn't realize the police were no safe haven for me either—I was terrified of them myself because I had my own minor misdeeds, like skimming off our plant, and was constantly afraid I'd end up behind bars.

"Only now do I see how utterly cowardly I was. I roamed from city to city, just to stay as far away from here as possible! But to be honest, I ran from Bahrom only in the first few years, not knowing he would keep pursuing me obsessively until the day he died. Yes, that's right—I often checked up on him, found out where he was and what he was doing—so that if necessary, I could face my enemy prepared. And recently, I learned by chance that my pursuer had, in fact, been arrested for some of his crimes and died in prison."

"Anyway, after that, I met someone… As things happen, we fell in love. No, we didn't marry—we're still legally married, you and I, Vika. But Anya and I had a son. Three years later, he became gravely ill and died. Anna couldn't cope with the grief. She turned spiteful and angry, blaming me for not finding enough money to cure and save our child! She ignored the fact that I was only human, that I was hurting too—maybe not as much as she was, but still. In the end, everything collapsed between us, and I left her. Many times I considered coming back to you, but… If I'm honest, I was ashamed. I'm still ashamed. It's hard to speak of all this. But believe me, Vika, there wasn't a single day when I didn't think of you at least once! It seems I've truly loved only you my whole life…"

"You should still have mustered the courage to come sooner," Viktoria Sergeevna said, shaking her head critically. "I would have taken you in. And forgiven you…"

"So, does that mean you still love me, too? That you can forgive me now?" Zakhar Ilyich asked hopefully.

"We're too old to hold grudges, wouldn't you say? We're not kids anymore. I forgave you a long time ago."

Zakhar lit up with relief.

"So, are you just passing through here? Or are you staying a while?" Viktoria asked, trying not to set her heart on a reunion of the Khaev family in vain.

"I've come here for good!" her husband declared brightly and confidently. "Now, where's that old hammer of mine? The small handy one for around the house? Show me. Perfect. I'll finally nail up that coat rack—it's been falling off the wall for ages!"

***

Moscow, 2006

Konstantin Koscheyev had invited his longtime acquaintance, Veronika Midiyatdinova—formerly Nemigaykina—to meet at a café. Veronika was reluctant to go, guessing the topic of the upcoming conversation, but she didn't want to get into an open conflict with Koscheyev just yet. Still, she sensed that a clash with him was inevitable.

He ordered them each a cup of cappuccino.

"So why did you invite me, Kostyenka?" she asked, pretending not to understand.

"How's it going, gorgeous?" Konstantin began, taking a roundabout approach.

"All fine. Can we speed this up? I'm in a hurry."

"In a rush to cook dinner for your husband?"

"Maybe dinner, maybe supper. What's it to you?"

"Well, I see you've grown a bit sassy! Forgotten how I pulled you out of those nightclubs, how I kept you from drinking yourself into oblivion and helped you get your act together? Then I handed you off to a decent guy! Now you're living it up, rolling in dough—has it been so bad for you? And who do you have to thank for that, eh? I'm asking you, Veronika! Silent? Fine, I'll answer for you. Thanks to me, that softhearted fool. Where would you be without me now, Nemigaykina-Toogoodyforyoukina?"

"That's all in the past, Kostya. There was a time you got plenty out of me in return. Though I hate even thinking about that now. But you were perfectly happy with it. So what do you want from me now? Why do you keep milking everyone like a leech?"

"Watch your mouth, girl! I might take offense and punish you severely! You know me… Now let's get to the point. How is it that after all these years, you still haven't ruined the life of that guy you're sharing a bed with, the one you're always around? Remember what I asked you to do? Sniff out all his secrets and report them to me. Did I ask, or didn't I? And you haven't told me squat. Plus, I gave you those special medications for him. Did you give them to him or not?"

"He doesn't have any secrets from you, what are you—"

"Shut it!" Koscheyev hissed, furious. "You're taking me for a fool, is that it? Lying there with your hubby day and night, and you can't worm out the info I need?"

"Stay out of my married life, dear. None of your business, honey. Got it?"

"Oh no, my lovely, it *is* my business! Because I'm the one who steered you to him and helped you marry him! Back then, you agreed to all my demands, swore up and down that you wouldn't let me down. Because I promised to pay you well—and I kept my word. Isn't that right? Or am I mixing things up?"

"I didn't know back then that… Now I love Kirill, and I don't want to harm him!"

"You… you what? Love him?!"

Konstantin burst into loud laughter.

"You, a dolled-up little doll, do you even know what love is?"

"I do now. And there's more—I'm expecting Kir's baby. Look, I'm already showing. And he loves me, too."

"What? Are you crazy? You got yourself knocked up by him? You're pregnant, and you didn't get rid of it?!"

"It's none of your business. And—oh, here…" She pulled out a thick envelope from her purse. "Here you go, Kostya, take this. It's the money you've been giving me all these years. I took the money, but I never hurt Kirill, because he never deserved it. I mean… He never did me any wrong, personally."

Koscheyev stared at her silently—glowering, angry, displeased.

"You'll regret this, Veronika," he threatened.

"What, arc you going to kill me, the way you've always wanted to kill Kirill? If anything happens to me, a video recording of all your plotting against Kirill goes straight to him—and a few others! Then he'll find out what kind of 'friend' he's really got. So just sit down, Kostik, and shut your mouth. I was this close to telling him everything already, but I spared you. Because if Kir knows the truth about you, he'll tear you to pieces. You won't even have a wet spot left behind. You know he's stronger and more influential than you now."

"Hey, hey, my dear!" Konstantin said more gently, trying to calm things down. "I didn't mean anything bad. Go on, love each other. And tell me—are you expecting a boy or a girl? Got a name picked out? If it's a boy, how about Kostya?"

***

Moscow, 2010

When Uzbek intelligence operative Artur Kiramov was inserted—under a false name—into a certain gang that had set up shop in Moscow, he had no idea that the new name of the outfit would so closely echo both his real and cover surnames.

He had been placed there in order to help neutralize the group.

"What did you say your name was?" Kirill Midiyatdinov asked him. "Say it again!"

"My name's Artyom Kiryushin," Artur said with an air of pride, as though it were some unique last name worth bragging about.

"Nah, too long, no good. Everyone here's got a nickname," Kirill replied, every bit as cocky. "Look at me, for example—they call me 'The King.' Now, what nickname are we going to pick for you? Want to be 'Kir'?"

Koscheyev, who was present, paused briefly in thought, then said to Midiyatdinov:

"Kirill, actually, Kir suits you more. Could I have a quick word with you in private?"

They stepped into another room. Koscheyev continued quietly:

"Hey, 'King,' I just had a thought. What if we keep calling you 'King,' and then we name our entire organization 'Kir'? In your honor! What do you think?"

Midiyatdinov loved the idea, feeding his ego.

"Hey, Konstantin, brother—thanks! So what about Artyom?

What's his handle?"

"He can be Kiryusha, or just Ryusha. That's all. But from now on, let everyone know that the most dangerous and fearsome gang is called 'Kir'! Maybe even in all caps 'KIR,' like 'TSUM'! Let people think it's named after Kiryushin, not Kirill. They won't realize you're the real leader. That keeps you under cover. Safer that way! If the cops bust in, we can pin all our sins on that dope Artyom, and you and I walk away. What, agreed?"

"Yes, Kostya! You're always on point! The brains! And I really like it: a gang called 'KIR'! I know it's really in my honour!"

Midiyatdinov was older now, already going grey, but still, in some ways, a boy at heart.

Meanwhile, Artur quickly got the hang of things in the gang, carrying out tasks for Midiyatdinov and Koscheyev.

So, Kirill is their top dog, Artur noted to himself. *But I still don't know if this 'KIR' in Moscow is the only one, or if there's one in Tashkent too…*

* * *

Moscow, 2012

Kirill Midiyatdinov—raised by the harsh, brutal Oleg, never having received any warmth from him, and then hardened by the streets, prison, and the vindictive Koscheyev—had long ago become a cold, unfriendly, and callous man toward the world at large. As a small child, he'd loved "aunt" Marina when she was just an occasional visitor who doted on him. As an adult, he helped her financially but couldn't bring himself to feel any real filial love or accept her in his heart as his mother.

Yet when Marina died of a heart attack, Kirill took care of the funeral and the memorial. After she was laid to rest, he stood alone by the grave of his unfortunate parent, quietly weeping like a child.

His "brothers," the gang members, of course, offered their help, but not wanting to disturb him, they hung back among the other mourners, waiting for their boss.

Kirill desperately wished Marina's husband—Denis's father—were there, the man Kirill had always gotten along with, even when he didn't know he was his biological son! But Kirill had been unable to find Denis; he'd only heard he'd left long ago for the far north.

"She loved you dearly all her life," a deep voice suddenly spoke behind Kirill.

A strong man's hand fell on the grieving crime boss's shoulder. Midiyatdinov turned and gasped.

"Uncle Denis?! Hello. How are you here? I looked for you and found nothing…"

"Why call me uncle? You know the truth, Kiryusha—I'm your real father… The neighbors of Marina had my number, and they've known me a while. She and I did live together for a long time—well, you know…"

Kirill threw his arms around him first, and Persiyev returned his son's embrace just as warmly.

How much these two had endured, how far they had come for this reunion! By now, Denis was in his seventies…

"Papa, move in with me, okay? There's plenty of room at my place. My wife and the kids would love to have you. You've got two grandkids—Lyuba and Kolya. And you didn't even know you're a granddad!"

"Thank you, son, thank you," said Denis Kirillovich, fighting back tears of joy. "I'll definitely think about it!"

"What's to think about? I've got it all worked out!" Kirill retorted, used to deciding and ordering everything himself—he still went by Midiyatdinov. "I'll give you a big room on the second floor of our house today! Where's your stuff?"

"At the hotel for now. Son, who are those men in black suits waiting off to the side? They look dangerous."

"Come on, Dad! Think before you speak—I'm the dangerous one! They're just my 'dogs,' loyal and obedient. Don't worry about them. Let's go home!"

35

Tashkent, 2012

The captive Konstantin Romanov shifted in his chair.

"Right now, I'm going to ask these thugs to at least let you go, madam!" he announced to Tamilla, striking a noble-hero pose. "Just watch—I'll talk to them, and they'll release you. You've no gold or diamonds, so why keep you locked up here for so long?"

"Perhaps you shouldn't risk yourself like that, Konstantin Ivanovich?" Tamilla Mahkamova said with genuine concern for her business partner and friend.

"For you, Tamilla Sardorovna, it's absolutely worth it!" Romanov exclaimed flamboyantly, no longer restraining himself nor bothering to spare her husband's feelings—though her husband was no less noble or courageous.

435

Rashid Batyrov, biting his lip, regretted that he himself had not proposed bargaining for Tamilla's release. Yet something about Romanov's behavior seemed to puzzle him.

"Hey, you there, come here!" Konstantin shouted at Dmitry, who had moved off a short distance. "Can you fetch… what's his name… Bahrom?"

"And what would you need him for, if I may ask?" Dmitry responded politely.

"It's none of your business!" Romanov snapped for no apparent reason. "Just call him!"

"All right."

Dmitry left to find Bahrom, who was somewhere nearby.

"Bahrom, I need a word with you," Konstantin said when the bandit approached the three captives—showing no fear or hesitation at addressing him informally. "But not here. Hey, untie me now, come on! I have important business with your gang leader, Midiyatdinov. Did I get that name right—the boss of your 'KIR' outfit?"

Bahrom appeared somewhat unsure—he clearly didn't know how best to respond. But hearing Kirill's name seemed to affect him: it carried weight and practically compelled him to act. After hesitating a moment, he walked over to Romanov, undid the ropes, and… led him away, unbound.

Once they were gone, Rashid leaned toward his wife and spoke in a whisper—although no one else was around, he still feared someone might overhear:

"Tamilla, my dear, listen. I want to warn you: do not trust Romanov! I know you're smart, but you're too kind and open—you trust that haughty, skinny upstart too much!"

"Darling, I'm sorry, but why shouldn't I trust Konstantin?"

Tamilla asked, confused. "He's been my long-standing, reliable partner!"

"Well, if we really think about it, he might not be so reliable. You yourself said there's been no contact from the kids in the USA. I think he—this Romanov—might be up to something. Sorry, but the more I talk to him, the more I feel he's a 'dark horse.' Plus… look at that expensive gold chain around his neck. Why didn't the bandits take it from him? And they led him out unbound! So he was only tied up in front of us. It all looks staged!"

"Stop it, Rashid!" snapped Tamilla, who was physically and emotionally exhausted. She was a bit cross with her husband too, for not stepping up to negotiate with the bandits himself. True, she would never have left without him—she wouldn't abandon her husband to certain peril. But he could at least have tried talking to the captors. Maybe they'd have let them all go free? "You're just throwing baseless accusations at a good man. I've never seen you act like this!"

"Wait, my love. Didn't you hear the name of their gang just now—the one he mentioned? 'KIR'? Which just so happens to be the initials of Konstantin Ivanovich Romanov!"

Tamilla stared at her husband, thinking: *What?! Surely not… No!!*

About an hour later, Romanov returned to the hangar.

"I spoke with their leader—Kirill Midiyatdinov," he told Tamilla and Rashid. "He agreed to let Tamilla Sardorovna go. But on one condition: If you truly have no diamonds—namely, the Koh-i-Noor fragments Pulat Gafarov discovered—then both of you, or at least one, must provide the exact name and address of whoever currently has them. They couldn't just have vanished into thin air!"

"We honestly don't have any such information!" Tamilla insisted, her spirit strong and fearless, though she felt hope slipping away.

And it's diamonds, diamonds again, Batyrov thought bitterly. *As if there's nothing else in the world that interests him!*

His suspicions regarding Romanov were reinforced more than ever.

***

Outside Boston, USA, that same period

Ivan Makonin had realized there was no way to free the students from the bunker without their involvement. The captives needed to understand what was happening and then team up with him to escape. But how would they grasp anything, how would they think and act rationally, if they were continuously kept under the powerful haze of hypnotic suggestion?

Ivan was quite a sociable person, easily making connections wherever he went. This allowed him to befriend one of Dr. Trabs's lab assistants—Lucy Norton—without much trouble. Lucy was privy to everything happening with the Uzbek students, all the medical experiments performed on them.

One evening, at Ivan's place, an apartment he rented under the alias "McConnley," Lucy revealed to him the terrible secret behind the students' captivity. She was sworn to remain silent about it under threat of severe punishment, practically under pain of death.

But Lucy was lonely, and she found "John" very appealing. So it was obvious to Ivan that her candor had a motive: the girl, who was being courted by him in compliments and sweet talk, saw him as a prospective husband. After all, what secrets could she keep from her future spouse? She reassured herself with that logic.

Because Lucy was quite attractive, and Ivan liked her too, he might indeed have considered a future with her… if not for one seemingly small but crucial factor that made any such plan unthinkable.

Namely, Ivan simply could not fathom how this seemingly kind girl could participate in such an immoral enterprise, or at least condone it if not openly enjoy it. It repelled his uncorrupted conscience and roused a fierce protest in his soul—one he had to hide behind a mask of cordiality around Ms. Norton.

Maybe Lucy will change someday, become better? he wondered hopefully. But in his heart, he knew he still loved Nadya—his former wife, mother of his child, who'd left him and taken their daughter in the divorce. Makonin still dreamed of reuniting them all one day!

He could not reveal his personal plans to Lucy, however, as that might cost the helpless students their lives.

Yet he also couldn't bear the idea of using Lucy ruthlessly—he pitied her and refused to deceive her in so callous a manner.

Ivan asked just one favor of his American friend:

"Darling, you said Darkness hypnotizes the kids daily so they won't understand what's really happening to them?"

"Yes, that's right," Lucy nodded.

"You don't happen to know if he does it first thing in the morning or later?"

"I believe it's in the afternoon. His hypnosis lasts twenty-four hours. Meanwhile, in the mornings, our 'guests' go to the gym, the pool, have breakfast, and spend time in the library. Dr. Moran says their bodies and brains need constant training and development."

"Got it, perfect."

Ivan handed Ms. Norton a small vial of dark liquid.

"I have a favor to ask, Lucy. There's a coffee break at eleven o'clock, yes? Could you discreetly slip the contents of this vial into Mr. Darkness's coffee? Don't worry—there's nothing in it harmful to his life."

"I've noticed you don't really like poor Greg for some reason, John!" Lucy teased, misreading the situation and assuming he was simply getting back at a rival who might have flirted with her. "But sure, let's have a little fun at that clumsy Darkness's expense! Is this a sleeping draught? He'll doze off at coffee break right in front of everyone?"

"Well… not exactly," Ivan hedged. "But I promise you'll find the result amusing. You'll get a good laugh at your 'secret admirer's' expense!"

Sure enough, the next day Greg Darkness—whose digestive system was hardly robust—drank just a few sips of coffee laced with Lucy's secret addition: a potent laxative. Almost immediately, he began passing gas in the middle of his colleagues, then spent the rest of the day practically confined to the bathroom. As Makonin had predicted, Lucy, far from sympathizing, found it hilarious. Compassion was not her strong suit.

For Makonin, Darkness being sidelined from the "battlefield" was exactly what he needed.

During the late lunch break, Ivan quietly crept up behind the carefree Yekaterina Solovyova, who was walking down the corridor, and—grabbing the young woman in his arms—dragged her into a small, vacant room.

"Katya! I have something very important to discuss with you and the two guys. Can you go back to the cafeteria now, discreetly call them over, and bring them here without anyone else noticing?"

"What for, Mr. McConnley?" a bewildered Solovyova asked, not having seen John in the bunker for quite some time. "And what are you doing here?? Oddly enough, I'm happy to see you. Why are you whispering like that? Are you afraid of someone?!"

She was about to laugh out loud at what she considered McConnley's amusing behaviour, but he quickly silenced her by clamping her own hand over her mouth.

The young woman was frightened and tried to scream.

"No!!" Ivan silently mouthed, forming the words with his lips only. "Don't make a sound, Katya, I beg you! I must speak with you all at once. Will you bring them?"

Three minutes later, everyone had assembled. It turned out that without the hypnosis they had grown used to, the boys were suffering from severe headaches. Katya was in better shape, although her face was flushed, and she had tachycardia—her blood pressure had risen slightly.

Ivan realized there was very little time to explain, so he did his best to quickly outline the crux of the situation. They listened to him closely…

"So in the end, do they plan on killing us here?!" Katya asked, horror in her eyes as she grasped the full tragedy of their predicament.

"Yes. Your lives mean nothing to them. To these monsters, you're just 'tools'—no different from a computer mouse, a chair, or a knife…"

"We have to think of something!" Daniil Shevtsov burst out, fighting through his headache. "We need to get out of here as soon as possible!"

"That much is obvious," muttered the ever-terse Aibek

Khashimov, whose headache was even worse than Dan's. "But the question is how?? Mr. McConnley, you're the one who brought us here! Why do you want to help us now?"

"It's a long story, truly, and not important right now," Ivan replied. "The main thing is that I'm sincerely on your side… Call me simply Ivan. I'm Russian, from Moscow."

The three young people exchanged surprised looks. Based on his sparse, broken English, they had initially suspected he wasn't a real American. But they couldn't understand why he had put on a show of being a Yankee. Still, they figured he must have had his reasons, and it really didn't matter anymore.

Could they trust this mysterious man? Yet Ivan spoke so earnestly, clearly worried about their fate, that in the end, they believed him.

"But since you're the one who led us in, don't you also know how we can get out?" Katya asked hopefully, fixing him with a pleading gaze.

"No, I haven't a clue yet. The security system here is extremely tight, and they guard you three most vigilantly," Ivan admitted, looking frustrated. "By the way, they could start searching for you throughout the bunker at any moment, and we still haven't come up with a plan!"

They all fell silent for a bit.

"Listen, I have an idea!" Daniil exclaimed suddenly. "Ivan, what if you go to New York and ask for help at the Embassy of Uzbekistan—or the consulate in Washington? I'm sure our diplomats would help us."

"That's probably true, and I would do that for you," Makonin agreed. "But it would take a fair bit of time to reach out to the embassy and then wait for effective help. And you, my friends, don't have any time left."

"Yes, exactly," Aibek chimed in. "Plus, the bunker has a secret basement. The villains could just hide us down there, and no one—diplomats or not—would ever find us."

Ivan pressed on:

"Tomorrow, that Darkness I temporarily sidelined will almost certainly be back on his feet, and he'll hypnotize you again so you won't remember any of what we're talking about now. Which is why, my friends, we have to act right away—today, now!"

"Then let's analyse the situation," Katya said warily, glancing at the door that bunker security had already knocked on once. "They could barge in here at any moment. We have to think fast! Mister Mac—sorry, Ivan, please explain: who exactly told you to bring us here? That's important. Professor Moran? Maybe Trabs?"

"No, no, I got my orders from… well, not exactly a 'boss,' but… basically someone I owe a large sum of money. He's forced me into a situation where I have to work for him. He told me to meet you at Boston's airport and take you to Moran's bunker. My boss and Moran have some sort of arrangement. Most likely, the Moscow businessman—and gangster—I've been working for supplies students for these experiments in return for huge payments."

"What's your employer's name?" Aibek asked.

"Konstantin Ivanovich Koscheyev."

All three students looked at each other, baffled.

"Wait, Konstantin Ivanovich?" Dan nearly whistled in surprise. "But we were sent to Boston on scholarship by a man also called Konstantin Ivanovich! Just a different surname—Romanov."

"That's quite a coincidence!" Katya exclaimed, now putting two and two together.

"I doubt it's a coincidence," said the rational Aibek. "I don't really believe in 'miraculous coincidences.' By the way, our K.I. is also from Moscow… Come on, in this day and age, how hard is it to change your last name? You can have two passports."

"True!" Makonin agreed. He knew from experience; he himself had two passports—one Russian, one American.

"But how?" Katya pressed on. "Our Konstantin Ivanovich was always so kind, generous, and courteous. He covered our travel expenses, and before that, gifted each of us laptops. And he wasn't working alone—he collaborated closely with our beloved Tamilla Sardorovna! She would never do anything to harm us…"

"Right," Daniil said. "It makes no sense. Could Tamilla Mahkamova really be in cahoots with these criminals—people who commit horrific crimes and keep us locked up like powerless slaves? She's the same as they are?!"

"Aren't you ashamed to spout such nonsense?" Katya chided him. "Especially about a woman who did so much for us! She treated us like her own children, helped us pass our preliminary courses, and made sure we aced them! She's nothing like these people. Ivan, is your Koscheyev skinny, older, slightly stooped?"

"Yes, that's him," Ivan nodded.

"So," Katya continued, "this cunning scoundrel Konstantin Ivanovich no doubt tricked Tamilla Sardorovna, just as he tricked us. I'm sure she had no idea about his cruel plans. She's a wonderful woman, a true friend! She might be in trouble herself, for all we know. We have no idea what's going on back home in Tashkent—or how our parents are faring…"

"Exactly—they're probably going out of their minds with worry, since we haven't been in touch for so long!" Aibek said gloomily. "My mom has bad lungs. How will she cope with all this?"

Suddenly, an idea struck Katya.

"Ivan," she said, trying to hide her excitement, though her eyes gleamed, "do you have a pen and at least some scrap of paper?"

"Not on me, no. But I have some at home. I can still move around freely in the bunker. I'll zip back to my place and bring you whatever you need."

"That's perfect. Tell me, in what language do Moran and your Konstantin Koscheyev correspond? English? Because I don't think Romanov knows the language…"

"Yes, English. You're right—my boss doesn't speak it himself, but he uses professional translators. Why do you—"

"Do you think Moran would recognize Koscheyev's handwriting? Actually, that might not matter if you have at least one of Koscheyev's official company letterheads—with the logo and all the usual features. Then you wouldn't even need a seal—just a signature. Are you able to forge your boss's signature?"

"A signature? A seal? But why would we need all that?" Makonin asked, still confused. "Though yes, I do have his company letterheads."

"Bring what we need, and I'll explain afterward. Hopefully, we can meet here again tonight without any issues! Try to make that happen, okay?"

"Yes, Katya. Of course. I'll do everything you say," Ivan promised.

…They told the staff who came looking for them that the unfamiliar American food had upset their stomachs, and that they'd all been stuck in the bathroom. Since Greg Darkness himself had been sick all day and barely left the restroom—and coincidentally, another lab worker had also come down with a stomach-ache—people accepted the story without fuss.

Another neurosurgery on the test subjects was being prepared by Dr. Trabs, but it was scheduled for the end of the following month, so for now, the kids were allowed to watch TV—educational and science programs handpicked by Moran.

That evening, Ivan met with Katya again and wrote down what she dictated to him. The kids weren't needed at that moment, but they were ready to act at a moment's notice. All three students were mentally prepared to stage a quick, coordinated escape from the bunker if necessary. They knew escape was nearly impossible, yet they still hoped Ivan would find a way.

In the end, though, they didn't even need to attempt a breakout. Katya's clever idea worked exactly as planned.

…The next morning, Professor Moran received a "letter from Russia" via his usual courier, John McConnley. Such letters occasionally arrived from his Moscow business partner, Konstantin Koscheyev.

The letter—written in English, in a tone suggesting a cautious and secretive correspondent—read as though it were in Koscheyev's own hand:

My dear friend George, please forgive me for what I must now share with you.

I am informing you that the fresh batch of product from Uzbekistan, which is currently in your custody, has suddenly been claimed by its original owners. They are demanding that I return this product to its homeland, intact. I respectfully request that you cover the costs of returning them. Please rest assured that, since you have already transferred a substantial sum to me in exchange for these three items, I am obliged to send you—free of charge—a new batch, larger in number. I give you my word, Mr. Moran, that you will not encounter such problems with this new shipment. After working through the new

material, you can then easily dispose of it with no obstacles whatsoever.
Respectfully yours, always, Konstantin Koscheyev

The company letterhead was genuine—Ivan, being Koscheyev's usual courier to Moran, always had a supply of the stationery, along with matching envelopes.

What was unusual was the *"fake"* content of the letter. Moran read between the lines: it meant the captives' relatives had raised a serious uproar. The professor wanted neither a scandal nor the risk of arrest.

For the students, luck was on their side—Moran believed the lie! The "young goods" were now handled very carefully, so as not to damage them. Moran ordered his staff to purchase three tickets from Boston to Tashkent without delay.

By the next day, all three were not only released from the ill-fated bunker but also back home in the arms of loved ones who had nearly lost hope.

They were escorted to the airport (supposedly on Koscheyev's orders) by none other than "John McConnley." The students were endlessly grateful to him. As for John—or rather, Ivan—he decided to return to Moscow. He kept wondering: how could he avoid being killed by Koscheyev–Romanov? And ultimately, how could he rebuild his beloved family?

* * *

Moscow, the same period, 2012

Kirill Midiyatdinov never did travel to Tashkent, despite Koscheyev's persistent pleas. Having learned that his old friend Konstantin—on another of his business trips to Tashkent—had taken two people prisoner (or at least taken part in their capture; Kirill wasn't entirely sure), Midiyatdinov, who had grown far more cautious over the years, decided not to get involved in anything that might see him charged with kidnapping. He had absolutely no desire to end up behind bars again.

Besides, he trusted the cunning and unpredictable Koscheyev less and less. Kirill sensed that Konstantin might well be trying to set him up—to have him thrown in jail. And Midiyatdinov was right! Indeed, in front of Tamilla and Rashid, Koscheyev–Romanov was deliberately playing the role of a fellow captive, so that once Kirill showed up, he could secretly call the police to the hangar and blame every "crime of the century" on Midiyatdinov!

In doing so, he would have exacted sweet revenge for that unforgettable apple core incident back in the orphanage.

Yet there was another reason Kirill didn't budge from Moscow.

And that reason was the Koh-i-Noor diamond shards—or rather, two shards of it—that had been in Midiyatdinov's safe for several years already. These were diamonds from the very cache discovered by Rashid Batyrov's late friend, the archaeologist Pulat Gafarov.

How had these jewels fallen into Kirill's hands? It happened like this:

Stanislav Zakharovich Levidovsky, having let slip to Kirill and Koscheyev that excavations were underway in Uzbekistan, discovered that Koscheyev, along with two helpers, had gone to the area around Kungrad. Levidovsky decided to follow them.

When Koscheyev and his cronies attacked the unfortunate Pulat in the dead of night—Pulat having a small bundle of diamonds wrapped in a calico kerchief in his pocket—the poor man fell backward. The kerchief slipped from his pocket, and two precious shards tumbled out onto the dark grass, unnoticed.

Koscheyev, unaware of this, retrieved only three of the shards. Returning to Moscow, Konstantin found a wealthy Indian buyer and managed to sell him those diamonds for a fortune.

He then chose not to let anyone know that he had become fabulously rich. Like the hidden millionaire Koreiko in Ilf and Petrov's novel, he kept dressing modestly and living a low-profile life, stashing his money in chests and commercial bank accounts.

Yet Konstantin was well aware that he had not recovered the entire "Uzbek Koh-i-Noor." He knew more fragments had to be out there somewhere. Precisely how many in total, he did not know. What he also did not know was that… the next morning, Stanislav Levidovsky found the other two shards in that very same patch of grass—thanks to his well-trained eye for diamonds!

…Years later, Levidovsky ended up in a wheelchair—his legs had failed him. Once a "tough" tycoon, he had become weak and defenceless. His son, Stepan, abandoned him, but his daughter Alexandra and granddaughter Nastya cared for him as best they could.

One day, Stanislav Zakharovich summoned Sasha and, holding a small box of diamonds, said:

"My dear daughter, I've wronged you in many ways. I feel I don't have much time left in this world. Please—take this, with Alyosha and Nastya. For good luck!"

But when Alexandra saw the diamonds—and already knew, through her husband Alexey Irmanov and his friend Rashid, about the search in Uzbekistan for precisely these gems—she immediately understood what they were.

"No," Alexandra Stanislavovna said firmly, refusing her father. "Those are stolen diamonds, and I know a good man died because of them. I'm sorry, but I won't take them."

Levidovsky was not offended; he saw his daughter's point. He then began to ponder what to do with the stones. He didn't want to pass them off to just anyone, nor did he want to hand them over to the Russian or Uzbek governments. Then he remembered someone who had once taken him in like family—someone who had been like a son to him.

Thus, the diamonds ended up with... Kirill Olegovich Midiyatdinov, who by then had changed his paperwork and become Kirill Denisovich Persiyev. He gratefully accepted the diamonds from Levidovsky.

Why, then, would Kirill put himself at risk and head to Tashkent for diamonds he already had at home?

Moreover, his father, Denis Kirillovich—upon learning the provenance of the jewels—said:

"Son, I want you to become a decent, honest man! Stop living on the wrong side of the law. I want to be proud of my son again—not, sorry to say, ashamed like I once was. And I beg you: take these diamonds to Uzbekistan and hand them over to the authorities. That's where they belong."

Thinking it over, Kirill decided that's exactly what he would do—later, once all the commotion about Koscheyev–Romanov's prisoners had died down. He planned to travel to Tashkent and deliver them to Rashid Batyrov, the friend of the well-known businessman Alexey Irmanov, who had overseen the excavation where the diamonds were found.

* * *

Moscow – Tashkent, 2012

With help from another undercover operative, Dmitry—the very same Dmitry who had been so humane in guarding Tamilla Sardorovna and Rashid Kudratovich—Artur Kiramov (a.k.a. Artyom Kiryushin) orchestrated events so that all the main players in the "KIR" gang would end up together in the hangar with their prisoners. The plan was to catch them all red-handed. But Artur feared he wouldn't make it in time, because two days earlier, he had overheard the gang boss ordering his men… to dispose of the two captives!

Tamilla's and Rashid's lives were now truly hanging by a thread.

Both of them realized this and—saying nothing to each other about it—tearfully thought of their daughter and grandchildren.

Saltanat, my darling daughter! How will you manage without us? Tamilla grieved.

My little girl, my own flesh and blood… If only you can go on being happy! Rashid thought.

…Artur had asked Saltanat not to do anything rash herself, because the gang had long been under surveillance by the security services, and gathering ironclad evidence of all its crimes was no simple matter. Artur, Dmitry, and their superiors in state security wanted to ensure the young woman wouldn't inadvertently sabotage their operation.

Artur already knew who was truly in charge of the gang. It had taken him some time to figure it out, because the person was very good at covering his tracks—constantly letting others take the spotlight so that, if necessary, law enforcement wouldn't be able to pin him down. The criminals had no idea there was an adept undercover officer in their midst!

Artur also knew about the coveted diamonds the criminals were trying to *shake out* of a baffled Rashid and Tamilla—who genuinely had no idea where the stones might be.

But Kiramov had not yet discovered one thing: why the head of "KIR" harbored such fierce hatred specifically toward Tamilla Sardorovna Mahkamova. That remained a mystery to him.

* * *

Tashkent, 2012

The republic's Ministry of Foreign Affairs was in a frenzy: the airline had just reported that a prince from India was unexpectedly flying into the capital of independent Uzbekistan! And not just any prince, but a descendant of their mutual forebears—the Great Mughals themselves, from the line of Emperor Shah Jahan!

He was welcomed with great honours: not only was he ushered through the VIP corridor, as expected, but there was also a red carpet, ceremonial music, and an honour guard in full dress.

"Actually, I'm here purely in a private capacity," remarked Prince Yakub Habibuddin Tusi, politely responding to the official greetings and the diplomats' courteous bows. "I came at the invitation of the UN Goodwill Ambassador—Lady Mahkamoff. She and I arranged about a month ago that I would come to discuss avenues of cooperation with her. But I haven't been able to reach her by phone for several days to confirm the details of my visit to Tashkent. Nonetheless, I decided to come anyway, because I know how conscientious she is, and it troubles me greatly that I haven't been able to contact her for so long. Can you help me find her?"

"Well… we'll do our best," the diplomats said, somewhat at a loss.

Along with his personal belongings, Prince Tusi had brought a valuable gift he intended to present to the government of Uzbekistan. First, however, he wished to show it to Lady Mahkamoff—then, possibly through her, deliver it to the state depositories of Uzbekistan.

Hence, the prince decided to wait until his esteemed business partner could be found and meet with him in person.

* * *

Tashkent, the same period

…Tamilla opened her eyes after a heavy, brief, and restless sleep in a chair. At first, she didn't understand what was happening.

Standing before her, wearing a haughty smirk, was someone she recognized from long ago—her former bandmate Irina, who had grown only harsher and more menacing over the years.

"Ira?! You?!" Tamilla exclaimed in genuine surprise. "Hello. What are you doing here?"

Irina let out a loud, rolling laugh, brimming with mockery. Only then did Tamilla notice the pistol in Irina's hand.

"Me? What am I doing here?!" Irina shouted indignantly. "I'm in charge here, got it? These people are my men. On my orders, they grabbed you and your husband!"

"Hold on," interjected a shaken Rashid upon hearing this revelation. "Isn't your organization called 'KIR'?"

"Of course it is!" Irina confirmed. "Exactly. It stands for *Korshunova Irina Rinatovna*—because I'm the boss here! Also, 'KIR' stands for *Kovarstvo, Intrigi, Razboi* [Treachery, Intrigue, Robbery]. It's our gang's motto. Clear?"

Tamilla remained silent. Irina continued, "performing" her little show:

"And Konstantin Ivanovich Romanov, who you thought was the boss here, was mainly carrying out my orders. However, in the case of your students, he acted at his own discretion—it was his independent business project. He's only here temporarily; he has his own business in Moscow, together with the boss of a group just like this one. But this is my territory, and everything here is mine!"

It seemed to Tamilla that her old acquaintance was simply not quite right in the head.

"Oh, how I hate you, Tamilla! You ruined my life! Why do you have to stick your bright ideas and projects into everything? Don't you see you just provoke everyone?… Everything falls into your hands, and you never ask anyone for help! I'll never forgive you for those successes! But I might let you go if you do everything I say. Hand over those diamonds—you know which ones I mean—or tell me where they are! Otherwise, I'll have you and that devoted husband of yours shot right now!"

No sooner had Irina blurted out this confession of her crimes than powerful special forces officers burst into the hangar. They swiftly subdued all the criminals, cuffed them, and set Tamilla and Rashid free.

As the commandos led Irina, Konstantin, and the other members of both "KIR" gangs out of the hangar, preparing to "pack them" into armoured vehicles, Irina spat out one last vile remark at Tamilla:

"But why, why?! Why is your victory guaranteed yet again?!"

"Because the one who truly works wins, not the freeloader; because good triumphs—not evil," Tamilla replied gently.

…Saltanat, waiting for her parents at the hangar's exit, rushed to embrace them both in turn, covering their grimy, tear-streaked faces with tender daughterly kisses and pressing them tightly to her—overjoyed to see them alive—her mom and dad! And they could hardly believe their eyes, reunited at last with their dearest Saltanat!

"My darling, how are our grandchildren?" was the first question they asked.

"They've been waiting for you, my beloved parents," Saltanat answered. "Let's hurry home!"

* * *

Tashkent, 2012 – a few days later

Gathered around were the family and friends closest to a now very frail Feruz-begim, who made it clear by her demeanour that she was expecting something unusual, mysterious—beyond a casual tea gathering. Standing at the head of the table was the Crystal hookah, an artifact from ages past. The fragrant smoke of herbal blends wafted through the air, creating an atmosphere of inspiration and wonder. The air was filled with the scent of mystery and the uniqueness of the moment…

He who has been beaten by life achieves even more.
He who has tasted a pound of salt cherishes the sweetness of honey.
He who sheds tears laughs all the more heartily.
He who has died understands that he truly lives!

Feruz-begim continued singing softly… and then… came the sound of firm but measured footsteps, and the doors to the hall opened.

Into the room stepped the newly recovered, ever-graceful, and striking Tamilla Mahkamova, arm in arm with her husband Rashid. Behind them followed another direct descendant of the Great Mughal Emperor Shah Jahan—Indian Prince Yakub Habibuddin Tusi.

Feruz-begim greeted her guests calmly and introduced everyone in turn. Delight and astonishment lit the faces of these happy heirs of Uzbekistan's soil.

"Dear, esteemed friends and relatives," Tamilla began proudly, "I am so pleased to announce that we are about to launch a truly important undertaking—the creation of an International Charitable Foundation! Founded on the rich, ancient heritage of the Great Silk Road, this foundation will promote friendship among nations and champion peace and progress. We will also dedicate ourselves to supporting gifted youth worldwide, caring for sick children and orphans! And we'll help women in crisis—those on the very brink—so they can become intelligent, courageous, educated, kind, and noble, like the heroines of our past…"

"That is wonderful news!" exclaimed Prince Tusi with approval. "I agree wholeheartedly, Lady Mahkamoff."

"I fully support this plan—and I want to help with the foundation as well!" chimed in Amin.

"Moreover," Tamilla continued, "I personally hope to aid a certain good man—Ivan Makonin—and reunite him with his family. Risking his own life in Boston, Ivan saved three of our university students—snatching them from the clutches of monstrous captors—and helped them all return home."

"We will absolutely help Ivan," Amin Fattakhov agreed. "He's a genuine hero. And regarding orphaned children, I'll be there to ensure they receive an education—and we'll make sure they have proper housing as well…"

"Thank you, Amin," Tamilla said, shaking hands with the Uzbek businessman.

"I also have a valuable gift for your country," the Indian prince added with a smile. "I believe it will serve us well in these noble tasks."

His Highness drew a small box from his briefcase. Inside were—like a tiny miracle—three shards of the Koh-i-Noor diamond once discovered by Pulat Gafarov!

Tears welled up in the eyes of the woman who had just endured such severe trials.

"I hardly know how to thank you, dear prince!" she said. "But please—tell me, how did you come by them?"

"Once you wrote to me, telling me that these jewels had long ago been sold in India to a certain individual," explained Prince Tusi, "I investigated the matter and discovered who the buyer was. I managed to repurchase them, since they truly belong—by right—to the people of Uzbekistan. After all, the Koh-i-Noor was originally owned by the Great Mughals—our mutual ancestors, who hailed from Uzbekistan!"

"Thank you from the bottom of my heart," Tamilla Sardorovna replied with a smile. "And now, it's my pleasure to invite all of you to the Alisher Navoi State Academic Grand Theatre for the *Tomyris* ballet, composed by Ulugbek Musaev—another chance to draw near to Uzbekistan's cultural treasures and behold, on stage, one of the greatest, bravest, and noblest women on Earth!"

Thousands of years will pass, and yet Queen Tomyris—and the wondrous Koh-i-Noor diamond—will live on forever in the memory of our people.

****

Reference – History of the Koh-i-Noor Diamond

Koh-i-Noor (<u>Pers</u>. کوہِ نور, <u>Urdu</u> کوہ نور, <u>Hindi</u> कोहिनूर — "Mountain of Light") *is a 105-carat <u>diamond</u> currently set in the crown of Queen Elizabeth (United Kingdom), and is one of the most <u>famous diamonds</u> in history.*

It is among the largest diamonds in the British Crown Jewels (the largest being the "Cullinan I").

Originally, the diamond had a slight yellowish tint, but after being re-cut in 1852, it became a pure white with a bluish sheen.

The documented history of the Koh-i-Noor can be reliably traced back to the <u>year 1300</u>. However, legends speak of events connected to the stone that go back even further.

Koh-i-Noor in Its Older Form, Pre-1852. Illustration from an encyclopedia

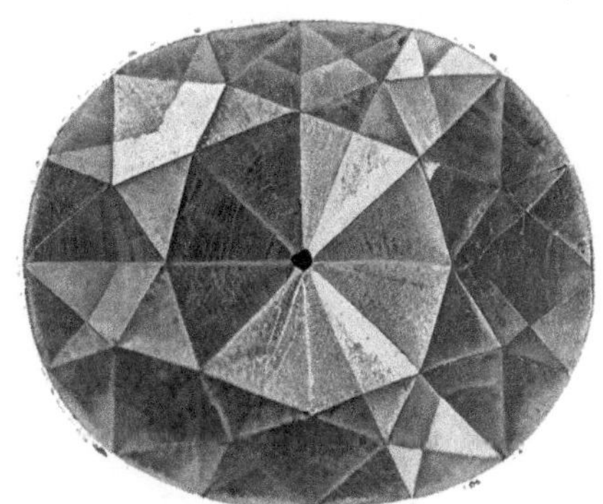

Koh-i-Noor in Its New Form, Post-1852, Illustration from an encyclopedia

For several centuries, the Koh-i-Noor adorned the turban of the <u>rajahs</u> from the <u>Malwa</u> Dynasty. Legend held that if the "Mountain of Light" were ever to fall from the rajah's turban, the entire people of Malwa would become slaves. And so it happened in 1304, when Malwa was conquered by the <u>Delhi Sultan Alauddin</u>. Among other captured treasures, the Koh-i-Noor passed into the victor's possession.

However, the diamond later returned to the rulers of Malwa—its new owner became <u>Bikramjit</u> (Vikramaditya), the Raja of Gwalior.

Another legend attributes the origin of the Koh-i-Noor to Alauddin's sons—Khizr Khan, Shihab-ud-Din Omar, and Qutb-ud-Din Mubarak. After their father's death, the three brothers vied for power and decided to divide the territory into three parts. To do this, they set off on a journey across their father's dominions. In the mountains, they were overtaken by rain and found shelter in a cave. Upon entering, they saw it was lit by an unusual light emanating from a diamond resting on a granite stone. The brothers began to argue over who should claim it and prayed to their respective gods: Khizr Khan prayed to Vishnu, Omar to Brahma—the soul of the universe—while Mubarak prayed to Shiva, the Destroyer. Shiva heard Mubarak's prayer and struck the diamond with lightning, causing it to split into three pieces. Each fragment weighed more than seven hundred carats. Khizr Khan took the largest piece and named it "Daria-i-Noor"—the "Sea of Light." Omar named his stone "Koh-i-Noor"—the "Mountain of Light," and Mubarak called his "Hind-i-Noor"—the "Light of India."

After they assumed their thrones, disasters befell the country. Famine and epidemics claimed tens of thousands of lives. Seeking Shiva's favour, Mubarak sold his diamond to the Shah of Persia. With the proceeds, he built a temple and placed at its entrance a marble statue of Shiva three times the height of a man. But the misfortunes persisted. Then Khizr Khan and Omar ordered stonemasons to set the "Daria-i-Noor" and the "Koh-i-Noor" into the statue's eye sockets. Immediately, all calamities ceased.

Later, the "Daria-i-Noor" and the "Koh-i-Noor" were mounted into the throne of the Persian shah who had invaded India, seizing these diamonds among other spoils.

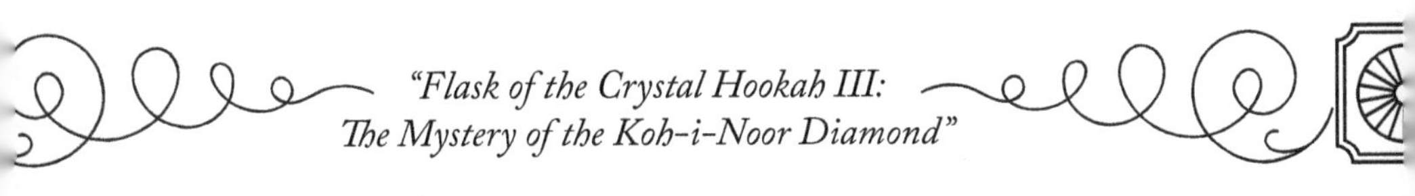

Over time, numerous legends arose around the Koh-i-Noor. One story claimed it was discovered about 5,000 years ago in southern India, in the famous Golconda mines, and that its first owner was <u>Karna</u>, one of the legendary heroes of India mentioned in the ancient epic <u>Mahabharata</u>.

In 1526, Sultan <u>Babur's</u> armies—Babur being a descendant of <u>Tamerlane</u>—invaded India. He was accompanied by his son, the warrior <u>Humayun</u>, the future founder of the Mughal dynasty. In the decisive <u>Battle of Panipat</u> that same year, Indian forces were defeated. During the battle, Raja Bikramjit was killed, and his family was captured while attempting to flee <u>Agra</u>. Hoping to appease the conqueror, the Raja's wife presented Humayun with all their treasures, including the Koh-i-Noor. The victors spared the Raja's family.

Humayun ceremoniously presented the diamond to his father, who, after admiring it, returned it to his son. From that time on, the rulers of the Mughal dynasty wore the Koh-i-Noor on their turbans until it was eventually placed in the famous <u>Peacock Throne</u>. It was believed that as long as the diamond shone above the throne of the Great Mughals as an unbreakable <u>emblem</u>, the dynasty would endure.

Before long, the power of the Great Mughals spread across India. Under Sultan Babur's grandson, <u>Akbar</u>, the country became more unified than ever before. Akbar showed tolerance toward different religions and treated the conquered peoples with kindness. As an educated man, he patronized the sciences and the arts, and schools were established throughout the empire.

During its golden age under <u>Shah Jahan</u>, the Mughal Empire produced masterpieces such as the <u>Pearl Mosque</u> in Agra and the world-

renowned <u>*Taj Mahal*</u>. *But the Peacock Throne remained the dynasty's most prized treasure.*

We know about the throne from the travel accounts of several visitors, including <u>Jean-Baptiste Tavernier</u>. According to his descriptions, the Peacock Throne stood in a special hall where seven other thrones were also displayed. It stood out among them because it was set on a massive marble platform decorated with precious stones. The seat of the throne was supported by six sturdy gold pillars. Silver poles inlaid with gold and jewels rose above, supporting an openwork canopy woven from fine silver wire, crafted in a botanical design—grapevines, leaves, and flowers with petals of green <u>emeralds</u>, buds of raspberry <u>rubies</u>, and cores of blue <u>sapphires</u>. Their crests and tails were formed from gold and silver wire and adorned with precious stones, carefully arranged to imitate the plumage of living <u>peacocks</u>. Large diamonds served as the peacocks' eyes. The Koh-i-Noor was mounted between the peacocks, positioned directly above the ruler's head.

Shah Jahan had four sons. The eldest, <u>Aurangzeb</u>, sought to seize his father's throne—and with it, the Koh-i-Noor—believing that possessing the diamond would grant him power over the entire world. After failing to persuade his brothers to join a revolt, Aurangzeb staged a coup, seized power, killed his brothers, and imprisoned his father in the fortress of Agra, transforming the throne room into a prison. He did not dare kill his father or take the Koh-i-Noor from him by force, fearing that doing so would provoke uprisings against his rule.

For seven years, Shah Jahan lived imprisoned among his treasures. Once Aurangzeb felt secure on the throne, he demanded that his father send him the largest gems from the treasury to adorn his turban in preparation for his formal ascension. Shah Jahan died in 1666 in the arms of his daughter, within his jewelled prison.

In <u>1739</u>, during the reign of Shah Muhammad, Persian forces led by <u>Nader Shah</u> invaded northwestern India. They seized all the Mughal treasures, including the Peacock Throne. But the throne's greatest treasure—the Koh-i-Noor—was nowhere to be found.

Thousands of people were sent out in all directions, and a large reward was promised to anyone who revealed the diamond's whereabouts. One of the former members of the harem disclosed that the Koh-i-Noor was hidden in Muhammad's turban. During a feast, the Persian shah proposed that Muhammad exchange turbans with him as a sign of friendship—an ancient custom in the East. Refusing such a proposal was impossible, and Muhammad had no choice but to offer his turban to Nader Shah, along with the diamond. The Persian ruler, not waiting for the ceremony to end, hurried back to his quarters, unwrapped the turban, and upon seeing the diamond, exclaimed: "Mountain of Light!" (Koh-i-Noor in Persian). Thus, the stone acquired its name.

Nader Shah returned to Persia. During his reign, he could not escape rebellions, poisonings, and betrayals—the fate that plagued all owners of the Koh-i-Noor. He nearly lost his mind, trusting no one, and in 1747 he was killed by the <u>Kurdish leader Salah Bey.</u>

After Nader Shah's death, the throne was seized by his younger son, Prince Rukh, but he was unable to retain power and was overthrown. Nevertheless, he managed to hide the Koh-i-Noor and refused to disclose its location, even under torture. Rukh gave the diamond to the Afghan Ahmad Abdali. Thus, the Koh-i-Noor ended up in <u>Kandahar</u>, Afghanistan, where <u>Ahmad Abdali (Durr-i-Durran)</u> seized the throne and founded the Afghan state, becoming the progenitor of the Durrani dynasty.

Following Ahmad's death in <u>1773</u>, his son Timur took over leadership of the dynasty and moved the capital to <u>Kabul</u>. After Timur died, power passed to one of his twenty-three sons, <u>Zaman Mirza</u>. Another palace coup followed, giving power to Zaman Mirza's brother, Shuja ul-Mulk. Zaman Mirza was tortured to reveal the diamond's location and was blinded. In prison, he carved a recess into the wall, hid the diamond there, and covered it with plaster. Several years later, it was discovered by a jailer, who handed it over to Shuja ul-Mulk. Yet another coup took place, transferring the throne to Shuja ul-Mulk's brother, <u>Mahmud</u>. Mahmud blinded Shuja ul-Mulk and imprisoned him. Shuja refused to reveal the stone's location, believing that as long as he possessed it, he would one day regain his kingdom and power. He eventually escaped from prison with the Koh-i-Noor and other treasures. Together with his family, he found refuge in <u>Lahore</u> under <u>Ranjit Singh</u>—known as the "Lion of the Punjab."

Upon learning of the diamond, the raja decided to extract its location through torture—not from the blind Shuja ul-Mulk, but from his wife. She could not endure it and agreed to surrender the diamond under certain conditions: the release of the captives, guarantees of their safety, and a lifelong pension. Singh agreed. He nearly lost his senses when the "Mountain of Light" came into his possession. He paid Shuja ul-Mulk 125,000 rupees and granted him an annual pension of 60,000 rupees for life.

Having taken possession of the Koh-i-Noor, Raja Singh united the Punjab and built a strong army. He also planned to rid India of British influence. Yet, being a clever and farsighted politician, he understood that he could not stand against Britain's growing might. Seeing the diamond's bloody history, Singh decided it would be best to part with it. He intended to present it as a gift to a temple but died before he could do

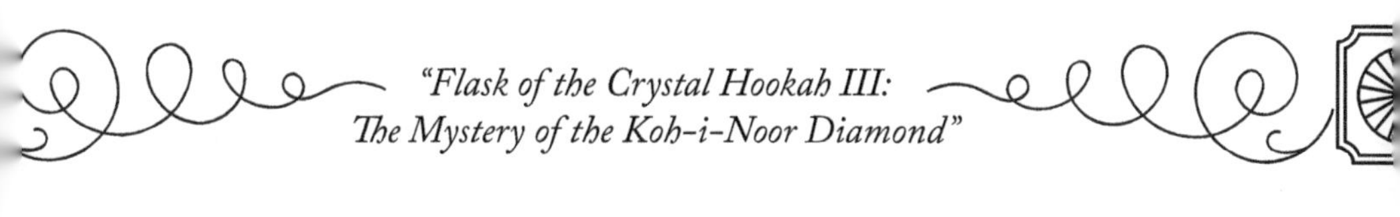

so. His heirs knew nothing of his plan. After the raja's death, the country was plunged into years of anarchy and disorder. The raja's army clashed with the British and, although it initially enjoyed some success, it was ultimately defeated.

In 1849, the <u>Lahore</u> treasury fell into British hands. The diamond first ended up with Sir <u>John Lawrence</u>, Governor-General of India, and was nearly lost: Lawrence did not appreciate its value, and it was only saved when a faithful servant discovered it among his master's belongings. On <u>April 6, 1850</u>, the Koh-i-Noor left India and reached Britain on July 2, 1850. The valuable cargo was received by J. W. Logg, Acting Chairman of the Board of Directors of the East India Company, who handed the diamond—along with other Indian treasures—to <u>Queen Victoria</u>. She noted in her diary:

The jewels are magnificent. They belonged to Ranjit Singh and were discovered in the Lahore treasury. I am happy that from now on they belong to the British Crown, and I shall see to it that the diamonds become part of the Crown.

In <u>1851</u>, the diamond was displayed at the <u>Great Exhibition in London</u>. Despite its reputation for bringing misfortune to its owners, the queen ignored the superstition and wore it in her diadem. Indian sources note that Queen Victoria felt uneasy about removing the Koh-i-Noor from India. In 1854, she invited Ranjit Singh's only son and heir, 15-year-old Duleep Singh, to Britain and granted him a pension of 15,000 rupees per year—against the government's wishes, which deemed the amount excessive.

Duleep Singh, who had relinquished his state at the age of eleven, was raised by an English tutor, converted to Christianity, and spoke fluent English. During his stay in England, at a personal audience with Victoria and at her request, Duleep Singh formally declared the diamond—already in her possession—to be placed under the queen's authority:

"Madam, it is my greatest pleasure as your loyal subject to personally present the Koh-i-Noor to my sovereign."

Until 1852, the Koh-i-Noor still retained its ancient Indian cut. English jewellers believed a new cut would enhance the stone's brilliance. In 1852, it was re-cut in <u>Amsterdam</u>, resulting in a flatter shape. Its weight dropped from 191 carats to 108.9 carats. The decision to re-cut the diamond was widely questioned and criticized, as it meant altering the world's most famous diamond—an object of immense historical and cultural value—at the cost of losing more than 42% of its original mass. In 1853, the Koh-i-Noor was set into the British Royal Crown alongside approximately 2,000 smaller diamonds. In 1911, it was transferred to a newly made crown for the coronation of <u>Queen Mary</u>. In 1937, it was moved again to a <u>new crown</u> for the coronation of <u>Queen Elizabeth</u>, where it remains to this day.

Currently, the Koh-i-Noor is part of <u>Queen Elizabeth's Crown</u>, kept in the <u>Tower</u> of London. In 2002, during the funeral of Queen Elizabeth the Queen Mother, the crown containing the diamond was displayed near the coffin as the procession passed through the streets of London.

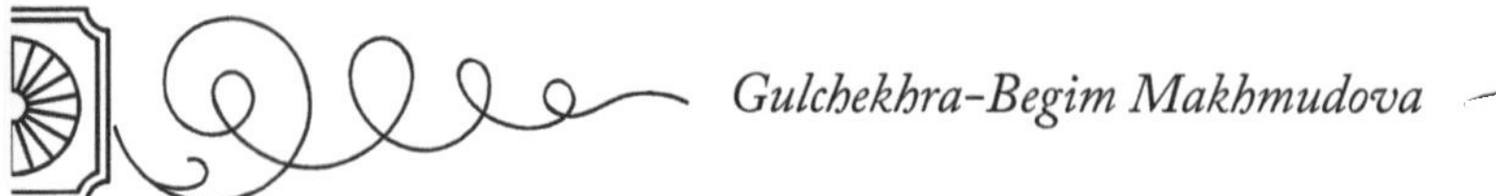

468

www.ingramcontent.com/pod-product-compliance
Lightning Source LLC
Chambersburg PA
CBHW051116300726
48981CB00002B/152